ANTWAN 'ANT' BANK$

PRINTHOUSE BOOKS PRESENTS:

I0650666

MADE III

Death Before Dishonor; Beware Thine Enemies Deceit.

FICTION, *Inspired by True Events...*

An Organized Crime Novel.

ANTWAN 'ANT' BANK$

PrintHouse Books, Atlanta, GA.   Published 8-4-13

www.PrintHouseBooks.com

VIP INK Publishing Group; Incorporated

This novel is fiction but also has been inspired by true events, most characters are fictitious no matter how true the event. Some characters remained the same as the events have been documented to the public and are on public record.

Cover art, designed by SK7.

ISBN: 978-0-991-1719-0-3

Library of Congress Cataloging-in-Publication Data

ANTWAN 'ANT' BANK$

MADE III;

Death before Dishonor; Beware Thine Enemies Deceit.

1. Crime Thriller 2.Mystery 3.Erotica 4.Urban Literature

5. Organized Crime 6. ANTWAN 'ANT' BANK$

Printed in the United States of America

Three years ago, I lost my wife and family to this messed up economy. After that nothing was there to hold me back, with no more support from Uncle Sam; I decided to pave my own way. Never one to break the law, I traveled down the straight and narrow but to no avail, thanks to this Bitch ass Cop; name Espinoza. So again I found myself in a corner. But as I gathered my thoughts and tried to come up with a plan; it was by fate that I met who would later become the love of my life.

Sabrina in her own fortuitous way introduced me to the life I have today. Still no wife nor kids in the picture, even though they constantly held a place next to my soon to be cold heart. I witnessed my life change in a split second. Now that I think back on it; mine did that very day I dropped Pharoah's punk ass in that back parking lot. I should have known things would never be the same after that day. I still get a thrill when I think about the look he had in his eyes when I took his life away and the smile that remained on Sabrina's all that day.

As I sit here smoking on this Cohiba, in this Mansion, with all this power, all this money and all the blood on my hands from those fools that stood in my way. My heart still beats fast at the sight of the cars, money, houses, women and the sound of hot bullets piercing warm flesh. See I live for this shit because there's nothing else out there for me; but this. Don't blame my mother, don't blame my pops. Blame Uncle Sam for placing that M16 in my hands and brain washing me to kill without feeling a damn thing. Blame this messed up economy; that has so many people struggling. Yeah I made a choice and I am happy with it. Because of that; me and my crew will protect what's ours until the day we die. See we don't plan on going to no prison, jail or nothing like that. Yes we plan to go out with a fight, last man standing! Death before Dishonor; that's how we roll! Gangsters make the world go round and Sin City is its axes. It's time for me to stop talking now; you have a story to read; see you on the inside. MADE III; Death before Dishonor; Beware Thine Enemies Deceit. The Final Chapter.....

Andy 'AC' Cooper; Don of Sin City.   -777

Dedicated to the Gangsters, Hustlers and Pimps that made it out of the game and to the fallen soldiers whose souls carry on.

ANTWAN BANK$

MADE III

Death Before Dishonor; Beware Thine Enemies Deceit.

VIP INK Publishing Group, Incorporated

Atlanta, GA.

Table of Contents

January; 1998

As the rain drops sparkle in the dark Vegas night and tourist crowd the strip awaiting the strike of twelve. Sirens sound while flashing red lights bounce off The Towers exterior as thousands of people parted to let the ambulance through. All AC could hear; is the sound of rain drops hitting the black body bag as paramedics zip up Sabrina's lifeless, yet warm body. This New Year's Eve would be one etched in his memory forever, one he would never forget. Excuse me Mr. Cooper! Yeah; what is it Chief? The paramedics gave me this ring and watch off the body; did you want to keep it? I was going to take it in for evidence but I knew you would probably want it. Coop looks down at the engagement ring that Chief Espinoza held in the palm of his right hand.

The red and blue flashing lights, rain and combination of fireworks overhead made it sparkle as he glance down at it. No man, go ahead, I'll get it when you're done. Are you sure? Yeah; I'm sure.

Happy New Year! The jovial patrons scream from the strip, adjacent casinos and hotel's as the clock struck twelve. Only the immediate on lookers and AC's crew stood there in disbelief as the officer's slid Sabrina in the rear of the coroner's truck. The rain hid Coop's tears as he watch his baby roll away as the crowd parted to let the coroner leave. Hey bro, are you alright? I'm straight Manny! Are you sure dog? Yeah Will! Come on baby; let's go inside out of the rain. Chill Mo; give me a minute! Nina; what the fuck happened? I don't know Coop; we were on the balcony drinking and laughing then all of a sudden she was falling! That's fucked up! Denna, did you see anything? Just the same as Nina baby. I refuse to believe that nobody seen anything! That's bullshit! Hey yall; I'm going back upstairs, I need a drink. Really Loon! Yeah Duck; really. This shit has me stressed out, besides; there aint nothing we can do about it now!

Yeah guys; Loon's right, let's just go in. Baby if you want to stay down here; I will stay with you. No it's fine Mo; come on yall, let's go in. You sure AC! Yeah Capo; let's go.

Detective Casey; you and Briggs start canvassing the area and find out if any of these folks saw anything. Detective

Ricky; go upstairs with AC and see what you can find out. I'm headed back to the precinct to look at some files. Ok chief we're on it; did you want us to bring the witnesses back to headquarters for questioning? Only if you have to Casey; the last thing we need is a precinct full of witnesses on New Year's Eve. Alright Chief; roger that.

Yo; this is messed up homes. I can't believe that chica's dead. I know Hector; I don't know what happened. Manny; do you think she jumped? No that's crazy, AC just proposed to her the other day; she was happy Hector. Somebody had to push her homes. Sabrina was pretty drunk Hector; she probably tripped or something like that. Ding! The crew walked onto the elevator, still quiet and in a state of disbelief. Tears continue to run down the sides of AC's face as he tried to maintain a firm expression as Monica places her left arm around his shoulders while holding his right hand. In dead silence and 45 flights later the crew exits the elevator, enters the hallway and walks into Nina's unlocked condo.

Hey Coop; I'm fixing me a drink, you want one bro? Yeah Loon; make it a double; I'll be out on the balcony. Monica; can you please stay here; I need to be alone right now.

11

Sure AC; no problem. His heart pounds harder than it ever did while he walked in the last steps that Brina ever took. The crew calmly looked on from the other side of the glass wall while he paced back and forth on the balcony. Nooooo! Why me! Why me! God how could you take her from me! She didn't deserve this; why didn't you take me instead God? Coop falls to his knees then leans his forehead against the balcony rail as his tears fall onto the ledge and drips down below. He takes one last breath; jumps up; pulls his nine from his waist and starts shooting.

Pow! One shot let off into the New Year's Eve sky. Pow! Pow! Two more shots. Pow! Pow! Bling-Bling! AC no! The crew ran away from the window as the glass shattered. Coop; stop it! Nina; fuck that window; get out of the way sis! No; let me go Denna; he's destroying my shit. Pow! Pow! Bling-Bling! Oh my God! He's losing it; do something Manny. Look guys just stay here in the room out of his way; we can get that window fixed later. Nina stop worrying; it will be taking care of. Pow! Pow! Bling-Bling. Bam! Bam! Bam! A strong gust of wind from the outside pulled all the doors closed inside the condo as AC turns towards the rail and lets off two more shots in the sky. Pow! Pow!

Mr. Cooper; put the gun down! Do it now! Detective Ricky; what are you doing up here? I came to check on you; now put the gun down please. What if I don't; are you gonna shoot me Amanda! If I have to Cooper; I will. I don't believe you Amanda! Look AC; I know that you're hurt right now but it doesn't have to end this way. Just lower the gun, come inside and talk to me and your friends. I don't want to talk right now, can't you see that!

Hold on Detective; let me talk to him. Ok come on, give it a shot. What's your name? I'm Manny Detective! Ok Manny; come on! Hey bro; it's ok man; we're all here for you. We just need you to put the gun down so you won't hurt yourself or anyone else. Manny; why did it have to be her bruh? I don't know brother; that's something for God to answer. Well; he aint fucking answering me Manny! Pow! Pow! Bling-Bling! Mr. Cooper; please put down your weapon; I will have to shoot if you do it again. Aww Amanda; I pay you too much. You aint gone shoot me! Manny fix me a drink brother; I'm coming in. Cool; I got you man! Did you want a double? Yeah and no ice!

13

Detective Ricky; you can have my gun now; there's no more bullets anyway. Hey Nina; I'll replace your window sis. Yeah you better, you crazy bastard! I aint crazy sis; just pissed the fuck off. Monica; come here! Yeah; what is it baby? Is this what you wanted? What do you mean AC? Me all to yourself, no more; skinny girlfriend. Coop you tripping; what are you implying?

Just what I said; it's me and you now baby girl. Well, you know I always had your back from day one, it's no secret! Hey guys; I'm sorry if I acted like a fool. I need to go lay down; Mo get my drink and let's go to my place. Amanda; thanks for checking on me. Hey Coop; you ok man? I'm good Will; you guys just do your thing; I need to get out of here. Come on Mo! Hey Mr. Cooper! Yes detective? I will call you tomorrow; I'm gone hang back and speak to your friends about what happened here tonight. Sure Amanda; do whatever you want!

Ring-Ring! Hello; Detective Briggs speaking! Hey Briggs; you and your partner get in here and bring your files on that cold case too. Ok Chief; on the way! Hey Casey; Chief wants to see us in his office. Damn; what about? I don't know partner; he said to bring our case files too. Ok come on, let's go then. The constant ringing of phones in the background and loud disgruntled inmates in booking, made it hard for any normal person to even think at the precinct. Hey chief what's up? Come in Detectives; close the door and have a seat. Did you bring those files like I asked? Yes Chief! We have the new ones as well as the cold case. Great Casey; you guys have a seat; I have to show you something.

Do you recognize any of these people in these pictures Detectives? Chief spread several photos over his desk for the detectives to look at. Yes that's the vic from the jailhouse murder a few months ago. I think his name was Victor Delgato! Correct Briggs! Is there any more you recognize? Yeah that's Bobby and Vinny Delagato; isn't it? Yes it is Casey! Keep looking detectives while I post these pictures on the bulletin board. Chief Espinoza tapes Vinny and Bobby's photos at the top of the bulletin board and writes their names underneath then tapes Victors photo below. Hey Chief; these photos are of all the guys we saw at the Towers on New Year's Eve.

Yes that is true Casey; we have to figure out how they all are connected to the Delgato's. Do you know any of them besides AC Chief? Not at this time Briggs. Isn't Detective Ricky working a cold case that involves some Towers residents; those murders last year at the drive in? Oh yeah; the girls and that taxi driver right? I think that's it Chief. Hold on a minute; let me get her in here. Ring-Ring! Hi this is Detective Ricky! Hey Detective can you come to my office please? Sure Chief, on the way. Ok she's coming. Chief walks over to the board and places AC's photo under Victor's. Hey Chief; what's up? Come in Ricky, have a look at those pictures on my desk. Hey Ricky! Hey Briggs, Casey; how are you? We're good Detective just trying to connect these photos; we were hoping you could help. Sure what do you need?

Do you recognize any of these people? Hmmm. Yeah all of them! Really? Yes Chief! Ok start naming them Ricky. This is Sabrina; the victim from the other night. This guy is Manny; AC's best friend. That's Big Will and that's Loon. This guy is Duck and these two ladies are sisters, Nina and Denna. How are they connected Ricky? From my understanding Briggs they are all childhood friends from the same neighborhood if I'm not mistaken. Oh really! Yes chief! Casey; tape these photos to the board and write their names under their pictures. I need to make a call. Ring-Ring! Hello! Hey detective; how is that undercover assignment going? Going good so far chief! Great; I need you to come in later this evening to look at some files. Ok Chief no problem; how does 7 pm sound. Make it 7:30! Ok chief; see you then.

Who was that Chief? I assigned an undercover to check out a hunch I had. I'm meeting with him later to see if he has any intel on these suspects. So right now we have AC, Manny, Duck, Loon, Big Will, Nina, Denna and Sabrina. There is a connection somewhere between these guys and the Delgato family. Once we find that out we can start building a case Detectives; I think this is going to be huge. From this point on; I want all three of you to focus on building this case and get any intel you can on the suspects. You guys are dismissed; call me if you find anything! Ok Chief; not a problem! Later detectives!

Ring-Ring! Evidence; Sergeant Brown speaking! Hey Serg; pull the evidence on that robbery last year at the Adult store; that double homicide at the bank and that murder at Clark County Jail. The Victim's in the last two cases were Delgato and if I'm not mistaking the Delgato's owned that video store in that first case. Ok Chief; did you want me to hold it for you or are you sending someone down to pick it up. Just pull it Serg, I'm sending my secretary down. Alright Chief; got you covered! Thanks Serg!

"Hello Las Vegas; this is Katie Strong with your 11 O'clock news." "We're only 5 days into the New Year and we already have our first death of the year." "While millions were celebrating this past New Year's Eve; A young lady fell to her death at the Towers luxury Complex." "She was a Las Vegas native and leaves behind her Mother, Farther and no siblings." "Chief Espinoza says the cause is still unclear but funeral arrangements are scheduled for this weekend." Mo! Mo! What AC! Turn that TV off; I don't want to hear that! Ok; I'm sorry baby; I'm making breakfast; get out of bed and come eat! Alright; give me a minute! Ok; I'm almost done; so hurry!

Damn; it does smell good in here! What you cooking? Some cheese grits, eggs and bacon. Cheese grits! Girl, what your west coast ass know about some cheese grits? Don't trip Coop; I got this. Well; I'll know in a minute. Yes you will Mr.! So are you going to the funeral? No; I don't want to remember her that way Mo. AC that was your girl;

you have to go. I don't have to do anything but stay black and die! I said I aint going and that's the end of it. Alright nigga; calm your nerves; damn. How many pieces of bacon do you want? Four is fine! Cool, fix us some OJ. I'll bring the plates to the table. The grease is still popping in the frying pan as it cools off while Monica places the bacon on their plates along-side the scrambled eggs. Did you want ice in your juice Mo? Nope; no ice! I already put butter in the grits while it was cooking; did you want more? Hell yeah girl!

I was just asking Coop; don't get fucked up in here; early today! Monica; you're always talking about you gone fuck somebody up and you know your behind can't fight a lick. Ha-Ha! Kiss my behind AC; I don't need to fight; I got a gun for that; piyah! Here; put these plates on the table while I fix the grits. Hey, hold up Mo! What is it? Why isn't my grits on my plate? I'm fixing it now baby! But why isn't it on the plate with my bacon and eggs? Ugh! That's gross; who does that! Girl your West Coast behind; I'm a country boy; put my damn grits on this plate. You can eat yours like it's cereal; I'm mixing mine with bacon, eggs, cheese, butter and some salt and pepper. Ugh AC! What Mo!

19

That's how you eat grits; not in no damn bowl woman. Ok give me your plate; I'll put them on it for you. Thank you Ma'am! You're welcome; now go sit down.

"Well it's official Las Vegas; it's only a few more days until The Star Trek Experience opens at the Las Vegas Hilton." "Our sources say; that ticket's for the first two days has already sold out." "Trek fans from all across the globe will be traveling to Las Vegas to enjoy the Star Trek Experience." "This has been Katie Strong; I will see you tonight for your 6 O'clock news." Are you going to see Doctor Spark Monica? Boy I ain't no Treke! Ha-Ha! I was just asking; you do eat grits out of a bowl with sugar on it. So anything is possible with you. Yeah; whatever AC.

Damn this is good; you should try it Coop! Girl you can keep that sweet ass grits. I was just kidding but on a serious note baby; I think you really should attend the funeral; especially when everyone else is going. Monica I've already made my mind up and its final, now talk about something else. How are things out at the ranch? Things are good but I think I can help you more if I was here in the city with you. How so? I could help keep an eye on things; you know watch for the snakes in the grass. Manny and the rest of the crew have that taken care of. Only so much though baby; they can't be here with you 24 7 like me. They have their lives and businesses to attend to. You can be my business and my only focus. All you have to do is point out all the players so I can watch their every move and report back to you. It sounds good Mo but whose going to take your place at the ranch? I still can work my days at the ranch and be with you when I'm off.

 That's my point exactly; so you really won't be with me every day now; will you? That may be true but who else can you trust to watch your back other than your crew. I'll think about it Mo; I know you got my back. Damn right I do baby; and don't you forget it. Now finish those nasty country grits you're eating over there. Shit; these grits are slamming girl! Ring-Ring! Ring-Ring! Are you gonna answer the phone AC? Nope! Ring-Ring! Let the answering machine get it! Ring-Ring! Ring-Ring! "Hi you reached Coop; leave a message!" "Hey Bruh! What's up; this is Jerm. I heard about what happened; I will be in town in a few days. I will come by when I get in. Later!"

 Who was that? My homie Jerm; out in LA; I don't remember if you met him or not. I don't think I did. I don't think so either but thanks; the food was good. You're welcome! Are you going out today? Nah; I'm chilling, gone roll up a few blunts and just kick it. Why; what's up? Nothing just asking because you haven't been out since the accident, that's all. No need to worry about me Mo; I'm good. Damn you smell that! Smell what AC! That smoke; it smells like something is burning! Did you turn all the eyes off? Yeah I did. Beep-Beep! Beep-Beep! Oh fuck Mo; the smoke alarm is going off! Something is still on! AC jumps up and runs over to the stove to check the eyes. Black smoke seeps out from below and brushes under his nose. Monica; open the slide door! Hurry up! Coop reaches down and opens the oven. God damn Mo! You done burn up the toast!

Oh shit; I forgot about it! Ha-ha! No kidding! This is the last time I let; you cook in my kitchen! You almost burn a brutha up in this muther. It was a mistake AC; I'm sorry! I know baby; damn this toast is black as charcoal though. Here; you want one! Boy; stop playing! Ha-ha! Well everything else was good Monica; this right here did you in though baby. Next time use the toaster. Now you got jokes huh! Nope I got crispy toast! Come on let's go get some fresh air. Monica and AC; both still in their night clothes; him in baby blue boxers and her in a long white tee made their way to the balcony.

Ahhh, fresh air! Do you have to go in today Mo? Nah; I work tomorrow. Do you like working there better than the perfume company? Nope! You're kidding right! Why not? Because you're not there! When I worked at the office; I looked forward to seeing you every day. I don't have that option at the ranch. But you do like the money though right? Yeah that's lovely, no complaints there. Well, that's all that matters; you can see me when you're off, like now. Yeah I guess; if that's how it has to be. Yep this is how it has to be. Don't be getting smart nigga. I ain't getting smart, just telling it like it is woman.

Do you miss her Coop? Of course I do; what kind of question is that Mo? I was just wondering that's all. Well stop wondering and most of all, stop asking dumb questions! Fuck you nigga; don't be going off on me like that! Then stop acting stupid girl; you got plenty of sense with your slick ass; the crew might not know you but I do; don't forget that shit Mo! That's the second time you came at me sideways Coop; do you have something you want to say? I just said it Bitch and lower your damn voice! Man you bugging; I will talk to your black ass later, you acting crazy. Yeah that's a good idea Mo; kick rocks! Bye AC; I'm getting dressed so I can take my ass home. Coop leans back against the rail, folds his arms and watches Monica as she storms off the balcony. His gut feeling just wouldn't stop telling him that Mo knows more about the accident then she's letting on.

Days later; as cool winds blew across the Mojave Desert's flat plane. AC's black Limo hastily approaches the empty desert where Loon, Will, Nina, Denna and Duck sat waiting on the hood of their vehicles for Coop and Manny's arrival. Out in the middle of nowhere on this 60 degree January evening as the sun began to set and mouths were mute, the obvious tension was thick enough to cut with a knife. Everyone was curious to know why their Boss and Capo summons a meeting out in the middle of the damn desert. The black limo finally approaches with clouds of dust still behind as Mick came to an abrupt stop, jumps out and opens the back door. What's going on soldiers? I don't know; you tell us AC! Slow your role Loon, it aint that serious. It seems serious to me Manny; yall got us out in the middle of bum fuck Egypt!

What's this all about Coop? It's about business Will; we need to tighten up. Why you say that bro; everything has been going fine; except for that accident. You may be right Denna but my gut is telling me different. Something is not right somewhere, I just haven't figured it out yet. I brought you all out here because it's safe and we can trust each other. This way there's no outsiders to worry about. Well; I'm glad you did AC! I know you just lost your girl but you've been kind of slacking since that shit happened. It's time to get back on the horse brother. We love you and you know we got your back. So whatever your gut is telling you, listen to it and do what needs to be done. Just remember Death before Dishonor, we aint going nowhere bro! Thanks Duck! No problem bro!

So what exactly is your gut telling you; Boss? I got that nervous feeling; like someone is too close. Know what I mean Loon? Yeah I feel you; who do you think it is? I have no idea but we need to put distance between us and these outsiders we're working with. From now on, be careful about what you say around them and trust your instincts.

Keep an eye out for anyone unusual and especially those asking too many questions! Alright; so say I come across someone that I think is a suspect. How do you want me to handle that? Just let me or Manny know and we will look into it Will. That way we can be sure before we handle business. Ok I can do that. Oh, I've been meaning to tell you that I met the Chief at that private party we did last year. What party was that Nina? The one with the Judge and the Senators, the Mansion party! Oh really; are you sure it was him? 100 percent sure Manny! I'll be damn; we've got some dirt on the Chief after all. Did he take a date with one of the girls Nina? Of course he did Coop; who can resist a beautiful Angel's Escort! Ha-ha! Good job sis! Did he remember you when he saw you New Year's Eve? I don't think so Manny; if he did; he didn't say anything. Hmmm; that's interesting, we'll just have to hold on to that card for now.

Hey Mick, hand me a bottle of water from the fridge please! Yes Sir! The driver enters the limo to retrieve a bottle of water from the fridge while the crew continues their conversation. Nina took the opportunity to whisper out a thought that she'd been pondering. AC what about him? Who Nina; Mick? Yeah him! He's not a problem; I hired him from the Towers driver's staff. Ok; I was just making sure. Here you are sir; one water! Thanks Mick!

Hey guys; what do you think about using the drainage tunnels? Use them for what Duck? For the weekly re-up Coop; I think it would bring down the probability of someone finding out our moves. Man those tunnels are full of bums Duck. I know that Manny but hear me out! Ok we're listening go ahead. Well; the tunnels already run under the warehouse on industrial anyway; all we have to do is take the operation underground. When the shipments come in, we can have it run through the tunnels instead of meeting at the warehouse and picking up duffle bags of product in broad daylight. That's sounds good Duck but I still have to convince Diego to dig a hole in his warehouse floor to the tunnels. He is a business man, so he probably would go with it. I tell you what, you guys chill for a second while I go call him. Alright Coop; handle your business Boss. I'll be back in a minute Manny, hold it down.

Ring-Ring! Ring-Ring! Hello, who is speaking! Diego; what's up brother, this is AC. AC my friend, what is going

27

on? I just came across a way to make us some more money and move more shipments safely. Oh yeah; tell me about it my friend. Let's have lunch; I can be in Vegas tomorrow. Cool, call me when you get here and we can have a sit down. Alright my friend, tomorrow we have drinks. Later Diego! Hey Mick, you got a light on you? Sure Loon; here you go. Thanks man! Will, you wanna hit this blunt with me? Hell yeah; light that shit up! So what did he say Coop? He's coming down tomorrow Capo for a sit down. Alright, that's what's up. Does anyone have something they want to put on the table since we're all here now?

Yeah Boss, I do! Go ahead Denna. Are you 100% yet, I mean after what happened with Brina? I'm good sis, aint nothing I can do about it now; let's just keep our minds on this paper and this business. Ok bro; I was just checking; you know we all got your back no matter what. Thanks Denna and I appreciate your concern sis. Yeah; no problem AC. Hey Loon; when you get a chance go by the health clinic or shelter and find us a kamikaze! The others look his way and responds all at once. Whoa! Hold up AC! Chill out guys; let me explain before you get crazy. Remember that operation during Desert Shield when the old bum walked up on Bravo Company. Yeah; the pan handler right! Yeah Duck, that one. Coop that motherfucker was tied to 3 pounds of C4! He killed half the damn platoon; what does that has to do with you sending Loon on a kamikaze mission. Here me out Capo! Ok; go ahead we're listening! We'll; say if my gut is right and we have to deal with the opposition. The way I see it; if they are coming for us they apparently already know who we are. If we enlist a kamikaze to act when we call on him and only then we can take them out with the element of surprise. That's cool and all AC; but who the fuck are you going to find to do a suicide mission for us? Just listen Duck; I already put some thought into this. We find someone that is infected with H.I.V and they don't have long to live. Make them an offer to take care of their family members and grant any last wishes they have before they complete the mission. A logical wish of course; and why would they refuse; they're dead anyway.

Coop you're crazy but that's a smart ass move; I guess that's why you're the Boss bruh; I would have never thought of that. Thanks Will; so are you guys down with it?

Hell yeah; all in baby! Great; Loon make it happen! I'm on it baby; I'll let you know when I find a prospect. Solid; ok then crew, that's it; Manny or I will let you guys know what happens with Diego. Head back to your post and be safe in them streets; things are starting to heat up! Mick; let's go player!

"Hello Gentlemen, welcome to Dolls Fabulous Lunch Hour!" "Eat all you want and please, please tip the ladies." "This is Dj Skillz; holding you down on the Day Shift!" Hey Red; what's up baby? Hey Dylan; how you doing girl? Are you working today? No Ma'am; me and Barbie are headed out of town! Damn girl, yall stay on the road. I know girl; it's only business though. What kind of business? It aint nothing; is Will in? Yeah he's in the office. Ok I'm going to holler at him. Alright Dylan! "Alright fellas we got Gia coming to the stage!" "Taking yall to Staten Island with this WU-Tang; CREAM!" "Cash rules everything around me; CREAM get the money!" "Dollar Dollar Bill yall!" " I grew up on the crime side; New York Times side." "Staying alive was no jive." Knock-Knock! It's open, come in! Hey Big Will; what's up! Hey Dylan; come in baby!

I just stopped by to let you know that me and the girls were headed out. Gloria and Trish are headed to LA this time. That's cool; where are you and Barbie going? We are hitting Arizona this time. And the other girls? Well; Shooter and ol girl going to Utah and Asia and Malibu are working Vegas. Alright that's what it is; check in with me Wednesday and I will let you know who is making the pick-up. Ok Will; later baby! Yeah; be safe and don't do anything stupid! Who me! That should be the least of your problems. I hear you Dylan; just keep it on the down low. I promise Will; I will behave! Bye Dylan!

"Fellas let's hear it for Gia; she will be stepping down from the stage now." "She is available for table dances and privates, so hit your girl up and spend some loot!" "Coming to the stage next; we have the lovely Remy!" "Once again; this Dj Skillz; rocking the day shift here at Dolls!" "Home of the sexiest entertainers in Sin City!" Bye Red; I'm out girl! Alright Dylan; see you next time babe! Yo; can I get a Crown on ice? Sure honey; give me a second! No problem; take your time baby. Ok you said a crown on the rocks; right? Yes! I've never seen you here before; are you visiting? Yes I am! Great; how are you enjoying Sin City? It's ok; so far!

Well; I'm Deb but everyone calls me Red; what's your name sir? Oh you can call me Jack! Ok Jack; here's your Crown on the rocks and welcome to Vegas; I hope you enjoy your stay. Thanks Red; are you originally from here? Yes I am; where are you from; if you don't mind me asking. Bridgeport! Isn't that in Connecticut? Yes it is. So what brings you to Vegas? I'm here for the Pawn Brokers Convention. Really; so you have a pawn shop? Yeah; three to be exact! Interesting; are all three in Bridgeport? Yes they are. So is that a good business Jack? I think so Red; I make pretty good money and I have been in business for 6 years now. That's great Jack; congratulations! Thank you Red!

Hey daddy; did you want a dance? Who me? Yeah you mister! Red can't give you no dance; she's just the bartender; all she can give you is a drink! So, do you want one or not? No thank you; I'll pass! What! You must be gay or something; you're going to pass on all of this right here!

Gia calm down girl, he said he didn't want a dance; so go about your business. Fuck you Red, stop cock blocking Bitch! What! Girl you better calm your nerves before I come across this bar! Come on Bitch; I'll fuck you up! Gia; just take your high ass to the dressing room and sit down somewhere; you're not worth my time. Um-hmm. That's what I thought; ol red headed skank.

Damn; is that how all the girls act in here? No Jack; excuse that mess; she's probably too drunk. I am so sorry about that; here, have another drink on me. Thanks Red; you didn't have to do that. No, it's on me; it's the least I could do. "Gentlemen we have Remy coming at you one more time." "Remember to pay the pussy bill; these ladies do work for tips and tips only." "Show some love for Remy as she entertains us while dancing off this Funkdafied!"

"So, So, So Funkdafied." "So, So, So Funkdafied." So, So, So Funkdafied." "Open up, open up and let the funk flow in" "From this nigga named J and his new found friend." "I'm hitting switches like Eric on the solo creep." "For yo jeep it's the B.R.A.T."

Night falls over the Las Vegas strip as traffic creep at a snail's pace while red tail lights illuminate the boulevard. 45 stories above watching it all below; Nina and Denna sit on the balcony of her newly renovated Tower's Condo. They did a good job on the window sis; looks perfect. Yeah; I still can't believe that AC shot them out. Nina; you know he was under a lot of stress then. I'm not tripping Denna; it's just hard to believe that Sabrina is gone and it's been a month already. Damn has it really been a month? Yep; it will be February in two days girl! Damn Nina; where did the time go? We only live once baby; let's start living life to the fullest. You can say that shit again Denna! I want some smoke sis; do you have some here? Yeah; look in my top dresser drawer and bring the bong off my bathroom counter. I'll fix us some wine while you're doing that. Alright bet!

Ooh wee! This is some strong chronic Nina! Where did you get it? Dupree! Damn; it smells good and green; just how I like it too. You're a hype Denna! Why, because I like to smoke; you got some nerve girl. I did just get this from your dresser drawer. So if I'm a hype; you one too chica! Shut up Denna; here, drink your wine. Hold on sis; let me light this first. The bubbles boiled as she lit the bowl while inhaling the indo smoke, held it in then passed the bong to Nina. She exhales then in a low voice makes a remark while Nina inhales. Yeaahhhh; this some good shit sis; good shit. She looks up at Denna; exhales then shakes her head. I know sis; I know.

I got a question for you Denna! What is it? How did you end up with Loon's whoring ass? I don't know girl, things just happened; I think he spiked my drink one night or something. We were at the wooden nickel having drinks one night and one thing led to another. The next thing I know; we were in a hotel suite making out! Yeah his slick ass probably slipped you a mickey. You think so sis? Knowing him; yep! Has he been faithful to you? As far as I know he has. Now that; I can't believe! Well; I already told him, I would kill his ass if he did! Shit; if you don't I will! Damn right sis; now pass me that bong! Ha-ha! Wow chica; you're a damn weed head aint you?

Nina; don't start that non-sense; give me the smoke. You need to get you a man; when was the last time you had some? Huh? You heard me! Damn it feels good out here tonight. Don't try and change the subject; answer the question! It's been too long sis; too damn long. So you need to fix that; you got this nice ass condo over-looking the strip and you sleeping here all alone. I'm gone set you up with somebody. Who Denna? I have no idea, but right now your ass doesn't have the right to be picky! Why not? Because you're getting older by the minute and pretty soon you're going to get used to being alone. That's not good sister.

Well just make sure he's not a bum! Beggars can't be choosey! I'm not playing Denna! Alright, alright I know. Enough of that; how are things out at the Ranch? Just crazy; all those girls do is have sex all day; they don't even leave the Ranch. It's a whore house sis; what did you think was going to happen! I thought it was going to be different but now I see. It's not that much different from what I do running the Escort agency. That's what I thought because at the Adult store we had peep show girls and I was under the impression that it would be similar. Well isn't it? Nope! How so? Look at it like this Nina; the Ranch is where they live and they don't leave. The girls eat, sleep, cook and fuck at the Ranch. They're on the clock 24 hours a day.

At least at the Club, Agency or Adult store they can have a, some-what normal life with days off and such but not at the Ranch. There; it's pussy, pussy, pussy! All day, every day in that joint and I'm the one that has to crack the whip to make sure they're giving it up! So, are you saying you don't like doing it Denna? I can care less about them hoes sis; I had to shoot one bitch in her foot the first week. Then just a few months ago I had to murder this pimp who thought he could just post up his RV across from the Ranch, and cock block our paper. Damn; that's too much drama! It comes with the territory Nina; I know our crew is making a lot of paper right now and there's going to be haters and stick up kids coming at us from all angles. I'm surprised no one crossed you yet. I am too sis but I'm sure it's coming. Well, here's to keeping the Nine locked and cocked for those fools! Cheers! I'll drink to that!

We need to get Monica out to the gun range though; I don't think she is comfortable with a piece yet. Girl all that damn desert out there where you at! You don't need a range; take her ass out behind the building and shoot some stuff up. Ha-ha! You're right sis, I never thought about that. How is she working out anyway? She's a natural at it Nina; got a lot of street sense. That's a good thing; once we get her right with the fire, she can roll hard. Yep; she's definitely gone need to be ready; especially now that she's gone be with Coop like that.

For all we know; AC probably taught her how to shoot already. I don't know if he did or not but I'm going to make sure she can; first chance I get. Well; one thing is for sure Denna! What's that sis? She's down for whatever; that Bitch came on the scene and months later; Sabrina's ass is ghost! What are you saying Nina? All I'm saying is; if it walks like a duck and talks like a duck; it's probably a duck. Nina gone with that bullshit; you really think so! Hmmm.

February, 1998.

Ring-Ring! Ring-Ring! Hello; thank you for calling Vegas Luxury Auto! Jackie speaking! Yes may I speak to Dubai! I'm sorry Ma'am he's with a customer at the moment. May I take a message? No that's ok; I'll call later. Ok and thank you for calling Vegas Luxury Auto. Excuse me! Yes Sir; what can I do for you? I'm here to see Duck! Ok hold on minute; he was with a customer. Ring-Ring! Yeah Jackie; what is it? You have a visitor; are you still with a customer? No I'm available, who is it? Hold on! Excuse me sir; what's your name? Hector baby! It's Hector sir! Alright send him in; I've been expecting him. Alright Mr. Dubai he's on the way. You may head back to the office Sir! Thanks baby!

Hector; come in brother; have a seat! What's up amigo; I see business is booming! Hell yeah and I love it! That's good homie; so what you got for me? I need three of those new Range Rovers, two Rolls and one of those new BMW coupes. We can do that; how soon did you need them delivered? Can you have them in a week? Maybe but let's say two weeks for sure; let's leave some room for error.

Does it matter what color they are? Nah man; I can sell whatever color you get; just get them for me player. Alright homie; I got you covered. Knock-knock! Hey baby; come in! I didn't know you were coming by. Hi Hector! Hey Karen; how you doing mommy! I'm great Hector and thanks for asking.

Hey Homie; I'll take care of this for you; I'm gone let you two love birds be. Alright Hector; thanks bro! Damn Karen; you looking fine as fuck in that dress baby! Oh yeah; you like it! Hell yeah! I don't have on any panties either! Shit; you never wear any panties girl! Ha-ha! You're funny Duck! Close that door and come over here woman. No- you come to me Sir! Duck rolls from behind his desk and slowly approaches Karen while sitting in his big blue office chair. Ummm; you smelling good too girl! Can I taste that kitty? Umm-Hmm; I just shaved it too! Karen leans back in the corner behind the closed office door and teases Duck by lifting up her dress just a little.

He rolls in closer so that she wouldn't have any room to run. Ummm-Hmmm! I'm stuck baby; I can't move! Shut up and hold up that dress; put your left foot on the arm of this chair and let me have that kitty. Oooh! Ooh Duck!

Dubai slides his right arm up under her left thigh and grips a hand full of her dress then moves in for desert. Oh that feels good; oh lick it right there. Yeah like that; damn you're eating the fuck out of my pussy. He strokes his tongue from the bottom of her wet wet then up inside her sugar walls. Slowly he licks inside her moist lips, starting from the top then around clockwise to the bottom then all over again. Oh! Oh shit! Duck! Duck! Slurp-Slurp! Slurp-Slurp! Dubai licks Karen's whole vagina sideways then sucks on her clit just a little and watch as she jerks spontaneously from moments of infinite pleasure. Oh my God; I'm about to cum in your mouth baby! Oh my God! Oh my God! Holy Shit! Uggghhhh; Yesssss!

Knock-Knock! Yeah what is it! I have your mail Sir! Hold on Jackie! Just keep it up front, I'll get it later! Ok! Bend over baby! Why; I'm finished Duck! But I'm not; now bend that ass over; put your head in the corner and try to hold your screaming down; I got customers out front. Alright, don't be trying to kill me with that snake of yours; go slow! Duck stands up from the chair; drops his dress pants then grabs both her butt cheeks; spreads them apart and slides his Johnson in slow like she ask. Umm, Umm, Umm, Umm, you're hurting me Duck. Umm, Umm, Umm, go slow baby. Karen's back arches a little more as she holds her head down in the corner while her silky black hair fall evenly off both sides of her neck. Damn you're dripping wet girl; back this pussy up and take this dick! Umm, Umm, Umm, slow down Duck! Umm, Umm, Umm, Damn baby; my- Come on girl; you're a champ; you can take it!

Umm, Umm, Umm, Oh shit! Shhh; hold it down Karen; I got customers remember. Umm, slow down baby, you banging my insides up. Ok I'm almost done! Put it in my ass Duck, you're tearing my insides up. Hell no; you will be screaming even louder. Well; let me suck it! Nope! Umm, Umm, Umm, Umm! Yeah that's it girl, take this cock! Umm, Umm, Umm, Umm! Ring-Ring! Ring-Ring! Get the phone baby! Fuck that phone! I'm about to nut girl, hold on; it's coming. Umm, Umm, Umm, Umm! You like that; don't you? Umm-hmm! Uh-huh! Uh-huh! Uh-huh! Oh shit; yeah motherfucker! Hurry up; turn around Karen; catch this nut; I don't want to get any on the floor! Karen stands up, turns around and sits in the blue office chair. Duck grabs the back of her head then slides his cock down her wet throat. Uggggh! Uggggh! Ugggh! Uggggggggh! Whew!

Damn that felt good! You get it all Karen! Umm-Hmm! Now that was good; did you enjoy it too baby? Yeah but we can't be doing it in your office because I like to scream and I can't scream here. Aw, but it was fun though right? Hell yeah it was; you licked the linen out of my pussy and tried to rip my guts out with that sneak but it was good though baby! You God damn right it was woman! Alright don't start getting all macho mister; you alright! Ha-Ha! What the fuck ever Karen!

"What's up Las Vegas; you know what time it is!" "It's 8pm and that means it's time for you guys to start calling in your request" "I'm Dj Glenn and I'm hanging out with you for the next four hours baby!" "So; start ringing these phones while I put on our first request from Rose Royce; Love Don't Live here anymore!" "You abandon me, Love don't live here anymore" "Just a vacancy, love don't live here anymore" "When you lived inside of me, there was nothing I could conceive." Ring-Ring! Ring-Ring! Hello Towers front desk; Dave speaking; how may I help you?

What up Dave; it's AC! Hey Mr. Cooper; what can I do for you? Can you pull out my Harley, I'm about to take a ride. Ok sir; did you want it now? Yes; I'll be down in 15 minutes! Ok it will be ready! Thanks David! No problem Sir; my pleasure. "In the windmills of my eyes" "Everyone can see the loneliness inside of me" "Why'd ya have to go away!" AC slips on his black leather biker pants and jacket along with his timbs then grabs the 357 off the kitchen table and heads down the hall to the elevator. A dead uncomfortable calm came over his body as his mind pondered on his ex-wife; his kids and Sabrina. It had been almost 2 years since he seen his children; that alone left a hole in his heart and a huge knot in his gut. The passing of Sabrina had only made the pain worst. He needed to somehow get that monkey off his back. As the elevator doors closed and he descended down; it finally hit him; he had made up his mind. Tonight no matter what happened he was going to see his kids and nothing or no one was going to stop him. Staring at his image in the gold mirror doors he watched himself closely; head hung down but eyes straight ahead. His mind was set. Ding!

Thick cigar smoke, seared steaks and onions along with loud drums, horns and soprano voices filled the lobby air from the live lounge band and busy Tower's Restaurants. Hello Mr. Cooper; you're Harley is waiting and here's your helmet. Thanks David! You're welcome Sir! Hello Sir, where's the destination tonight? Oh you're good Mick; I'm taking my bike; take the night off; I'll see you tomorrow. Ok Sir; have a good one! I will Mick, you do the same and wash that Limo; it's filthy. Yes Sir!

Hey David where can I get this thing washed at this time of night? Are the lot attendants still here? No man, they clocked out at 7! Do you know of anywhere close then? I think everything is closed Mick, shit just park it in back and wash it yourself man. I don't think so Dave; I'm not getting this suit wet. Oh; I don't blame you but I don't know what to tell you my man. Thanks anyway, I'll figure something out. You're welcome! Oh that's the first time I've seen AC with that bike; does he ride often. Not so much now but he used to ride a lot around this time last year. Oh ok; alright later David; have a good one. You too Mick!

15 miles and 20 minutes later AC arrives in Summerlin; his heart pounding and palms sweating as he slowly approaches the front door of his old home. Knock-Knock! Knock-knock! Hey AC; what are you doing here? I came to see the kids! It's almost 9 o'clock on a school night; they haven't seen you in two years; why haven't you called!

45

Don't start with me woman; you know why! Hey baby; who is it? Oh it's my ex-husband! That was a man's voice; who the fuck you got in my house bitch? Hey calm down brother; I'm her husband now! Oh you got married again and didn't tell me! Tell you for what! It wasn't your business! You know what; you're right! I just came to see the kids; can I see them. Look man, it's late and.... Hey nigga; if you know what's good for you; you'll shut your face before something bad happens; mind your damn business.

Rodney; go back inside; I'll handle this; it's ok. Are you sure babe? Yeah I got it! Alright AC; I'll let you see them; just a few minutes ok, they have school in the morning. That's fine! You can come in and sit down! Thanks! Coop enters his old house but stops just 5 steps in. His body went numb as he gaze over the pictures that hang on the wall; the familiar living room furniture he purchased just years ago was still sitting right where he left it. The pictures and statues he brought back from over-seas sat on the mantle over the fire place and off in the corner sat his favorite stereo system and cd collection. Hey I'll just wait outside; ok! Why; what's wrong; you can have a seat!

No, that's ok! I'll be on the porch. Daddy! Daddy! Daddy! Coop's heart pounds rapidly as the three little ones ran up to him then jump in his arms.

Hey; I missed you guys; how are you? Good; where you been daddy? I've been working a lot; sorry I didn't come by sooner! How is school? It's fun; we made some rockets and painted some pictures too! That's great! I'm so proud of you guys! Are you coming home daddy? No; I don't live here anymore baby but I promise I will come by and see you again soon; ok! Yeah daddy! Ok, you guys get to bed; I love you! Muah! Bye Daddy! Bye Bye! Alright; thanks for letting me see them; I really do appreciate it. You be safe and I will call you next time I want to see them. Ok sure; just not so late! Alright; no problem!

Ring-Ring! Ring-Ring! Hello! Hey Fool; where you at? Whose this! Jerm man! Oh what up boy! Me and Tammy just hit town; where you at? On the way to the Towers; where you guys at? We're stopping by Denny's to get a bite. Which one homie? Over by Odyssey Records! Ok; I'll meet yall over there; order me a Grand Slam! Ok no doubt; see you in a bit fool! Hello; welcome to Denny's; you guys may sit where ever you like; your server will be with you shortly. Thank you Ma'am! You're welcome Sir! Where do you want to sit Tam, a booth or a table? Let's sit at this booth Jerm; it looks clean. Ok baby!

Hello folks; I'm Jason; and I will be your server today. Can I start you guys off with something to drink? Sure; I'll have a sprite and glass of OJ for my girl. Alright I'll be right back with your drinks Sir! You buggin J; what if I didn't want OJ! You always get orange juice woman. I'm just saying; maybe I wanted a sprite too. Ok then, we'll tell Jason when he comes back. Nah I'm fine; I was just saying that's all. Tammy you crazy; that's your problem! Don't call me crazy boy. I love you baby but your ass is off a few tics. Kiss my red ass Jermaine. Aww baby; I'm just fooling with you! Ok here's your OJ Ma'am and a sprite for you Sir! Thanks Jason! My pleasure; do you guys know what you're having yet? Where are you from Jason? West Las Vegas Sir! Cool, maybe you can help me. Help you with what Sir? Call me Jerm man; Sir is not necessary. I'm sorry; what did you need help with Jerm?

I'm looking for that white girl; have you seen her? For show; she's around. That's what's cracking player, what time is she coming through? Whenever you want her to man! It usually takes her 30 minutes to get here, sometimes 60; but if you want to wait until you guys are done eating she can be here in an hour and a half. Ok that's what's up Jason. Hey Tam; let me have that c-note and those three twenties out of that money I gave you earlier. Here you go baby! Thanks Tam! Here you go Jason, make sure she's here in an hour and a half and keep the change. Alright no problem; are you guys ready to order? Yeah let me get two grand slams, my boy is on the way up here. What are you having Ma'am? Uh, let me get a moon over my hammy.

Ok I have two Grand Slams and one Moon over Hammy; will there be anything else? Yeah bring another sprite for my partner and don't forget to tell that girl to be here in an hour and a half. Got you covered Jerm; be back shortly with your order. Baby; why did you give that guy your money; you don't even know him! Shit that fool aint going nowhere baby; plus I know where he works. He'll be a dumb ass to stiff me out of $150. He just might be that Jay. Be what girl? A dumb ass! Ha-Ha! Tam I love you; your crazy ass! It's all good he aint going nowhere! I hear you Jermaine and it was $160; you never know what someone is going through. He might have a bill he needs to pay or it could be anything! Woman would you please chill; damn!

Jerm; what up boy! There he is! AC what up fool! Aint much, just kickin it; you ordered my Grand Slam! I got you homie! Hey Tam! Hey AC; how are you? I'm great, can't complain; just thankful for another day. Hey I'm sorry to hear about Sabrina my man; that was crazy. Yeah it was but life goes on right. So what brings you two to Vegas; you were supposed to be here a few weeks ago? Tammy wanted to come for Valentine's Day weekend. Ok I hear that; you guys tying the knot this weekend? Nigga don't start her up with that marriage stuff. He's scared AC; I'm gone leave his ass if he don't hurry up. Girl you aint going nowhere, stop tripping. Alright; aint no ring on this finger; so that means, aint no lock on this pussy either; play-boy! Ha-Ha! Yall crazy as hell! Tammy cool it; will yah? Just say you scared Jerm; Coop knows you're a punk anyway. Ha-Ha! Boy Tammy is giving you the business. Yeah you started it nigga! Who? You; aint no owls in this bitch! Ok guys; here's your meals! One Moon over my hammy for the lady and two Grand Slams for the fellas! Thanks Jason!

You're welcome Jerm; let me know if you all need anything else.

Damn this smells good! I know right; I'm hungry as a cow! So what you been up to fool; are you still trying to be a Mafia Don around this joint. I'm handling my business; you need to come and work for me. Hell nah fool; Vegas aint for me; I love the L.A life; Sun and Beaches; this I can't do. I'll pay you more money! Man I aint no gangster; I'm a lover not a fighter; you feel me. I feel yah home boy; but the offer is always on the table. You never know when you might change your mind. AC please; Jerm is not changing his mind. He wants to stay at that record label and hang out at the L.A clubs and party with the celebrities. He thinks he's a star! I am a star girl! See I told you Coop! Ha-ha! Yall funny to me!

How is everything guys? We're cool Jason! Oh this is for you sir! Jason slides a small black desert box over to Jerm while he's eating. Thanks my man! You're welcome; enjoy your meals and call me if you need anything. Damn fool; you already ordered desert and you haven't even finished eating your food yet. You still greedy like always. This aint no desert fool! Then what is it! Here look for yourself.

Coop takes the box from Jerm and opens it up. Aww nigga; you still on this shit; how much did you pay for it? Just $150! Man I could have gotten you the stuff for free; why didn't you just wait?

Because he's a fast ass; that's why; I told him not to even get it from that dude. We don't even know him! Jerm you're a head case; I hope that this isn't just baking soda. You'll be a mad nigga if he just went in the kitchen and bagged your ass up some gold medal flour; huh? Shit; I'll bust that fool head open with this plate! Man; you're my boy and all but sometimes I wonder about your ass. AC; both of yall can kiss my ass; eat your food and let me worry about my business. Ok playboy I was just saying but you got it. Where you coming from anyway fool? Oh; I stopped by to see the kids. Oh yeah; how are they? They're good; it's been almost two years since I saw them last. Damn; why so long Coop? I know Tammy but the ex-wife tried to put me on supervised visits but I told her that wasn't gone work. I only went tonight because I finally said fuck it and just went!

Sometimes I wonder about these women; doing all this crazy stuff to their kid's fathers; then be mad when they don't come around. I don't even let it bother me Tammy; I just keep busy and stay focus on making this paper. This was good, thanks Jerm. Where you guys headed after you leave here? We're going to check in the Luxor; wash up then hit the town. Alright; hit me up when you get out; I'll be at the Towers. Thanks again; it was nice seeing you Tam. Nice to see you as well AC. Ok fool; we'll see you later!

Hey; I like that outfit Remy! Where did you get it girl? Bitch I had this custom made! Wow; it looks nice; who made it for you? This old lady over on Desert Inn; the same lady that made all of Sabrina's outfits! Meagan used to wear some hot ass stuff too! Yeah I miss her ass; it's still hard to believe she's dead Gia! I know right; that was so sudden. Did they ever find out what happened? I didn't hear anything else about it Gee, who knows! Damn, she was so happy the last time I saw her; AC had just proposed to her at the Christmas party that night. Wow, really, that's so sad; I had no idea she was getting married Remy! Yep; she was so excited too! Alright girl; we better get on this floor before Will comes back here fussing.

I need some money; whose Dee jaying today? I think Tru is Remy. Good because Skillz be fucking up a bitch set with his drunken ass. That fool comes to work tore up! Well at least we don't have to worry about him begging for ass all night like Tech! Begging! Girl please; that boy a trick; he paid for this pussy every time he hit it. You better tell that fool to come off some ends the next time he starts begging. Girl; stop lying! Gia you're the fool honey; closed mouths don't get fed and neither do legs, so use that ATM God gave you and cash in fool. Unless you like being broke! Hell nah; I need all the money I can get! Then you better start taxing these niggas and stop fucking for drinks and chicken wings. Ha-ha! Fuck you Remy aint nobody fucking for no damn drinks and chicken wings. Might as well; you aint getting paid; are you?

Shit; from now on I will be! Hey; what are yall waiting on; get on the damn floor already! We're going Will; we're going, hold your horses. You two are always the last ones to get out here. I don't know what the hell I'm gone do with yall asses! Hurry up; I'm taxing yall a late fee next time, you hear me! Yes Boss; we hear you Boss! Remy you crazy Bitch! Why! Making fun of Will like that! Girl he just needs some pussy; I'll go give him some later! What; you fucking Will girl! Gia, you better lay off them drugs girl and get in the game. The sooner you learn that your pussy can get you anything you want. The better you'll be sister! Well; I'm just gone stick to your ass like glue then Remy. That's fine but it's gone cost you a drink! What! Yep; hey Red, let me get a double shot of Crown baby; Gia's paying for it. Bitch you a trip! Ha-ha! Thanks for the drink girl! What's up Gia; did you want anything? Yeah Red; a double shot of Jose'!

Ok one double Crown and one double Jose' coming up! Thanks baby! You're welcome Remy! "Alright guys; it's Friday and I know yall fools got paid; so it's time to come off the pussy bill" "Coming to the stage; straight from Bangkok Thailand we have the gorgeous Mystery" "This is her first night at Dolls; so give her a warm Vegas welcome" "And I don't mean clap; ass holes; give up the money!" "So without further a due; here's that new booty" "Dancing to this hot ass track from Dru Hill!"

She's cute Remy! Yeah she is but can she dance! Ha-ha! Yeah right; she might be like the last two that was here from Germany. Ha-Ha! Didn't Will send them ho's to escort? Yep; I think he did Gia! She's doing ok though; she can dance better than you Remy. Girl please; she can't get none! "I got this feeling and I just can't turn it loose" "That somebody's been getting next to you" "I don't want to walk around knowin' I was your fool" "Cuz being the man that I am, I just can't lose my cool."

Hey Red! What's up D; what you having hun? One Corona and a shot of Rum please! Coming right up! Hey baby; what you doing here? I came to have a drink with my Remy. Hey Gia! Hey Derek! Here you go; one Corona and your shot of Bacardi. Thanks Red! It's kind of dead in here huh! It will pick up in a few D; did you make some loot today? Yeah I did ok; about 8 stacks. What! That's my white chocolate; make that paper honey! That's what it's all about baby; stacking this cheese, aint it? You damn right sugar! Hey, I'll be back in a few; I need to holler at Will for a minute. Alright Derek!

The fluorescent pink lights flickered just above the mirrors over the corner booth where Will was sitting; observing his operation. The club had begun to get busier from the after work crowd and 2nd shift dancers that populated the floor as beautiful naked women scrolled back and forth. Yo D; what's up playa; come on and have a seat man! Hey Will; what's poppin? Aint much, just out here making sure these fools working, that's all. Speaking of work; how's business going for you. Are you keeping up with those orders? Oh yeah; I have that all under control. Cool, that's what I like to hear! Did you want a dance or something; a sandwich, a drink? Nah I'm good; I wanted to put a bug in your ear. Oh yeah; spit it out then; what's on your mind? Remember when I made that drop for Duck a few months ago. No refresh my memory! The Lexus truck! Oh that Paco drop! Yeah that one! What about it? Well; that fool asked me to cook up a new batch for him. Ok; go ahead continue! But he didn't want to go through the right channels to get it! Let me understand this; you're saying he wanted to buy from you direct and skip paying us! Yep!

That motherfucking snake! What did you tell him Derek? I told him, if he wanted something he needed to go through AC or Manny like always and that I couldn't help him. What did that snake have to say then? I didn't stick around to hear him; I got in the car and left. Last I know he was standing in the middle of the parking lot shouting as we pulled off. We? Yeah; Remy and I were together that day remember; I dropped her off at work after. Oh yeah; I remember that day. Thanks for telling me that D; I'll make sure we take care of that punk ass before it's too late! It's no problem Will; I've been meaning to tell you sooner but it kept slipping my mind until this morning when I was driving over. Well, I'm glad you did! Grab yourself a drink on me; I need to go handle some business! Ok thanks bro! Don't mention it!

Hey Detectives; how are you guys today? Did you want this dirty car wash; we got a special going; half off the original price. That's a full wax, armour all and vacuum. Nah, we're looking for your Boss! Oh Fat Boy; that's him right there walking to the Tahoe! Ok thanks! You guys almost missed him he's about to head out to the Rebels game. Go ahead Casey; park this thing while I go chat with this Fat fuck! Alright Briggs; I'll be over in a second. Hey! Hey! Are you Fat Boy? That depends whose asking! I'm detective Casey; Homicide with LVMPD and that's my partner Briggs walking over here now. What can I do for you guys; I'm running late for my game. We just have a few questions about this missing person.

Nobody that I know is missing; who you guys talking about? Everything ok over here Casey? Yeah Briggs; Fat boy has been kind enough to be late to his game to answer some questions for us. What! I didn't say I was answering shit! Look Sir; you can answer them here or come down and answer them at our place. We got a nice smoke free room with a cold AC and a window you can look out of.

Alright, alright, go ahead what did you want to know? That's more like it Fat Man! It's Fat Boy! Whatever dude, we're looking for this fellow from New York named Crash. I don't know anyone by that name. What makes you think I do anyway? We had a phone call from one of his relatives yesterday. And? They said he came down here to your shop looking for one of your acquaintances. Detectives; I don't know anything about him, how does he look. Hold on; I'm glad you asked. We have a picture right here. Well, let me see it! Lower your voice Sir or we can do this downtown. Did you ever see this man? Nah, I aint never seen him around here detective. Thank you Sir; for your cooperation! Yeah no problem, can I go to my game now? Sure and call us if you remember anything! Um-hmm! What did you think Casey? That boy was lying through his teeth; he knows something. Well what do you want to do? Let's wait until he's out of sight then we can question these employees. Ok, I'll be back, I'm going to notify dispatch of our 20. Alright Briggs!

Excuse me young man! Yes Ma'am! Have you seen this guy around here recently? Umm; no don't think so detective! Can you please look again and take your time; I know you're trying to work but this man is missing and his family is worried about him. You can understand that right? Yes Ma'am I understand but I haven't seen the guy. Alright thanks for your time; you can get back to work. Sorry I couldn't help you detective, hope you find him. Yeah thanks! Excuse me! Nope don't ask me nothing; I aint seen nothing and don't know shit!

Excuse me Sir; how was that? You heard me detective; don't know nothing and I aint seen shit! What's your name sir? Number 4578904 CCDC! Oh you got jokes huh? Nope I just aint seen nothing; and that's the name I went by for 5 years straight. So can you please let me work; I'm trying to be a productive citizen. Oh really; what was that name again? I forgot detective; my doctor says I'm crazy because I always forget things from one minute to the next. Is everything ok over here Casey? Yeah we got a smart mouth convict over here, that's all. Did you want to take his ass in? Take me in for what Detective! You asked did I know something and I said I didn't! How in the hell are you gonna arrest a working man for that? You got a smart mouth convict! Can I just get my work done detective; that's all a felon wanna do; damn! Come on Briggs; nobody seen anything over here. I don't believe that Casey; somebody knows something; they're just scared I think.

Hey let's get out of here; come on. Hold on Casey let's talk to this transient over by the sidewalk, he probably knows something. Hello Sir! Howdy Ma'am! I'm detective Briggs; what's your name? My friends call me Walt but you can call me Walter if you want. God damn; it smells over here! Briggs hurry up; he stinks! Wait a minute Casey! Walter we're looking for this man, have you seen him around here? You have to hold it closer detective; I'm kind of blind without my glasses. Oh I'm sorry, here you go, is that better? Well; I think so but I need to eat so I can be sure of it. How was that Sir? My memory gets kind of shady if I don't eat and the garbage cans haven't been kind to me for two days. Nobody is throwing away food

61

anymore, just cups and wrappers. What did you want to eat Walter; will a burger fill you up?

How about some Jack in the Box! That will work fine Ma'am! Ok come on Walter, you can ride in the back seat; let's get some lunch! Briggs; are you kidding me; you're putting him in the car! Yes; he may know something? What if he doesn't? Then we've done our good deed for today! Come on Walter; have a seat in the back, it's only a few blocks. Thank you Ma'am, God bless you! We need to drop him off at the gym so he can take a shower; I'm about to puke. Really Casey; it aint that bad! Hey there's a Jack in the Crack right there; turn; hurry!

Park here Briggs! I need to get out, this is ridiculous! Alright, come on Walter; let's get you something to eat. What did you want? A chicken sandwich and fries will be lovely Ma'am. Ok, did you want a drink too? Yes a large Ice Tea! Hey Casey; are you coming? In a minute Briggs, there's no way I can eat with that smell around me. I'll be in shortly; I have to air out. Suite yourself; we'll be inside partner. After you Ma'am! Thanks Walter! Welcome to Jack in the Box; what can I get you guys today? Hello young lady; get my friend here one of those chicken combo's and a large Ice Tea! I'll just have the cheeseburger combo with a coke. Ok I have a number 3 with a large Ice Tea and a number 2 with a large coke.

Yep that's it! Ok it will be up in a second. Go wash up Walter, I'll get the food. Thank you detective! You're welcome! Here you are Ma'am, enjoy your lunch! Thanks! Where's your friend Briggs? In the restroom washing up; we're sitting over by the window. Bring some napkins when you come over will you? Sure partner. Hello Ma'am; what can I get for you today? How you doing today young lady; give me a large order of those seasoned curly fries and a large sprite. Did you want a sandwich with that Ma'am? No just fries; I'm trying to watch my figure. Ok; that will be $2.89! Here you go, can I have some extra ketchup too! Sure no problem! Oh and some extra napkins too. The napkins are on the counter Ma'am; you may help yourself to them. Alright thanks!

Here you are; one large curly fries and a large Sprite! Thanks! Briggs you love those damn burgers don't you? Yes I do; that's your ass trying to be skinny partner; I'm eating. I'm not starving for nobody! Umm-Hmm; thanks for the food guys. You're welcome Walt; sit down and let's talk. Casey did you bring the photo in? Yeah it's right here! Now take a close look at this picture Walter and tell me if you've seen this gentleman around the car wash.

Walter slid the photo over in front of him to take a closer look. His dirty hands and fingernails wrapped around his drink while he took a bite of his sandwich that he held in his left hand. Yeah-Umm-Hmm; I saw him. He was driving one of those Lexus cars with New York plates; I think it was New York. Good Walter; how long ago was this? Maybe a few months ago; towards the end of last year! Good; can you remember what color the car was? Brown or Gold I think! Did he get it wash over at the shop? He didn't stay too long; the guys were washing it then I saw him walk inside. This is important Walt; did he come back out of the building? Yeah Detective but he ran out! What do you mean; he ran out. Miss Briggs he ran out; you know running! Did it seem like he was scared or in a hurry? He didn't look scared to me Miss Casey; he pushed the guys away from his car and took off! But it seems like I heard a few gun shots before he came out of the building. Gun shots! Yes Ma'am more than one! Did the police come by or the ambulance? No Ma'am; everything went back to normal when he left then that Big guy came outside and called someone on his cell phone.

This big guy; was it someone you saw before at the car wash Walter? Yeah; it was that Fat white boy that owns the joint. Can you remember exactly what month or day it was? Miss Briggs; I don't even know what day and month it is now; hell, what year is it? Ha-ha! That's ok Walter you done good; finish your food and we can drop you off at the shelter own our way to the precinct, so you can shower and shave. Thanks Detective Briggs! You're welcome! Good; we need to wash our car after we drop him off too! Casey shut up; come on and let's get out of here! What; don't act like the car isn't stinking! Come on Walter let's go; don't pay my partner any mind. You can ignore it all you want Briggs but I'm rolling all the windows down. Ha-ha! Suit yourself Casey; if that makes you feel better. Bye guys; have a good day; come again! Thanks; you do the same, the food was great!

Ring-Ring! What up this Paco; whose speaking? What up playboy; this Dupree! Hey Amigo; what's crackin? I'm on your side player; you at the meet? Yeah I'm here! Good; my bitch is bugging me about a damn Gucci bag; you got any? Yeah man of course! I aint talking about no knock off shit now! Only real for my people; how far are you? I'm pulling on the lot now playboy! Ok; I'm in the office waiting on you. Alright; I'll be there in a few shakes. Park over by the office door Deac! I'll be back in a few; let me see what kind of bags this fool got. You want me to come with you? Nah stay with the Rover; these fools over here will jack my shit as soon as you walk inside. Don't you know where you at old man? Pree them niggas know this your car; they won't even think about jacking it. Old man that's exactly why they will take it; they want that street cred. You may be an OG Deacon but you don't understand these new baby gangsters out here I see.

Just keep your gun cocked and ready I won't be long. Alright Pree; I got you. Cool, be back soon playboy. Pac where you at fool! What up Amigo; I'm back here in the office. I thought you had a secretary pimpin; why that bitch aint on her job? Oh she's on her break right now. Come in, come in amigo, have a seat. Damn Paco! How many pairs of boots do you have playboy! Is them shits snake skin? Yep and alligator too! Every time I see your ass you got on some old exotic boots and shit! Anyway where the bags at; I aint trying to be in your hood too long fool! Come with me; there in the closet in my back office. Ok lead the way playboy! So how is business over on MLK? Everything is lovely playa; more money than I can count! That's good my friend! How's business over here? It's great amigo but I want some better prices on that meth! Here are the bags; take what you want? Oh yeah she gone love these; I want all of them. How many models you got? Five right here! Right here; damn you got more? Yeah but there over at the warehouse! Ahh, fuck that, give me one of each. How much I owe you?

Your money is no good here amigo, go ahead and take them. Are you sure playboy? Yeah my friend; take them. Thanks Paco and what were you saying about the Meth prices? I think we should get better prices, what you think? I'm cool with the way everything is right now; you know we have to pay that Sin City Tax; that's how it always been. It doesn't have to stay that way Dupree! So what are you saying Paco? I think we should buy straight from Derek; fuck AC and Manny! Well, did you speak with Derek about that? Yeah I did! What did he have to say? That punta is scared; he wasn't trying to hear it. That's a smart man!

Damn Amigo; are you scared too. Nigga; Dupree aint scared of no man; I just think money is too good right now to be shaking shit up; you dig. Dupree you need to think about it and team up with me. We can run Vegas amigo! Paco; my pops only told me one thing when it came to money. What's that Amigo?

He said anytime that you leave for sure money, for more money; you end up with no money. Think about that playboy; I'm out of here. Thanks for the bags; hit me up when you're on my side. Ok my friend later; tell your ol lady I said hi! Alright playboy; be safe and don't do anything stupid! Come on Deac; get me out of here! What's wrong Pree? Nothing; just drive old man! Be careful over here too, po po's hot on this side. I got this youngster; just sit back and ride. What's the speed limit anyway? 55 I think! Where we going? Let's head back to the church, I got some folks coming over in a few. How many bags did you get? Five I think! Damn; she need that many? Deacon you know my bitch greedy; that girl got to have everything. Your ass is her meal ticket; that's all that is. Old man what you talking about? I'm talking about you spending all your cheese on that girl of yours. So you think I shouldn't?

You're a grown ass man; do what you want with your money. Then why you bring it up playboy? I just don't want you to be blind youngster; that's all. The way I see it Deac, she's my bitch, so she deserves it. Ok I hear you and why do she? Do she what? Deserve it! Because that's my girl; she aint got to do nothing for it as long as I'm fucking her. What makes her different from any other skirt you jabbing? Gone with all that non-sense Deacon! You didn't answer the question Dupree! Shit I don't know man; because she's always there for me I guess! Oh yeah; in what way? Man I don't know! Exactly; she aint no different than the rest of them chicks you fucking man. Just admit that you paying for the pussy because she damn sure don't do anything for you besides fuck you my nigga.

Now don't get me wrong; I had my share of sluts in my day but I just want you to really understand what's going on. Until she start's doing things for you on her own time and dime without you asking; she aint no different. Recognize game young man; a lot of bullshit comes with this paper you making. It just so happen that most woman are in it for the money; I don't give a damn if it's your momma; sister, aunt or grandmother! They're all the same until they show you different. If you go into all your relationships knowing that; you will stay two steps ahead of them. Ok old man; I hear you! Yeah, but are you listening Dupree? Oh I heard you loud and clear; I got it! Oh shit! Eeerrrr! Boom! This motherfucker hit his breaks at a green light!

Aint this a bitch; why that fool jam on breaks like that; the damn light just turned yellow. Stay here Pree; I'm going to make sure he's alright. Ok hurry up before the cops come; I'm not trying to see no police. Alright I'll be right back.

Excuse me young man; are you ok? Yeah fool break yourself! Hey hold on a minute! Shut up old man; back away from my car and stay your ass still. Look man; put the gun down; I was just coming to make sure you weren't hurt! I'm good fool; empty your damn pockets and give me the keys to that Rover pops! Pow! Pow! Pow! Take that you punk ass motherfucker! I bet you won't jack another nigga! Deacon; hurry your ass up; get in the car; leave that dead fool! Damn Dupree; did you kill him? Old man come on; he was about to smoke your ass; let's go! Errrr!

Just get me out of North Town; these BG's crazy over here! You alright; you didn't wet your pants did you! No; he just caught me off guard; that's all. See; didn't I tell you these streets were crazy. They don't have any respect for the game no more Deac; all they want is a rep! I tell you one thing God dammit! What's that old man? I thought I was a dead man back there. Not today Deacon; it wasn't your time; let's get back to MLK; stop by Popeye's when you get over there too. I want some of them red beans and rice and some of that spicy chicken with some jalapenos. Alright man; I can use one of those hot biscuits and some honey too! Step on it then playboy; I'm hungry!

Hey David; what's going on brother? Hey Manny what's up? I'm good brother are you holding things down over here? Yeah I got it under control. Cool; that's what I like to hear; if you need something don't hesitate to call me bro. Thanks Manny! It's no problem; is AC up stairs. Yeah as far as I know! Great; do me a favor; call him and let him know I'm down stairs will you? Oh sure thing Manny! Thanks; I'll be over there having a smoke! Ok; I'll go do it now! Ring-

Ring! Hello! Hey Mr. Cooper; this is David! Hey Dave what's going on? Manny is here; he's outside waiting on you. Ok thanks; tell him I'm coming now. Alright sir; will do! He's on the way down Manny! Cool; appreciate it! You're welcome!

Emanuel pulls down the tailgate of his freshly waxed El Camino; takes a seat and continues to smoke on his Newport while waiting for Coop. Traffic at the Towers was unusually calm as patrons and residents alike stroll in and out of the luxurious building. Slot machines chime every other minute instead of seconds like usual; the lobby was clear of smoke and no music could be heard from the lounge; only plates and glasses clashing as the bus boys clear the empty tables left from the lunch hour rush. What's up Capo; you ready to get your ass whipped. What up Boss! Aint shit; let's go shoot some hoops! Damn this sucker is clean; you just waxed it? Yep; you know I got to keep it clean for the honeys! Man Sophie gone kick your ass; keep that shit up! I know you aint talking AC with your whoring ass! But I'm not married bruh; you is! Man I just be flirting with those girls. Yeah whatever; you say that now but if one of them let you hit; you hitting! Damn right

I am! Pitiful; come on let's go ho! Ha-ha! Whatever Coop! Flip the switches on this bitch; let's hit some three wheel motion on the strip pimp! Drag that bumper!

I'm not getting a ticket for your ass! What; you scared Capo! You be hitting switches out here with those chicas at night. Yep; that's at night; it's broad day light now; them fools will write me a ticket in a minute! Alright man; whatever; let's hit the park with your scared ass. I'm gone show you scared when I start busting those three pointers on you player. Manny you aint got no game boy; stop dreaming. On the real though Capo; I need you to start putting a plan together for the re-ups! That's what's cracking; when will Diego have the warehouse set up? He's taking care of it as we speak; it should be up and running for the next re-up. I want each crew to have a designated pick up spot in the tunnels. Just make sure them homeless cats are out of the way or put them on the payroll as look outs if you want; do something with em.

I can make that happen; no problem. You might want to go down to the clerk's office and pick up copies of the tunnel maps though. How am I supposed to get those with-out them being suspicious AC? Don't we have some construction workers on the payroll or something? I don't think so! Well make it happen Manny; that's why you're the Capo; right player! I got it! Cool brother; slow down you're going to pass the park fool. Oh shit; my bad! Yeah you're just trying to get out of this ass whipping I'm about to give you. Man whatever! There's a park right there Manny; right by that picnic table; pull in there. Ring-Ring! Ring-Ring! Is that your phone Capo? Nah; I think it's yours. Ring-Ring! Ring-Ring! Hello! Hey is this AC? Yeah who wants to know? This is Detective Ricky; we need to talk ASAP! About what Amanda? Where are you; it has to be in person. I don't know about that; I don't trust cops that well. Mr. Cooper; you'll want to hear what I have to say; I assure you! Oh really! Yes really; where are you? I'm at Sunset Park behind the airport. Ok; I'm on Eastern now; I will be there in 5 minutes! Ok Amanda; see you in a minute.

Is everything straight Coop; who was that? I don't know Manny; that was Detective Ricky; she's on the way over to tell me something. Isn't that the one you've been peeling 10 stacks off on? Yeah that's her. Just turn off the car; we'll wait here until she comes. Do you have any beers in that cooler back there? Yeah there's a case of Corona's. Cool; I think we're going to need it; she sounded serious about what she had to say. I'm going to sit on the tailgate and drink me a beer Capo; you coming? Yeah; right behind you. She should be here any minute; keep your eyes open and make sure she's alone when she pulls up. Ok I'm on it. If anything looks fishy, smoke her ass; I'm not going to jail for nobody. You already know AC; I will lay that ass down without a problem. That goes without saying; I aint going to jail either; fuck that! Alright; be sharp she just turned on the lot I see her now; you see her? Yep; I'm on it! She's alone Coop; no one else is in the car and nobody seems to be following her. You want me to stay close or stay on the look-out. Wait over there by that other bench and keep an eye out for anything suspicious. I'll signal you if I need her dropped. Alright let me know.

AC waives at Detective Ricky as she enters the park while he stood beside the El Camino as she approaches in her dark blue Crown Victoria and parks beside him. Hey; what's up Detective; what seems to be the problem. What's so damn urgent that you had to track me down? Did you get me some information on that murder case? No

Ma'am; still cold, no one's saying anything right now but it will work itself out sooner or later. What you got to tell me? You have a big problem my friend. What do you mean? Chief Espinoza is building a case on you and your friends. What are you talking about Detective? We had a meeting a few weeks ago about some cold cases and your name came up along with some of your associates. Go on; keep talking! He had pictures of you; Sabrina and some of those people that were at the Towers that night she died. What did he say about the pictures? He thinks that there's a connection between you and some cold cases involving a family by the name of Delgato. I just moved here; so you know I'm not making this shit up.

You said he was building a case; on what grounds is he doing that? I don't know; all I know is that me and Detective's Casey and Briggs were in the office with him and we're going back next week for another briefing about the case. He's building intel on you and I don't know where he's heading with it but the Chief is focused; only because he has a gut feeling. I'm only telling you this because you're looking out for me with my case. Thanks Amanda; I appreciate it! Yeah; don't mention it just be careful. I have to go; there's a homicide over in West Las Vegas I should be at. Later Detectvie!

Hey Manny! Come on Capo, we need to get out of here! What did she say Coop? She said that the Chief is building a case on me and he has photos of all of us. He's trying to connect me to the Delgato's. What the fuck; we covered our tracks; he don't know shit! Let's hope we covered them good Manny or we got big problems. Fuck that Espinoza motherfucker; I'll smoke his ass if I need to! Just calm down Manny; let this thing play out; let them show their hand first. I'm calm AC but I aint going to jail brother; for no one! I'll leave in a body bag first; Death before Dishonor; that's how it is; you dig! Oh no doubt Capo; that's the only way. Start this car up and let's head back to the Towers we need to put a contingency plan together. Alright; you want me to call the crew and let them know? Not yet Manny; it's too early to say anything. We'll just make sure the crew is on their toes. Ok AC; whatever you say!

March; 1998.

Ring-Ring! Ring-Ring! Yeah; Chief speaking! Hey Chief there's a guy out here; say he's your U.C and he had an appointment. Oh yeah; send him in LT! You can go in sir! Thanks LT! What's up son; you still alright? I'm good Chief; I found out some more info on Cooper. Great what you got; I need all I can get. This thing is still puzzling me but I know it's all connected somehow. Have a seat son; and I really appreciate you coming from Cali to work this undercover assignment for me. It's all a part of the job Chief; that's what I signed up for. Yes indeed; so what you got?

Well I know that your boy Cooper is running things and Emanuel is like the underboss or something; I haven't quite figured out their set up yet. The twins; Denna and Nina also have some kind of business affiliation with him also and so does that Duck guy and Loon. What about William? Who the big guy; no I don't think he's involved but they do associate with him from time to time. Hmm; that's interesting I was under the impression that he was close to them also. Well as of right now Chief; it's still too early to tell. I haven't really had a chance to catch all of them alone at one time in the same room. When that happens I will get a better understanding of things. Did you at least know what kind of illegal activity is going on; it has to be some. Not for sure Chief; that AC doesn't really be around illegal stuff that often. Just hang in there son; something will come up and when it does; I'm coming down on his ass like the Hulk on a fly.

There is one thing though! What's that? I over-heard Manny talking about some new girls from overseas one evening and that they were starting work at some club soon. Hmm; did you hear what club? No, he was on the phone; so all I could catch was his end of the conversation. Ok; just hang in there and try to get a little closer without blowing your cover. I know we're close; I can feel it; it won't be long now. Did you want me to assign you some help? No I got it; besides, a new face now would definitely cause some suspicion. Yeah maybe you're right; well, get out of here before they miss you; call me with any updates. Alright Sir will do; have a good one! You too and be safe out there! Yes chief; of course Sir!

Espinoza takes a seat at his desk and gazes at the files he collected a few weeks ago. Several cold cases; some property deeds, some arrest records and a bulletin board with photos of AC, Manny, Loon, Duck, Nina, Denna, Will and Sabrina was all he had at the moment. Nervously he taps his pen repeatedly on his steel desk and leans back in his chair while staring at the board of pictures he scoops up a pack of crackers with his left hand. Ring-Ring! Ring-Ring! Yeah what is it? Chief there's a lady on the other line; she says she knows where Hoffa is! What; are you kidding me; take a message! I don't have time for that non-sense LT! Ok Sir; no problem! Jesus Christ!

Ring-Ring! Ring-Ring! LT speaking! Come here for a minute LT; I need you to do something for me. Ok chief; coming now! He gazes over the papers while talking to himself as LT enters the office. I'm gone get to the bottom of this if it kills me! Something is just not adding up and it's right in front of me! I know it dammit! Yes Chief! Do me a favor and run background checks on everyone up on that board; contact the Department of Defense and see if they have anything on them also! Ok chief; anything else? Yeah;

run their names by the FBI too! Alright I'm on it! Thanks LT!

"Good evening Las Vegas; this is your boy Dj Glenn." "You know what time it is; time for your picks at six baby." "Number one on the list we got that hot ass track from SWV!" "I don't know what it is that you done to me" "But it's caused me to act in such a crazy way." "Whatever it is that you do when you do what you're doing...." I get so weak in the knees I can hardly see! I lose all control when you take over me!

Mo! What! Stop fucking up that song; you done skip about four versus girl; let the radio play! Kiss my ass AC! Ha-ha! I'm for real though! Yeah; yeah whatever! It smells good in there though; I know that much; you can't sing but you damn sure can cook girl! Umm-hmm! When is it going to be done? Another hour maybe! I just put the corn bread in the oven; the chicken, greens and Macaroni are done. The yams are almost done too! God Damn; you doing it up aint you! Yeah; didn't you say Jerm and Tammy are coming by? Yep they should be here soon. Dang those yams smell good; got the balcony scented up out here! Hell the neighbors might be knocking too before it's all over.

81

Come out here and give me a kiss; looking all sexy in them jeans with that fat ass. Hold on a minute; let me turn these yams down ok. Alright baby, bring me a cold beer when you come out too! Ok! "I try hard to fight it" "No way can I deny it" "Your loves so sweet" "It knocks me off my feet." Muah! Here's your beer! Thanks Mo! You're welcome. Oh; I've been meaning to ask you about your visit. What visit? The kids! Oh it was cool; I didn't stay long it was late. Did your baby momma trip? Not really but her punk ass husband tried too but I nipped that shit fast. So were they happy to see you? Yeah they were; and I was happy to see them too. When are you going back; you should bring them over sometime.

I thought about that but their mom is still on that supervised visit bullshit and I aint trying to hear it. Besides this isn't a good place for them to come anyway. Why not? There always drugs, money and gangsters up here; this is no place for kids. Then you should get a house Coop; all this money you got, I don't know why you're still up here anyway. Maybe you're right; I'll think about it! Yeah please do; two years is a long time to not see your kids nigga. Knock-Knock! Oh that must be them now! You go open the door Coop; I'll turn the yams off and take out the cornbread. For sho!

My nigga come in! Hey Tam! Hey AC! Jerm what's poppin? I'm hungry fool; that's what's poppin. Hey Mo! Hey Jerm; how you doing Tam? I'm good girl; it smells good up in here. Thank you; you guys are just in time too; everything just got done. Umm; is that cornbread? Yeah child; it's Jiffy; AC's country ass won't eat no other kind. That's alright girl, that's my favorite too. Really; it doesn't matter to me. So Jerm; what did yall do the other night? Man we went to see the Crazy Girls over at the Rio. Was that a good show; I haven't had a chance to check it out yet. Yeah it was straight; boy it was some fine bitches up in there though! No, you're kidding. Coop stop clowning; you know what I mean. Yeah I'm just messing with you fool; you want a beer. Yeah let me get one! Meet me on the balcony, I'll bring it to you; I have to ask you something anyway while the girls are fixing the plates. Alright bro; cool!

Here you go J. Thanks! So what's up; everything straight right? I don't know man; this detective came to see me the other day with some disturbing news. What kind of news;

are you going to jail fool? She said that the Chief is building a case against me. How can he do that when he aint got nothing. That's what I said but she said he has it out for me for some damn reason; I need a good ass lawyer. Don't worry about it man; I know a cat in Hollywood that can make anything disappear but it's gone cost you. Money isn't a problem; just make sure he can represent the whole crew. No doubt; I will call him as soon as I get back to Cali. Thanks brother; I appreciate it! It's nothing pimpin; I got your back cuz. That's why you're my boy; ride or die. And you know that fool; now let's go eat before Tammy eats all the chicken. Man stop tripping; your girl aint gone eat all the damn chicken.

AC my girl can eat bruh; it's like feeding an 18 year old growing boy; I aint playing; come on. Ha-ha! Jerm you stupid! I maybe but I'm serious as hell, play with it and you gone be starving. Ha-ha! Come on nigga with your crazy ass. Alright guys the food is ready; come eat. We coming Mo; I have to wash my hands first though. Mine are already clean; thanks Mo this looks delicious. You're welcome Jermaine! So how does it feel to be the HNIC Coop? You making a lot of paper now and that come with haters, gold diggers; stick up kids and all that! How you handling that pimpin? We got it under control fam; I got the crew and we got a few henchmen on the payroll too, you dig. Alright; I'm just checking because I know you will murder a fool in a minute. You don't need any bodies on you player; let your soldiers do that work. Jerm I aint no rookie bruh; I got this. Yeah; plus I got his back too; I wish somebody would try my baby! Oh yeah and what are you gonna do if they do Mo? Nigga what; you better ask somebody. I handle mines!

 AC you got a thug girl over here don't you! Man; don't be following Mo up; she never even shot a gun. What does that have to do with anything Coop? Everything girl; that's what gangsters do; they shoot people; you need to learn to shoot before you jump bad in some bodies face. I don't need a gun; I'll stab their monkey ass. Last I check MO; a knife never stopped a bullet. Tam clears her throat and addresses the conversation. Hey guys; eat your food and cut that out. Mo I know you got my back baby and I appreciate that but you do need a gun. We'll give me one then Mr. Big shot; Sin City Boss! Don't worry baby, I'll take care of you soon enough. Now let's enjoy this nice meal you fixed! Hey Jerm pass me the chicken please babe. Hold on Tammy; can I cut mine before you get another piece? Hurry up then; you guys arguing about a damn gun; I thought yall wasn't hungry. See Coop; I told you! What bruh! Tam ass can eat; that's what!

Jerm I know you wasn't talking trash about me! No baby; I just told AC that you can eat. I wasn't lying! Hey Tam; help yourself to all you want girl; don't pay those two knuckle heads no mind. These greens are slamming girl! Thanks Tammy; I'm glad you like them! Told you AC; a damn teenager; look! Ha-ha! Bruh leave your girl alone; she's fine. I know; I'm just messing with her; Tam knows she's my baby. I hear you over there Jerm; keep it up you won't be getting any head from me tonight. You know you want some too! Alright, alright, I'm cool; don't be taking the head away now. Umm-Hmm; you better be! Pass me some more cornbread MO! Sure baby; did you want anything else? Nope just that! Here you go! Tam; can you pass this to AC please! Sure! Monica you put your foot in this baby; we have to visit more often; if you going to be cooking like this. AC you're going to be fat the next time I see you; all this home cooking. Hell nah I aint either; I'm not eating like this every day. Why not man? Jerm I'm cool with my weight like this; I'm not even trying to get any bigger.

You're better than me bruh; I would be chowing down every day! Ring-Ring! Ring-Ring! Hey Mo; where's my phone? On the counter! Ring-Ring! Ring-Ring! Thanks! Hello! AC what's up bother? Hey Capo; just having dinner what's the word? I'm out in front of Dupree's now; about to make this pick up and let him know about the tunnel situation. Did you figure the logistics out already? Yeah it works perfect; tunnels run through all the territories so no one has to leave their hoods to re-up. Perfect; go handle your business than; I'll get at you later! Alright Coop!

Slowly the rain starts to come down harder and harder as Manny leaves his car and walks up the sidewalk to the rear entrance of the Church. Deacon as usual stood just outside the door way as he approached, standing tall, holding an umbrella over his head. Hello there Sir; I see you brought the rain with you this time. There's nothing wrong with a little rain Deac, besides we need it; don't you think? Nah; I can do without; Dupree's in the last room on the right at the end of the hall. Go ahead in; he's expecting you. Thanks man! No problem youngster just doing what I'm paid to do.

Yo Pree; where you at! Down here Manny; keep walking! Please man; it was a mistake! I swear! Shut up playboy; I don't want to hear excuses; just answers! Where is my five thousand dollars? I misplaced it Dupree; I swear man! Hey youngster, sit that fool down in this chair and tie him up. Put your gun up; I got mine on him; go ahead lil man; tie his ass up! Damn brother; what you got going on in here? Manny; my amigo! How you doing playboy? Better than that fool! Ha-ha! Sure you right! Come in man; you want a beer or something? Nah; I'm straight! You sure? Yep! Well; your money is on the table. Thanks, I see it. So what did this poor dude do anyway? This knuckle head claims he lost $5,000 of mine; all he had to do was pick it up and bring it back here. But no; this fat fucker goes to Popeye's; leaves my shit in the car! Comes back outside and it's gone! Then gone have the nerves to bring his big fat greasy chicken eating ass back here and tell me he lost it.

Damn; that aint good my man! Tell his ass again Manny! He thinks this is a game! Boy do you know how many shoes and bags I can buy my woman with $5,000! No I don't man, but I'm sorry! Of course not; you aint got no bitches! You spend all your money on chicken, pancakes, burgers and that damn Del taco! Tie that rope tight lil man! I'm gone teach you not to lose nothing else of mine you fat fuck! Hey Manny! What up bro? Hand me one of those Bible's off that shelve! Sure; here you go! Thanks playboy! Listen up; you hamburger eating nigga; you see this Bible! I said; do you see this Bible! Yes I see it! Good; you know God don't like liars; right! Yeah! I'm gone ask you one more time where my money is and if I think you're lying, I'm gone smack you with this Bible until the pages fall out. Now; where is it?

I swear Dupree, I don't have it! Someone must have stole…. Bap! Bap! Ouch! Damn man! Now let's try this again! Where is it? I don't kno.. Bap! Bap! Please man; stop! Playboy we can do this all day; this Bible don't look like it's coming apart anytime soon! Now where the fuck is my loot? Dupree listen man; I left it in the car and… Bap! Bap! Uggh! See; I told you God don't like liars! I want my money playboy and I want it today; I don't care how you get it! Get me my ends! How Pree! Bap! Bap! Uggh! Ok, ok! So when will you have my cash boy? I don't know Pree!

Bap! Bap! Ugh! Come on man! Manny; look at this fool begging like I'm wrong! This here is business playboy; you owe me 5 stacks! But I ain't got that kind of money Dupree! Shit; you better figure out something quick! I can work it off Pree! Hell nah nigga, I want cash; all at once; fuck that working shit; I got plenty people to do that! But I don't know wha... Bap! Bap! Bap! Bap! Uggggggh shit! Stop it man, please! Didn't you buy a house over in the Lakes last month, fat ass? Yeah um hm! Good; where's the deed at? What you mean? Did I stutter player; where's the damn deed? Give it up or lil man is going to earn his stripes tonight and you won't see tomorrow. How do you want to play it playboy? Alright man, alright, it's under my mattress. Under your mattress; man you kidding right? No, that's where it is! Ok lil man get his keys; you and Deac go over there and get that deed; bring it back to me!

Ok Pree! Well, what are you waiting on lil man; go ahead! See that's the kind of drama I have to go through Manny. I'm sorry about this amigo! It's all good brother; I need to talk to you alone for a minute though. Alright; we can talk in the hallway. Don't try nothing stupid fat ass; I'll be right here in the hall! What's on your mind Manny? Well, we have a new re-up spot that's going to work better for everyone. Oh yeah and where is that? Just over by the bridge not far from here. The bridge; what do you mean? You know about the drainage tunnels right? Yeah I do. Well, Diego and AC agreed to drop the product at the warehouse then distributed it through the drainage tunnels that run under the city. Diego has made an entrance through his warehouse floor where he can drop the shipment's; then have the runners deliver them through the tunnels to every ones pick up spots in their territories.

Damn; that's genius playboy! We can pick up like three times as much now without all the damn risk. Yep; that's the plan! Well; it's a damn good one. I'm all in amigo. Cool; pick up your next re-up there; I will call and let you know the date and time. Alright say no more; oh I almost forgot! What is it Pree?

Yall need to watch Paco; that boy has an agenda. What do you mean? He tried to get me to link up with him so we can buy product direct from Derek. No shit! Yep; I ain't got no reason to lie playboy. Is Derek in on it too? Nah but he did ask him. What happened? He said D told him he had a death wish; I told that fool to let things be; everything is gravy how it is; you dig. Thanks for telling me bro; we definitely have to handle this problem. Yep and fast; playboy is eager too. Alright brother; hold it down, I'm out of here and good luck with that $5,000! Playboy I don't need luck I got the deed; you dig! Ha-ha! Later Pree!

"Good Morning Phoenix; you're tuned in to KKNT; News Talk Radio" "I'm your morning jock Kenny Madenna" "Well folks it has been crazy around here for the past few weeks, since we had a visit from our friends from another planet." "The Air Force base now claims that all of us here in Phoenix only seen a training exercise!" "Yeah you heard me people; Now get this; they said what we saw was several flares that were lit during the exercise." "You and I know that's a bunch of BS if we ever heard it." "Hell at least 50 people saw this thing close up as it glided over their homes and neighborhoods!" "When will the Government stop lying to us?" "Never; that's when!" "My phone lines are open if you guys want to call in and comment!"

Ring-Ring! Ring-Ring! Hello! Hey girl; are you at the bank yet? Yeah Dylan, I've been here for 10 minutes already;

listening to this radio show! Did you make the deposit yet? Yep just now! Good because we need to leave Phoenix! Why bitch; we just got here, we have 4 more days to go before we can leave! Dylan I just heard on the radio that some UFO's was flying over the city and shit! Barbie you tripping! No I'm not either; they're talking about it now on the radio! Yeah whatever, go get that money so we can hit this other bank then go grab something to eat. Alright; I'm going but I'm serious Dylan; check it out if you don't believe me. Uh-huh; you're taking out $5,000, don't forget!

Ok bye; I will call you when I'm back in the car. Alright; I'm headed to the other bank, just head over to the one on that side of town and deposit that check when you leave there. Yeah, yeah, I know the routine. Well hurry up bitch, I'm hungry! Bye Dylan! Only a few cars were parked outside of the bank as Barbie exited her car. Cactus trees align the sidewalk leading to the entrance of the building. Barbie's heels made a clicking sound as she walk down the warm cement while the cool Arizona desert breeze; blow her yellow sun dress, gently wrapping it around her toned thighs. The tinted glass doors slowly open as she approach.

Thank you! You're welcome Ma'am, you better hurry before the lunch crowd comes; it's amazingly slow right now. Oh really; I guess I better get up there then. Yep; have a good one!

Hello Ma'am; welcome to Phoenix Bank & Trust! How may I help you today? Yes, I would like to withdraw some money from my account. Ok sure; that's not a problem; did you need a withdraw slip? Yes I do! Here you are, just fill that out and I will need your I.D to complete your transaction along with that. Alright just a second! Take your time Ma'am. Here you go, all set! Thanks, it will only take a minute. Did you want this all in large bills or does it matter? All large please! Ok, here's one hundred, two, three, four, five, six, seven, eight, nine and one thousand. Oh you don't have to count it all out honey; I can see how much it is from here. Well, thanks for your business; here's your cash and have a nice day! Thanks Honey; you too!

Ring-Ring! Hello! Hey Girl, I'm leaving the bank now! Did you get it all Barbie? Yep! Cool, head to the other bank and deposit that check; call me when you're done. Damn! What's wrong Barbie? I just opened the door and this sun is blinding my ass; hold on while I put on my shades. Ok girl! Alright what were you saying now Dylan? I said go drop that check so I can make my pick up, then we can go get some food. Oh ok, did you listen to the radio? No; what for? The aliens bitch! Girl; stop tripping and take your ass to that other bank! I'm almost to my car; it won't take long! Click-Click! Barbie pause after hearing a loud clicking sound and feeling cold metal against her skull. Give me your purse Bitch! What! Shut up; let the bag go and don't turn around! Barbie what's going on? Dylan help- Pow! Barbie what was that! Oh my God, Barbie! I said shut up bitch, next time I won't shoot in the sky. Drop the damn bag! Ok, ok! Good girl, now don't fucking turn around or my face will be the last one you'll ever see! Got it! I said do you got it! Yes! Yes! Barbie! Barbie! Oh my God, Barbie can you hear me? Vroom-Vroom! Errrrrr!

She could hear a vehicle peel off as she turns to catch a look at the car. Her empty purse lay on the sidewalk, keys beside it with an empty bank envelop and only her check-book cover. Barbie! Barbie; please can you hear me! Hello! Girl what happened, are you alright! No; I just got robbed girl! Oh my God, I'm on my way now! Are you hurt? No just a little shaken up! Don't come over here; let's just go to the hotel. Are you sure? Yeah; we better call Will; they took my check book too. Did you see who did it? I only saw the truck; it was a red bronco with Florida plates; I got some of the numbers and it was two people. Ok good, I'm calling Will; meet me at the room; I'm headed there right now. Alright Dylan, I'm coming.

Hello Dolls; Will speaking! Hey Will this is Dylan! Hey baby, how's Phoenix; everything good? No, we have a problem! What kind of problem? Well, Barbie just got robbed! What the fuck! Is she ok? Yeah she's fine, it happened after she made her pick up from the bank. They got the 5 stacks and her check book! Damn, that's not good. Did she see who robbed her? Not really but she saw the truck and got some of the plate. Cool that should be enough to find those punks. You ladies hang tight at the hotel; I'm sending a crew down there to take care of this mess. We'll get them baby; don't worry! Ok Will; I'll let her know. Alright Dylan and stay in that room until our people get there. Ok, we will. Alright later!

Ring-Ring! This Hector; what up? Hec; this Will player! What's up homie? One of the girls got robbed in Phoenix; she got an ID on the punks and we need to handle that as soon as possible. Say no more homes; I'll send two of my best people down there. Cool, they're at the hotel where we make the weekly pick-ups from. It's Barbie and Dylan, Barbie is the one that got jacked. Ok don't worry my friend it's my problem now, it's handled! Later amigo; I'll call you when it's in the bag. Did you want them chumps dead or what? Yeah waste them fuckers. My pleasure homes! Thanks Hector! Anytime mane, anytime!

Yo Chino! What up aye? Come here homes; I got a job for you and your lady esse'. Hold on a sec; let me finish painting this bumper! Later for that; Carlos can finish it! This is important homes! Ok what is it Hector? I need you and Mya to ride out to Phoenix; go see Dylan and Barbie at that hotel we use in town over there. They got some marks that need to be canceled homes. What kind of marks esse'? These punta's robbed them homes; and that means they're robbing us; our money come out of that loot at the end of the week. Say no more esse'! Those punta's are canceled; I'll go get Mya from the crib and head to Phoenix right now. Yeah, you do that homes and call me when it's finish! Comprende'? Yeah man! Good; go handle that homie! Make it a quick good trip!

Damn it's slow today boss! I know Josh; it's a nice day out too; I guess everyone is outside enjoying the weather. I guess so Denna but somebody always wants some pussy. Don't worry Josh; it will pick up sooner or later. Let's just sit out here on this porch and enjoy the weather while we got a chance. That's fine by me, I don't get outside often. Why not Josh? If I'm not working; I'm usually home asleep or watching TV. You should always try and enjoy life outside of work Josh. Yeah I know but I have plenty of time for that. Tomorrow is not promised to any of us, remember that fact young man. Tsssss! Tssss! Did you hear that Denna? No; what? Tssss! Tssss! There it is again! I heard it that time. Tssss! Tssss! Josh! Yeah what is it? Don't move; stay still. What! Why not? Tsssss! Tssss! There's a rattle snake, right behind your chair; stay still I'm going to try and shoot him. Are you serious Denna? Yes just stay calm, don't move and be quiet. Pow! Pow! Pow! Got it! Damn, that sucker didn't want to die! Whew! Thank you Denna! Don't mention it! Hey what the hell is going on out here! Mo, Denna just killed that thing! What thing? That!

Oh shit! Is that a snake? Damn he's big! Oh my God; where did he come from? Calm down Mo; that was the only one, for now anyway. I'm taking my butt back inside; yall can have the reptiles and wild animals. Hold on a minute Monica; I need to teach you how to shoot anyway, might as well do it now. What? AC said you wanted to learn; so now is a good a time as any. Josh; hold it down for us; while I take her around back to get some practice. Ok Denna; I got you guys covered. Come on Mo; follow me honey. Are you sure about this Denna? Yep; couldn't be more sure; besides you can't roll with us and not be able to shoot. Alright if you say so miss. We're just going around back to take a few shots, so you can get comfortable with firing. What are we going to shoot at Denna? At one of those old trash cans back there Mo. Ok because I don't want to hurt anyone! Girl relax, there's nothing back there but the damn desert.

Alright this right here is a clip; it holds the bullets. It's 8 rounds left in this one but it holds 12. What are rounds? Bullets girl! Oh ok. You really don't have a clue do you Monica. No and I don't see why I need to learn anyway. You're dating AC, The Don of Sin City; that job comes with crime and it can happen any given day at any given moment. What if someone rolls up on him while you guys are out and he doesn't see them but you do, then what? I will tell him to watch out! No fool; you need to be putting a cap in their asses until he can help you. Oh! Now do you understand? Kind of. Well look at it this way; remember how someone kidnapped Sabrina last year? Yeah! Why you think that was? I don't know; maybe they didn't like her. No Mo; they were after AC and his money! This is not a game baby; if you're going to be fucking with my brother you will be packing. You got it! Yeah I do know. Good girl, now hold this gun, aim at that trash can and pull the trigger! Take your time when you pull it; don't jerk it! Grip the handle; place your pointer finger on the trigger; then rest your hand and grip in the palm of your left hand and pull. Remember to take your time and aim at that trash can. Alright go ahead, take a shot. Pow! Ok you jerked a little; try it again.

Pow! Again! Pow! Again! Pow! How did that feel? Powerful girl! I like it! Good, take some more shots. Ok! Pow! Pow! Alright you have two shots left, take your time. How do you know how many shots I have left? Because you only had 8 when you started; you just shot 6. Oh yeah; I remember. Now aim right at the trash can and hit it this time, you missed the last six. Ha-Ha! Did I? Yeah you did! Go ahead, take your time. Pow! −Bing! Good job, one more time! Pow! −Bing! See that wasn't so hard was it? Nope; when can we do this again? Maybe later; we have to get back to work now though. Alright; thanks Denna! You're welcome girl; come on, let's get inside. We can't leave Josh by himself for too long. Why not? Mo that boy doesn't know how to do anything but serve drinks. Ha-ha! Oh ok!

Beep-Beep! Beep-Beep! Hey man; move up some; I can't get to the pump. Alright, alright my bad Ma'am! No, it's ok; I know you don't want anyone close to your pretty BMW. Ha-ha! It's not even like that, besides this is a nice Beamer you got yourself! Oh this is my sisters; I'm just borrowing it. Ok it's still nice! Thank you! Well, I'm Winston by the way and you are? I'm Nina; nice to meet you Winston! So can I pump that gas for you? Sure, go ahead. I'll go pay for it! No I got it; I'll just put it on my gas card. Wow; look at you, are you a real gentleman Winston or is this a pick up scam? Ha-ha! It's no scam Nina! Well, that remains to be seen. I tell you what; come by my place later and have a few drinks and we can talk a little bit and get to know each other. What do you take me for little man; you think because you drive a Beamer and paid for my gas that you can get some. Plus you're only like 5'2", I don't date guys shorter than me sir. I'm 5'7" and damn near six feet with heels.

Wow Ms. Nina; that was a lot to take in! Well, it's the truth! I'm sorry if you took it the wrong way Nina but I was inviting you to my Comedy Club to have a few drinks, not my house. I am very comfortable with my height, so you can save that one. This BMW is my work vehicle, I drive a Bentley for leisure and I think that you are a wonderful person thus far. But that remains to be seen, saying how you just judged me a few moments ago. Now that your gas is all done; here are two comp tickets to my club for tonight. If you're interested stop by for drinks and some laughs; if not I'll understand. It was nice meeting you Nina; do enjoy the rest of your day. I have to be going now! Vroom-Vroom! Nina now speechless stood there watching in disbelief as Winston peeled off the lot then onto Sahara blvd and disappeared into the flow of traffic.

Ring-Ring! Ring-Ring! Hello; Rose speaking! Hola Senorita! Who is this; Paco? Yeah you know it mommy; how you doing babe? I'm doing great sir; about to stop at Olympic Gardens and grab a drink or two. What you want? I know you want something; that's the only time your butt calls. Why it got to be like that mommy. What's up Paco? I wanted to talk to you about this business opportunity. Don't even ask me to sell those hot ass Gucci bags you got. Nah it's on some other business; we have to speak in person. Alright, I suggest you bring your yellow ass to OG's; I'm pulling up now. Cool; I'm only two blocks away; be there in a minute. Ok honey; see you when you get here; I'll be in there somewhere. Ok Rose, on the way.

Welcome back to OG's Ma'am, I can park that for you. Thank you Hun and don't scratch my Hummer, I just got it waxed. I won't Ma'am; here's your ticket, hang on to it. Honey this is not my first time in Valet, I know how it works. Sorry Miss; I didn't mean anything by it. Don't apologize honey; just go park my baby and be careful. Yes Ma'am, right away. Thank you; now I need a drink, it's been a long day. The Doorman greets her as she enters. Hello Rose; welcome back to OG's; I see you're alone today. Hey Buddy; how are you? I'm doing fine Miss Rose, enjoy yourself. Of course hun, I always do! Oh; I have a friend meeting me here; tell him I'm sitting in the corner booth by the bar. He'll be the short Latin fella wearing some snake skin or alligator boots. No problem; I will make sure he finds you Ma'am. Thanks buddy!

Rose enters the club confident as usual, gazing through the smoke filled foyer and patrons that fill the front bar. Loud music bounced off the white plastered walls while 5 strippers dance simultaneously on the five Octagon shaped stages that are scattered through-out the club. Huge Palm trees align the walls and touch the ceiling as water stream down the glass rocks that protruded from the walls in the hallway entrance. "What's up people; welcome to the world famous Olympic Gardens. Home of the sexiest dancers on the strip!" "It's 4pm and second shift is just starting; we got the drink specials flowing and over 200 beautiful women are working just for your entertainment pleasure." "You can tip any of the five girls on either one of our World Famous Five Stages or get yourself a table dance from one of the other 195 gorgeous ladies." "I'm your Dj for this evening, I go by Dj Big Gee and

I do take request for a small fee of course and please, please remember to tip the girls, the waitresses and don't forget the hard working bartenders" "Again Welcome to OG's!"

Hey honey; let me get a glass of Merlot please! Sure Ma'am, one Merlot coming up! Thanks hun! Oh yeah; this is my song; go Dj! I love me some Keith Sweat! "There you go tellin me no again" "There you go, There you go." "I wanna be more than just your friend." "Don't you know, don't you know." Here you are; one Merlot! Thanks! You're welcome, did you want to start a tab or pay now? Go ahead and start a tab honey; my friend should be here soon, we'll be having a few. Okay Ma'am, do you have a card I can use? Oh I'm sorry; sure! Here you go honey; use this AMX. Thank you! You're Welcome! Sing it Keith! There you go! There you go!

Hey, I see you already got started without me! What! Startled; Rose turns to see Paco standing behind her. Oh hey Paco! Don't be sneaking up on a sister like that; you almost got the elbow boy. Ha-ha! Damn mommy; you violent! I'm just saying; that's all. Hey hun; get my friend a drink will yah? Sure what are you having Sir? A double shot

105

of Jose' baby! Ok coming right up, did you want lemon and salt? Hell nah, make it straight up! On the rocks; or no? No ice; just straight up! You got it, coming right up! So what kind of business did you want to discuss Paco? Damn, you don't waste any time; do you mommy? Not when it comes to business I don't. Hello, how are guys doing? Would you two like a table dance? Not right now mommy; we're talking business! Come back later! Ok thanks anyway! Hold on hun! Here you go! Aw thank you so much! You're welcome honey. Paco you're so damn mean; you could have tipped the girl. Rose we're talking business, she can wait. Besides, she should be happy; I seen that 50 you gave her. Yeah whatever hun; that's no money to a stripper; believe me! Anyway go on; what's the opportunity you're talking about?

I'm not happy with these new arrangements that AC has in place. Things were a whole lot better when Vinny and Bobby ran things. That maybe so Paco but Vinny and Bobby are dead! Coop is Boss now and he does things his way. I'm making more money than ever; aren't you making money? Yeah I am but I want more. See that's the problem; Greed! That will get you killed honey; quicker than you can ever imagine. I'm not afraid to die Rose, when it's my time; it's my time. Listen Paco; I do understand where you're coming from with wanting more money. AC has his way of making sure everyone is happy. He offered me in on the meth gig but I don't want that stuff around my clientele, so I passed. Did you pass on it? No I'm in and making good money but there's so much more to be made if we can cut out the middle man. So you want to buy directly from Derek and Diego and just say fuck AC. Yep that's the idea!

You have a death wish honey; I hope you're not serious! I am very serious Rose. Do you have any idea how much money and power AC has? Not that much more than me; that's why I can take over, I know I can. Paco, he has a hit squad, a crew of Lieutenants, a gang of soldiers, Diego in his pocket, not to mention Derek and you can't even count the amount of money he's worth. Do you realize what Coop's role is in our business, yours and mine I'm talking? Yeah a greedy pig! News flash Paco! Without him you couldn't operate in Sin City; your ass would be dead or back in Mexico right now. AC is not a drug dealer honey; he's a business man, a Crime Boss! He owns Dolls, The Ho

Ranch, The Escort service, The Car lot, The Adult Store and the streets. He's the one that allows Diego to distribute dope in Sin City.

But! Hold on Honey let me finish because you don't have a clue about the kind of shit you're about to step in. He came up with a way for all of us to make more money with the Meth if we wanted it and all he wants from us for doing business on his streets is a tax! Yeah Rose; a tax that's been in place before he came along! Paco he could have changed it but he didn't honey. Think about what you're saying here; before you move forward. I thought about it already Rose! Well here's one last thought for you hun; this guy you want to take out had the smarts and the power to take over these streets and had the balls to murder Vinny, Bobby and the last of their name sake; Victor; who he got taken care of in CCDC. Honey; stop dreaming and make your money; do yourself a favor and don't bite the hand that feeds you. Hey hun, cash me out I'm about to leave! Where are you going Rose? I have a meeting lined up Paco; I can't bullshit with you all day. Oh and I will keep our conversation to myself. Do yourself a favor; forget about that crazy move; you won't last hun, trust me! Here you go Ma'am! Thank you honey! Later Paco! Don't do anything crazy! Yeah, yeah, bye Rose!

Chino I'm ready to go back to Vegas! It's been four days and still no sign of these dudes! Just be patient Mya and keep looking for a red bronco with Florida plates. Ugh, ok! What numbers did Barbie say they were again? Umm, look on that napkin, right there under the arm rest. I wrote it on that. This is only three numbers! That's all she could get baby but we know the truck is red and the plates are from Florida, so we will know it when we see it. If you say so Chino! What's the numbers? Oh it's 569! Okay let's go hangout over by the bank where she got robbed at. Why? Do you think they're coming back to the bank? Maybe or that might just be the spot where they scope out their next target. Sounds good to me baby; let's go; I'm ready to merc these bastards so we can go home. Yeah me too Mya, make sure your nine is cocked and ready! I'm set Chino, ready to pop off as soon as we lay eyes on those punta's!

Isn't that the bank on the corner? No not that one; it's like two more blocks up. Are you sure Chino? Yeah chica, calm down! Oh shit; hold on baby! What? I think I saw the truck; turn in this Denny's parking lot. Where is it Mya? I think that's it; parked four spaces away from the entrance. Okay let's check it out then! You see it Chino? Yeah hold on; let's check the plates! Look at that napkin and see if those number's match while I get closer. Damn; it has California plates; not Florida Chino! Alright; let's head back towards the bank. I sure hope those guys are still in Phoenix; you've been driving around all day and we haven't seen anything close to the truck except just now.

 Just be patient Mya; if those punta's are still here we will find them, don't you worry. I sure hope so! Ring-Ring! Ring-Ring! Get that baby! Ring-Ring! Hello! Hey Mya; where's Chino? He's right here Hector; hold on! Here! It's Hector! Hey mane what's up? Damn homes; it's been two weeks; yall ain't find those fools yet? Not yet amigo; I'm gone ride all night if I have to! You better do something homes, by the time you find them it might be Christmas; as long as you're taking. Do you want me to send Poncho and Carlos? Nah I got it Hector. Ok handle that shit and get back to Vegas; we got business back here to handle. No problem amigo; I'm on it! Good; hurry the fuck up Chino!

Hey baby; there's an el Pollo Loco by the bank; let's get something to eat while we're waiting. Ok Mya; I'm hungry too, we can do that. Yes; because I am starving! Oh shit! That's it right there! What Chino! The truck! Look! Florida plates; look at the napkin and check those numbers! Hold on! Hold on; let me get it! Let's see; it says 569 Chino! What's on the plates? TNK 8569! Yep that's close enough! Is anybody in the truck? No; they must be inside; I'm parking so we can go find them. Get your nine ready Mya! It's ready! Cool, now be calm I'm going in like a normal customer. How are we going to know who they are Chino. That's easy; I'm going to tell the cashier that someone is outside breaking into a red truck with Florida plates. You wait here by the door and follow them when they walk out. I will be right behind you. Wait until they get to the truck then we dust their asses; one shot to the back of the dome. You got it Mya! Yep I got you baby! Good; wait here; I'm going to make my move. Okay, go ahead!

Hello; welcome to el Pollo Loco sir. What can I get for you today? Hey mane; I just seen two guys breaking into this red bronco parked right outside here. It has Florida plates! Oh no! Hold on, let me page them. "Excuse me; will the driver of a red bronco with Florida plates; please come to the front." Thank you for telling us sir! Oh it's no problem mane. Chino leans sideways against the counter waiting to see who was going to approach. He notices two guys getting up from their table and walking towards him. Both dark skinned black males, wearing brown dickie shorts, long white socks, black slippers and black shirts. One guy was bald and the other wore a jerry curl. Hey young blood; you said you wanted to talk to the drivers of a red bronco with Florida plates. Yes sir; is that you guys? Yeah it is; what's up? A customer just said that he seen two guys breaking into your truck a few minutes ago. Oh shit; come on bruh; let's go! Chino raise off the counter then hastily walks behind the guys as they rush out the door while Mya walks only a few steps in front of him. Man what the fuck, aint nobody breaking in our shit! Mya points her nine at one of the robbers and let two go. Pow! Pow! The first guy falls to the ground while the other stands there stunned. Whoa! Hold up lady! What you want money; the truck! You can have it; don't shoot! Nah she don't want nothing from you home boy! Hold on man; let's talk about this; what yall need bruh! You robbed my people a few weeks ago at the bank homie.

No man; you got me mixed up! I aint even from here; look at the plates bruh! I'm from Miami! Yeah we know! The girl you robbed saw your plates. Chino do that punk; we have to get out of here! Hold on man; please don't shoot! Pow! Pow! God dammit Chino; you could have waited until I moved. Now I got his blood and guts all over me! Forget that; let's get out of here; you can wash at the hotel and throw those damn clothes away! Come on; get in the truck! Yes; finally we can go back to Vegas! This place was getting on my nerves! Mine too Mya; mine too! Hey; call Hector while I get us out of here! I will; give me a minute to take off this damn bloody shirt. Damn; which way is the hotel? Turn left Chino! Ring-Ring! Ring-Ring! Hello! Hey Hector! Who is this? It's Mya! What's up baby; did yall get those punta's? Yep it's done! Good; tell Hector to get back here as soon as possible before the cops start crawling. We're stopping by the room to get our stuff then we're headed back. Alright that's what's up, see you two later tonight. Cool, later Hector! What he say Mya? He said to hurry back! Ha-ha! He didn't have to tell us that; huh baby! Ha-ha! Hell no.

April; 1998.

Loon; do me a favor and call Nina; I need you two to meet me over at The Texas for lunch; we have some business to discuss. When AC? Right now knuckle head; I'm already headed that way; get your assistant to watch the store; go scoop up Nina from the agency and meet me there ASAP. Alright Coop; we'll see you in a bit. Cool; see you later. Hey Mick; open this sun roof and let some fresh air in here. Ok Boss; no problem! Thanks! And take me over to The Texas; I'm meeting Loon and Nina there for lunch. Ok Sir! Why do you guys call your friend Loon? Ha-ha! Why do you think Mick? I don't know but if I had to guess. I'd say because he was kind of crazy!

Yep that boy is crazy; we gave him that name back during Desert Shield. Oh you guys were in the service together? Yeah the Army! Why; did you serve Mick? Who me; nah; no sir! So how long did you stay in the Army? A few years and that was enough for me! Was it that bad Mr. Cooper? Actually it wasn't bad at all; I just wanted more for myself. Well if I must say; you're doing pretty good for yourself now sir! Thanks Mick! You usually don't talk this much; why so many questions today? Ahh; no reason Sir; just having a conversation! Oh ok! We're pulling into The Texas now Mr. Cooper did you want me to park or come back for you? Just drop me off at the entrance and wait over with the other Limo's. I have no idea how long we're going to be. Ok no problem! Mick came to a complete stop in front of the casino entrance as the valet approached AC's door.

Good afternoon Sir and welcome to The Texas! Thanks man! No problem Sir; please enjoy your stay! Hey bruh; say I need a private suite for a business meeting; you guys have any vacant? Sure we do; I can help you with that; walk with me over to my booth and I can get you a key. Cool that's what I call service! How much is it? It's $1,900.00 for the suite but you pay the attendant at the desk when you get to the 19th floor. Alright thanks; I appreciate that! You're welcome Sir! Here take this for your trouble! Wow; thank you again Sir! Just call me AC man; no need for all that Sir shit! Thanks AC! That's more like it! 19th floor you said right! Yes 19th!

Ring-Ring! Hello! Hey Nina; where are you guys? Hey Coop; we're only 5 minutes away. Ok great; when you get here come to the 19th floor; I got a private suite; there will be an attendant at the desk up there. Your keys will be at the desk. Alright thanks; see you in few minutes. Several lines of patrons congest the lobby as AC enters the Texas Casino. Bells chime from the slot machines as the lines move slowly toward the movie ticket counter to enter the Texas Casino Theaters. He weaved in and out of the crowds, steadily making his way to the elevators. Excuse me Ma'am, can you hold the elevator for me please! Sure no problem! You're welcome young man; which floor? Oh, 19 Ma'am; Thanks! Um-hm.

It sure is pretty busy downstairs. Yeah it's always like this around lunch time; they have specials on the buffet. You must not be from around here young man. Oh I live in Vegas Ma'am; I just don't get over this way often. Well if you plan on eating something, you better get back down stairs in a hurry. It gets busier than this around 1:30. Ding! This is my floor young man, I enjoyed talking to yah; have a good visit now. Thank you Ma'am; I enjoyed talking to you too. AC places both hands in his pockets then leans back against the elevator wall with his eyes closed and head titled back. The buzzing sound from the movement of the elevator car seemed to relax him as it continued up to the 19th floor. Ding! He jumps up from the wall and exits. Hello sir; did you have a suite? Yes I do; here is my key, I got it from down stairs; the gentleman said I was to pay here.

Yes that is correct! Cool; you can charge it to my visa and I will need two more keys also. Great; I'll be happy to take care of that for you; here's your receipt and your extra keys. No, keep them up here at the desk. Excuse me Sir? Well, I have two friends arriving in a few minutes. The keys are for them, can you make sure they get them? Yes Sir, that won't be a problem. Great; it will be a bald head black male and a Latin female; my name is AC. They will be asking for me when they come up. Alright we will make sure they get the keys Sir. Great, I appreciate it; now which suite is it? Oh I am sorry about that; it's the 2nd door on the left; suite 1902. Thanks!

Hey Nina; just park right there by the door. Boy I'm not parking by the door; we're going to valet! Alright sis; my bad, damn! Loon; don't start with me today! What I do! That's the problem; you don't know! Aww girl whatever, stop the car. Hello folks, welcome to the The Texas! Yeah, yeah, what floor are the business suites on man? The 19th

floor sir! Alright hurry up Nina; we have to go upstairs. I'm coming; don't rush me. Damn it must be that time of month; what's with the attitude today? I don't have an attitude Loon; you tripping. Shit; I'm not the one tripping sis! When was the last time somebody knock the dust off that kitty of yours. Ha-Ha! What did you just say boy? I don't have any dust on my kitty. Well something's wrong with your ass. What is it? Nothing; where's the elevator? It's right past the movie theater. Ok I see it; let's hurry, Coop's waiting.

I think you need some dick in your life; you're just uptight for no reason. Shut up Loon; you don't know what you're talking about! Ding! I think I do Nina! Be quiet and get on this elevator crazy. Yeah I need to speak with Denna about finding you a man; you're to tense right now sis. You and Denna need to mind your own business and stay out of mine. Girl you are our business; you're family so that makes you our business. Loon; just drop it already; I'm fine! I promise! Are you sure Nina? 100% sure brother! Alright but I got my eye on you. Yo why aren't we moving? Oh shit my bad! See you got problems boy; push 19. Ha-ha! Damn; don't tell anybody that happened. Don't worry;

I'm sure you will beat me to it. Don't say I did it either. But it was your fault Nina; you were the first one on the elevator. Loon; go to hell; our floor is coming up, let's go. Ding! Hello guys; did you have a suite reserved? No but we're supposed to pick up some keys. Ok, who are the keys from Sir? That would be Andy Cooper; we call him AC! Alright; here you are; it's the second door, right over there; suite 1902. Thank you! You're welcome Ma'am.

Man the door is cracked already, we don't need the keys. AC! Hey; in here guys! What's up bruh; why you left the door opened. Was it open? Yep! I don't know; I thought I closed it! Hey Nina; how are you doing sis? I'm good AC; what's going on; you got us out here in the middle of the day like this. Sit down; I have something to tell you guys. Aww shit; what the fuck done happen now! Calm down Loon and listen! Ok man; I'm listening. I don't know how else to say it; so I'm gonna give it to you raw. Las Vegas Metro is building a case on us. I don't know how much information they have yet but my source told me just the other day and it's a reliable one. How reliable AC? It's that Detective that I've been paying off; she came to the park the other day and told me. Damn, what tipped them off;

did we fuck up somewhere? No not really; it's that damn Chief Espinoza; he's been out to get me before we got into this business. This just made him more eager; now that we're making all this money. Well, did she say anything else? Like what Nina?

Like are they going to be indicting us or what? No, she said it was too early to tell and all he really had right now was all of our names and faces. Damn that aint good bruh! I know Loon; that's why we're having this meeting. Did you find that kamikaze patsy like I asked? No but I've been looking, I have my eye on a few prospects. Well speed that shit up; I want to be ready as soon as I find out who is leaking our information. Say no more bruh; I got you. So what do we do now AC? Let's play it cool Nina; stay the course and don't make any new friends, associates or any kind of contacts.

I know this stubborn ass Espinoza; he's like a pit bull; he aint letting go unless we bust him in the fucking head with something. I wonder what he has on us Coop. From my understanding; nothing right now; he's just building a case off his gut. Damn that's messed up; if he's that eager; he's bound to find something. Yeah that's what I'm afraid of

Sis! I say we smoke the fool, myself! Hell; that's the way I feel too Loon, but we need to make sure we can do it clean before we move on that bastard. If we kill a cop there can be no mistakes; no room for era. You dig! Oh I understand bruh, trust me I do. That's why we need that patsy Loon! We need the element of surprise; remember. I will be taking care of that immediately AC; say no more about it. Good; well that's what I wanted to tell you guys. Manny already knows and he's telling Denna, Duck and Will right now.

Don't hire any new employees until this thing rolls over. What about Hector Coop? What about him Nina? Should I tell him? Yeah go ahead but only him not his goons. Man; we gone need a good ass lawyer if this hit the fan. I already got one out of LA Loon. Jerm turned me on to him! Cool; well I'm hungry as a bear; we getting room service or what? Yeah Loon; go ahead order something! Nina you can get something too; order me the Steak and Lobster while you at it and a bottle of that Cristal. Make that, two bottles! Alright; how you want your steak bruh? Medium well Loon! Nina what you want? I'll figure it out by the team you order; go ahead and call room service. Say no more! Ring-Ring! Hello Room service!

"What's up people; welcome to Dolls; I'm your Dj for tonight and I go by the famous Dj Tech!" "I hope you all enjoyed this Easter weekend with your families, now it's time to have some fun baby!" "Get your drink on, get plenty of ones because this next girl coming to the stage is a sexy red motherfucker!" "Let's hear it for that sexy ass Dylan; jamming to one of my favorite Jay-Z cuts; Can't Knock The Hustle!"

"I'm making short term goals, wonder whether foes" "Just put away the leathers and put ice on the gold." Hey Red; how you doing baby! Hey Manny; what's up! Who are these two handsome fellows you got with you? Oh this is my son Manny junior and his friend Tony! Guys this is Debbie but we call her Red! Hi Debbie! Hello young men; you guys hanging out with the big boys today huh? Yes Ma'am! Cool, he looks just like you Manny! I know, I know, he got his good looks from me and smarts from Sophie! Ha-ha! Manny you're a trip! Hey, give them a pitcher of beer will you; I'm going to speak with Will. Sure no problem! Thanks Red! Hey Son why don't you and Tony go have a seat in that booth over there when you get your beer and buy yourself some dances. But we don't have any money dad! Oh shit, hold on! Yo Red! Yeah Manny? Give them 500 ones a piece too! Ok, got you covered baby! Thanks; you're the best! Yeah, yeah, go talk to Will! I got the boys covered. "Taking out this time, to give you a piece of my mind" "(Cause you can't knock the hustle)" "But though you think you are" "Baby one day you'll be a star."

Knock-Knock! It's open, come in! Big Will! Hey what's up Capo! Man we got a problem! What problem Manny? Paco is trying to make a move on us. Stop bullshitin; Paco's cool bruh. What reason do I have to lie man. Who told you that crap? Dupree told me when I went by the church to collect his taxes. Damn, how did he find out? Paco approached him about joining up with him. Does this fool know who he's messing with! What's his problem? Pree says Paco wants more money and even tried to buy direct from Derek. Yeah Derek did tell me something about that; I brushed it off because it was Paco. I had no idea that fool was trying go John Gotti on us! Turn on the speaker phone we need to call AC and see what he wants to do! Alright, give me a second Manny. I have to take a piss.

Hurry up, go piss then! Hey; don't rush me Emanuel! Go to the bathroom already; I'll call him while you're in there. Ok go ahead! Ring-Ring! Ring-Ring! Ring-Ring! Ring-Ring! Damn, he's not answering his cell! Call the Condo Manny; he's probably home. Yeah I'm doing that now. Ring-Ring! Ring-Ring! Hello! Hey Mo; is AC there? Who is this? It's Manny! Oh, hey Manny; he's busy, what's up? Tell him it's urgent; I need to speak with him. Alright; hold on! Is he there Manny? Yeah, Monica is going to get him now. Ok cool! Mo holds her hand over the phone and waits about 60 seconds and brings it back up to her mouth. He says he's taking a dump, just tell me what it is and for me to tell him. What! You heard me Manny, is that a problem?

No; just tell him that Paco is making a move on us and we need to act fast. Ask him if we should take him out or wait to see what happens. Ok; hold on Manny! Mo covers the phone once more, this time for 90 seconds then brings it back to her mouth. He said to go ahead and take that fool out before he gets to one of us first. Are you sure Mo? Yes; didn't I just say it! Do you want me to repeat it Manny? No that's ok, thanks! Bye Manny! So what's up Capo? He said to take Paco out before he tries to make a move. When did he want us to do it? I guess soon; he didn't say. Well, I hope that fool got his shit in order because he's a dead motherfucker now. You can say that again Will! These fools will never learn, they aint built to take us out. Seems like every month; we're dusting somebody off! Hey; it comes with the territory Capo; it's not our fault that they can't play by the rules. Yep; you're right about that shit. Alright hold it down Will; my son and Tony are out there getting some table dances; I'm going to join them. I will holler at you later Big man. Cool; tell junior I said what's up, if I don't get out there before you guys leave. I need to finish up these beer orders. Okay, will do!

"Alright Gentlemen; coming to the stage is one of the newest members here at Dolls." "All the way from Thailand; this is Mystery dancing to Seal's, Kissed by A Rose." "There used to be a graying tower alone on the sea." "You became the light on the dark side of me." What's up Junior; you guys having fun? Hey Manny! Hey Dylan; what are you doing here? We had to take a break; someone robbed Barbie while we were in Phoenix. Oh yeah I heard about that; is she ok? Yeah; she's in the dressing room now getting ready. Oh ok. So son, you like it? Yep! Is this your boy? Yeah that's my little man! He's handsome; he must get it from his mom. Whatever Dylan; you know where he got it. Go easy on him; don't make him lose his mind now. Oh; I'll be gentle poppy; I promise. Tony how you doing over there; you haven't said a word since I walked over. He's fine Manny; I'm taking good care of him! Aint I baby! Um-hmm! See; look at that! Hey Tony; Remy has a lot of ass; you sure you can handle all of it! Anthony sat there mesmerized as Remy bent over in front of his face. All he could see was naked ass and fat shaved pussy. She bounced up and down on his lap while rubbing her right hand through his silky black hair. Remy could hear him moan as her back touched his young chest.

Damn that boy is out of it over there, Remy done blew his mind. Leave him alone Manny; he's having fun. Yeah; yeah, I'm just messing with him Dylan. Junior I'll be at the bar; let me know when you guys are ready to go. Ok dad; oh can we have some more money? What! Hell no; that's all you get! Don't get caught up son; just enjoy the moment; these girls are working! That means; they get paid to make you feel how you are feeling now. Get your thrill and keep it moving; I'll be at the bar! Ok pop! Aww;

give them some more money poppy! Dylan; don't even try it! Yeah come on... Remy; you either! Ha-Ha! Bye Manny! Bye girls! "Ooh, the more I get of you" "The stranger it feels, yeah." This song is about to end Junior; you want another one? Yep! Okay big boy; let's do it then. "Now that your rose is in bloom" "A light hits the gloom on the gray."

Slurp! Slurp! Slurp! Yeah, I like that; keep going. Ummm, your mouth feels good girl. Slurp! Slurp! Slurp! Whoa! Whew, slow down baby. Slurp- Slurp- Slurp- like that! Yeah like that. Slurp- Can your girl- suck your dick- good as me? Slurp- Slurp- Huh? Slurp- I said; can your girlfriend- suck your pipe like I can? Slurp- Slurp- Umm, no- Stop talking; keep slobbering baby. Ummmm, Slurp- Slurp- Slurp- Damn; whew, oh that shit feels good! You like? Hell.... Yeah girl. Slurp- Slurp- Slurp- Are you about to cum? Umm- hmm! Ooh; nut on my face. Slurp- Slurp- is it coming now? Ahhhhh.. Slurp- Slurp- Slurp- Ohhhhh, damn! Yes, give me that nut nigga! Put it on my face, oh yes! Ughhhhhh! Ummmmm, rub it in baby. God damn Chocolate; you missed this dick huh! Whew that was good girl! Nah, you miss this good head Loon, that's what it was. You know

Denna aint got no skills on the mic like me. Ha-ha! Choc you are crazy.

Well, I'm going to the back so I can get dressed; you better go wash up before we get some customers, standing there with your dick hanging out. Shit, I'm still in the moment; you got me on that one girl. Don't I always handle my business Loon! Sure you right; let me get it together; tell Candy to come watch the front while I go to the bathroom. Alright baby; I'll tell her. Loon runs from behind the counter, jeans hanging halfway off his ass and makes it to the bathroom. Hey girl, can you watch the front for Loon while he's in the bathroom. Sure no problem and wash your face bitch you got something on your chin. Ha-ha! Stop playing; do I for real! Choc you nasty, Denna gone kick your ass; keep on!

Denna aint gone do a damn thing because she don't know shit. I'm just saying girl. Candy; just mind your business and you better not tell her or it's gone be me and you. Bitch whatever; you don't want none of Candy! Try me and see; your ass will be chocolate covered candy in this piece. Ha-ha! Choc kiss my ass! Ha-ha! You know that was funny girl, don't be hating on my Eddie Murphy skills.

Girl you are not a comedian, just a broke ass stripper, college student, like me. Bye Candy; just go watch the front of the store! Yeah I'm going.

Ding! Hello; welcome to Vegas Video; how can I help you today? Yes Ma'am, I'm looking for some Jenna Jamison flics! Oh that's on the third isle Sir; is there anything else I can do for you? No that will do it! Thank you! You're welcome. Hey Candy, thanks for watching the store, I heard the bell ring. Was it a customer? Yeah he's on isle three. Ok thanks, how are you today? I'm good Loon, what about you? Couldn't be better baby! Well that's good to hear. That dress looks good on you, look at you with your matching boots too. Aww, thank you Loon! I had it made last week! They did a good job on it. It fits your body just right; tight up top so your boobs pop out and it hangs just below your ass cheeks, enough to tease. Did they make the panties too? Oh no, I don't have on any! Stop lying; yes you do. No I don't, wanna see? Yeah, let me see.

Candy leans over the counter just enough to give him a peek. Wow, you aren't wearing any. You have a nice snatch too. Really, I don't know if I should say thank you or be offended. Why you say that Candy? No one ever called my pussy a snatch before. Hold that thought Candy let me get this customer. Sure. Ok this is the one I'm looking for; can I have a box of those ribbed Trojans as well? Sure sir, will there be anything else? No, that it will do it man. Ok your total is $14.98 for the movie and $2.95 for the condoms for a total of $17.93! Are sure that's the total sir? Yes I'm sure of it, 14.98 plus 2.95 is 17.93 all day. Well, what about the tax? Oh you must not be from around here man, there's no sales tax in Vegas. Wow, really! Yep! Ok thank you, you guys have a good day! You too sir!

Now I was saying that you shouldn't be offended baby, that's a good thing. Oh it is, is it? Yes Ma'am, it looks so pretty just sitting there; can I touch it? I don't know about that Loon, I don't want any trouble! What kind of trouble are you talking about Candy? Don't you have a girl? Yeah but we have an open relationship, besides she's way out in the desert. I'm not gone tell her, are you? No! So can I touch it? Yeah I guess.

Candy leans over the counter to make her ass pop up a little higher as Loon starts to massage her vagina slowly. With his left hand he runs his fingers lightly across her lips, back and forth. Ummm! Does that feel good Candy? Umm-hmm. Loon takes his two middle fingers and slowly penetrates her sugar walls. In and out with a slow motion he went for several seconds until it begin to make popping sounds from the moistness as her lips separated her from one another. Ummm! It feels good don't it Candy? Umm-hmm. He gets closer behind her until his body meets hers with his hand still penetrating her juicy womb. Loon looks down at the pretty wet muscle as it moves slowly back and forth on his fingers then bends over and drops just a little spit on her pussy. Ummm! Yes that feels so good.

He reaches back behind him and pulls a condom from the wall with his right hand, places it between his teeth, then reaches down and unzips his jeans while finger fucking her with the other hand. Loon's Johnson now erect, he rips open the magnum, slides it on then shoves his black love into her throbbing wet hole. Ohhhhh shit! Ummm, ummm, ummm, damn! What's wrong Candy? Ummm, ummmm, oh shit; you're in my stomach! Yeah, you like it don't you, don't you! Umm-Hmm! In then out, in then out, in then out, in the out he went, watching his every stroke as her pussy juices bubbled on his cock. Oh God! Oh God, it hurts so good! Bam! He jumps back. What the fuck! Loon, you sorry as piece of shit! Whoa Choc, hold on! Bam! Stop throwing shit girl! You sorry dog you! Wait Choc! Shut up Loon! And you bitch! Bam! Choc I'm sorry! You two sorry ass niggas! Choc calm down and stop throwing shoes and shit! Bam! Fuck you! Oh girl; you better not hit me! What you gone do Loon! You make me sick! Candy; bring your ass here! Stop Choc! You better run bitch! Ding! Now look what you did Choc; why you ran that girl out of the store! Go get her! What! You done bump your head boy; you go get her! And how are you gone fuck this girl, right under my nose!

Wait I can explain! Explain what, how your dick fell in her pussy! I stood there and watched you finger her Loon! I thought maybe you would stop or she would; but no! Yall two sluts, was all into it! You get on my damn nerves Loon; I'm going home and don't bother calling me either. But Chocolate I need you at work; I'll be two girls short! You should have thought about that before you stuck your dick in that skank bitch! Bye Loon! Choc come here! Don't touch me; I'm going home and Fuck you, whore ass nigga! Come on; don't leave Choc-

Hello; thanks for calling The Flamingo Laugh Factory! Hi; may I speak with Winston please? Sure; can you hold a second? Yes! Yeah; this is Winston! Well hello mister! Hey, may I ask whose speaking? This is Nina! Excuse me; you must have the wrong number; I don't know a Nina. We met at the gas station a few weeks ago. Oh the beamer right! That's right! Well; it took you long enough to call; I was starting to think I've lost my touch. Ha-ha! Oh really! Nah, I'm just kidding! How are you? I'm doing pretty good; I was going through my purse and came across your card. I thought I had lost it. I'm glad you called; when are you coming by to see a show? I don't know yet; but I am coming. It depends on my schedule. Is your schedule too busy to come by one evening? Yes it is; for now. Wow; you're a busy lady. That I am! Well, you know what I do Nina! What profession are you in; if you don't mind me asking? Right now I do mind, maybe I'll tell you later. Ok mysterious woman; I can wait.

So I see your club is on Flamingo blvd; is it closer to the strip or further out. It's right on Flamingo and Koval, that same corner Tupac got shot on. Damn, was that bad for your business? Nah, it brought more business if anything;

don't ask me why! That's crazy Winston, really? Yep! My sister lives on the strip and Flamingo at The Towers; that's only a few blocks from your club. Yeah it is; you guys can actually walk here, don't even have to worry about finding a park. Maybe; I will let you know though but I have to get back to work. I just wanted to call and speak. Alright thank you for calling and I'm looking forward to seeing you. You're welcome Winston; take care and have a great evening. Thanks Nina; you do the same.

Ring-Ring! ILona get that other line will yah! But what do I say Nina! "Say Hello, thank you for calling Angel's Escorts; can you please hold!" I'll be over there in a second; I have to put my cell phone on the charger. Just place them on hold! Ok, ok! Hello; thank you for calling- Angel's Escorts! Can I help you? Yes I would like to book a date for this evening. Ok sir; can you please hold! Yes I can. Give me the phone ILona!

Hello; you said you wanted a date for this evening; is that correct sir? Yes Ma'am! Did you have any particular girl in mind? No I'm not picky as long as she's sexy with long hair and big tits! Ha-ha! I believe we can accommodate you with that. Great; I'll be ready around 9pm; is that fine? It most certainly is! I will need your name, just like it is on your I.d and an address too. My name is Robert Williams and I stay at 4589 Shadetree Lane, Las Vegas. Thank you Robert and is this where you want us to send your date? Yes Ma'am! Ok great; she will be there 9 O'clock sharp; please have your I.D ready so that she can verify who you are. I sure will and thank you! You're welcome Robert; enjoy your date. See that wasn't hard ILona, was it?

No it wasn't but you didn't tell him how much the date was. The dates are always $500 ILona; unless they ask for a double or some crazy shit, that's out of the norm. Ok I got it! All you have to do is remember to be nice and make sure you always send them what they ask for. It's too many agencies in Vegas slanging pussy to be fucking up. If we lose a customer we may never see him again. That's the part you have to pay close attention to; keeping them happy. So what if we don't have the type of girl they want? You make that bitch up girl; that's why we have wigs; fake nails, tanning lotion, color contacts, etc. They get whatever they want! Wow; I never looked at it that way Nina. I know baby; that's how come I'm telling you now.

At the end of the day, all they want is a warm pussy to slide their cocks in or to eat out; whatever their pleasure. All that blonde hair, blue eye crap is just for show baby. The sooner you learn that, the better! Hell that even goes for these square ass guys out here that don't trick. The same principals apply. Do you know why? Not really Nina! Because we got what every man wants mommy; this cha cha! There shouldn't be any reason for a woman to be broke, especially when her pussy is working. What if she is ugly? ILona there is somebody for everybody, trust me some guy will fuck her. But I don't know about paying her for it though! Ha-ha! Nina you're funny! I'm just telling you how it is baby; that's all. Now go get freshen up so you can go on this date. Robert is your trick tonight; you got an hour and half. Alright I'm going to change then head over. Ok baby; see you when you get back and don't forget to check his I.D! Oh I won't!

Damn, it's warm out here today! Hey Manny; how you been man? I've been good David; is AC upstairs? Yeah he's up there. Cool! How are things over at The Towers now? It's pretty much the same Manny, not much has changed since you left. Oh yeah; so you making good tips? The tips are alright. What's alright David? I mean, I do ok! So what are you making a day $100, $200, what? No; more like $350! Hmm, that's not bad! What you mean Manny; I think it's pretty good. Well when you're making $600 on a bad day and at least $1,000 on a good one then you're doing something. No way, you made that much while you were here? Yes Sir, so see you're not doing so hot; are you David. Hell no, not when you've been making that much. At least now, you know that it's possible David. Just remember to know your guest, residents and patrons from one another then cater to what they need. You make it sound so easy Manny. It is Dave, just focus and you will get there. It was good talking to you player but I need to go handle this business with Coop. Alright Manny, see you later. Yep, later!

Knock-Knock! Who is it? The F.B.I.; open up! Manny cut that shit out, come in its open! What up Coop! How did you know it was me? Because your ass is crazy like that! Well, I need to know how you want to handle this Paco situation. Should I get Hector to knock him off or should one of us do it. What; knock off Paco! Why would I want to do that, he's a good earner! He has North town on lock!

You're talking crazy Capo; what you been smoking. AC; you told me and Will the other day to handle him after we told you what he did. Man; what the hell are you talking about; I never spoke to you or Will about Paco! What's this non sense you're talking?

Damn, you better sit down AC; you're not gone like what I have to say brother. Go ahead and spit it out; this better be good because you're not making any sense right now. Yo boy Paco is trying to make a move on us; he's already tried to get Dupree to join him as well as Derek. And you know this how? Dupree told me when I stopped by the church to make a pick up. That's how I know about Derek too! Did Derek tell you or you only heard it from Pree. I only heard it from Dupree but Derek had mentioned something about it to Will. Has he tried to recruit anyone else? I can't tell you that Boss but he's serious about it; that's for sure. So what this craziness about me telling you to knock him off and I haven't spoken to either of you?

Coop as soon as we found out we called your cell. I don't remember you guys calling me. That's because when you didn't answer; we called here. Then what happened! Monica answered the phone and I asked to speak to you.

She said to hold on because you were in the bathroom. What? Hold on, I'm not done Coop! I say to her; go get him and tell him it's urgent! She put me on hold again then comes back this time and says you said to tell her what I want. I told her about the Paco situation and wanted to know if you wanted us to hold on before we made a move or should we take him out. She came back and said. "AC says take that motherfucker out and do it now before he moves on us." What! Are you kidding me right now Manny? Nope! That black bitch! I wasn't even here Manny; she made all that shit up! I need to go handle that ho ASAP! Where is she? She's at the Ranch now Capo but don't worry; I'll handle her ass and that punk Paco! Are you sure you don't want Hector to handle it? Nah, this one is mine.

But you can visit Hector and let him know that North Town is about to be wide open; we're gonna need somebody to take Paco's spot. What, you want Hector to run it? Not Hec, but maybe one of his goons can. They get respect on that side anyway; that'll make it a smooth transition. This way if it's any heat from Paco's crew; Hector can handle it his way. Alright I like that plan, I'll go by there right now and let him know. Yeah you do that Capo; I got some things I need to take care of too. Later Boss; I'll hit you up tonight. Later Manny!

Ring-Ring! LT speaking! Hey LT; I have Detectives Casey, Briggs and Ricky in my office; could you come join us and bring those background check files on our suspects. Sure chief; should I get the Captain also? Nah; he doesn't need to be in this one. Ok; on my way Chief. Thanks LT! Detectives; make yourselves comfortable. We got some good intel on our suspects. These guys are no amateurs either; here's LT now. He will tell you all about them. Good Morning Detectives! Good Morning Lt! Alright; I'm just gone get right to it; I know you guys have cases to work. So I won't take all day! Here we have our first suspect; AC aka Andy Cooper; he's originally from the Carolina's. Joined the Army in 1990, won a few medals, and has a Top Secret Clearance; his job was to build and destroy inferred missile equipment. Mr. Cooper was also an Airborne Ranger, was in Special Forces, Air Assault, and pretty damn good with a rifle. He qualified expert every year that he was enlisted. This guy lead a Platoon of soldiers on a covert mission in the Desert and returned back home with no casualties and all enemies were deceased. Mr. Cooper was ordered to bring back prisoners but he refused because he thought the enemies would serve America better off dead.

Excuse me LT? Yes Casey! Did he get discharge for breaking that order sir? Hell no, son of bitch got a purple heart! Wow! That's what I said when I read it too Briggs! Next up is Emanuel Ortega aka Manny; he served as Corporal under Cooper's watch. His specialty was field training. He could train anyone to survive in the field, in any conditions, any terrain and anywhere. Mr. Ortega was also an expert with his rifle but better with a bayonet. Detectives these aren't your everyday boy scouts we're dealing with. These guys were trained by yours truly, the U.S Government and their damn good too.

Next on the list we have Dubai Patel aka Duck; he's originally from India but moved state side when he was a boy. His parents owned a chained of hotels in the states but he didn't want to be in the family business; so he joined the Army. This guy is dangerous Detectives; probably more than the others because his specialty is explosives. It's rumored that he acquired the nick name Duck because he would have bombs going off unexpectedly with no warning. Hence, telling his peers to duck! This next one was my favorite!

This guy here; Looney aka Lionel Massey is a loose cannon; please be careful around this guy. He's known to lose his temper for the smallest thing. I'll explain! Mr. Massey still had some time left on his orders when the rest of his platoon left the Army. He wanted to leave with them, so how does he fix it! Well, during a road march, this guy pulls out his Rifle and Shoots his Sergeant in the ass! Wow! Yep, my reaction too Ricky! They let him go on a honorable medical; they blamed the incident on PTSD. Damn; what was his specialty? Oh, good question Briggs! This guy was a sniper! Whoa! Did you say sniper LT? Yes I did Ricky, so be careful. A sniper, with a loose cannon, is not good!

Hey Chief; I think we're gonna need some back up when we do move in on these guys and I'm not talking about no street cops. I'm already working on it Casey! Good; thank you! Ok detectives these next two suspects are Nina and Denna Sanchez; originally from Rio but moved to America as kids then joined the Army on a buddy system straight out of High School. These two ladies were straight A students and aced the ASVAB with flying colors. Because of that the U.S Army; General at the time personally recruited them to be on his Military Intelligence team. Both of them speak and read 15 different languages; completed the highest level of Taekwondo and are excellent with any weapon. People we're talking, hand guns, rifles, swords, knives, and even Bow and Arrows. Please don't let these girls good looks fool you. On the streets they're known as the twins, but they're actually 5 minutes apart so.... You know what I mean!

This is a lot to take in Detectives, I know, but we want you to know who you're dealing with. Now to our last suspect; Mr. Tosi! His real name is William Tosi; born in Hawaii to his native father and Indian mother. Mr. Tosi aka Big Will; is the enforcer of the crew; during his time in the Army; he was a gunner with several infantry platoons before he landed with these guys. For the most part this guy is quiet but has a temper. He stands about 6'7" as you have all seen and he's very heavy too. So please don't piss this guy off without back up. His hands alone will crush anyone of us in this room. We're calling these guys; the Sin City Seven! Detectives; our mission is to infiltrate their organization and bring it down! Is there any questions?

Yes LT! Go ahead Ricky! Do we have a projective date to bring the Sin City Seven in? As of right now, that answer is no detective. We're still gathering some intel on their operations and developing some contacts with known associates. Anyone else- Alright great; I hope this helps detectives! Thank you LT; that'll be all! You're welcome Chief; anytime! Alright detectives; this is what we're working with; so be careful out there and go work those cases so we can bring these bastards down! Roger that chief!

May, 1998.

Welcome to Vegas; Asian Sun Spa! Hey Honey, how are you doing today? I'm doing lovely Rose; did you want the full treatment today? No not today, I'm just doing the Sauna and a full body. Ok you go sauna for ten minutes then I come get you for your full body; ok Rose! Yeah girl that's fine. Oh; hold a minute; I need to make a call before you put my stuff in the locker. Ok Rose, no problem. Ring-Ring! Hello, Will speaking! Hey big guy! Hey, who is this? It's Rose Mr.! Well I'll be damned; it has to be snowing outside! Ha-ha! Funny! It is funny; what made you call me woman. I mean you did give me your number; isn't that's the reason you gave it to me. To call you! Yeah; about a year ago! Well, better late than never!

Rose you are too damn much; what's going on with you? I'm at the Asian spa about to step in this Sauna then I'm going to enjoy a full body massage. Don't even ask if I want to come; the answer is no. Why not Will? I just don't feel like it today; maybe another time. Aww; you promise? No; I don't make promises. Well, that's not why I called anyway! Alright why did you? Because; I wanted you to meet me for dinner tonight! Damn, are you sure it's not snowing out!! Will cut it out, I'm serious. Did you want to go or no? Sure I guess I can, what time were you thinking? I leave here in 30 minutes; you can pick me up from the spa and we can ride together. Look at you; got it all figured out don't you? Well, kind of! Oh really; so where are we going for dinner? I was thinking the Top of The World at The Stratosphere; they have a really nice menu.

Do they really; I've never been! Aww; you'll love it Will! You think so? I do! Ok; what time will you be ready? Let's say 40 minutes! Alright Rose; I'll see you in 40 minutes; if you're not outside when I get there; I'm leaving. What do you mean? Just what I said woman; if you're not there waiting when I get to the Spa; I'm leaving! You wouldn't! Try me and see if I won't! Ha-Ha! William stop being mean! I'm not being mean Rose; I just don't like waiting! Alright; I will be there; waiting on you! Is that better? Yes Ma'am it is! Great see you in a few Hun! Yep!

You done with phone call Rose; come let's go Sauna now. Ok honey; I'm ready; you got that steam adjusted right for me. Yes, hot and steamy, just how you like!

Rose steps out of her clothes then into the thick white robe that her host is holding for her. The bamboo walls permeated from the heat evaporating off the hot coals while the glass door panel fogged up from the steam.

Ok Rose; come in; you sit down and read paper; relax yourself. Thank you hun, set that timer for 10 minutes! Sure; ten minutes no problem. Thank you!

Total quietness and the heat; made it hard for Rose to concentrate on reading the paper. Sweat rolled down her face and onto the robe as she sat there; patiently waiting out her ten minutes.

Hey Honey! Honey! I'm coming out now; it's too damn hot in here. Why you come out! It no finish; you have 4 minutes left. I said it's too hot; I'm ready for my massage anyway. Alright, go in room and lay on table, I come massage you. Thanks hun and can you make it fast; I have a date in a few. Sure, I go fast for you! Ummm, what's that smell you got in here; it smells great. That is rain forest candle; helps you to relax Rose. It smells wonderful, where did you get it? I have to get a few for my house. Don't worry; I'll get some for you today! Aww; really; thank you honey! No problem, you my best customer! Yeah; now you're just buttering me up; aint you! Oh no butter; that's candle! Ha-ha! No hun, I was just saying that to be funny. Oh ok; you turnover for me please; on your stomach. Sure hun; I can do that.

Let me know if I massage too hard for you; ok! Oh you're fine; that feels great hun. I don't want you to take long today; I have to meet my friend in a few minutes. I will hurry; it's no problem for me Rose. You turn back over now so I can get your legs and feet. Damn; yall need some bigger tables in here honey. I know you catch hell massaging your big clients. What you mean big clients? Fat honey; fat! Ha-ha! Oh yes; really hard to do on this table. Don't they make bigger ones? No, no big ones, this is it. Wow; that has to suck for the big person. No problem, we put them on side! Side! Yes; right here; the side! Oh ok; on their side! Doesn't that take longer? Yes but cost more money! Right; I bet it does honey; all that damn extra work! Here; let me get your arms for you.

Ummm, I feel so much better now! Ok, you all done now; get dress for date! Thank you honey; I'll stay longer next time, I promise. You welcome; no problem Rose! I be right back with your clothes! Great; you're the best!

Beep-Beep! Will blows on the horn as he pulls in front of the Spa; looking for Rose just as she exits.

Look at you; all on time! I almost left you woman! Yeah whatever; you knew better Mr.! Well, are you getting in or what? Hold your horses; don't rush a lady! Rose you're a bigger gangster than I am, talking about lady! I'm still a lady; none the less, Will! Alright; you have a point there baby; I apologize! Thank you; apology accepted. Now let's go get some food and chat; we have some catching up to do! You're right about that; a lot of catching up too woman! Hey; good things come to those who wait Will, haven't you heard that before? Yeah; we'll see about that Rose....

Yo Mick, start this thing up and take me to the Ranch; I have some business to handle. Make it fast too; I don't have all day! Sure Mr. Cooper; on the way sir! Open the sun roof and turn on some music. I need to ease my mind; you can roll up your glass; I'm about to smoke some chronic. Ok; no problem Sir!

Coop sat in the back of the limo frustrated and on pins and needles because of what Mo did. He rocked back and forth, looking up at the clear black sky as the limo cruised away from the city and into the desert. The surround system bumped in the background as he lit up his blunt; pondering his next move. Monica had gotten out of line; she was taking her position too seriously. All he could say to himself was. "Who the fuck do she think she is!" As he inhaled the chronic and blew the smoke in the air; he bopped his head back and forth to the lyrics of Cee Lo as they came through the speakers.

"Lord it's so hard- living this life-" "A constant struggle- each and every day" "Some wonder why- I'd rather die-" "Than to continue, living this way." This right here is good music Mick, that dirty south shit, you dig! Yes Sir; I agree! Man; what do you mean; you agree! Where are you from anyway Mick? Me! Yeah you! San Diego Sir! So you moved to Sin City to be a limo driver? No; I wanted to be a singer Mr. Cooper. No shit; a singer huh? Yes sir! Well, you came to the wrong city for that playboy; aint nothing here but gangsters, pimps, prostitutes, degenerate gamblers and union folk! Why you aint take your ass to Hollywood? That place is too saturated with wanna bee's Sir! Ha-ha! Mick if you knew how you sound right now; you would slap yourself. Excuse me Sir! Never mind man, keep driving; how far do we have to go? About 20 minutes Mr. Cooper! Cool, step on it!

It's a nice night out here in the desert. Just look at it Mick; all that desert covered in total darkness! Does that scare you; not knowing what lurks in the night. I just try not to think about Sir; that's a whole lot of empty space under the night sky; you can barely see pass the street. Yeah I know; that's why you should always ride out here with a full tank. There's not a gas station in sight until we reach Pahrump. Oh and another thing, always, always keep your piece on you; just in case! Just in case of what Mr. Cooper? Just in case you have to defend yourself from one of those wild animals out here Mick. What kind of animals, should I fear in the desert Sir?

Wolves, coyotes, hell, snakes too man! No way! Shit; yes way! I've never seen either one since I've been driving out this way Mr. Cooper. That's because you haven't had a reason to go in the actual desert; you've always used the road. Trust me Mick; they're out there partner, I can promise you that. Not to mention these crazy ass Rebels that live out there in the middle of nowhere. Those folks will shoot you dead for trespassing on their land. Wow; it looks so calm and peaceful out here; I would have never thought it. Yeah don't forget it! I won't Mr. Cooper! We're at the Ranch Sir; shall I turn off the car? No, I'll be right back, this won't take long.

AC jumps out of the Limo and slams the door behind him, runs up the brothel steps, opens the door and rushes inside.

Josh! Hey AC! Where the fuck is Mo! Over in the cashiers cage sir! Monica! Monica! Yeah what is it babe? Get your ass out here! Right now! Hurry the fuck up Mo! Hold on, I'm coming, I'm coming!

Ouch nigga! Coop grabs her by the left arm then pulls her outside to the limo. Man what the fuck is your problem? Shut up and get in the damn car! For what! Mo; don't make me say it again Bitch! Who you calling... Get in the fucking car! Ok, ok, damn, why are you tripping! AC slams the door as they get inside. Baby why are you tripping? Shut your damn mouth and listen; don't say a fucking word! But.. Shut your mouth! The next time I ever hear of you giving orders to any God damn body, you're a dead bitch! Don't you ever in your life pull that shit again! This is grown man business and you aint got no damn authority over nothing!

You had the damn nerves to order a hit on one of my people and lie like I ordered it! You lucky I found out before they clipped his ass because we wouldn't be having this conversation right now. Don't think just because you're sucking my dick that I won't make your ass disappear! I'm talking disappear forever; do that shit again and your Momma gone be crying over your damn casket. But..... Shut the fuck up and get out of my sight bitch! When I see you again, you better have your mind straight and play your damn role! Now get your trifling ass out of my car! But- Get out Mo! Mick let's go player! Where to Sir? Vegas dummy; where else! Yes Sir, on the way!

"Good evening out there in radio land, Dj Glenn here." "We interrupt our regular scheduled program to make a sad but very important announcement on this 15th day of May; 1998." "One of our beloved has moved on to that Copa Cabana in the Sky." "It saddens me to announce that

Old Blue Eye's; Frank Sinatra passed away yesterday from a Heart attack." "Tonight we; The City of Las Vegas will honor him by dimming the lights on the strip to show our love for old Blue Eyes." "On that note here's one of my Sinatra Favorites; My Way!" "And now the end is here" "And so I face the final curtain" "My friend, I'll say it clear" "I'll state my case, of which I'm certain" I've lived a life that's full" "I traveled each and ev'ry highway" "And more, much more than this, I did it my way." Knock-Knock! Knock-Knock! Red! Red! Girl why are you knocking on my car window like you're crazy!

Hey girl; I'm sorry, but you're taking up two parking spaces. Can you move over some, so I can park! Oh my bad Gia; I was in here listening to Frank Sinatra. Frank Sinatra! Yeah girl, he died last night and they were playing one of his songs on the radio. It's called My Way; that thing was deep; it was like his farewell song or something. Ok that's cool but can you hurry; I don't want to be late! Will can be an ass hole sometimes. Alright; don't get your panties all in a bunch, I'm moving. Thanks Red! Yeah whatever!

There you go; you should be able to fit now; see you inside. Thanks again Red! Yeah um-hmm! Gia pulls up;

straighten her wheels then backs her side kick in the empty space between Debbie's Cadi and Remy's Maserati. Oh shit; I have 2 minutes! Let me hurry my ass up before Will curses me out. Damn, this car is pretty; old lucky bitch. Why she get to drive a Maserati; I'll fix her ass; she aint special. Skreeeeeeeet! Skreeeeeeet! Hey Gia; hurry your ass up! I'm coming Red! Skreeeeeet! What was that noise? What noise Red? I heard a scratching sound; you didn't hear it? Nah; I didn't hear anything! Hmmmm, that's weird! Hey girls; yall cutting it close! I'm sorry Will; I've been here! So why are you just getting in then? I was in the car listening to Frank Sinatra. Frank Sinatra! Yeah man; he died yesterday.

Oh I did see that on the news; they're dimming the lights on the strip tonight in his honor. Yep! Hey Gia; what's your excuse? I'm not late Will! You're damn close, the other girls are almost dressed for work and you're late as usual. Hurry up!

Ok, ok, I'm hurrying! Yo Will; come here let me holler at you about something. Hold on Deb; let me turn off these bright ass lights first. Sure go ahead; I'll turn on the sign. Thanks Red! Yeah, no problem; how many girls are on the roster? We have 45 for now; 35 more schedule for late shift. Cool; that should be enough for tonight. Yep, now what's up? You had something to tell me! Yeah, you might want to check the cameras and take a look at Gia getting out of her car before she came in. Why? I think she keyed Remy's car. Get the fuck out of here! I'm serious Will! Did you see her do it? No but I heard what sounded like keys scraping on metal. You heard it? Will; just look at the tape; I'm almost certain. Ok Red; I'll take a look but I don't think she's that stupid. You can never be too sure Will; these girls are unpredictable. Shit; aint that the damn truth. They never surprise me man, I done seen it all Will. Alright; I'll go rewind the tape and take a look before we get busy. Hold it down out here and tell Skillz when he gets in; he owes me $50 for being late! It's 15 minutes after and he's not here to relieve Tech yet. Ok got you!

Hey Red, what's up? Hey Dylan; where's your side kick? Oh she stayed home tonight; it's that time of the month. What you saying; Barbie too good to dance while her period is on? Don't ask me child; that girl be in her moods sometimes. I could care less; I'm about my paper. I hear that Dylan, and that's how it's supposed to be. What you drinking? I'm taking it easy today; give me some absolut and cranberry. Coming right up! Hey what yall bitches over here talking about? What's poppin Remy; we just kicking it! That's what's up; I sure hope it's some money in here tonight. Yeah me too; it's been slow this week. I'm surprised you've been working this many days girl; wasn't you and Barbie working out of town? Yeah but we needed to take a break from the road a bit. Cool; I can understand that, where Barbie at anyway? Home on her period! What; that girl gone let that stop her money. It aint like she fucking; she better cut that string and stuff that motherfucker up her crouch. Ha-Ha! Remy you're a damn fool! Dylan please; you know what it is; better school your girl. I aint got nothing to do with it; I'm here for me! I know that's right girl! One absolut and cranberry! Thanks Red! You're welcome! Hey Remy; what you drinking baby? I'm good for now Red; I'm higher than a kite. Ha-ha! Ok baby!

Alright let me rewind this tape and see what Debbie is talking about. Ok there's Red backing in; Remy's car right there. Hmmm, where's Gia? Oh here she comes now. She's getting out to talk to Red. Red's moving her car; Gia pulls in, Red is walking towards the building. Gia is getting out, stops looks up at Red, then starts walking with her…. Oh; I'll be damn! This crazy bitch did key Remy's shit! Fuck, let me go out here and look at this car. Man these girls are just like a bunch of kids. I swear, it don't make any sense.

Knock-Knock! Who is it? Skillz! Come in! Hey Boss; Deb said you wanted to see me! Yeah, you owe me $50 for being late! Aw man, come on! I aint playing with you Skillz; give me my money. Try it again and you gone be looking for another job. Ok Will; I'm sorry but I had to… Yo, I don't want to hear it! Go relieve Tech and get to work. Ok I got you. Good, now kick rocks and move, I have to check out something real quick. Damn, I'm moving, my bad.

Hey Will! Hey girls! Red I'll be right back, I need to run outside for a minute. Damn, what's he in a hurry for; is there a fire or something? I don't know Remy; it's probably nothing. Will walks in the parking lot then makes his way over to the white Maserati and looks at the driver's side, which is closes to Gia's side kick. Ummm, ummm, ummm. This fool scratched up this woman's car! Wow, how am I gone handle this shit. Will stands there in disbelief; leaning back against the red side kick, starring down at the damage Gia has done. He takes a deep breath, stands up straight then walks back inside.

So Remy; when are you and D getting married? Red what are you talking about girl? You heard her Remy; when is the big date? There is no date Dylan, we haven't even discussed marriage! Well, it won't be long now, watch and see. Yeah whatever; yall tripping! Hey Remy! Yeah Will, what's up? Come to my office! Huh! Meet me in the office! Ok- I'm coming. Girl what you do? I don't know Dylan. I'll be back yall. What's up Dylan? Hey Gia; you better stop being late before you get in some damn trouble. I know Dylan; Will warned me when I got here. What you drinking Gia? A Corona Red! Alright coming up!

Knock-Knock! Come in, it's open. You wanted to see me? Yeah Remy; lock the door and come have a seat; I have something to show you. Alright; what is it? Just sit down and watch this tape. Remy takes a seat in one of the chairs in front of the desk and faces the security monitor as Will plays the tape. What am I looking at Will? Just keep watching it. Isn't that Red and Gia; I don't understand. Just watch! Ok damn, I'm watching! Oh hell no- What the- is that bitch keying my shit! Yep, I went outside just now to confirm and- it's keyed! I'm gone whip that ho's ass! Remy jumps up to run out of the office. Hold on Remy! Let me go Will; that aint right man! I know, just sit tight; I'm gone call her in here so you two can handle it. I don't want the entire club involved. Will; I'm gone kill that skank! Remy I don't care what you do; anything you give her; she deserves. Just don't damage my office; I'll lock the door and you can shoot the slut for all I care. Just don't bring your guys business out of my office. Ok I'm cool, call the bitch. Alright; hold on. Ring-Ring! The Bar! Red; send Gia to the office. Ok Will, no problem. Hey Gia; Will wants you in the office. Who me? Yeah; did I stutter! Ok; watch my drink! Sure go ahead I got you.

Damn, she must be in trouble Red; you looking all crazy. What the hell is going on? I don't know what you're talking about Dylan. You know something Red; you just aint telling. Knock-Knock! Come in! Yeah what's up Will? Gia come have a seat; I think you owe Remy an apology! Apology for what Will? Gia, we both watched the tape and saw what you did. Well; I'm gone leave you two in her to work it out; I'll be right outside the office door. Sit down Gia; we need to talk bitch. Will leaves the office and locks the door from the outside then stands in front of it while facing the bar.

Remy what's this all about? Bap! Bap! igh! igh! Stop Remy! Bap! Bap! Act stupid, go ahead! I'll smack your ass again! Why you do it? Do what? Bap! Bap! igh! igh! Why you key my car ho? I didn't know it was yours Remy! Bap! Bap! igh! You're a motherfucking lie! Gia curls up in the chair afraid to retaliate as Remy continues to smack her again and again. Bap! Bap! igh! Hit me again, I'm gone kill your ass! What! Bap! Bap! Kill me ho! igh! Kill me Gia! Bap! Bap! Ouch, that's it God dammit! Gia stands up then swings hard with a right to Remy's head. Bam! I said don't hit me again bitch! Bam! Get the fuck up off the floor! Bam! Remy tries to get up then falls back to the floor as Gia slaps her in the head; over and over with the office phone. Bam! Now what! Bap! Bap! igh! Gia get off of me skank! Bap! igh! I'll kick that raggedy pussy off your pelvis bitch! Bap! Bap! igh! Remy now on the floor kicks Gia in her vagina repeatedly as she tries to hit her with the phone. Bap! Bap! igh! Stank pussy ho! Remy thrust the heel of her six inch heel between Gia's legs again and again. Bap! Bap! igh! igh! Remy stop; I'm bleeding! Bap! Bap! igh! igh!

Ok, ok, enough, enough! No fuck that Will, I'm gone kill this ho! Remy, go to the dressing room and get cleaned up. You've done enough; I got it from here. You're lucky Will saved your ass skank. You're gone pay for my shit too!

Remy get out and lock the door. Ummmmm, ummmmmm, ummmm, it hurts. Stay down there Gia; I'm getting you some help. Ummmmm, ummmmm, ummmmm. Gia lay on the floor ball up, holding her pussy as it bleeds from the hard strokes delivered by Remy's six inch heels. Ring-Ring! The Bar! Red; send one of the bouncers to the office to get Gia and have a taxi waiting out front to take her to UMC. Sure; I'm on it now! Thanks Red! Gia; this is what happens when you disrespect other peoples shit; I hope you've learned your lesson. I have a taxi waiting to take you to the hospital; once you're all better, come clear out your locker; you're fired!

Paco stood on the sidewalk outside of his swap meet; admiring the baby gangsters as they slap boxed with one another in the doorway. Dirt stained the outside of the huge blue, tin, warehouse sized building that was home to local vendors and weekly patrons. The North Las Vegas police sat out in the parking lot; monitoring the busy weekend shoppers. Yo BG; come here let me holler at you lil homie. Yeah; what's crackin Paco? I got some work I need done; you and your homie wanna make 2 stacks? What! Hell yeah fool! The two young gangsters, now excited; stood in front of Paco awaiting instruction. What we need to do homie? I need you two to shoot up some things for an OG! Just name it Paco; we got you homes! Oh yeah; you sure? Hell yeah man; whose the mark? Alright check it; yall got some fire right? Yeah we packing; that's everyday OG.

Cool, head over to Fat Boy's detail shop; over on Sahara and spray a few of them cars up. Don't kill anybody; I just need to give him a warning. Make sure; you cover your faces and shout out this. "This is a message from AC nigga; next time it's on!" Can you remember that BG? No doubt; I got it! Repeat it then, so I know you won't fuck it up! Man I can remember! Say it youngster; go ahead; lemme hear it! Ok, ok! "This is a message from AC nigga; next time it's on!" Yeah that's it homie; alright, go do it now before it's too late! Hold on Paco; where's the paper homes? It's right here and this is where it's gonna stay until you handle that business. Now hurry up and get it done; your money will be here when you two get back! Alright, that's what's poppin; come on homie let's go do this. We'll be back Paco; you better have our money! Oh that's gone be here; just hurry the fuck up already! Calm down Paco; we're going. Hold on youngster; on second thought; I'll take you guy's; come on, let's take my Lexus truck.

Oh yeah; that's what's up OG! Yeah calm down and come on; I'll drop you two off a block away. Alright; that's what's poppin right there homie! Man this is hot right here Paco; I need me one of these! Youngster you don't even have a driver's license. I know how to drive OG; what I need a license for! Ha-ha! Man do you fools remember what to say? Yep! "Yo this is a message from AC nigga; next time it's on!" See, we got this!

Good; and don't kill nobody! Just shoot up a few cars; scare those punta's a little bit. Ooooh weee, this is tight big homie! I got to have one; how much was it? Get me 30 stacks and I can get one for you little gee. Hells yeah fool; I'm about to rob me some banks, some dope boys, liquor stores; all that. I'm gone get you that 30 gees big homie! I want me a black one though; so I can tint the windows all black and be incognito up in the city homie. Yo get your mine right; we're almost there. Yall got some mask? Nah but we got our flags; we can wrap our face with, up under these LA fitteds. Ok, get out right here and walk up the block and handle business. And remember- We know; no bodies! Alright go ahead!

The BG's jump out of the Lexus, tighten their blue chucks, pull down their caps and wrap their blue flags around their nose and mouth; showing only their eyes. Both youngsters retrieve a nine from inside the waist band of their khaki dickie's and run up the sidewalk, creeping onto the detail lot. Pow! Pow! Pow! Bling! Bling-Bling! Yo; hold on player; don't kill me! Shut up fool! Pow! Bling! Sit your punk ass on the ground! Alright; I'm sitting, I'm sitting! Where's your fat ass boss? Inside man! Pow! Pow! Bling! Bling! The youngsters shoot the windows out of a few cars. Tell that nigga this is a message from AC; the next time it's on! Pow! Pow! Bling! Bling! Next time we won't be shooting cars fool! Pow! Pow! Bling! Bling! You got that! Yeah man; I'll tell him! Pow! Ouch my foot! Yeah motherfucker; you better tell him! Come on homie; let's get out of here! Yo why you shoot that fool; Paco said no bodies! He aint dead homie; so there aint no bodies! Man your ass is crazy! Later for that; keep running; the Lexus is around the block!

Hey man; what the hell just happened! Two, baby gangster's shot up the cars and shit then shot me in my damn foot! Which way did they go? Man I don't know Fat Boy; they said this was a warning from AC and that the next time it won't be just cars they're shooting! What- AC! That's what they said! Damn; get this glass cleaned up and move those cars to the back before the cops come. Dude; can't you see I'm injured! Hope on your good foot, I don't care, move these cars. I got to call Manny and see what's going on! Fat Boy you're a sorry ass boss; see a brother shot and still want me to work. Damn; it's hard out here for a felon! Man; shut your ass up and clean this mess up; I'll be back in a minute.

Ring-Ring! Hola this is Manny! What up fool; why your people shooting up my place of business. What; who is this? It's Fat Boy! What are you talking about? Some BG's just came over to my shop and shot up two cars and shot one of my best workers in the foot. They said it was a warning from AC! Amigo; that's some BS; that wasn't our work; believe me! I'm gonna make some calls to get to the bottom of this. I'll call you back and I'm sorry for your worker; is he alright? He's good but this is fucked up Manny; if this wasn't you guys then who was it; we got a problem. Yeah; I agree with you there Fat Boy; I'll be in touch. Yeah do that!

Knock-Knock! Hey Detective; come in and have a seat; close that door behind you. How are you doing today? I'm good Chief! That's great; did you get some more information on this Sin City 7? Yeah I got a little bit. Well, everything helps, as long as we're moving forward with this case. Are you still comfortable over there though; no one expects anything? Yeah I'm good; they don't have the faintest idea. Great; now that's what I call good undercover work; keep it up detective. Thank you Sir and it's an honor. So what you got? Well, they're not quite set up like we thought Chief. What do you mean? You know how the Mafia has the Boss, Under Boss, Capo then soldiers. Yeah! Well these guys are more of a Military operation not so much the Corporate Company that's set up like our Italian friends. Ok, go ahead keep talking.

AC is like the Major or the General; he's the highest ranking officer. Manny is his Captain; he filters all orders through him and vise a versa. What do you mean vise a versa? Let's just say Manny has the power to give orders to the lieutenants without permission from AC. How is that so? It's like a military operation; the Captain knows his day to day missions via the Major and he can execute it how he see fits. Hmm, that's interesting. Yeah, I thought so too, that just means these two guys really trust each other. Yeah they do.

Next you have the Lieutenants; which are Loony, Will, Duck, Nina and Denna. Each of the LT's has their own soldiers that follow their orders, according to their day to day mission and standard operations. Well; who are their soldiers and what's their standard operations? I'm still working on that part Chief; I only have bits and pieces, I still need time to make it all make sense.

Tell me something Detective! Yeah what is it Chief? Who is Mr. Cooper's new girl; now that Sabrina is dead? Oh some woman named Monica, Chief! Oh really; that's interesting; she worked for him back in the day. So you know her then? Yeah, I know him too! We had a few run ins in the past; that's how I know he's up to something. Well, your hunch has proven positive so far Chief! Hey, you should always trust your gut Detective, it's right most of the time. Roger that Chief; did you need anything else from me? No detective that's it; get back on that case and keep up the good work; we're making some leeway. This is great intel! Alright; later chief! Yep, later!

Ring-Ring! Yeah what is it LT! Hey Chief, they need you on a crime scene; they just found something out at one of the new housing developments off the interstate heading out towards Utah. Thanks LT; I'm on it, call CSI; have them meet me out there also and call the officers, tell them to keep the press off the scene! Yes Chief; Roger that!

"Good evening Las Vegas; this is Katie Strong coming to you live from Shady Pines; a new housing development just off interstate 15." "An area that contractor's has been using to build new housing developments; to help supply our cities rapidly growing population!" "We are here tonight because one of the families upon deciding to add a swimming pool in their backyard; came across a gruesome discovery!" "Pools Inc., the company hired to install the home owner's pool while digging up the back yard came across several dead bodies!"

Oh shit! ILona; turn that up! Hurry up! Ok Nina; I'm getting it! Thank you, now move out of the way, I need to see this! "The family; wishes to remain anonymous and doesn't want to speak with us about this horrible discovery but the driver of the bull dozer is here with us live!" "Ok Sir; please tell the people what you found while digging in this poor families backyard." "Well; I don't know any other way to say it Katie; I found several bodies in a huge hole!" "When you say several Sir; are we talking ten, eight, six, how many exactly?" "I believe it was four or five Katie; it's mostly bones; so there could be more or could be less." "I'm no expert!" "Thank you Sir!" "You're welcome." "This has been Katie Strong for your evening news; we'll have more on this story as it develops."

Damn, damn, this isn't good. What is it Nina? Nothing ILona, hand me that phone! Ring-Ring! Hello, Manny speaking! Hey this is Nina; did you see the damn news? No why? They found the bodies! What are you talking about Nina? Hold on a minute Manny! Sure! Hey ILona; run over to Sunset and pick us up some wings and a large sausage pizza! Ok Nina; should I get some drinks too? Yeah, that's fine! What do you want to drink? It doesn't matter honey; whatever you get is fine. Ok; I'll be right back. Manny, I'm back! What bodies Nina? They found like four bodies out in one of those new housing developments; you know the ones you guys visited last year.

It's probably nothing sis! Manny; I think it's something; you need to check it out. Well, how did they find the bodies? Some family was getting a pool installed and the contractor was digging the hole and uncovered the bones, deep underground. You're right; this is not good! I know, I know, you better tell AC; we need to fix this, quick poppy! Alright; just stay calm sis, I'll call you later and keep you posted. Ok Manny; don't forget! I won't Nina; I promise, talk to you later.

Ring-Ring! Ring-Ring! Good Morning, this Coop! Man where the hell you been; I've been calling you all night! Calm down Capo; what's up? We have a situation; well two situations. Manny, what are you talking about? Somebody shot up Fat Boy's detail shop the other day and said it was a message from you! Hold on; what did you say? Someone shot up Fat Boy's detail shop and said it was a message to him from you. What the fuck, did you speak to Fat Boy yet? Yeah; he's cool; I told him that it wasn't us. I got Hector beating the streets for some information on who the shooters were. Alright what else you got?

Nina called me all upset after seeing the news last night, because they found some bodies in the desert. Why was she upset about that; this is Vegas; there always bodies in the damn desert! No Coop; this was at one of those new Housing developments that they built last year. Ok and why is that important Manny? They found like four bodies deep underground when one of the families were getting a pool installed in their backyard. Damn; how many bodies? Four or five; I think. Ok, round up the fellas and go check that out after the heat cools down; this is the last thing we need with those po-po's trying to build a case on us. Damn, make sure you take care of that Manny; I'm gone handle this Fat Boy situation; I got a gut feeling whose behind it! Alright Boss; I'll keep you posted! Later Capo! AC hangs up the phone and walks into his guest room, pulls out his black Levi jeans, black long sleeve fitted top, black biker jacket then pulls his 357 from the drawer. Coop loads his gun then fills the spare cartridge.

The warm Vegas sun rays beamed in through the balcony window as he took his belongings up front, sat on the couch and slipped them on then laced up his black leather biker boots. The condo was silent, no music, no TV, just the sound of the refrigerator motor running and speckles of dust in the sun light was all he could hear and see while he finished getting dressed. Ring-Ring! Hello Towers; David speaking! Hey Dave this is AC; bring my Ninja up will you! Yes Sir Mr. Cooper; what time are you coming down? I'm leaving my Condo now David. Alright Sir; it will be here when you get down. Thanks Dave! No problem Sir!

Ring-Ring! Hello! Hey Nina; I heard the news sis! Hey AC; that's crazy right! Yeah it is, we're taking care of it though, don't worry about it. Cool because that has me paranoid. Listen, I need a favor from you. What is it Coop? Call Paco for me and tell him you're on the way over to the Swap meet to buy some bags or something; call me back and let me know what he says. Ok no problem; what's this about AC? Oh nothing; he was supposed to order some Gucci bags for Mo but he's giving me the run around. Alright, let me call him; I'll call you back. Thanks Sis! Ring-Ring! Ring-Ring! Yeah; this Paco; who this? Hey Paco; it's Nina! Hey sexy girl; to what do I owe this pleasure? Poppy I need a new Gucci bag to go with my outfit; I got a hot date tonight. Do you have something for me? Sure baby, anything for you! Cool, can I come check them out now? Yeah I'll be here for a few hours, stop by, maybe we can grab some shrimp Taco's from across the street after. That sounds good poppy; I'm on the way! Alright see you later baby!

Ring-Ring! Yeah! He's there bro! Thanks Sis; I'll holler at you later! Sure; no problem. AC exits the condo and enters the elevator, leans back against the wall, head back, staring up at the ceiling as he descends. While slipping on his black gloves, a familiar feeling came over him, one he haven't felt since he and the crew left the Iraqi desert. Inside; his body felt empty, a shell of blackness, no thoughts or emotions ran through his head, only one mission. The outside world didn't exist; people had no voices, cars, trucks and buses no sounds, all he seen was glaring stares as he exit the elevator and glide towards the exit.

Here's your helmet Mr. Cooper! He gaze at David, took the black helmet then walks over to his Ninja. Everything and everyone moved in slow motion with no sound as if it were a dream; but it wasn't. Sweat poured down the side of his face and his back as he raced down Maryland Parkway in route to North Las Vegas. The Sun rays intensified his body heat as it warmed the black attire that shelled him, while the silver metal from the 357 got warmer and warmer as it lay tucked against his right side.

A few miles, three lights and two intersections later he rolls into the parking lot of the North Las Vegas Swap Meet. The blue tin building, now barely busy, had only a few cars in the lot as he pulls up behind a gold Lexus truck parked just out front of the office. Coop turns off the bike, slowly gets off then walks towards the glass office door while pulling the 357 from his waist. The blue tin building reflected in the face glass of his black helmet, as he opens the office door. Hello Sir; how can I help you! Pow! Pow! The secretary lay slump over her desk after two shots to the chest. Hey what the fuck is going on out there! Paco runs through the door way. Pow! Oh my leg! My leg! Hold on man! Hold on; what you want? You want money! AC walks towards Paco as he sat on the floor bleeding, just in front of his office. Man I got 50 thousand in the safe; you can have it! Just don't kill me! Paco could see himself begging in the face glass, of Coop's black helmet.

AC gets closer and closer then takes a knee on the floor, just in front of him; lifts the face glass of his helmet, then looks dead in Paco's eyes. He places the barrel of the 357 in the center of Paco's forehead. Oh shit AC; hold on; let me explain man! It was— Pow!

June, 1998.

"What's up; Las Vegas! This yah boy Shi C checking in live on your radio!" "It is hotter than Hell out there today! Yall be careful out there in that Vegas heat!" "Drink plenty of water and stay inside if you don't need to go out." "If you're here visiting, welcome to the devils playground; this heat should give you an idea of why Vegas is called Sin City" "Here we break all the rules and it even feels like Hell too" "Whew it's 104 degrees at 12 noon; it's going to be a long day people!"

Mo; turn that radio off; I don't feel like hearing that fool talk today; he don't ever play no music! His big ass mouth! What are you doing around there anyway? Nothing! You're mighty quiet woman; you're up to something. AC; why is there a closet full of money in the guest room? What! You heard me nigga! How did you know about that Mo? Because it was locked, so I got your keys to see what was in it.

Your ass is nosey; you know that? Well, forget all that; answer my question. It's just some extra cash that had lying around; ones, fives, tens and some twenties. Extra huh! Yep; that's what I said. Can I have some then? Sure; have all you want; it's just extra! Are you for real AC? Yep go ahead baby; that's where I got the money to take you shopping that one time. Oh yeah; then why did you only spend five thousand dollars, if this is throw away money. Because that was Sabrina's stash; it's yours now I guess! Aww; aren't you so considerate! What's that supposed to mean Monica! You can lock the damn closet and leave it in there for all I care. Nah, don't be acting like that; I was only playing with you AC.

Yeah I bet you were! Well, I actually was gonna hide something in here that I got for you but since there's no room; I'll give it to you now! Oh you got me a gift Mo? Yes I do baby; close your eyes. Come on girl; why I have to do all that! Close them AC! Alright there closed! Ruff! Ruff! Hey; who is this? His name is Pete, baby; I got him from the neighbor; her Pit had puppies a few weeks ago. Ruff! Ruff! Aw; he's a handsome fella; all white with the black patch around his eye. Thanks Mo! Ruff! Ruff! There's one more thing Coop! Wow; why so many gifts? Here you go! What's this key for Mo? I got the locks changed and did some redecorating over at the Mansion. We're moving in tomorrow and I arranged for the movers to box up our personal belongings and take them over. Damn, who said I wanted to move? You did remember! No I don't remember! Ruff! Ruff! Be quiet Pete!

Don't yell at him AC! I wasn't yelling at him; why did you do that Mo? Because you're going to be a good Father to your kids and we need to be in a stable environment for that to happen. So Vicky and ILona are moving in here and the other girls are moving to the house in Summerlin. Damn; yall got it all figured out; don't you? Yep; so get over it, we're moving tomorrow morning baby. Ruff! Ruff! See; Pete is happy; aren't you happy too? Yeah I guess Mo! Good, now I'm getting dressed so I can go shopping! What are you going shopping for now? Remember all that stuff I saw at Caesar's that I couldn't get! Umm-hmm!

Well; I'm going to get it! Didn't you say that was my money in that closet? Umm-hmm. Ruff! Ruff! Come here boy; momma's going shopping; let her get dressed. Ruff! Ruff! Are you coming? Hell no woman; I'm not staying in the mall all day with your ass. Call Nina or somebody; me and Pete gone stay here and smoke a blunt. AC! What!

Don't give him no weed! I was just playing girl! Yeah you better be; because your slick ass will do it. Can you bring me a pair of all white shell toes back? What is that? Adidas girl! Oh ok; what size? 10 and a half! Alright; did you need some socks too? Yeah get me some of them too!

Hold on; wait a damn minute! Why; what's wrong AC? Where do you think you're going with that thin ass dress on? To the mall; it's 104 degrees outside; I damn sure aint wearing no jeans. You don't have to wear no jeans, but you better put on some shorts or something up under that thin ass dress. Aww; are you jealous? No; but your ass gone be hurting from my foot; if you walk out of here like that! Alright nigga; stop tripping. You aint my daddy and my name aint Sabrina! It might not be, but that's my pussy right there, and you gone cover it up! Ha-ha! Ok daddy; I will. Ha-ha! Yeah, you better!

Ruff! Ruff! See Pete; you always got to keep your woman in place; if you don't; they will be on some crazy ass shit boy. Ruff! Ruff! Now, is this better Sir? Yep; and don't forget my shell toes. I won't; see you in a little bit! Alright Mo; see you when you get back! Ruff! Ruff! Aww, bye Pete! See you later AC and don't give him no weed either!

Bye woman! Ruff! Ruff! Come on boy; let's go on the balcony and smoke this chronic. Ruff! Ruff! Yep; it's that good smoke too!

Good Afternoon Detectives! Afternoon Chief! Well, I called this meeting because we finally got the break we have been waiting for! The Captain and LT will be joining us today Detectives, this is the first solid information we have that links all the suspects to racketeering. As you can see; right here on the board behind me! I have the pictures of all seven suspects and I've written their roles in black marker under each of their photos. At the very top here; I have Andy Cooper aka AC as the General. Right below him, I have Emanuel Ortega aka Manny as Capo or Captain. Below him, on the third row, starting from the far left; I have Lionel Massey aka Loon, Dubai Patel aka Duck, William "Big Will' Tosi then Nina and Denna Sanchez aka The Twins. These five are all labeled as Lieutenants. Collectively we call them the Sin City Seven.

Hey Chief! Yes Briggs? I noticed you said racketeering; are we treating this like a Mafia case? Good question Detective Briggs and that answer would be yes. So what kind of evidence do we have to prove that Chief? Hold on a minute Ricky and I will explain. Yeah; I was wondering the same thing Chief. Casey be patient; you guys are about to find out. I'm patient Captain! Ok a few weeks ago; on a hunch, I had LT go pull the deeds on a few properties. What properties Chief? Detective Ricky; we checked out Club Dolls, Vegas Adult Video, Angels Escorts and Angel's Bunny Ranch. What we found was amazing! All of those places were owned by Vinny and Bobby Delgato! Interesting enough the beneficiary on those properties was Victor Delgato! Now, what do all of these people have in common besides their last name Detectives? They're all dead Chief! Right you are Briggs!

Now here's the kicker! Who runs all of those places now? The Sin City Seven! Yes Casey that is correct! Now, do you guys think it's a coincidence that Vinny and Bobby died in a bank robbery and Victor got shanked in a jail house brawl? Well I'll be damn, they set it up! Bingo Detectives; this is our case; we have to bring them down! We still have to prove the Delgato murders but we got them on human trafficking, murder, prostitution and money laundering. Are you sure we can make all of that stick Chief? Yes Ricky; I have a very reliable informant that will testify to it. So what's our next move Chief? We have to link them to the Delgato murders Briggs. I know they're responsible! Ricky do you still have that tape from the Towers cold case? Yes Chief! Great we're going to need that; some evidence maybe on it. Sure no problem, it's at my place; I'll bring it tomorrow. Great; that will work. Did you guys have any questions for me? Do we have enough to serve warrants yet Chief? Not enough to charge them for what I want to Ricky. You guys concentrate on linking them to those murders and I'll work on their known associates. This thing is going to be huge, I can feel it; we're just at the tip of the ice berg.

 Since AC runs those businesses now; has he been paying the taxes Chief? Hell no Casey; that's how we got him dead to rights. Umm, now that wasn't too smart! No Briggs it wasn't but I guess he didn't think it was important. Are you sure Chief; Cooper seems like a pretty sharp guy to me! Well Ricky, I've checked the records for the businesses and no taxes have been filed for the past two years. Maybe he owns a Corporation and incorporated all the businesses together under a different name than the Delgato's had in the past. Did Bobby and Vinny have the company listed as a LLC or Corporation Chief? I'm sure it was a Corporation Briggs; I saw the past tax records where they paid every year up until their deaths. Ok, in the normal scheme of things the named beneficiary would take over control of the company. That was Victor Detective Briggs; and we know what happened to him! I'm willing to bet chief, that he has all of those businesses incorporated under one Company.

You may have a point Casey; so go down to the clerk's office and run his name through the public records data base. If he did file for a Corporation, it would be public record. And if that is the case, we would have a cause for motive. Alright; did you want me to go now Chief? Yes Casey; go ahead, and call me as soon as you find out something! Roger that Chief; call you later. Detective Ricky; when you get home; go over that tape and see if anything sticks out. Pertaining to what exactly Chief? Anything that has to do with AC and anyone that you see associating with him on that tape! It has to be more on that tape than what we were looking for initially. So I'm not just looking for any evidence on the drive through murders but anything that looks suspicious when it comes to AC and his associates. That is correct Detective!

Great; I'll go ahead and get started on that now Chief. Thanks Detective! Briggs; do you remember that cashier getting murdered over at the Adult Video store? Yeah, old timer; he was Victor's good friend. Well; go through the evidence on that case and see what you can dig up. We covered every detail in that murder chief; I don't think we missed anything. Now you're looking for something different Detective; so maybe you will find something! Roger that Chief! Glad you understand; this meeting is adjourned; you guys get to work and call me if you need me! Later Chief! Yep; later detectives!

Good Afternoon Mr. Dubai, welcome back to Nevada Bank and Trust! What can I do for you today? Hey; how are you doing lady? I'm fine Sir! That's good; I would like to make a deposit. Sure; how much did you want to deposit Mr. Dubai? $55,000.00; all cash! Wow, another big deposit huh; I see business is good over at the car lot. Yes it is; you should come by and get you one. Nah; you have those luxury cars on your lot. That's out of my price range Mr. Dubai; I'm only a teller. Aww, come on; I'll give you a great deal! Really! Yes Ma'am! Ok then; I'll think about it. Cool, just let me know lady. I sure will; here's your deposit receipt. Thanks! Have a good day Mr. Dubai! You do the same baby!

Ring-Ring! Hello! Hey baby; what you doing? Getting dressed; I just got out of the tub. Do you have any plans? No I don't Duck; why what's going on? It's seafood night over at Sam's Town; you wanna go get some shrimp and crab legs? Sure baby; what time? I'm leaving the bank now; I can be at your place in 30 minutes. Alright; that's cool; I'll be ready when you get here. Ok Karen; see you in a few. Hey; can you bring me a box of Tide? Tide! Yeah Duck; I do wash clothes you know. Sure; no problem! Thanks! You're welcome baby!

"Hello Las Vegas; this your afternoon Jock Shi-C" "Police are in search of anyone that has evidence on two murders that took place over at the North Las Vegas Swap Meet a few weeks ago." "If you have any clues or know of anyone that maybe connected to the murder of these two individuals; please call LVMPD crime hotline." "Your identity will remain classified and there is a $5,000 reward for any information leading to the capture of the suspect or suspects." Damn man; play some fucking music already! They need to fire your ass; always talking or got the damn news on! I hate that! "Oh and make sure you guys stay out of the- "Wow; this guy can't shut up! Angry; Duck turned off the radio while entering Sav-way parking lot, parks then walks inside. Excuse me Ma'am! Yes Sir, how may I help you? What isle is your washing powder on? That'll be 12 Sir! Ok thanks! No problem; is there anything else I can help you with? No that's it!

"Attention shopper's, don't forget to take advantage of our summer sale" "We have Bryers ice cream; buy one, get one free and fresh watermelons for half off!" "Thank you for shopping with us, we appreciate your business." "Attention customers; checkout line 3 is now open with no waiting for 15 items or less!" Duck picks up the Tide and rush to line 3, looking around and thinking to himself. "Hell yeah; let me hurry up; it's crazy in here. Must be payday or something; this place is packed!" Oops; excuse me Sir! Damn lady, you gone knock me over! I'm sorry Sir! You shouldn't be in this line anyway; you got like 20 items. This line is for 15 or less. I know but I'm in a hurry and I only have 17 items; you won't mind would you? Go ahead; I'm in no hurry! Thank you so much! Um-hmm.

How are you doing today Ma'am? I'm fine; just doing a little shopping; I will be using my food stamp card; is that ok for this line? Oh sure; it doesn't matter what line you're in. Great; thanks! Did you want paper or plastic bags? Plastic please! You can leave your sodas in the cart; I'll just type that sku number in for you! Ok thanks! Alright that's $23.79! Oh yeah; I almost forgot the sodas! Now we got it; your total is $25.87! Here you go! Just slide it and punch in your pin Ma'am! Beep! Can you slide it again for me Ma'am! Beep! There we go; now put in your pin. Beep! Beep! It says that you're over your limit Ma'am. Really! Yes! How much over? $21.00!

Damn; that can't be right! Run the card again! I did it twice already Ma'am, do you have a credit card or cash that you could use? No; this is all I have. Well, did you want to return what you can't get and keep what you can? No I need all of it! I don't know what to tell you miss but you need to make a decision, you have people waiting behind you. Hey go ahead and bag it up; I'll pay for it! Oh my God; thank you so much! You're welcome! How can I thank you? Don't worry about it! Are you sure? What is your name? Duck! Thank you Duck! May God bless you! It's no problem; glad to help! That was nice of you Sir. Hey it was nothing; it can happen to any of us. Yeah; I guess you're right about that. Your total is $3.87 Sir! Here you go; keep the change. Thank you Sir; have a great evening. Yep; you do the same young lady.

Knock-Knock! Yeah who is it? It's Vicky and the girls from Angel's! Oh hold on; I'm coming! Hello Mister; is this the Gang Bang Party? Yes it is! Well my name is Vicky; this is Missy and that's Donna. Hi ladies; come in and make yourselves comfortable! These are the fellas; I'll let you introduce yourselves. Why thank you! Oh I already paid Nina over the phone! Yeah you did but that was only for us to show up. And since this is a Gang Bang party and it's like twenty of you horny bastards; we have to set some prices and guidelines. Ok; what's the rules Vicky? Well Missy is the head doctor; she will make any man toes curl with that mouth of hers. Donna has that super wet pussy, plus she's a squirter! Wow and what about you? Oh me; I'm the DP Queen baby; double penetration anyway you want it; pussy and mouth, ass hole and pussy, mouth and asshole, you get the point! Whew we! Let's get this Gang bang party going then!

Hold on a minute Mister; you fellas are gone have to pay us for those exclusive services now. Well, how much Vicky? Missy charges $200 for each head job; Donna charges $300 for that super soaker and I need $500 for the DP! Oh and so that there is no misunderstanding; those prices are for each guy. Now if you all can handle that; we can get this bang started! Hell yeah; we can handle it! Great; Missy you take the first bedroom, Donna take the office and I'll take the master bedroom. Gentlemen; have your condoms ready, dicks hard and cash in hand. Whew wee baby; let's get it on!

Hey girl; I need some cocaine before I start fucking all these damn drunk ass men in here. Hold on Donna; I got some in my purse; I'll do a few lines with you. Thanks Vicky; I already know my damn stomach is going to feel like a punching bag tomorrow. Yeah better you than me girl; I can't do it. I don't see why not Missy; you gone be sucking cock all night; so your ass aint no different! Hey girls; cut this arguing out and let's get ready to get this money. Yo we're ready to get this thing popping girls;

what's up! Hold on babe; we need to go powder our noses first. Can we use this bathroom? Sure go ahead Missy and hurry up too! We won't be long babe! You guys just get out your money and condoms. Alright bet! Hey fellas; it's about to go down. I'm getting me some of that mouth first then I'm gone fuck that thick ass white bitch Donna.

Missy did you want a line too? Yeah lay me one out! The fluorescent white lights over the bathroom mirror, bounced off the cream marbled counter top as Vicky took her credit card and divided the powder into three thin lines. Donna pulls her brunette shoulder length hair back into a ponytail then bends down over the counter and snorts up one line. Ummmm, yeah that's what I'm talking about girl; this is some good blow Vicky! Go ahead Missy; snort that! Don't rush me Donna; let me do this.

The two white lines of blow along with Vicky and Donna's image reflect in the lenses of Missy's black and brown Gucci shades but disappears the closer she gets to the counter. Missy's blonde hair falls over her face as she holds one nostril close with her left hand and snorts with the other. Ummmmmm! Yeah, it's some good blow; huh girl? it is Donna. Alright my turn; you two can't be high without me! With one swift swoop; Vicky leans over the cream marble counter top; holds her left pointer finger over her left nostril then sucks up the last line of coke with her right!

Knock-knock! Hey hurry up in there! Hold on we're coming! Ok ladies; let's go do this! I don't know about you bitches but I'm trying to make three gees tonight! Well; your ass better snort a few more lines Missy because it's going to be a long night! Fuck you Donna! Damn girls come on; it's about time; we ready to hit! Then yall need to line up outside whatever room you're going in, have your money out with your condom, and all you get is 30 minutes! Damn; that's it for $300! Yeah dude; it's 20 of you! Damn Vicky; come on! I'm sorry man, but those are the rules. What if we want more time? Then you pay double! Damn! Hey bruh; stop all that arguing and let us get our groove on! Nobody in this room needs more than 30 minutes, so stop tripping.

See that's a smart man; you need to listen to him! Yeah, yeah whatever Vicky! We're ready, let's get started. Ok girls; it's show time; see yall in a few hours! Vicky, Missy and Donna look at one another; straightens their hair and heads to their rooms to handle business.

Knock-Knock! Come in Mister! God damn your fine as hell. Thank you baby; put the money on the dresser and come over here. You got your condom? Umm-hmm! Well; put it on baby; we don't have all night. Oh; I'm sorry. Why are you so nervous? I've never had sex with a woman as fine as you before Donna. Is that right? Yep! Ha-ha. You better calm down before you burst a nut; you at least need to put your dick in my pussy first. Come on; it doesn't bite! Yeah that's it baby; stroke this wet pussy. Ugh! Ugh! Faster baby, faster! Ugh! Ugh! Oh; it's so good- Ugh- Ugh! Is it good to you baby, you like this pussy! Oh yeah- Ugh! Ugh,ugh,ugh,ug... See, that wasn't hard baby; it didn't even take you 15 minutes. Damn, can I go again? You got $300 more dollars? But I didn't get my whole 30 minutes! That aint my fault baby; this is a business. Damn, you gone do me like that? No; you can go again; it's just gone cost another $300. Aww girl, don't worry about it then! Are you sure; it's still wet! I'm not paying another $300! Alright; I understand, send the next guy in when you go out! Yeah, whatever! Aww, don't be like that baby; maybe next time you can go a little longer before you cum. Go to hell Donna! Bam! What's up man; why you slammed the door! You done already! Yeah; your turn man; break that bitch back! Oh I'm about to!

Knock-Knock! It's open, come see the doctor! Hey Missy! Hello there, how are you? I'm good, ready for some of that head action. Are you sure about that; I've been known to bring a guy to his knees. Shit, bring me to my knees, I want you to girl. Ha-ha! Ok, put the money on the table, drop your pants and come over here. Alright; let me put this jimmy on. I like my head sloppy wet, you can handle that right Missy? I got you; come here. Ummm! Oh yeah, you got that juicy mouth girl. Ummm! Ummm! Suck it baby! Ummm! Yeah I like that! You like that- Ummm! Stop talking and keep sucking; I'm paying for this! Ummm! Ummm! Yeah, go slow Missy. Just like that girl; suck this motherfucker! Ummm! Ummm! Go ahead and lick them balls girl. Umm-Umm, nope! Why not! Umm-Umm! You got some more money; that's extra! Ummm! Ummm! How much extra! Umm- $100! Hell nah; keep sucking! Ummm! Ummm! Oh yeah, that's it girl! Ummm! Ummm! Get this nut bitch! Ummm! Ummm! Ugh! Ugh! Ugh! Ugh.......

Whew, yeah you got a vacuum on you. Damn, I might be coming back for seconds. I'll be here daddy; all hot and ready! I don't know girl, it's like six fellows after me. Oh, that aint nothing I can't handle. Damn bitch; you go on like that! Yep, got to get this paper daddy! I do this for a living; I'm a pro at it! Well, I'll check back later and if you're still in commission; we can do this again. Ok daddy, that's a deal! Thanks Missy; later! You're welcome daddy! Next!

Knock-Knock! Its open guys! What's up Vicky; we've been waiting to double team your ass! Oh yeah! Yep! Ok put the money on the table, strap up and let's get to it! Look at her bruh; she thinks she's hardcore! Guys; they don't come any more hardcore than me; I'm sure I've done worse back home in Germany. Well, this here is Vegas and you aint seen nothing yet until you've experience some Sin City fucking. Ha-Ha! Really now! We'll just see about that fellas! Get your cocks ready and let's have a go at it. Ha-ha! You hear her dawg; she thinks she's a G; let's fuck this ho! I'll get the cat, you get that ho's throat! Ugh! No, don't scream now Vicky; you said you can take it! Ugh! Ugh! Ugh! The two guys had Vicky up on the bed doggie style, one standing on the floor with his Johnson down her throat while his boy stroked her from the back.

Uggggh! Uggggh! Yeah, um-hmm take this dick ho! Ugggh! Ugggh! You aint so tuff now Vicky, huh! Ugggh! Ugggh! Ummmmm, ummmmmm, ummmmm. Yeah cuz, choke that bitch! Uggh! Uggh! She rocks back and forth as they double penetrate her simultaneously, one down her throat and the other with his dick touching her kidneys. Ugggh! Ugggh! Hey cuz, this bitch is cumin, got nut all on my dick. Jam her throat some more; she said she can take it! I got her bruh! Uggh! Ugggh! What's wrong Vicky, you tryna tap out girl. Ummmm, ummmmm, ummmm. Yeah, this is Sin City fucking girl! We told you; you weren't ready! Ugggh! Ugggh! Oh shit; throw that pussy girl! Oh yeah; I'm cumin! Oh yeah bitch, throw it! Uggh! Uggh! Oh-oh, I'm about to bust girl Uggh! Uggh! God damn! Ohhhhhhhh shit! Uggh! Uggh! Ugggghhhhhh! Ahhhhhhh. Yeah, now what; how many girls can make two guys cum at same time! One for you, two for Germany! Pull up your pants American and send in the next victim. Ha-ha! Damn, good job Vicky! Uh-huh; I told you!

Hey Mick! Yes Mr. Cooper! We're headed over to North Town! You know where the Swap Meet is over there? Yes Sir! Cool; that's the destination. Hey Mick, what's up bro? Hey Manny; how are you sir? I'm great brother; thanks for asking. Alright Mick, step on it player, we got business to handle. Yes Sir; on the way! Did you call Hector and told him what time he needs to meet us? Yep! Cool, how does he feel about this new move? He's with it. That's what's up! He says that Chino and Mya will run things for him. Capo; I don't care who does it; as long as that cash flow keeps coming! Oh without a doubt; that's our main concern right there. I'm glad you understand Manny. Come on brother; you know I got this thing covered. I sure hope so player. Whatever came of those bodies they found in that backyard? I haven't heard anything else about it AC.

Well, keep your ear to the street; we already have enough heat on us. We damn sure don't need that coming back! I have our people on it. Cool, how's Sophie? She's doing pretty good! How about junior? Man that guy is getting big; eating up all the damn food in the house bro! Ha-Ha!

Really! Hell yeah! How old is he now? 18 man and still growing!

Wow; he grew up fast! I know right; how about your kids? Did you speak with them again since you visited? Nah but I'm making plans to start seeing them more. Monica and I decided to move into the Mansion. What; you serious? Yep! That's a good move AC; maybe your ex will stop tripping and let them come over now. That's what I'm hoping Capo but you know how baby momma's can get when another woman is around. Man I could never understand that; especially if a guy wants to see his kids. I feel the same way Capo but they don't seem to get it. Mick how far we got? Not long Sir! Alright step on it! So, are you and Monica getting real serious? I don't know really bruh! What do you mean by that? I've been fucking with her for a while but our relationship isn't like the one I had with Sabrina. How so? Manny; Mo is a different breed; she's more of a G! Sabrina was that spoiled ass; only child, model type chic. Monica on the other hand; watches every move I make, you make, Will, Nina, Duck, hell you get the point! Ha-ha! Yeah she's more like us! Exactly!

You know; good and damn well, Sabrina would have never had the guts to pull a stunt like Mo did! What stunt, that Paco shit? Yeah that! Um, that did take some balls. That's what I'm saying; she gone make me put my hands on her and you know I don't hit women. Don't worry Coop; you got Nina and Denna for that. That's what I'm afraid of; they will kill that girl if they knew she was tripping like that. You didn't tell them; did you Manny? Nah; it didn't cross my mind, that's your business Boss; I'll let you handle that one. Ha-ha! Thanks a lot Capo! Hey don't mention it! Ok Mr. Cooper; we're here! Cool, park by the sidewalk in front of the office.

What's up homes! Hector; what's poppin brother? Waiting on you two criminals; ready to get to business; AC what's up amigo? Hey Hector; I'm good baby. Let's go inside the office so we can talk. Ok give me a sec., let's wait for Chino he's in the 64 hitting some of that dust. That fool's smoking angel dust? Yeah Coop, you want a hit? Nah; I'm good Hector! Come on AC; it'll give you some wings esse'! Shit, I don't want those motherfucking wings! Ha-ha! Okay; no problem, here he comes now! Hurry up homes; we got business with the man! I'm coming Hector,

I'm coming. Manny; what's up amigo? Hey Chino, how you feel? Ha-ha! I feel good- Ha-ha! I bet you do! Hey Hector; is your boy gone be straight talking business? Yo, don't worry AC; it's no problem, I'm good amigo. See, he's good homes! Ok; let's go inside. Mick, keep the engine running, leave the AC on too. Yes Sir!

Come in guys; have a seat up front here. Coop, we have to remodel this office man. This place looks like we stepped back into the 70's. Ha-ha! I know Manny; I was thinking the same thing, that old receptionist he had must have decorated it. What you think Chino? It doesn't matter to me amigo; show me the money mane. See; I like you already Chino! Alright Hector; what's your plan on getting the word out over here in North Town? Me and the crew are gone hit up every block and lay it down homes. If they with it then it's what it is. If they're against the homies then we drop them punta's where they stand. What about you AC; did you want me to do it different? Nah man; handle your business how you see fit. Cool homes; say no more about it. So Chino whose gonna be helping you here at the office. My girl Mya; I don't trust anyone else but Hector and he can't do it so- that's who it is AC. Is this Mya dependable Hector? Yeah she's a soldier; no problems amigo.

Ok Chino; here's how this thing works. You and your girl are now responsible for any drugs that are sold in North Las Vegas. Nothing comes in or goes out with you touching it. If anybody tries to infiltrate, lay them fools down and ask questions later. You got that homeboy? Yeah I got it mane! I said; do you got it Chino! Yes I have it AC. That's better! Now all you have to worry about is paying your taxes to me; that's do every week before you re-up. Manny will let you know how much your taxes will be, it all depends on how much product you move. The more you push the higher the tax! The more money you make the higher the tax. You understand? Yes AC. Cool, your first three weeks will be your probation period; we need to see if you're really cut out for this game. If you are; then you get more product! Your contact person will always be Manny; unless I come see you personally and Chino- you don't want me to come see you personally. Understand? Yes AC. My taxes are due every week; don't be late and never ever be short. If you're short or even late; the gig is up and so is your life. Understand Chino? Don't look at

Hector man; I'm talking to you. This is serious business; I don't fuck around with my paper. So, do you understand Chino?

Yes AC! I mean; if you're having second thoughts Chino; speak up! By no means do I want you involved in a situation that you can't handle. Hector won't be able to help you out of anything; now I'm your Boss, judge and jury; my man. Now I'll ask you one last time. Do you understand the rules as I laid them out player? I understand clearly AC. Cool, let's do this shit then. Manny; show Chino where the keys are in that back office. Hector, take your crew on that mission and put the word out. I'm on it amigo; I'll call you if we run into any big problems. Cool; do that bruh. Manny; I'll be in the limo waiting on you Capo. Make sure Chino knows the value of that product. Ok Coop; I'll meet you out there in a minute; I'll square him away. Well, welcome to the crew Chino. We're gone start you with 2 pounds of chronic, 2 keys of snow and one key of meth. Don't be getting high off the supply amigo, this here is business. AC is giving you a chance; don't fuck it up! I won't mane, I'm ready. Ok cool, when is Mya coming? She should be here anytime now! Alright that's what's up; do you have any questions? Nah; I'm straight Manny! Are you sure brother? Yep! Well; you have my number, if you do; just call me. I'm out; go ahead and start getting your product ready for the street. Alright Manny; later mane!

Hey Mick; are you hungry? Yes Sir I am. Me too; let's go across the street and get some of those shrimp tacos when Manny comes out. Ok Sir! Here he is now! About time Capo! I had to make sure the homie was straight Coop. Is he? Yeah he's good! Come on then; close the door; we're going to get some shrimp tacos. Bet! Yo Mick; let's go eat! On the way Sir!

Hello ladies and gentlemen; welcome to a night of comedy. I'm Winston and I wanted to come out here tonight and thank you all personally. This is our 4 year anniversary here at the club and we could not have done it with your support! So to show our appreciation; I'm sending two bottles of Dom to everyone's table! Please enjoy the show; your champagne, and again, we thank you! Yay! Yay! Clap! Clap! Clap! The patrons applause.

Ok, ok that's enough clapping dammit! He's my boss; I'm the comedian; yall supposed to clap for me; not his short ass! Winston is so short; he needs a rope to climb in his bath tub. Ha-ha! Ha-ha! Ha-ha! That boy so short, he needs a life vest in the baby pool and that thing only 2 feet deep! Ha-ha! Ha-ha! Ha-ha! Ok, ok, that's enough; I can't crack on my boss no more tonight. He told me- Mo-Mo; I'll give you two jokes; after that I'm taking $100 out of your check for each joke. So that's it, stop laughing at Winston! My check aint but $400; his cheap ass! Ha-ha! Ha-ha! Hey; stop laughing; that wasn't no joke! Hey Winston; that wasn't no joke man. They trying to make nigga go home broke! Ha-ha! Ha-ha!

Alright; yall is a funny crowd. I see the waitresses bringing everybody their bottles of champagne and shit; where the hell is my bottle? I'm up here doing all the work! I'm just saying! Ha-ha! Ha-ha! Ok let's welcome our first comedian to the stage all the way from, North Las Vegas! Ha-ha! I'm just kidding; let's give it up for Val Miller from Chicago!

Well hello lady; it took you long enough. Hi Winston; this is my friend Georgia. Georgia this is Winston. Hello Winston! Hey Georgia, nice to meet you! Nice to meet you as well! So are you ladies enjoying the show? Yeah; Mo-Mo is too funny. Yes, that guy is a character. I'm glad you finally made it out Nina. I told you I was coming. I'm glad you did! This is a nice place you have here. I'm impressed! Why thank you! Did you guys want something to eat; our steaks are really good. Sure why not; you want something Georgia? Sure! Ok Winston; surprise us; we're not picky; send us your favorite dish. No problem girls; you two go ahead and enjoy your Dom and the show. I'll go put in those orders. Oh Nina; if you need anything baby; just have one of the waitresses come get me. Aww, thanks Winston; I sure will.

Hey yall; it is hotter than a 400 lb bear in a brick oven, set to 375 degrees down here in Vegas. Ha-ha! Ha-ha! How in the hell do yall do it? Damn, this heat right here; make a bitch miss the windy city! Give my black ass some cold winds and snow any day! I can-not do this! Ha-ha! Ha-ha! Girls; how yall wear weave in this place? I know as soon as you go outside the damn glue be melting and a bitch weave be sliding down her face! Right! Ha-ha! Ha-ha! Be at work! Your girlfriend be like! "Shonda; come here girl; yo high lights glued to your chin bitch!" Ha-ha! Ha-ha! And what is up with yall water! I took a cold shower because I was so damn hot. So I turned up the AC in the room; laid across the bed naked; trying to cool off. I happened to look at my leg, then my arm. I did not believe what the hell I was seeing. It's 139 degrees outside; so a bitch aint putting on no lotion. It is too damn hot for that! Yall tell me why my black ass, turned white as Pee Wee Herman. Ha-ha! Ha-ha!

No, no, that shit aint funny! If it's hot in Chicago or any other damn city; you don't need no lotion, no Vaseline, no coco butter! But in this damn place! Ha-ha! Ha-ha! How in the hell, you still turn ashy and it's 139 degrees outside! Ha-ha! Ha-ha! I was confused; so I peeped in the hallway and caught the house keeper. I said. "Excuse me Ma'am!" She said "Yes can I help you" I said. "Look sister, you almost as dark as me, so maybe you can tell me why I'm so damn ashy." "If it's hot at home in Chicago, I don't need any lotion." "What's going on here?" She said. "Ma'am it's the Vegas water." I said, what do you mean? She said. "We have hard water in here Vegas, the locals we don't even drink it." "We all have water filters on all our faucets at the house." So I said to the house keeper. "Let me get this straight; Vegas has bad water, so you guys don't drink it, don't wash in it, don't cook with it and don't even wash dishes with it." Then she looked at me with smirk and said. "Yes Ma'am that is correct." I almost lost my mind! I said lady. "If the people who live here don't drink the water, cook with it or wash with it." "Then why you motherfuckers let the tourist; wash with it, drink it, cook with it and all kind of shit!"

She said! "Baby; what goes on in Vegas, stays in Vegas, the water aint no different!" Ha-ha! Ha-ha! Yall been good; I'm Val Miller, Love you; Las Vegas!

July; 1998.

Gloria; why are you and Trish back here at the Ranch? You guys should be in Cali until Friday! I know Denna but we had to leave because we got robbed; they took all of our money, clothes and food too. Who Gloria? Some Bloods! When did this happen? Late last night; I tried to call Will but he didn't answer; so we drove straight here to you. Are you guys alright? Yeah; just a little shaken up. Trish; you haven't said a word the entire time; what's wrong? I just can't believe it happened to us; we were minding our business. Don't get all crazy on me now; no one got hurt and that's the important thing. You guys just relax and have a seat at the bar while I call Will. Ok Denna.

Hey Trish; Gloria! Haven't seen you two around here in a while! Where have you been? Hey Josh; we were working out of town; we just got back. Oh ok, well, welcome home ladies! What are you two having to drink? I'll take a Malibu and pineapple! Got you covered Trish; and how about you Gloria? Two shots of Crown on the rocks baby! Ok coming right up!

Ring-Ring! Hello Dolls! Hey; can I speak to Will please! Sure, hold on a sec! Will line one! Ok thanks! This is Will! Hey bro; this is Denna. What's up sis? Gloria and Trish just pulled up here about an hour ago. I know you're kidding, them ho's should be in Cali! I know but they said they were robbed last night; some bloods, took their money, food and clothes too. Bullshit; why didn't she call me then? Gloria said she called but didn't get an answer. Sis that girl aint call me. That's what she said Will. She's a liar! What kind of vibe you get from them; do you think they're telling the truth. Well, Gloria was kind of convincing but Trish was a little hesitant. They're trying to pull a fast one sis; I don't think they got robbed. Drill them again and see what you find out. Alright bro; I will call you when I know something. Yeah, later Denna!

Hey Trish! Yes Denna! Come help me get these groceries out of the car. Ok, I'm coming. There're only four bags, you can grab two and I'll get the other two. Are you sure you're ok Trish? I'm fine. Are you sure; you seem a little nervous to me. It's nothing Denna. Well I don't blame you; I would be nervous too if some crips robbed me at gun point. Did they rob you guys at the room or what? Yeah it was during the night; they followed us in the room and held us at gun point. Damn, that's why I keep my piece on me; it's some crazy people out here. Yeah; I have to get me one. Yeah; that's a good idea. Here grab these bags and take them in the kitchen; I'm right behind you. Ok, I got them! Cool, go ahead in front of me; I have to lock the doors.

Hey, you guys need some help Trish. No Gloria; it was only four bags, Denna has the other two. Ok cool! Josh; pour me another double please. Sure no problem Gloria! Did you get some lemons Boss? Yes I remembered the lemons Josh; I'm going to put these bags in the kitchen. I'll bring them with me, when I come back. Great I appreciate it! You're welcome J! Where did you want these bags Denna? Put them on the table then separate everything and put the groceries up. Ok no problem. Oh, I need the lemons! Sure here you go! Thanks!

Here you go baby; one double crown on the rocks. Thanks man! Josh! Yeah! Catch! Whoa! Two more coming! Whoa! Thanks Denna! Don't mention it! So Gloria; did you get a good look at the guys who robbed you. Nah Denna, they had red bandannas over their mouths and noses.

Where they catch yall slipping at? They caught us while we were leaving the bank! Trish was in the passenger seat as I was getting under the wheel. Then they popped up out of nowhere with sawed off pumps! Damn girl, yall need to invest in some protection. I have some pepper spray but I didn't have time to pull it out. And what would you have done with it, if you did pull it out? Blind that fool, so he couldn't see; that's what! Baby, the last time I checked; pepper spray was no match for shot gun shells. Well, I've never shot a gun before. Oh really! No I really haven't. Ok, come with me; let me show you. Josh hold it down, we're going out back! Sure Boss! Come on Gloria! Are you serious Denna? Yep, come on.....

Where's Gloria Josh? Oh she went outside with the Boss lady; did you want another Malibu? Yeah why not! Alright, coming right up! So are you guys going back out of town or you staying here for a while? I'm not sure man; we're probably gone be hanging around here for a bit. That's cool; I miss you guys being around. Say; did that cowboy ever come back around? Who the one you tried to rob? Ha-ha! Yeah him! Nah, I haven't seen him since that incident. Damn! I don't know why you are upset; it's your fault Trish. I know it is but I was so wasted that night; I don't remember what I did. You took the man's wallet and helped yourself to his cash; that's what you did! Umm, umm, umm, I need to stay off those drugs. You got that right lady, they only get you in trouble.

Ok Gloria, this is a 9mm handgun with the 12 round clip! This right here is a silencer. What's that for Denna? Oh this; I like to use it when I'm sneaking up on someone or when I don't want anyone to hear the shots. Damn that's cool! Yeah I know; it's my favorite tool. Are you ready to shoot a few rounds? I don't know Denna; you go first and I'll watch. Are you sure? Yeah go ahead. Alright, when you're shooting to kill someone; you need to aim one or two places. Where is that Denna? That's in the head or in the heart! We call that one shot, one kill. You put the silencer on like so! Click! You cock it to put one in the chamber. Then you aim at your target and pull the trigger.

Remember the two targets that you aim for when going for the kill Gloria? Yes! What were they? You said the head and the heart! Right! Denna places the cold black steel barrel on Gloria's forehead. Yep, the head. Whoa that's cold! It won't be after I shoot it! Trust me, don't ever touch a barrel after it has been fired; it will burn the hell out of you. Now the second place is the heart. Where's your heart Gloria? Right here! Well, not quite; you want to make sure you're dead center so you don't miss it. Denna places the nose of her nine over Gloria's heart. Now that's dead center. Can you feel it Gloria? Yeah I can? Good- Pow!

Ring-Ring! Hello Dolls! Will please; it's Denna! Oh hey Denna! Hey Red! Hold on hun; Will line 1! This is Will! Bro they jacked us; both their stories are different; one said they got robbed after they left the bank by some bloods and the other said some crips robbed them at the room. I knew it Sis! Cancel those bitches! Don't worry bro; Gloria is done; I'm about to take care of Trish in a minute. Good; those trifling ass whores, they deserve it! Calm down Will; it's handled, enjoy your day brother. Thanks Sis! Anytime bro, anytime! Denna hangs up the phone; places her nine in the small of her back and removes her white leather belt off her ck1 jeans.

Damn Trish; you better slow down on those Malibu's; you're gonna be wasted soon. I don't care Josh; make me another. Are you sure? Yep, pour it up baby! Ok, coming up! Hey Trish; are you alright honey? Yeah Denna, just having a few drinks. Where's Gloria? She's out back! What's she doing out there? Smoking on a blunt! Oh that's what's up. Come on let's go join her! Ok but I need my drink first! Nah, you don't need it now; Josh will keep it cool for you. Alright; then let's go smoke. Come on; I'll follow you. Hey Josh; keep her drink chilled; we're going outback for a bit. Sure Boss; no problem. Hey; I spoke to Will a few minutes ago. Damn, was he upset? No, not really, he said that Dylan and Barbie had gotten robbed recently too. Damn, did they? Yep! So now he's thinking about ending the whole check scam gig. Why Denna? It's getting too dangerous; he doesn't want any of you girls to get hurt.

Hey it was fun while it lasted right; you girls made some good money. Yeah it was; and we did make a lot of paper too. I don't see Gloria; where is she? Gloria! Gloria! She's just around the building Trish, just ahead, keep walking. Gloria- Ugh... Denna walks two steps closer behind her then wraps her belt around Trish's neck. It's ok Trish; Gloria will be waiting for your thieving ass on the other side. See; I asked Gloria what happened and her story was different than yours. Ugh... Trish falls slowly to the ground while looking up at Denna, her eyes now blood shot red; veins bursting across her forehead. Ugh... I told you bitches when we took this place over to never cross us. But you two had to try it; now look at you. Ugh... Trish's body got weaker and weaker as saliva foamed in the corners of her mouth while her lifeless body collapsed to the desert floor as Denna released her white leather belt from her neck. Ring-Ring! Hello Dolls! Let me speak to Will! Hold please! Will line 1! This is Will! It's done bro! Cool! Later; I need to clean it up. Click!

Ring-Ring! Hello Ranch Security! Yeah this is Denna! Hey Boss what's up? Grab your partner and some shovels; meet in back of the house. Ok Boss on the way!

Over at LVMPD the undercover agent knocks on Espinoza's door and pays him an uninspected visit. Come in its open! Hey Detective; what's new? Hey Chief; I have some new intel for you. Great have a seat; let's hear it. Well Duck is running the Vegas Luxury Auto car lot; I'm almost 100% certain that they're washing money through that business account. Good job detective; where are they getting the cars? As far as I know they are legit but it's still too early to say for certain. Ok keep a close eye on that operation; there can be some good evidence there. What else do you have? Remember that double homicide over at the North Las Vegas swap meet? Yeah not too long ago; it's still open. Well, get this Chief! What! Word is; AC owns it now, he has some Spanish kids running it for him and they're making moves in North Town as we speak. Hmm, wasn't that Paco guy, a known drug dealer? I think so Chief! If all of this is true detective; our friend is tied into the drug game as well; I'm going to take a closer look into this deceased Paco and his associates. Maybe this is the break we've been waiting for, to finally put this Sin City 7 away for life. It very well could be Chief! Good work detective, stay low and don't blow your cover; we're almost home. I won't Chief, see you next time. Sure thing, I'll be in touch.

Hello Towers; this is David! Hey Dave; pull out the Harley and the Ninja; Manny and I are coming down to take a ride. Sure thing Mr. Cooper; I'll have the valet get them now Sir. Thanks David! You know; he's been doing a good job Capo; almost better than you. Yeah whatever AC; you wanna hit this Chronic one more time before we leave.

Nah; I'm good; can't be too damn high on that Ninja. You got a point there Coop! I'm glad that you think so; because if you wreck my Harley you're buying me another one. Relax brother; I'm good to go. You better be! Come on; are you ready? Hold on; let me turn off my bedroom lights. Man aren't you gonna miss this place? I don't know Manny; I really haven't thought about it much. Well; I know I am; you were the only reason I had to come back over this way. You still can Capo; Nina's upstairs remember! I know but that isn't the same. You'll get over it bruh; get Duck on the phone for me while I lock up. Alright; hold tight.

Ring-Ring! Hello Vegas Luxury Auto! Jackie speaking; how can I help you? Yes; can I speak with Dubai please? Sure, hold a sec! Mr. Dubai; line two! Ok; I got it Jackie! Hello this is Dubai! What's up Duck! Hey who is this? It's Manny; you nut case. Hey bro what's going on! Hold on; AC wants to holler at you. Sure! Duck my man; how's business? It's good Coop; we're kicking ass this quarter. That's what I like to hear bruh. Yep; it's running real smooth. Cool, listen up! I'm all ears. I think it's time I do something special for the crew; it's been a productive year so far and I want to award you guys. That sounds like some good shit there Boss; what you got planned? Well Duck; I want you to call up the Bentley manufacture and custom order 7 of those new 98 Bentley's. One for each of us; call the guys and see what colors they want theirs to be and get them any features they desire. No shit Coop! Yep; can you handle that Duck? Hell yeah bro; no fucking problem. Good; jump on it and order them from the manufacture like I said; not from Hector either! Ha-ha! No doubt! Yo make mine's black Duck; fully loaded! Ha-ha! Did you hear Manny; Duck? Yeah I heard him! Cool, get busy and handle that for me; I want them to be here by Christmas. Ok bro; I'm on it! Good deal; later Duck!

Here's your helmet's sir! Thanks; David! You're welcome Mr. Cooper! Damn, what made you do that AC? What; the cars? Yeah! It's something I've been thinking about for a minute. Hell Capo; it's not like we don't have the money. Oh; we have plenty of that brother; the guys are gonna love that gift! Ok man; keep up; we're headed over to McCarran Airport! What are we going over there for? You'll see, just keep up rookie! Man I can ride a motorcycle! Oh yeah! Vroom-Vroom! Errrr.. Hey Man; wait up! AC burnt off the lot then onto the strip as Manny follow on the Harley. All he could see is Coop's tail-lights weave in and out of traffic as they speed down the strip. Traffic came to a crawl as AC approach the red light at the Tropicana and Las Vegas Blvd. intersection as Manny finally catches up with him. Hey bro; that wasn't cool. I told your ass to keep up man; you said you knew how to ride! I do but this is a cruiser and you're on a damn Ninja. Capo; stop crying! Vroom-Vroom! Errrrr.. Hey! God dammit AC!

Coop quickly leaves Manny and the other traffic behind as he makes a left onto Tropicana, Manny now following closer behind than before. The fellas cruise down Tropicana then make a right onto Maryland heading to the Airport entrance. AC; peels off to the right doing about 45mph with Manny on his tale. The huge airplanes sitting on the run way; fades in the distance as loud engines roar from the ones taking off over head. AC slows down then comes to a stop at a private run way off in the far right corner of the Airport. Two rows of Jet's, sit along-side a small hanger with an attached office and glass doors and tan brick walls. Manny looks puzzled as he pulls up and stops beside Coop.

Come on Capo; there's someone inside I need to see. AC; what the hell are you up to? You'll see bruh; just chill. Hello Sir; how can I help you? Yes; I'm Andy cooper; I spoke with Miguel earlier! Oh yes; I am Miguel; how are you Mr. Cooper? I'm good my man; this is my friend Manny! Hello Manny; how are you sir? I'm fine brother. That is good! Ok Miguel; what you got for me? Well; I have only three Jets at this time but they are all new and I'm sure you will love them. Alright; let's get to business; show me what you have. Sure; right this way Gentlemen! AC what's up! Manny; chill bruh! They're just outside by this hangar Gentlemen.

Mr. Cooper this is our 1997; Bombardier Phoenix CRJ 200. It's one of the fancier; business Jet's that was produced last year. It has dual FCC Long Range Auxiliary Tanks; that's 300 gallons each and that's also 8,729 lbs of thrust each. What the hell did he just say? I don't know Manny; just be quiet; we can ask questions later. Now it's equipped with an integrated Collins Pro Line 4 Avionics suite. If you Gentlemen would follow me up the steps; I can show you the inside. Wow; this is nice AC. I know Capo; I've been dreaming about this. Really; you're kidding right! Nope; I'm serious as ever. Coop; are you planning on buying this thing? As you can see guys; this is one of the finest Jets on the market today. It's equipped with a dual flight management system, electric window blinds, twelve inch stereo system with three subwoofers, three telephone handsets; the works.

Now it can also be configured to a 15 or 16 passenger jet. You have the cream leather seating and two closets, storage cabins, bar, TV's and pull out tables for group meetings, etc. Do you have any questions for me Gentlemen? Yes, I have a question! Yes Manny! Does this thing come with a pilot? Because none of us can fly! Ha-ha! Capo; stop tripping! I'm serious AC. No; it does not Sir, but we do provide a list of licensed pilots that are for hire here in the Las Vegas area. Thank you Miguel! You're quite welcome sir! How much does this one go for Miguel? The Phoenix is listed at $20,500,000.00 Mr. Cooper. Cool, thanks! You're welcome Sir! Damn man; did you say $20,500,000.00? Yes I did Sir! Wow; I'm in the wrong business AC; I need to be selling some jets brother. Ha-ha!

You aint kidding! Would you Gentlemen like to see the other two jets? Yeah let's see them! Okay right this way!

Now, what we have over here is the 1998; Bombardier Challenger 604! It's the latest model in the business jets class of the Bombardier's. It's equipped with an integrated; six tube Collins Pro-Line 4 avionics suite. The Challenger is a bit sleeker than the Phoenix; it comes with two bars, cd player, cassette player, 8 speaker stereo system and two subwoofers. Follow me up the steps and I can show you the cabin. Now as you can see, the leather in this one is more of a caramel than cream but just as soft. You have your TV's mounted inside the walls and they are equipped with Video cassette players as well. This one is only equipped to fit 9 to 10 passengers; it also comes with micro wave, coffee maker, hot temp oven, ready hot instant hot water dispenser and Hot liquid container. It is a bit narrower but was built for a more private passenger, hence all the amenities. It's pretty cool though Miguel. What's the price tag on it? This one is listed at $23,995,000.00 Mr. Cooper. Ok; is this the one you told me about on the phone; that price sounds familiar. Yes it is Sir. Coop this one holds less people and it's more than the last one that held almost double. Yeah, but it's a 98 that one was a 97 Manny. I don't know AC; I like the first one better bro! Did you guys want to see the last one? Yeah why not; let's see it! Ok follow me.

This one is what we call the Rolls Royce of our Jets, guys; it's the 1998; Cessna Citation X. Equipped with 8,000 lbs. of thrust, a Honeywell Primus 2000 Avionics suite and a WSI Satellite weather system. How many passengers does this one hold Miguel? It holds a total of 8 Mr. Cooper. How much is it? It's listed for $21,000,000.00 Sir! I tell you what Miguel, get me the list of pilots and go ahead and get the paper work started for that Phoenix. Yes Sir; right away!

Oh one more thing Miguel! Yes Mr. Cooper; what is it? I had my accountant draw a check for $23,995,000.00 because I had my mind set on that 604. Since I'm getting the Phoenix and it's only $20,000,000.00; I have a few million left over. Yes sir. So why don't you take $1,000,000.00 for yourself and hire me two of the best pilots off that roster you got with the other 2,995,000.00. Tell them they will be flying exclusively for me. Can you do that Miguel? Yes Sir; it would be my pleasure and thank you so much. You're welcome Miguel; get the paper work ready and my partner Manny here will sign it for you. I will see you boys later; I have some place I need to be! Alright Coop; I'll hit you when I'm done! Yep; later Capo!

Hey Loon! What's up Candy; did you talk to Chocolate? Nope; but there's some homeless guy outside in the parking lot, bumming money! What guy? I don't know; they all look alike to me man. Thanks Candy, I'll go check it out. Yeah you need to; he's gone scare our customers away. Just get dress woman, I'll handle that. Loon makes his way out to the lot to see what guy Candy was talking about, moving quickly so that the he wouldn't be away from the store for too long. Hey bruh! Hey you! Sir; I don't won't any trouble! What you doing out here man; you begging in my parking lot? What's your name? Walter; Sir! Whew; dude you need to wash your ass! Don't call me Sir; my name is Loon! Besides you look old enough to be my Grandfather. I'm sorry Mr. Loon. Man just Loon is fine.

Now you want to tell me why you're in my parking lot begging. I'm hungry, sick and homeless man. I make it the best way I can. You haven't always been homeless I know! No Loon I haven't. Well, where's your family, aint there someone to take you in. They all disowned me after I got hooked on that crack. Wow, there you have it! I bet you stole from your family too; didn't you? I'm afraid so Loon, but it was the drugs; I had to have it man. How old are you Walter? 59 this month man! So are you still on that shit? No, been clean a year now. That's good; did you see your family since? I tried but they're still mad with me for selling all their stuff. You need a job or something; if you clean yourself up; I'll let you keep the place clean. You know; pick up the trash; clean the bathrooms, sweep the cigarette butts up off the lot.

I appreciate the kind jester Loon but it won't matter much no way. Why not? I have terminal cancer; Doc told me all I have is 6 months to live. Well, it's more like 5 now. Damn, what kind of cancer is it? Colon cancer Loon! Wow; I'm sorry to hear that. Nah, we all have to leave here one day besides I'm about dead anyway; living out here in the streets like I am. Did you at least tell your family! No, for what; they don't give a damn if I live or die. Do you have any kids? Yeah I have two boys and a daughter. All of them are studying at UNLV. That's good Walter but you have to at least tell your kids.

Loon you're wasting your time man; nobody cares. So what kind of work did you do before this streak of bad luck? I retired from the Army! No shit! Yep; why, did you serve Loon? Yes I did soldier. Oh yeah; what was your M.O.S.? Me; I was a sniper with the 555th attached to the 82nd. Well; I'll be damn, so was I but I was assigned to Ft. Hood. You sure; you don't want this job Walter? I'm positive soldier; I'm just gonna die peacefully with no worries and all by myself. I hear that! Hey; when was the last time you fired a weapon? It's been a minute but I'm sure I still have it. Why you ask Loon?

My friend has a covert job that requires someone with your skill set. I would do it but he wants the shooter to be a non-associate. Hmmm, what's the target? I can't tell you that, until you take the job. I told you I don't need any money Loon; I'll do it for free. I'm going to be deceased in a few months anyway. No I can't let you do that; you have to get paid Walter. I don't want it! I tell you what then; if you do the job; I'll make sure your kids over at UNLV get $40,000.00 each; that should help them out. That sounds like a deal soldier but they can't know it's from me or how they got it. I'm sure we can arrange some kind of scholarship or something to make it look official. I like you already Loon, you got yourself a deal.

Now we're talking man, come inside and we can talk about the details. Sure; lead the way soldier. Cool but you have to promise me one thing Walter! What's that Loon? You have to take a shower man; you reek! I don't have a room or a house to take a shower at and the Salvation Army is closed for tonight. Man I have some showers in here you can use; just wash, that's all I'm asking. Ok; you got yourself a deal. Alright; come inside.

Two large moving trucks block the drive way over at the mansion in Spanish Trails as Monica instructs the movers where to put what. Ok fellas just sit all the boxes labeled kitchen and living room down right here, in the foyer by the statue. The ones marked bedroom and AC's clothes; you can take up stairs and leave them in the hallway outside of the master bedroom. Ok Ma'am; no problem! Ruff! Ruff! Move Pete! Thanks guy's; I really appreciate it! Soooo, baby what do you think? What do you mean Mo? I've always liked the Mansion; I just never thought too much about moving in it. I don't know why not; you're the Boss of Sin City; this is more your speed. Not that bachelor's pad you have at the Towers. Well; you wasn't complaining while I was knocking your back out in that King size bed over there or eating your pussy on the balcony. Nigga; you aint never ate my pussy on that balcony. Don't get knocked out in here.

Whatever woman; you get the point! See; you still have that skinny, model chic, dead girlfriend on your mind; that's the problem. Get over her baby; she aint ever coming back. I know you guys were in love and all that but it was her time and now it's mine. Don't you worry about nothing; Monica is not leaving you baby. You can count on that Mister! Oh yeah! Yep; now come here and give me a kiss; you sexy man you! Muah! Ok Ma'am; we're all done. Did you have anything else for us to move? Ruff! Ruff! Pete; be quiet! No; that's it fellas! AC can you tip them; my purse is upstairs. Sure! Hey bruh; here you go; we appreciate it! Thanks man, and call us anytime; you two have a good evening. You're welcome and we will if we have to move anything in the future. Ruff! Ruff! Pete; get back over here! AC, get him! Come here boy!

Those guys were nice Coop. Girl, they're supposed to be; that's what you call customer service. Ha-ha! Don't be getting smart with me Andy Cooper! Damn; you're just gone call my whole damn name out huh? Stop tripping; aint nobody in here but us! Yeah; yeah! Coop; where are you going; come here! Nope; I'm going out by the pool to smoke this chronic and ease my mind for a minute. Aren't you gone help me unpack these boxes? What do you think? AC; don't be like that! Those boxes can wait girl; I'm hungry anyway. What are you cooking? Why do I have to cook nigga? Because I'm about to smoke and I'm gonna be hungry once I'm high. Well, I don't feel like cooking. That's fine; there's a good Chinese restaurant right outside the gate. Just go pick up something. Ummm; that does sound good; what did you want? Get me a large shrimp with lobster sauce and two egg rolls. Ok; I'll be back in a little bit; I'll probably go by that Target and get some new sheets while they're cooking the food. Ok that's what's up baby; grab a bottle of Merlot too. Ok, where're the keys to the Rover? Look in the bathroom; I left them on the counter! Alright; be back shortly. Yep! Ruff! Ruff! Pete come on boy; let's go smoke.

The 102 degree heat felt like a sauna as Coop exit through the slide doors; walk down the steps and sat pool side. Millions of stars shine bright above in the dark Vegas summer sky as the moon light beam across the blue chlorine water that fill the pool. His skin became clammy from the humidity as he sat there in his blue shorts; feet dangling in the cool pool water. The loud fan from the AC unit, along with frogs croaking in the distance; play a familiar melody he hadn't heard since his teenage years down south. He pulls the lighter from his right pocket, lights the blunt, inhales, holds it in for a bit, exhale then places the lighter down on the warm cement then leans back while looking up at the stars, both hands, palms down behind him, inhaling again. It all seem so clear now; life itself and how he found himself here. Pete calmly sits beside him, glaring up at his master with puppy dog eyes. Every past day, month, hour, year, even second ran through AC's mind as he exhale the chronic smoke then take in another toke while looking up at the stars as the sky turns to a movie screen; he saw his life then and now in living color.

"So; you're just gone forget about me and move on; huh daddy?" Oh shit; what the fuck! AC snatches the blunt from his mouth and sits straight up! "Answer me daddy!"

Sabrina! That you! "Daddy!" He looks to his left, then to his right, shakes his head in disbelief, takes another toke and continues to look up at the dark sky. "You know she threw me off the balcony; right daddy!" Whoa! Man this is some potent weed! Fuck this; I don't need no more chronic tonight. "Where's my ring daddy; did you give it to her?" "Daddy!" Sabrina; stop this; you're dead! Stop it! Man what the hell am I doing; talking to myself. Here; I'm gone put you down buddy, no more green for me tonight. Splash! He dives in the pool then swims to the other side, climbs out and walks back inside the Mansion.

30 minutes had passed as he came to grips with himself while looking in the bathroom mirror. Baby! Baby; are you in here? Yeah; I'm in the bathroom; you get the food? Yep; but they didn't have the Merlot we like; so I got some Sauvignon Blanc. That's cool! Where's that smoke; you burn it all? Nah; it's outside on the table but you don't want none of that Mo. Why not? It had me seeing things and hearing voices, I'm done! Damn; you sure that was weed and not no LSD! Monica I rolled it myself; it was chronic! Ha-Ha! What kind of things did you see AC? I was looking up at the sky right, then I starting seeing my life

from the past to now; it was like a damn movie, and it was in color. Wow; really! That sounds like some good ass weed to me nigga! Oh yeah; well I didn't tell you what I heard! And what did you hear? You don't want to know Mo! Yes I do; tell me! Come on babe; tell me.

Nah; where's the food; I'm hungry? So you're not gonna tell me? You don't want to know; trust me. Yes I do; now come on and stop tripping; tell me baby. Sabrina was talking to me Mo! Ha-ha! Yeah you tripping; what did she say? She asked me how come I forgot about her and said something about me and you moving in the Mansion. Damn; did you answer her back? Hell no! Ha-ha! Yeah right nigga; yes you did. No; I didn't but the last thing she said really got under my skin. What was that baby? She said you pushed her off the balcony that night. Wow; yep, that wasn't no regular weed for sure! Monica grabs the food from the bags and began to fix their plates while shaking her head at him. You definitely can't smoke no more of that shit; come on; let's eat; I'm hungry!

August, 1998.

"Damn it's hotter than fish grease in here!" "Welcome to the Crazy horse; I'm Dj Royal." "You guys have to excuse me tonight; we only got 5 girls in this dungeon!" "But none the less; get yo lap dance on, drink on, you know what to do!" "Do yo thing while I play this Mase and Puffy for yall; let's go!" "Uh-huh, uh-huh" "We like it" "Uh-huh, Uh-huh" "Yeah Kid Harlem on the rise" "This is the Remix '98!"

Hey Bebe'! Man Hector; what the hell do your sorry ass want! Chill chica; I came to see you; don't you miss me? Hell nah punta! Damn home girl; why I got to be a punta! Where your girl at? What girl? The one you had with you when you came in here the last time. Bebe'; that was my cousin and that was like 2 years ago. Exactly and now you come see me! That's the BS I'm talking about punk ass. Well look; I'm sorry Bebe'; I'm here now though. Yeah; what you want? I came to tell you that my crew is gone be running North Town now and you're going to be seeing a lot of me. Why; I don't want to see your ass. Can I have a drink first and then I'll tell you. What you want sorry? Just a Corona! Um-hmm; I should of known that; when are you gonna try something new? Why; I like coronas! Whatever; here you go punta. Thanks bartender!

Yeah whatever, now tell me why I'm gone be seeing you? We need a place to have our meetings and this is on the edge of town before we get to the North side. So; it's plenty of clubs around here; why this one? Paradise is up the street, Crazy Horse too is a few miles that away and Cheetah is not far from there. So why here Hector? Damn; look around chica; it aint like yall don't need the business. Oh we need the business but those fools you got with you are crazy. Aint no damn security guards up in here; so don't be bringing no trouble Hector. Bebe'; it's about the money; I'm trying to take care of my favorite girl. Oh; so now I'm your girl again huh! You've always been my girl chica! Hector; shut up and drink your beer before I slap you! Damn chica; stop being so mean. Um-hmm.

"I been around" "Yea-yea, yeah-yeah" "I been around the world (I been around)." Hey sexy; can I give you a dance? Yeah go ahead! Wow; you're just gone get a dance in front of me like that? Bebe'; it's a strip club, you're the bartender; what the fuck am I supposed to do? Splash!

Damn; why you do that girl! Hector you're not gone be coming in my job disrespecting me! I'm serious; you're lucky I didn't throw this glass at you! Here let me wipe your face baby; that bartender be tripping. Come on; we can go sit in a booth. Yeah go sit in a booth Hector! Bebe'; you need to chill out! I'm going over here to finish my dance and I'm gone deal with your crazy ass later. Come on baby, let's go! Fuck you Hector! Yeah just keep showing off Bebe' and watch what happens. Is she your girlfriend sexy? Nah, just a friend; I'm sorry about that. Oh it's ok; you want to wait for the next song? Yeah that's fine.

Ring-Ring! Ring-Ring! Hold on baby; I need to answer this. Hello! Hector what's popping? Yo who is this? It's AC! Hey homes; what's going on? How's that move coming on the North Side? It's going as planned homes; my soldiers are taking care of the corners now. We should be setting up shop in a week or so. That's what I like to hear my man; call me if you need anything! No problem amigo; I can do that. Later Hector! Alright homes! Are you ready for your dance sexy? Yeah; come on and let me see that cha-cha! Oooh; you got a nice one home girl. Thank you sexy! Is that a tattoo on your lips chica? Yes; you like it! Hell yes!

It's a butterfly! Ummm, ummm! I'd sure like to spread those wings. Ha-ha! You're so silly! Nah, I'm serious though. Uh-ah! Why not chica? Because; your girlfriend; that bartender is crazy and I don't want to get fired. Why are you gonna get fired baby? Because I will shoot her crazy ass; I'm too pretty to fight. Ha-ha! You're too pretty huh! Yep! Ok, just keep dancing mommy; I'm leaving when you're done anyway. Why are you leaving? I got some important business to handle, and it can't get done if I'm playing in pussy all day. Well, are you coming back to see me? Oh; I'll be back mommy; you'll be seeing plenty of me.

That's great because I like you? Oh is that right? Yep; what's your name? I'm Hector; what's yours? Me; I'm Sunny. Nice to meet you Sunny! Nice to meet you too Hector. So where are you from Sunny? Costa Rica. Oh ok; that's why you got that pretty skin and nice black hair. I got it from my momma. Ha-ha! Is that right? Yes it is; my mom's a fox! I bet she is; especially if you came out of her pussy. You have a nasty mouth Hector. I know I do but I can't help it. It's just the way I am. Oh; I don't mind; I kind of like it. That's good Sunny because I wasn't about to change. Well, your song is over; did you want another dance? No; I have to go; I'll see you next time. Ok; bye Hector! Later Sunny!

Yeah; you better leave punta! Hey; I'll deal with you when I come back Bebe'. I need to teach your ass some manners! Fuck you Hector! How about mind your business and serve some drinks. Yeah; whatever punta! "Sunny to the stage please; Sunny to the stage!" I'm coming, I'm coming!

Ruff! Ruff! The vicious Rotts bark as Remy and Derek enter the shop lot. Ruff! Ruff! Hey Carlos! Hey Derek; what's up bro! We came to pick up the Maserati; is it ready? Yeah bro; we got it looking real fly for you too! Oh yeah; I hope so because that bitch fucked my paint job up! Don't worry Remy; we got you covered mommy. Come in the garage; Poncho just finished putting the head lights back in. What! Why he got my head lights out? Calm down baby; they had to remove them so they could paint the car. How do you know D; you aint no painter! Because I know Remy; that's why! Carlos; please tell Remy why yall took the lights out. Yeah; he's right Remy; we always remove them when we paint a car. Oh, ok! See; are you happy now? Yep, can I see it? There it is mommy! Wow; that's looks brand new! You guys did a good job Carlos. Thanks mommy! Where's Hector; so I can thank him!

I don't know where the homie is mommy; but I'll tell him you said thanks! Please tell him for me Carlos. I will; don't worry. Alright bro; we need to go meet Chino and Mya over at the Swap Meet. Cool, be easy Derek; you too Remy. Don't get a speeding ticket in that race car now. Ha-ha! They have to catch me first baby! I hear that home girl; you guys be safe over in north town; in that car. I got my heat man; I aint worried. They got heat over there too Derek; don't get caught slipping home boy. We won't Carlos; take it easy! Yeah you too!

Alright Remy; start this baby up and let's drop off these keys. I don't know D; maybe we should take the other car instead. Remy; we're already late; let's just go. Besides, we don't have time to go get the other whip anyway. Ruff! Ruff! Aww; shut up! Ruff! Ruff! Damn D, those are some big ass Rotts! They're not gone come to the car Remy; just start this baby and head to the North side. Okay, ok, I'm going! Ruff! Ruff! Vroom-Vroom. The vicious Rottweiler's continue to bark as Remy's; cocaine white; Maserati pulls

238

off the chop shop lot and onto Industrial Blvd. What cd's you got in here baby?

Tupac; who else? Girl; is that all you listen to? Yep; that's my other boyfriend; so don't mess up D! Yeah, whatever Remy!

Yo check this new south cat out! Who is that baby? It's Silkk the Shocker and Mystikal; this joint is hot Remy; trust me! It better be D; put it in! You gone like it watch! Yeah; we'll see mister. "Ohhh; it aint my fault!" "It aint my fault!" "Yeah all yall nickel and dime motherfuckers-" Hold up D; that sounds like that Master P dude talking. It is; Silkk the Shocker is his little brother. Oh ok; I like the beat though; I'm gone add this to my dance set. See I told you! Alright; I'll give you that one baby; turn it up! For sho! "Ohhh; it aint my falut!" "We can't stop now bitch; we can't stop!" "It aint my falut!" "You can't stop us; and Bitch don't try!" "We TRU soldiers and we don't die!" "It aint my fault!" Damn; I'm really feeling this baby; them country boyz putting in work huh. Yep; the south is on some other shit; in a few years they're gonna have all the Dj's bumping their music. I don't know about that Derek; Bad Boy doing their thing and we got Snoop; Cube, Dre and Short over here and E-40. Them South boyz alright but they got a long wayz to go.

Remy you got it all wrong baby; trust me! Ok; since you're so smart; why do you think the South is gone have their music played everywhere when clearly, the East Coast and West Coast running the Rap game! It's common since Remy; let me ask you two questions! Ok go ahead D, ask! When you think about the east coast; what cities do you think about? That's easy! It's New York, Jersey, Phila and D.C. Ok and when you think about the West Coast; what cities do you think about? Shit; Cali! That's my point Remy! I still don't get it D; explain what you're saying! Explain it like I'm in 1st grade! Ok answer this Remy; when you think about the South what cities do you think of? Let's see; Georgia; The Carolina's, Alabama, Mississippi, Tennessee, Florida, New Orleans, Texas, Virginia and maybe St. Louis.

Now, you just named like 11 or 12 states baby. Hell if you put the East Coast and West Coast together, they barely cover half of that. So what's your point D? You still don't get it; do you girl? Nope! Well, remember that the West Coast just really started getting some recognition in Hip

Hop when Death Row started smashing hits like crazy. Before that; nobody showed us no love! It was all New York! Yeah I agree with you there. Cool, now we're getting somewhere. Now let's take the South artist for example; you got OutKast; So So Def, TLC, No Limit, 8 ball & MJG, Under Ground Kingz, Goodie Mob, Mystikal, Cash Money, Rap-A-lot and God knows how many more. It's just simple logistics Remy; the South has more Artist combined than the West Coast and East Coast. Right now they're building a fan base, and New York and Cali is helping them build it because they're not giving the South any respect in this rap game. In a few years; those same country boyz are going to figure out this business and start feeding off each other. Then the game will change and the South will be running this rap thing. Mark my words on that Remy; it's just common sense. Anytime you push someone in a corner, that's when they fight the hardest.

Man whatever; the South aint gone be running nothing; the West Coast gone be Boss in this Rap game. You mark my words on that Derek! Ha-ha! Ok Remy; we're here just pull in front of the office and I'll drop this package off to

Chino. Cool; no problem and hurry up; I'm hungry too. Alright; I'll make it quick!

Yo Chino! Where you at! Hey Derek, come in; he's in the back. Thanks Mya; how you doing? I'm good D; you can go on around there; he's waiting on you. Alright; cool! Chino my man; I got something for you homie. It's about time Derek; where the hake you been white boy. We just left the chop shop; we had to pick up the Maserati remember. Oh yeah; did Carlos do a good job on it? It looks brand new man; he hooked it up. That's cool; how much you got in the bag there? This is three keys; I threw in one extra because business has been good on this side.

Thanks; I appreciate that mane, does AC know? I'm sure he does; I asked Manny before I packed it up. Cool, because I don't need no problems white boy! Aww; you straight Chino; I wouldn't play you like that man. You want a beer or something? Nah, Remy is waiting on me outside. Did you guys drive the Maserati over here? Yep! You better go ahead and leave then mane; these baby gangster's will try and jack yall if you're not careful. Chino; do I look worried; them fools know me; I come over this way every week. Yeah but do you drive a white Maserati when you come? Nah but I see your point Chino.

You'll probably be alright though; since they know your face. Yeah but I aint taking no chances with my girl in the car; I better be going. Alright Derek; be safe and I'll see you next week, don't bring that car next time though homie. D daps up Chino then heads for the office door, stops, looks down and notices something on the carpet near the doorway. Hey Chino; what the hell is this on the floor; is it blood? Oh that! Yeah, that's Paco's blood; Mya tried to clean it up but it aint helping much. Dude; just get some new carpet; why your ass being so cheap. I thought it could be cleaned up but- Chino; get some new carpet bro; don't explain! I'm out; see you next week! Alright mane!

Mya it was good to see you again baby. Good to see you too; Derek! Ok you take it easy and tell cheap ass Chino to get some new carpet; that blood stain aint coming up! Thank you for saying that; I tried to tell his cheap ass! Ha-ha! I just told him too; maybe he will do it! I sure hope so D; have a good day! You too Mya; see you next week!

"Ohhhh it aint my fault!" "It aint my fault!" Alright Remy; let's get out of here baby; you like this song don't you? Hell yeah; this is my new shit! I hope Skillz got the cd! I'm sure he does baby; now step on the gas and keep it moving. Why you rushing D! Why you think Remy? Oh yeah! Vroom-Vroom! Errrrrr... Damn; baby; don't get a ticket! Shut up Derek and buckle up; I'm driving this Maserati!

Ring-Ring! Hello; this is LT! Hey LT; grab the Captain and you guys meet me in my office; the D.A is on the way over. Ok Chief; we'll be right there! Knock-Knock! Come on in Ma'am! Hello Chief! Hi Attorney Rollins; come in and have a seat; the Captain and LT will be here in a sec. Ok great; how are you today? I'm doing pretty good; I'm excited about this case. I am too chief; it sounds like this could be a big one. It is Mrs. Rollins; it is. Knock-Knock! Hey Captain; LT; come in and join us. Hey Chief! Attorney Rollins! Alright guys; I'm here to see if you all have enough on this Sin City Seven to issue a warrant.

Chief I'm ready when you are! Ok Ma'am; right now I have an undercover agent from Cali working the case! He has provided us with a wealth of information so far. Right now we know of several properties that have been obtained through a hostile takeover; which involves several murders. Do you have any proof of those murders Chief? Not yet but we're working on it; the motive and evidence is there; we just need to link it all together. Ok and who is at the head of this Crime Organization? Well; if you look over here at the board Ma'am, I can show you who the players are. This guy at the very top is AC aka Andy Cooper; the General if you may. Right below him is Manny; his Captain or Capo. The five people on the third row are the Lieutenants and they all run their own squad of soldiers if you will. From the far left is Will, Duck, Nina, Denna and the last guy is Loon. What about their soldiers; you don't have any photos of them? No Ma'am; we're working on that too.

Right now Chief; all that I am hearing is circumstantial; there is not enough here to get any kind of warrant. Didn't you say that there was some property involved? Yes Ma'am! How about tax evasion, can we get them on that? We're close to working that angle Mrs. Rollins; I have a few detectives working on that. Ok, how's that going? It's going well; it's just taking us some time to go through all the paperwork. What kind of properties are we talking about here? Let's see; there's a Strip Club, Escort Service, Whore House, Adult Video Store and a Car lot. Really! Yes Ma'am!

It has to be some illegal narcotics in there somewhere; with all the strippers and prostitutes; don't you think Chief? Yes I do Mrs. Rollins! Good; I think you guys should implement the RICO act in this situation; if you do that we can build our case quicker and obtained that warrant. I agree with you 100 % Attorney Rollins, do you think it's anything there now that warrants one. I don't know Captain; you tell me; it's you guys case; you all have the evidence. You may want to look up the RICO act and compare what you have to what you need. You might get lucky!

Excuse me Chief! Yes LT! It says right here that we need to have at least two acts of racketeering before we can charge them with the RICO act. The acts listed are Murder, Gambling, Drug Trafficking, Extortion, Kidnapping, Arson, Robbery, Bribery, Counterfeiting, Theft, Fraud, Money Laundering, Murder-for-hire, Slavery and some corporate crimes. If all we need are two of those acts then we don't have far to go guys. You're right Chief; so make it happen! But if you want my advice; I would concentrate on getting AC on tape confessing to one of those acts; that would get the ball rolling. Do you have any wires in place?

No we don't Mrs. Rollins; just eye accounts. Chief this must be your first big case! You cannot run an efficient undercover operation without tapes Chief Espinoza. Ok; I'll take care of that Mrs. Rollins. Great; call me after you do because right now you don't have a case. Get me something! Yes Ma'am; we will take care of it! Ok; you gentlemen have a good day and good luck with this case; it can be big if you do it right.

Wow; we have our work cut out for us Chief. It's not as bad as you think Captain; we just need to prove that the Sin City Seven were responsible for the hits on the Delgato's, the tax evasion, money laundering, drug trafficking or just any combination of two acts. We have them on the hook; let's just keep working our leads. Ok Chief; I'm with you, just let me know what you need from me. I'm headed to lunch; you guys want something? No Captain; I'm good! How about you LT? No; I'm good sir. Alright; see you in a few gentlemen. Hey Chief; we really are close with the murder for hire because the motive is already there. Yeah you're right LT; let's hope the detectives can get the information. Maybe you should have your U.C take pictures also. That's a thought LT; I just might do that!

The base from Janet's; I Get Lonely; pulsated through the club speakers as Pink, Green, Yellow and Black lights; sliced through the smoked filled atmosphere. An at capacity crowd stood captivated while Thailand's new additions to Club Dolls mesmerized them from the Stage. Mystery and Rebel both whore bright yellow thongs which attracted even more attention from the capacity filled titty bar. Their thick silky black hair flowed effortlessly, under the cool air that blew from the vent just above the stage, during the sensual doubles routine they performed as Rebel twirled around the tall brass pole and Mystery worked the front of the stage, sensually massaging her perky D cup tanned breast.

"I get so lonely" "Can't let just anybody hold me." "You are the one that lives in me, my dear." "Want no one but" Hey Red; how are you doing honey? Rose; hey girl I haven't seen you in a few weeks; where have you been hiding woman? Just handling business hun; it's a big crowd in here tonight huh? Yeah; it's the weekend baby and there's a few conventions in town too; so- Well, this is what Sin City is all about right; Sex, Gambling and Drugs; what better place to enjoy it than here at The World Famous Dolls. Ha-ha! I couldn't have said it better myself Rose; what can I get you to drink babe? Hmm, give me a shot of 1800 and a bottle of that Cristal. I'm gone let my hair down and enjoy myself a little bit. Alright; go ahead now; did you want a VIP table too? Of course Honey! Cool; just take the Company one; it's already RSVP. Give this ticket to the bouncer and he'll let you in. Thanks Red; oh, phone Will and let him know I'm here; will you hun? No problem babe! Thanks a million!

Ring-Ring! Hello; what's up Red? Hey Rose is here; she's at the Company booth. Ok; thanks baby. You're welcome! "Gonna break it down, break it down, break it down" "Gonna break it down, break it down, break it down" Hey lady; take this bottle of Cristal over to Rose please; she's sitting at the Company V.I.P booth. Ok got you; did you get my order for table 9 yet? Yep; I'm finishing up your margarita now- and here you go! Thanks Red! Um-hmm!

"Alright ladies and gents, thank you for tipping the lovely Mystery and Rebel visiting us all the way from Bangkok!" "I'm your boy Dj Skillz; remember to tip the waitresses, dancers and the bartenders as well." "Now let's show some more love for the ladies from Thailand" "Coming at you with their second song; Let's Ride by Montell and Master P!"

Damn, it's some money in here tonight! Why you aint call me Red and told me to come in early girl? My bad Remy; I was too busy to think about calling somebody; what you having the regular? Nah; let me try something brown tonight. Ok; did you want whiskey, cognac, rum, bourbon? I don't know; just make me a good drink. Ha-ha! I'll fix you a Courvoisier on the rocks. What's that? It's a top shelf cognac. Cool, do your thing baby; oh this is my joint right here; let's ride! "Uhhhh, you like that huh?" "Remember me?" "Let's get rowdy!"

Remy what's up bitch? Aint shit; what's up with you Dylan? It's all good girl; damn I should have come in early; it's busy as hell in here. Me too; I was just telling Red that. Hey girl what's up! Hey Barbie; you looking all sexy; I like that hair cut child. Thanks Remy! Um-hmm; you're welcome. Here you go babe; one Courvoisier on the rocks. Oh snap; look at you, drinking something new; huh? You know I have to try something new, every now and then Dylan, you know how I do. Yeah, I see you been acting brand new since you got that pretty ass Maserati! Ha-ha! Aint it pretty girl! Remy, shut up your crazy ass. Don't be telling me to shut up Barbie; it is pretty! Anyway- Red can I have a glass of Pinot please? Sure; and what did you want Dylan? I'll have a double shot of Grey Goose! Ok coming up! "Let's ride" "All night" "I don't doubt it" "Your love is bout it, bout it" "And I'm so excited" "Girl, I wanna ride it" Oh shit Barbie; look who just came in. Who Dylan? Turn around Barbie!

Hey ladies! Hey Sam, Smiley; what you two doing here; you brought some more bitches from out of town? No Dylan; not this time. Wow; that's a first! Hey Red! Here's your wine and your goose Dylan. Thanks Red; come on Barbie let's go get some dances. We'll see you later Red. Ok girls! Hey fellas; what brings you guys back to Vegas; you got some new chics? Nah; we have some other business with AC and Will. Oh ok, Will's sitting at the Company V.I.P booth with Rose and I haven't seen AC tonight. Yeah it's no problem; we just spoke to him over phone. Great; did you two want anything to drink? Sure; send a bottle of Dom over. No problem Smiley; anything else? No that's it! Cool, it will be over shortly.

"Now baby was more than incredible" "She did her thing" "5'5" 146", swinging nothing but a G string" Damn, this is a surprise! What, a girl can't come visit her friend at his place of business? I'm just surprised that's all but I'm happy you came. Good; sit down and have a drink of Cristal with me. Sure pour me a glass; I can chill for a bit. If you're busy Will, you can come back later; I'll be here for a while. No it's fine; I'm expecting some people but they're not here yet. Are you sure; don't let me hold you up. Rose; pour the Cristal already baby. Ok, ok I'm pouring.

"Hell yeah; this is how you do it!" "We got the sexy Rebel and Mystery working the main stage for you!" "There's over 100 girls working the floor and V.I.P area!" "Guy's you can't go wrong with all this sexiness walking around up in here tonight!" "I'd like to give a shout out to all the people visiting Sin City; thank you for stopping by The World Famous Dolls." "Please enjoy yourself and remember; what goes on in Vegas; stays in Vegas!" "Alright coming back at you for their last set; let's give it up for the Thailand beauties; jamming to that Nicole Ray and Missy!"

"But uh anyway" "You can catch me any day" "Sippin Hennessy" "With Nicole Ray" Hey my friend! Sam; Smiley; when did you guys get here? We just walked in! Cool; you fellas know Rose don't you? Yes; hello Rose! Hi guys; sit down and join us. Yes of course; we have some Dom coming over. Great; now this is about to be a party. So AC told me that you guys found a spot in Puerto Rico. Yes; we found a nice building. What size is the building Sam? Maybe 8, 000 square feet, two levels. Oh really, was it a club before or what? Yes it was same kind of club that we want. The owner went bankrupt, uh, a few years ago. Smiley has photos for you to see. Ok cool! Here you go my friend; look here. Thanks Smiley. Yeah this is nice; needs some landscaping and little work on the inside but it will definitely work. Why are you guys looking at a building in Puerto Rico Will, are you trying to leave me already? No Rose; we're expanding Dolls to two more locations, that's all. Oh that's a great idea; it should be nice. Thanks Rose.

Here's your Dom Perignon, gentlemen! Thanks baby; here, this is for you! Aww, thank you so much Sam! You are welcome! Let's say we make toast to Puerto Rico! Let's not toast just yet Sam; we still need to get AC's approval first. But he is not here Will. No he isn't but we'll go in my office and call him after we finish our champagne; I'm sure he's going to approve it anyway. Just not this location; so why don't we toast to- say um, new beginnings. Ok, to new beginnings! Rose, Sam, Smiley and Will all held their glasses above the table, clinked the tips together and made their toast. "I got what you want (Got what you want)" "I got what you need (Got what you need)" "Can I get another Shot" "This time I'm a make it hot."

Hey Red; fix me a shot of goose real quick; me and Barbie have to get on stage in a few seconds! Damn, Dylan, you still get nervous from going on stage girl? Yeah bitch; hurry up! I'm coming, I'm coming! Barbie, don't leave me girl! I aint gone leave your crazy ass Dylan! Come on Red! "Ok guys, that's gonna do it for Rebel and Mystery, they will be available for table dances and V.I.P's after they freshen up for you." "Coming to the stage next jamming off of one of my favorites; Swing my way by K.P and Envyi!" "Let's welcome the gorgeous Dylan and Barbie to the stage" Here you go! Thanks Red! Dylan grabs her shot; turns it up and runs to the stage alongside Barbie; just as the song starts.

"Shorty swing my way" "You look so good to me" "Now would you please" "Swing my way" Damn; it is packed in this piece bruh; come on let's go to the V.I.P table. Hold on Loon; let's go tell Will we're here first. Duck I swear your ass is blind; look over at the V.I.P booth. You can't see Will and Rose over there. Man I wasn't even looking that way. Yeah whatever; Karen you might want to take your man to the eye doctor; that boy is blind. Leave my Duck alone Loon! Yeah whatever! Hey Red; what's poppin! Hey Loon; just mixing these drinks baby; how you been. I'm good girl; when are you gone holler at a brother. Don't you have a girlfriend Loon? I don't know what you're talking about Red; I'm single! That's not what I heard! Huh! What did you hear? You already know Loon, so stop it!

Nah, I was just messing with you; send us a couple of bottles of that Crissy over to the booth. Ok I got you player! Hey Red! Hey Duck; how you doing babe! Hi Karen! Hey Red; good to see you again. Good to see you too girl; did you guys want something besides the Crissy. No that's it. Ok, enjoy yourselves. Thanks Red! "Shorty swing my way" "You sure look good to me" "Now would you please" "Swing my way." Oh so yall was just gone have a party and not invite a brother! Loon; what's up boy! Aint shit Big Will, me and Duck and his ol lady just dropped by to get some drinks and check on that new deal. What up Sam, Smiley; yall fellas alright? Yeah my friend; how are you? Fantastic man; about to get my drink on and enjoy some of this adult entertainment Will got going on up in this joint.

Hey Rose; how you doing? I'm good Loon; thanks for asking. Yeah, so you and my partner are a couple now or something. You have to ask your partner that Lionel. Damn, no she didn't just use my government name like that. Ha-ha! Will what's up with your girl bruh? She's just messing with you Loon. I know that but that aint what I asked you. Man I didn't hear you ask me anything! Are you two dating; are yall a couple, is yall fucking? Was that clear? Man; mind your damn business! Yep, yall fucking; I know you Will, you can't hide nothing from me. Aint no need for yall to keep it a secret; hell, me and Denna aint no secret! Show your love player, I'm glad you got a woman. I was starting to get worried about your ass.

What! You heard me fool. Somebody fix this boy a drink; he's bugging.

What's up people! Hey Duck; hey Karen! I see you guys got a party going over here. Nah; just chilling man discussing this Puerto Rico project! Well; how's it looking? The place is nice Duck; we need to do some landscaping and some general work on the inside but it can work. Here look at the pictures, Sam has them right there. So when do we start on it? I still need to call AC and get the final word; I'm going to do that after we finish drinking our champagne. Ok that's cool! Yeah; this is a nice spot Will; we should make plenty of cheese over there boy. Hell yeah; I can't wait either Duck. Loon what you sweating them girls for; you better calm down before Denna put a bullet in your butt. Go to hell Will, that aint funny. Ha-ha!

"Oh boy; damn Dylan and Barbie are working that pole" "Come on fellas; pay the pussy bill!" "These ladies don't work for free in here now" "We got Dylan and Barbie coming back at you; dancing off of that Big Pun, Still not a player." We'll be back guys; come on Sam and Smiley; let's go call AC and close this deal. Alright Will; we'll just finish this Crissy for you. Loon; don't drink all my shit bruh! I won't; I'll leave you a glass. Loon smirks and shakes his head at Will. You need to stop tripping; we on the place Will; what's the problem!

"I don't wanna be a playa no more" "I'm not a playa I just crush a lot" "But Big Punisher, still got what you looking for" "For my thugs, for my thugs!" As the music pierce through the crowded club of patrons and naked beauties, Will and his colleagues from another country, slice cautiously through the smoke fill room and into his office. Have a seat fellas; I'll get Coop on the phone. Ring-Ring! Hello! Hey Coop; it's Will! What's up bruh; did Sam and Smiley make it? Yeah they're here now; I have you on speaker! Hey guys! Hello my friend, how are you? I'm good guys but I will be even better if you got some good news for me. Now tell me about this property in Puerto Rico. My friend; it is a nice building; 8,000 square feet, two levels and only needs minor work. Thanks Sam! Will; how does the photos look; is there much work to be done from what you can see? It looks good to me; we have to do some landscaping and some general work inside to fit our floor plan but it looks like a sure shot. Cool, thanks bruh.

Smiley you said that the previous owner went bankrupt; was that because of the economy there or from his own negligence. It was definitely negligent AC; this guy had gambling problem. Oh ok; I see. What about the girls there; are they receptive to stripping or will we have to ship in our own girls, Sam? The ladies are ok but I think a good mix would be; you know better. Some other girls and Puerto Rican girls too; this will be good for tourist and locals. Ok what about staff; will we need to bring in some Dj's and Bartenders to set the pace, Smiley? Yes that will be good idea; because we can train them your way. So how much is this building? It is $179,805.00, AC. Is that it? Yes! Alright; I say let's move forward; Sam call the agent over there and close the deal. Will have the agent contact you then wire them the payment in full, no financing. Alright Coop; I'm on it!

And one more thing Will! Yeah what's up! Tell Dylan and Barbie that I will be sending them to Puerto Rico for 6 months to help get this Club jumping; they can show those girls how to hustle the right way. Ok Boss; will do; who do you want to go in the Dj and Bartender spot? Send Tech for the Dj and find one of those part time night shift bartenders; I'm not sending Red no- where; we can't afford to be without her for six months. That's what's up; I'll handle that ASAP. When should I tell them to be ready? Let's shoot for the end of next month; we'll get the construction crew in there as soon as the deed is signed. Ok no problem! Great; you guys take it easy; go celebrate or something; I'll see you all later! Sam and Smiley; good job! AC; thanks my friend! Yep!

Pork sausage links; scrambled eggs with cheese and toast mixed with chronic smoke; smelled up the lavish kitchen downstairs at the Spanish Trails Mansion as Mo stood there naked; preparing breakfast. Hey baby! Baby! AC do you hear me? Coop walks out of the Master bedroom and stands over the stairway balcony in his ck1 boxers. Yeah I hear you woman; what you cooking; breakfast or dank? Breakfast baby; aint you hungry! I am, but I want some of that weed too; that skunk smelling up the house girl. Oh my bad baby but, I did roll a blunt for you too. I didn't know it was that strong though; you really can smell it over all this food. Yep; I'll be down in a minute, let me wash my face. Ok baby; I'll fix your plate. Cool; be down in a minute.

Monica's smooth brown skin; manicured nails and pedicure toes reflect off the onyx marble walls in the kitchen as she prepare their plates under the soft white fluorescent lights that beam from the 20 foot high ceilings. She places the plates atop of the onyx marble top island that sits in the center of the kitchen. Her foot prints appear and disappear on the smoke gray marble tile as she walks back and forth over the automatic temperature floor. Smack! Ouch! AC that hurt; why you smack butt so hard baby! That wasn't hard girl; I had to pop it though; you just look so sexy; all naked in the kitchen.

You're just saying that because you just got up and your dick is hard. Well; that's part of it; can you blame me? Let's eat AC; your horny ass. Alright; but I'm tapping that ass when we get done. Um-hmm; what you want to drink? I'll take one of those cold buds! Boy; it's too early to be drinking! Mo; you aint my momma; give me a damn beer! Alright-alright; you don't have to yell. Sometimes you can get slick at the mouth woman; so that's needed every now and then. Nigga don't act like that's some brand new shit. I've been this way ever since you met me. Yeah, you're right but its different now; you're living with me. How so

AC? Before; it was just at the office or a quick hook up here and there. But now I can't get rid of your crazy ass. You're always here; I have to put up with your mouth more than usual. So what you saying; you want me to leave? No baby; just don't have diarrhea of the mouth so much.

Coop; you know how I am; I'm not about to change. Mo; just turn it down a notch; that mouth can get on my nerves. Now don't say I didn't warn your stubborn ass. I'm not stubborn boy; you're the one stubborn! Damn; these sausage are good; what kind are these? Don't try and change the subject AC! Um; these eggs! Mo this is good baby; you need to eat yours before it gets cold. You think you're funny AC. Um; this is some good breakfast Mo; pass me that blunt. Here! Thank you baby; eat your food it's getting cold. You think you're so slick; don't you mister?

Coop places the blunt in his mouth; flicks the lighter and lights it as he looks at Mo while inhaling. I know you hear me AC; you better not start tripping on me; I aint Sabrina. He exhales the chronic smoke; pauses then looks at her. What's that supposed to mean? Just what I said; you aint gone be talking to me any kind of way. Girl, this weed done got you talking crazy, you don't want none of me woman. I aint scared of you Coop! Sin City Don, Boss, AC, whatever they call you. What you gone do if I bust you in the head; hit me nigga? Nope; Denna or Nina gone be the ones to handle that; I don't hit woman! Why; you scared?

Mo; eat your food; I know what you need! Bam! Girl is you crazy; throw something else! What I need AC! I know you better not throw no more food at me or I'm coming across this counter top. You aint gone do shit! Try me and I'll pull your ass across this island by them blonde micro braids! Bam! Ugh-Stop it! AC; let my hair go! Didn't I tell you not to throw anything else; Huh! Yes! Bring your naked ass over here! Cling! Cling! The food and plates crash to the floor as Monica's naked body slides across the onyx marble counter top. I'm sorry AC; I'm sorry. No; don't apologize; you were all bad a minute ago. Coop places his arms under hers then snatches her up off the counter top. I'm sorry baby; don't hurt me! Shut up Mo; turn your ass around! Ummmm, AC, ummmmm. AC; damn baby! Ummm, that shit feels good. Um-hmm; I told you I knew what your ass needed! Ummm, ummmm, ummmm. Mo lay bent over the counter; gripping the opposite side with both hands while Coop is stroking her from the back.

The right side of her face rest against the black marble; her back arch inward, ass up, now with both arms stretch out, one gripping the left side of the counter top, the other the right. Ummm, ummmm, ummmm. AC strokes her wet pussy from behind, over and over again as she moans louder and louder from every thrust. Ummm, ummm, ummm! You like this dick; don't you girl! Don't you! Yes! How much you like it bitch! What! You heard me; I said how much do you like it bitch! I like it baby; I like it! I can't hear you Mo! I like it AC, I like it! Ummm, ummm, umm. No, say I like it Daddy! Huh! You heard me girl! Ummmm, Ummmmm, Ummmm! Ohhhhh shit; ummmmm. Damn AC, ummmm! Say it! I like it, I like it!

Coop reaches down and grabs her by her braids and pulls them while he's stroking her. Ummmm, ummmm! Say it Mo! I LIKE IT DADDY! SAY IT AGAIN! I LIKE IT DADDY! Damn right; that's what I'm talking about. Ummm, ummmm, oh your cock feels so good in me. Ummmm, ummmm, I like it daddy! I like it! Fuck me Daddy; Fuck me! Yeah; whose your daddy now bitch! You Daddy, you! AC releases her braids; palms her butt cheeks while placing both thumbs in the crack of her ass. Oh my God; it feels so good Daddy. Ugghhhh! Uggggh! Oh shit; is that your- thumb in my ass daddy! Ummmm, ummm, ummmmm. You like that Mo! Oohhh hell yeah; don't stop! Ummm, ummmm, uhh, uhh, uhhh, uhhh, uhhh, uhh, UMMMMMMMMM! That's right; call me Daddy bitch! Uuuuhhhhhh; DADDY!

Hello this Pree; who this! Hey Dupree this is ILona. Hey playgirl; what's crackin? Can you bring me and Vicky some snow? How much you trying to spend playgirl? Ah, we have $600. Sure; where you girls at; the club? No we at our new place. New place; where is that playgirl. We are at Towers; in AC's old place. What you mean old place; where Coop at? He and Mo move to Mansion. Oh ok; that what's crackin; what time you want me to come through playgirl? Now please. Ok; I'll be there in about 30 minutes. Ok; thank you Dupree! You're welcome playgirl.

Vicky; where are you? Out here Lona; on the balcony! What are you doing out there? Tanning; it's some good sun today; you need to join me. No thank you; I'm not lying on the balcony naked; people can see you. So what; they never seen tits before! Vicky you are crazy. Yeah whatever; is he coming? Yes in 30 minutes. Cool! Knock-knock! Is that the door Lona? Yes! Well, are you answering it? No; you answer it! Why can't you Lona? I have to go to the bathroom; I've been holding it for an hour already. Ugh! You suck Lona! Vicky jumps up from the patio chair and runs to the door. Yes who is it?

Hello Ma'am, it's David the concierge; I have your welcome basket. Ok just a minute! Yes Ma'am. Hi David! Hello Vicky; I'm sorry did you want me to come back; I didn't mean to intrude. No; don't be silly; I'm only naked. You've seen tits and ass before; right David! Yes; of course. Good; you were making me; how you say- nervous; just looking at me like that. Oh; I'm sorry Vicky. Well; come in; what you got? It's just our new tenant welcome basket; there's some chocolate; a bottle of Cristal, shampoo, soap and bubble bath. Aww; thanks David! You're welcome Ma'am; have a nice evening and call me if you guys need anything. Great; I sure will! Who was it Vicky?

Just David; he dropped off a welcome basket. Really; let me see what's in it. Go ahead; it's in the kitchen; I'm going back to tan. It's some Champagne in here; did you want a glass Vicky? Sure; why not! I think I'm getting in the

Jacuzzi; come get in with me Vick. Not right now Lona, I need to stay out here a little longer. Well don't get sun burn; here's your champagne; I'll be inside. Knock-Knock! That must be Dupree; I'll be back Vicky don't come in here naked. Knock-knock! Who is it! Dupree! Come in; it's open. Hey playgirl; what's up. Hey Pree; thank you for coming. It's no problem ILona; this is what I do. Did you guys want me to split this up or leave it in one bag? One bag is fine!

Cool, I'll just leave it on the counter; where's your partner? Oh she's on the deck tanning. Tanning! Yes; why are you surprised? This is Vegas; it's like 120 degrees outside; she's going to burn up out there. I told her to be careful. Shit; that's crazy; I couldn't do it. She'll be ok, Dupree. I sure hope so; oh you got that $600? Oh yes; hold on; it's right over here in my purse. Sure; take your time. I see you got the Jacuzzi running; are you about to get in ILona? Yes I am; I'm not in to the tanning thing. See; you're a smart woman; that Vicky got issues. She's gone look like a pickled pig feet when she comes inside. Pickled pig feet; what is that? A pig feet playgirl; you never ate no pig feet? Eat; God no; are you serious; have you? Hell yeah playgirl;

with some Texas Pete hot sauce! That's good eating; playgirl.

I don't think I want to try any of that Dupree. You should ILona; you might like it. No I don't think so; here's your $600. Thanks playgirl; you guys have a good day and call me if you need me. Ok; thank you for coming. No problem; I'm always available 24 hours a day; remember that. Great; we will keep that in mind. Alright; later ILona!

Vicky; come do a line with me! Ok; give me a sec; I'm coming. ILona opens the baggie; pour some on the kitchen counter, separates it into two lines with her driver's license. Rolls up a twenty dollar bill, bends down over the counter; closes her left nostril with her left index finger; sticks the rolled up twenty in her nose then snorts her coke. Ahhhhh! This is good Vick! Oh yeah; watch out, let me try it. Here; use this twenty! I don't need that, watch out! Snort! Snort! Yessssssss! Get two more lines ready Lona; let's hit it again. Go ahead; do it Vick; the bag is by the stove; I have to stop the water in the Jacuzzi. I love Vegas Lona; I'm never leaving this place! ILona wipes her nose and walks over to the Jacuzzi then turns off the water then looks at Vicky. Me too!

September; 1998.

Good Morning Mick! Hello Mr. Cooper, where to today? I'm headed to Miami on some business; we need to stop by the Rio, to pick up my business partner first. Ok Sir; this is a nice place you have here. Thanks Mick; I would invite you in but I'm on a tight schedule. Oh it's ok Mr. Cooper that's fine. You're not taking any luggage Sir? Nah; it's just an overnight trip; I'll pick up a linen outfit on South Beach tomorrow before we head back. Man that must be nice; I've never been to South Beach before. It is Mick; you should go visit one day. Yeah maybe I will. Why maybe Mick; just do it. Pack some bags; get your girl and just go! That sounds great Mr. Cooper but I don't have a girl to take with me. Man you're kidding me right; why don't you have a woman Mick? I work all the time Sir. Bullshit Mick; you're not driving me around every day! Do you have another job or something?

Ummm, not really; just the same, but for another hotel! When did that happen Mick; I hired you to drive for me exclusive. Do you need any more money? No Sir; you pay me more than enough. I just have so much free time when I'm not driving you around. Well; if you need some more to do; I'm sure we can keep you busy Mick. Is that what you want to do? No Mr. Cooper; you don't have to do that; I'm fine. Alright man; just let me know; because it won't be a problem finding more work for you. Ok Sir; thanks! Yeah no problem but I'm calling Nina; so she can send you a date. It's too much pussy around here for you not to have a woman. But! I don't want to hear it Mick; it's a done deal. The limo turns off Tropicana blvd. then on to the Rio Casino lot.

Hey, just pull in front of the entrance; my friend is standing by the valet booth. Yes Sir! AC rolls the back window down as they come to a stop in front of the valet. Diego; what's up my man? AC; my friend; where you been? I wait an hour already! Get in man; I'm here now; how you been? I'm good amigo; ready for Miami. Me too brother! Hey Mick; head to the airport! Yes Sir; Mr. Cooper. So Diego; tell me about this Club your friend is selling. It is nice building; my friend is moving back to Brazil and wants to sell it. What's his name Diego; do I know him? His name is Angel but you don't know him my friend. Is he in the business? Nah; just the club; this guy don't have guts for our business. Him like a little pussy cat; he loves the girls too much. He never even shoot gun before. Damn; really! Yes man; but a good guy he is; good guy.

Ok that's what's up; I'm looking forward to this trip; this would be a good addition to my company. Yes my friend; Miami has good money; sex, drugs and all the pussy you want; just like Vegas! Not like Vegas Diego; Miami has beaches; we have the damn desert but I understand what you mean brother. Enough about Miami; how's the business in Vegas my friend. Oh; I'm on top of the world Diego; those lawyers of yours really got us in the game. Hell; we can buy two fucking Casino's if we wanted brother! Yes; crime pays well my friend, crime pays well.

Mick; make this right up here and go to the private strip! Yes Mr. Cooper. Diego; wait until you see this Phoenix man; I had to have it. Every- since I rode in your helicopter; I've been wanting me a Jet. Yes the chopper is nice; you can have it if you want amigo. I have a jet now Diego; I don't need one. AC; you'll always need a Chopper; a jet can't go where a chopper can. You can have mine amigo; I have another. Thanks Diego! No problem amigo. Mick slows down as he approaches the private landing strip. Wow! Is that your Phoenix? Yeah Diego; aint that shit nice! Hell yes amigo! Mick; stop here! Yes sir. AC and Diego step out of the limo and walks over to the pearl white and royal blue business jet. Hello Sir; I'm Daniel your pilot; are you AC? Yes I am man; where's Miguel? He went to lunch sir! Ok cool; well are you gassed up and ready Daniel? I am Sir; Miami is the destination right? Yes it is. This is my friend Diego! Diego this is my pilot Daniel. How are you doing Diego? Good my friend; let's fly this baby! Ok; right this way Gentlemen! Hey Mick; I'll call you and let you know when to pick us up; take off for today. Ok Mr. Cooper and thanks!

All three guys made their way up the steps to the Phoenix. This is nice amigo; holy shit! Yeah; aint it Diego! Wow; I have to have one my friend. Hey; I'm sure Miguel can help you out brother. Good; I must see him when we get back from Miami. Alright Gentlemen; just make yourselves comfortable and I'll prepare us for take-off. Cool Daniel; we'll be back here relaxing brother. AC; I'm impressed my friend. Ring-Ring! Ring-Ring! Excuse me Diego; I have to take this. Sure amigo!

Hello! What up Coop! Hey Loon; what's crackin? I got that kamikaze in place man; just give me the word when you're ready. That's what's up Loon; I knew you could get the job done boy. Death before dishonor my nigga; you know how we do. For show playa; I'm about to head to Miami. Alright bruh; are you taking the jet? Yep! Cool; I'll talk to you when you get back then. Alright Loon; see you later.

"Hold on back there guys; we're taking off; we should be in Miami within the next three hours." As the Phoenix elevated away from Sin City and disappeared into the Sun Set; AC and Diego popped their first bottle of Cristal and lit a cigar while kicking back and relaxing in the plush butter leather seats.

I've been meaning to thank you my friend. Thank me for what Diego? You know; that idea you guys planned. Your welcome brother; we all are making more money because of it. That's right and that's only possible because of you AC. I'm glad we can be business partners; my net worth has tripled since you took over Sin City. You're welcome Diego; now drink your Cristal my brother. Besides; I'm sure you would have done the same for me; if you had to. At one time I wouldn't have AC but you have proved to be a great business man. Well I'm glad you're being honest Diego; and I'm also glad that you went along with the idea.

Sure; it was a no brainer; besides I didn't want to be at war with you my friend. I'm sure if I said no to the underground tunnels; you would have found another way to do it. Ha-ha! You think you know me; don't you Diego? No; I know a real business man when I see him; that's all my friend. Here; let's make toast to a great business relationship. Yes my brother; here's to good business!

Say bruh! Yes Sir; can I help you? Yeah; give me a Henn and coke and keep them coming too. No problem Sir! Thanks bruh, and where yo ho's at! Excuse me Sir! This a whore house aint it; where's the ho's! Oh we have to call them up Sir; so you can choose a date. No shit; that's how yall do it in Vegas! Hell; in Chicago them bitches on the track 24 7; half naked too! Here's your Henn and Coke. Thanks bruh; what's your name? Josh sir! Well call the bitches out Josh and whose the pimp in charge around this place? Denna turned away from the bar then looked up at the 6'4"; dark stranger who whore two long braids down to his shoulders and gold teeth across the front of his mouth. A long; Royal blue, silk shirt hung from his tall frame and over his black slacks that draped his Royal Blue, Mauri gators. That will be me; can I help you? Oh you the head bitch; how much you charge to suck my dick?

Excuse me! What; did I stutter or something? I said; how much you charge for head ho! I would love to slide my 12 inch cock down that pretty Latin throat of yours. Look buster; I'm not the one to play with. I run the joint; the girls will be up front in a minute; you can pay one of them to suck your dirty dick. I said I want you; you sexy ass motherfucker! Hey; get your hands off of me; unless you want to draw back nub! You're a feisty something; aint you! Josh; give me another drink bruh! Yes sir! What's your name Boss lady? Denna; what's yours? My friends call me Chicago Slim but you can call me Slim. Well Slim, the ladies are coming out now; take your pick!

Hold on a minute Denna; where are you going? Minding my business; and please stop touching me Slim. Josh; hold it down; I'll be right back. Sure Boss! The ladies walked up front and hung out in the lounge area so that they could mingle with the customers. Slim takes a seat at the bar then orders some more drinks. Keep them coming bruh! Yes Sir! When I came this way a few months ago Josh; there was a RV across the street with two fine broads working. Man I had a good time that night, how often do they come out this way Josh? Oh that was just an accident Sir; they were never supposed to be there in the first place. Why not Josh; it's a free country! Because they were interfering with our customers! Bruh; it's enough money to go around; besides it was only two girls and you guys got like 20 in this place. I don't see how they coulda harmed yalls business. Well, from my understanding; they were under cutting our prices; so they had to leave!

So you're telling me; those girls just left because yall said so! Nah; it wasn't that easy; Denna had to go over there and handle business. What do you mean by handle business bruh? See there was this guy over there with the girls; I guess he was their pimp. Boss lady sent word for them to leave but he wasn't trying to hear it! That guy had his mine made up; he was staying! I hear that; then what happened? Denna went and introduced herself then they left. Just like that; no fighting; fussing or nothing; Pimp just got his ho's and left? No it didn't go that easy but they went; well the girls did anyway. What do you mean by that Josh? Let's just say that when the RV left; the girls were the only people on it and there is one less pimp in the world. Damn; what happened to him bruh! Last I heard Slim; he was a part of the Mojave Desert. Get the Fuck outta here! I'm serious Slim! Who did him in; not Denna? Yep; the one and only; she's a bad girl man. Be careful how you talk to her; I've seen her put guys bigger than you to shame. Whatever bruh; this Chicago right here; home of the original Gangsters bruh!

I see you're still here; sitting at my bar. I thought you wanted a ho Slim? Slow your roll Denna; I aint the one. Excuse me; what did you say Slim? Chicago stood up from the bar; pulled his right hand from his pocket then swung it up to Denna's head. Click! Yeah Bitch; that pimp you smoked in the RV; that was my cousin. His ho's told me you shot him too. Now your pretty little Latina ass is about to join him! Click-Click! Pow! Thump! Chicago Slims; Royal Blue, Silk shirt turned darker as he laid on the floor while his blood oozed from the buck shot holes; Josh left in his chest. Good job Josh; that's how you get rid of a problem. Now put that gun down and come around here; quick, help move his body.

Yes Ma'am; I'm coming! Several of the Girls stood at the edge of the bar in aww. As Josh and Denna; picked up Slim's lifeless body and took it through the front door. Get back to work girls; aint nothing to see here! This is not the first time yall seen a dead body. We had to kill him; he was about to hold the place up! You guys should be happy; we caught him. Josh; open the door with your back and be careful. Yes Boss.

When you get outside; head around back. We're gone burry him right beside his stupid cousin. Yes Ma'am! Why are you calling me Ma'am so much? Are you nervous Josh; is this your first body? Yes Ma'am! Dammit Josh; don't call me that again. Ok Denna! That's more like it; drop his ass right here and go inside; I'll get security to finish. Josh laid Slim's body on the red desert floor, held his head down and walked back inside. Josh! Yes Denna! Good job, keep your head up; you did good man; don't go getting soft on me now! I won't Denna!

What's up Chief? Detective Ricky; how are you? I'm good Chief! Well, I'm glad to hear that, come in and have a seat; where are Casey and Briggs? They were right behind me Sir. Ok we'll wait on them; so did you find anything that we could use on that surveillance tape? I didn't see anything out of the ordinary Chief and I watched that thing at least 10 times. Damn, that's too bad. Hey Chief! Briggs, Casey, have a seat we've been waiting on you. I'm sorry Chief; we stopped by the break room to grab some coffee. That's fine Briggs, have a seat and let's go over this case. Chief Espinoza stands up from his desk, walks around to the front of it and leans back against it while looking at the three Detectives.

Alright Briggs; whose names were on those property deeds for the Club, Store, Whore House and that Escort Agency? The Delgato's Chief! So; there weren't any changes in ownership and no new Corporation listed as owner? That's affirmative Chief! Thanks Casey! Good job Detectives; that gives AC motive to murder the Delgato Family. I went over the tax records and no taxes have been filed since the owners died. That means we have them on Tax Evasion too; right Chief? Yes Detective Ricky but we need one more charge to charge them with the RICO act. That is two charges Chief! Yes it is Briggs but Tax Evasion isn't a part of the Rico act. As it stands right now; we can only charge the Sin City Seven with the Murder-for-Hire. The only chances we have on sealing that RICO charge is to get them on Murder, Money Laundering, Robbery and Drug Trafficking.

But Chief Espinoza; if I'm not mistaking; we do have them on Robbery! How is that Briggs? Well, if we secure the indictment for the Murder-for-Hire then we got them on Robbery because the Delgato's were both murdered in a Bank Heist. Good work Briggs; that should do it; we just have to convince the D.A! We're getting close to bringing the Seven down; let's keep our ears and eyes open for anything else that we can use to bring them in. Ricky I want you to look into that Swap Meet murder over in North Town; I got the word that AC is running that place now too. Yes Chief; no problem! What about us Chief; is there anything else we can do? Yes Casey; you and Biggs can head back over to the Towers and start asking questions about AC and Manny. Let see what runs out of the bushes when we shake things up! Ok Chief; we're on it! Great work Detectives; go handle those new assignments and I'll call the D.A and let her know where we stand! Ok Sir; talk with you later! Roger that Detectives; be careful out there; these guys are pros! Yes Chief!

Ring-Ring! Ring-Ring! Hello; District Attorney Rollins office! Hi; this is Chief Espinoza; is Mrs. Rollins in? Sure Chief; hold on a second. Hi this is Mrs. Rollins! Hello Ma'am; this is Chief. Hey Espinoza; how can I help you? Well; we have evidence that AC had motive to murder the Delgato's Ma'am. What kind of evidence do you have Chief? He now owns and runs the day to day operations of all the Delgato businesses. It looks to be a hostile take-over Ma'am and from the looks of it; he's not finished. Okay that may work Chief, and why do you say that he's not finished? My undercover officer told me that he's almost 100% sure that Cooper was responsible for that Swap Meet murder over in North Town. How sure is he Chief? Word's on the street is; AC and his crew are running the place now. If that is true Espinoza; you guys really need to work fast; if this guy gets too far gone we may never catch him.

Yes I know Mrs. Rollins; I have my Detectives working some leads at the Towers and canvassing the Swap Meet. Good job Chief; keep me posted; the sooner you get me more information on that Swap Meet murder; the faster I can take this case to the judge for a warrant. Yes Ma'am; I'm on it! Great and Chief; did you get your U.C to wear a wire? Yes Ma'am but he doesn't have anything yet? Ok push him to get all he can; the more evidence we have, the better chance we got at putting this Sin City Seven away for good. Yes Ma'am and one more thing; we got Mr. Cooper on Tax evasion also! That's great, now we're really getting somewhere Chief. Thanks, Mrs. Rollins! You're welcome Chief; keep up the good work!

Ring-Ring! Ring-Ring! Yeah what's up! Hey Coop; how was the Miami trip bruh? It's was cool Loon; it's some fine ass girls down there boy! Damn; did you hit any of them? Nah; didn't have time; had to get back here to handle some other business. Well, are we adding a club in Miami? I'm not feeling Diego's friend; my gut is telling me to keep stepping; you dig. Go with your gut dawg; it aint failed you yet. No doubt; what's up with you though Loon? Oh check it; I'm throwing a little surprise get together for Denna and

Nina tonight, over at Club Ritz. That's what's up; what's the occasion? Coop; it's their birthday man! Damn; that is right! So are you coming? Of course man; what time? Around 9, playa! Cool; I'll be there Loon; I can't believe it's the 26 already. Yeah; this year is flying by. Yep I'll see you in a few hours Loon; it's 6 pm now; I'm headed to the Mansion to pick up Mo and change clothes. Alright AC; see you later bruh; I'm pulling up to the Towers now; to meet Los at the Ritz. That's what's up; see you in a few!

Hello Loon; how have you been? I'm good David; what's up with you playa? Just another evening at the Tower's; preparing for this busy weekend! Beep-Beep! I'll talk to you later Loon; let me take care of these patrons! Beep-Beep! Do your thing Dave! Beep-Beep! Several cars, trucks, taxi's and Limo's jammed the Towers entrance and Valet area as Loon entered the Towers. Loud music from the Restaurant band echoed through-out the lobby area while freshly grilled shrimp, steaks and onions created a mouth-watering aroma in the air. The evening was still young and the loud chatter from the row of bars and Restaurants that aligned the hallway in route to Club Ritz was filled with laughter and joy as Loon scrolled by. It's about time you got here fool; it's almost 7! Calm down Los; I'm here now baby; is everything set up? Yeah I got you guys the Deluxe V.I.P. Section, 8 bottles of Cristal, 3 bottles of Moet and 4 bottles of Dom P! My man; good looking out! No problem Loon; just have my $300 fool. I got you bruh; I got you; stop tripping. I'll be at the door all night long; come see me. Carlos; you know what! Loon stops just inside the Club entrance; reaches in his front pants pocket; pulls out a bank roll and peels off 5 one hundred dollar bills. Here you go bruh; thanks for hooking a brother up. Shhhiiiitttt; you're alright with me fool! Let me know if you need anything else! You're welcome Carlos; now let me go make sure this table is right. Cool, go handle your business.

Hey Pierre! Loon; what's up bro! Hey dawg; I'm throwing a surprise party for my ol lady tonight. Los said my table was ready. Yeah it is; follow me; it's just over here. Damn; yall hooked this shit up boy! Loon you know I had to look out for my partner. Hey; I appreciate it man; she's going to love this. You're welcome Loon; I threw in three waitresses too; just make sure you guys take care of them. Thanks Pierre; and you know we will! Cool; that's all I ask; so go ahead and do your thing bro. I need to make sure all my people are in place; doors open in an hour. For sure man; appreciate it!

As the lights dimmed; the chrome poles that held the red Velvet rope; glimmered under the strobe lights while the music funneled in through the huge speakers that sat mounted on the wall. 8 huge round tables, covered with red crushed velvet cloths, held several platinum buckets of Champagne on ice and tall Crystal glasses. The cool air that blew from the ac vent above swayed the white silk curtains that hung flawlessly behind the V.I.P. section. Loon took a seat in one of the huge, white plush leather chairs that surrounded his section. Now 15 minutes pass 8pm; crowds of patrons poured inside, surrounded the bar and began filtering their way through Club Ritz while some occupied the other V.I.P. sections. Amidst the crowd; Loon spotted Manny, Sophia, Duck, Karen, Rose and Will walking towards him with gifts in hand, as he sat there under the flashing lights while sitting on the edge of the white leather chair.

Loon; this looks nice babe! Thanks Sophie; how you been? I'm good; thanks for asking. What's up Loon! Hey Manny; I'm glad you guys could make it bruh. Come on man; you know we support family. Where did you want us to put these gifts? This one is Denna's and the others for Nina. Just put them on the table Manny. Cool, got you. What's up my man; I see you got the V.I.P. all plush out! You know how I do Will; only the best bruh. Yes Sir; it looks good too. Thanks Will! Hey Loon. Hi Rose; you still hanging in there I see. Boy; don't make me pull out on you in this club; where should I put the girl's gifts? Ha-ha! You can place them on that table with the others Rose. Alright thanks.

Duck my nigga; what's up! I'm good Loon; we got the girl's some gifts. Where did you want them? Put them on the table bruh! Cool, no problem. Hey Karen baby; you can put them up there with the others. Ok Duck; I got it hun. So what time are the girls coming Loon? They're upstairs getting ready now at Nina's; it shouldn't be long Sophie. Oh I hear Nina's got a boyfriend now Manny; did you meet him yet? Nah Will; I think she said he was coming tonight. It's about time; hell this will be the first time that I've seen her with a guy. Nina's ass is always so secretive. You know how she is Duck; most guys can't even deal with her. Shit; you're right about that Loon!

"She was a Friend of mine, she left with my man" Oh yeah; this is my song baby! Sophie please don't sing; let Kelly Price sing; please baby. Shut up Manny! Ha-ha! What you laughing at Loon? You bruh! "She was a friend of mine; she used what she knew." "She lied, cheated and left me confused." The female patrons in the club, swayed back and forth as the song played while the guys seemed to be oblivious to the lyrics. Two well-dressed figures emerged from the crowd and made their way over to Loon and the other guest. Monica's voluptuous figure turned heads as she paraded through the crowd in her red fitted body suit, red stiletto heels and matching Diamond ear rings; necklace, watch, rings and bracelet. AC lead the way as she followed close behind while grasping the belt loop of his black slacks with her right index finger. His red Versace shirt and leather shoes; complimented her body suit and the silver and red gift wrapped boxes that he held under his right arm as they approached the crew.

What's up Gangsters! AC; what up bruh! Hey Loon; it's almost time to get this party started; where's the guest of honor? Still upstairs getting dressed Coop. Will; Capo; what's going on family? We good brother; you looking suave! Hey; Mo picked this out; and don't start Manny. It's tight though Boss; that's all I was gone say. Yeah, yeah; whatever! Ladies; you all are looking lovely tonight. Thanks AC! You're welcome Sophie! Monica where did you get that body suit girl? It is sexy as hell! Thanks Rose! You're welcome girl but you still didn't tell me where you got it. Ha-ha! OH; I got it over at Caesars Rose. Ok girl; I see how you want to be; you don't have to tell me; it looks good on you though. Mo takes a seat in one of the white leather chairs; cross her legs then run her fingers through her freshly bob cut hair doo then looks up at Rose. Thank you Rose, I'm glad you like it. Rose looked down at Monica then squint her eyes from the glare that the flashing lights caused as it bounced off Mo's Diamonds. Yeah; you're welcome. Will I need a drink; I'm going to the bar! Hold on Rose; just have the waitress get it. Fuck that; I'm walking; you coming? Nah go ahead baby! Alright Will; be back in a minute!

Wow; there are a lot of gifts up here! Yep; Nina and Denna are going to be so surprised; they think you invited us all to meet to celebrate the new club in Puerto Rico. Loon; your ass is crazy boy. Hey, I had to tell her something AC or I would have given it away. Well, they'll both like this celebration, just two days before their birthday. Damn Coop; I thought it was tomorrow, not in two days. No Loon; it's on the 24th bruh; not the 25th. Ha-ha! Good thing I planned this huh? Yep, good thing! Will what's up with your woman? What are you talking about Mo? She has an attitude with me or something. Monica you need to check yourself. What; check yourself nigga! AC; get your boy! What's wrong Mo? This fool gone tell me to check myself! Will; what's she talking about? Bruh; she's coming at me like she's somebody special. Got the nerve to ask me what's wrong with Rose. Hell; Monica's the one acting like her shit don't stink! Is this true Mo? What! What he just said girl; that's what! AC I aint do nothing to Rose; that ho just mad because I wasn't paying her no attention when she was trying to talk to me. Damn Mo; you got something against Rose?

Fuck that sassy Bitch! AC and Will looks at one another with disbelief. Hold up Mo; why are you tripping on my girl; she didn't do anything to you. Well you need to tell her to play her position; walking around here like she's the Top Bitch. I'm the one sleeping with this nigga every night;

I'm the one who cooks for this man every day and suck his dick in the mornings. He's the Don of Sin City and I'm his woman; that makes me the Top Bitch. Check your girl Will! Wow; Coop I'm going to get a drink bruh; you got a problem my man. AC stands in between Monica and Will; shaking his head with his left hand covering his eyes. What; don't be shaking your head at me AC. Girl your behind is crazy; come here let me rub that fat ass. Mo smirks, laughs then walks over to AC and backs her ass up on him while he leans back against the white leather chair. Ha-ha! I aint crazy either nigga! Look; just tone it down for me; Rose is my biggest earner; I don't need your jealous ass messing my money up. I aint jealous AC! I just know what my eyes are telling me. Girl that's Will's ol lady; me and her are just business partners. Um-hm, that's all she better be.

Oh my God this is nice; what's up everybody; this is my friend Winston! Hey Nina; happy birthday sis! Thanks Sophie! Hey man; I'm AC; nice to meet you. I'm Winston; nice to meet you too man. This is Loon, Manny; my girl Monica, Duck and Karen and that's Sophie; Manny's wife. Hi Winston! Hello guys; nice to meet you all. So what's all this on the table Loon? It's presents sis; for you and Denna. Wow; did Denna know about this Loon? No; it's a surprise; where is she anyway? She's coming; she stopped by the gift shop to get some gum.

What's up sis; happy birthday! Thanks Duck! Happy Birthday honey! Aww, thank you Karen! Your welcome hun; where's Denna? Oh; she's on the way. Now filled to capacity, lights flashing, music blasted and patrons crowding the dance floor, Club Ritz had come to life. A tall silhouette appeared from the crowd and made her way towards the crew. Long black hair fell to her shoulders as the air conditioned breeze blew just a few strands across her pink lip glossed Latin lips. Denna's perfectly shaped body, only seemed to be a mannequin, as her soft pink dress, flowed around her frame, revealing her erect nipples and no panty line, as she walked closer towards them. Loon stood erect like a dear in head lights, tuning out the music, his friends and anything that didn't look like Denna. Her soft tan skin glistened of body oil as her toes sat perfectly in her open toe, soft pink heels with the walnut wooden bottom.

There she is; there's my baby. Damn Loon; calm down bruh; you act like you never seen Denna before. Will; mind your business. Hey baby; Happy Birthday; damn you're looking fine as all out doors gurl. Thanks baby; I see I'm the last one here. Hi everybody! Hey Denna! Happy Birthday! Aww; thank you guys! Nina grabbed her sister by the hand then helped her up the three V.I.P steps. Happy Birthday Sis; look at all the presents for us. Wow; for us! Yep; Loon planned it. Really! Yep! Aww, it's nice baby; thank you! You're welcome Denna; anything for my woman. Ok people; now that both the Birthday Girls are here; let's pop these bottles and drink some champagne to my baby and her sister Nina! AC stands up, grabs a bottle of Cristal; pops the cork, then makes a toast. Here's to our favorite sisters; Nina and Denna; Happy Birthday ladies! The others follow suit. Happy Birthday! Thanks you guys; now let's party!

"Alright party people; this is DJ Al on the mic; welcome to Club Ritz!" "I like to give a shout out to the Birthday Girls in the House tonight!" "Nina and Denna; this song is for you ladies; Happy Birthday!" "Alright yall; it's time to party in this mutha!" "It's DJ Al and this is that JUNIOR

M.A.F.I.A! that Playa's Anthem!" "Niggaz, Bitches." "Uhh" "Niggaz grab your dick if you love Hip Hop" "Bitches rub your titties if you love Big Poppa." Come on sis; let's dance girl! Hold on Nina; let me takes these shoes off. Hurry up chica, come on; rub your titties if you love Big Poppa! Denna left her shoes under the table then followed Nina on to the dance floor as the rest of the crew watched them and admired the love the sisters had for one another.

Loon and Winston, you two better go join them before someone else does. Manny; don't make me kill a fool in here tonight over my woman. I'm just saying Loon; get on your job brother. Winston bypassed Loon and Manny and joined Nina on the floor. Hey; hold up man; where you going! Ha-ha! Shit; he's doing the right thing; you need to be following him Loon. Come on AC; not you too! Alright then; suit yourself Lionel; don't say we didn't warn you knuckle head. Ok Coop, I'm going, I'm going.

Capo; you believe this guy? You know how Loon is Boss; he'll come around eventually. Yeah; I guess you're right. Damn where's Will; he's been gone a while? He went to the bar with Rose Manny. Oh ok; I wonder how long those two are going to last. Aint no telling bro; Will never stays with one chick too long. I think he likes Rose though AC. What does that mean; his ass liked the last three women he was with too. Ha-ha! Yep, we'll just have to see; want we Coop? Yeah; enough about that shit; how's our books looking Capo? We're good man; there's an extra 2 Million dollars profit this month compared to this time last year. Come on baby let's dance. Hold on Mo; can't you see I'm talking to Manny. AC this is a party; stop talking about business for once. Yeah Manny; come on and dance with me honey. See Coop; Sophie agrees with me; so come on. AC and Manny looks at each other, smiles and shake their heads while following Monica and Rose to the dance floor.

Hey bartender, can I have a double shot of Bacardi please? Yes Ma'am, anything for you sir? Yeah man; fix me one of those flaming Dr. Peppers! Really Will; you're getting a flaming Dr. Pepper? Damn right; what's wrong with that Rose? Nothing; I just took you for a Vodka type of guy; not a flaming Dr. Pepper dude. Dude huh; what's that supposed to mean Rose? A big huge guy like you drinking a flaming drink is hilarious to me; is it even strong enough to give anybody a buzz? Ha-ha! You never had one

I see! Bartender; make that two Flaming Dr. Peppers! Yes Sir; coming right up! We'll see how much shit you talk, after you drink one Ms. Rose.

The bartender places two shot glasses on the counter top then fills them 3/4 way with amaretto then top them off with 151 proof rum. Will why is he putting 151 in the shot? Just wait and see Rose; then I want to hear what you have to say. Yeah whatever; it's still a sissy drink Will. The bartender places to empty ball glasses on the counter beside the filled shot glasses then sat the shot glasses inside the empty ball glasses. This looks stupid Will; why is he doing that? Rose, shut up and watch. Oh no; I don't drink beer, I've seen enough. Rose he's pouring the beer in the glass to level it off with the top of the shot glass. But why! Whoomp! Oh shit did he just set our drinks on fire? Yes Rose; that's why it's called a flaming Dr. Pepper. I'm not drinking that fire Will. No, you have to let it burn for a second then blow it out and drink it.

Ok big shot; go ahead, let me see you do it! Will blows out the fire over his flaming Dr. Pepper; picks it up and slams it back in one long gulp. Ahhhhh! That's good; try it Rose. Ok hold on; let me get my nerves right. You should blow that fire out now Rose. Ok; ok, hold on mister. She leans over the glass, blow out the fire, picks it up and slams it back just like Will. Whew! That was strong! It does taste like Dr. Pepper! See I told you woman; now let's go join the party. Ok, but if that bitch even looks at me wrong; I'm putting these size 8 Gucci pumps through her chest. Damn Rose; why are you so violent woman. Nah that's not it Will; I just don't tolerate no disrespect. Alright; I understand but she's not worth it. I don't know about you Will but I don't give a damn who she's fucking; I will do that child. Come on woman; let's just go to my place, this is not going to work. Now that's the best idea you've had all night sir. Lead the way; I'm right behind you.

Ring-Ring! Ring-Ring! Hello, thank you for calling Vegas Luxury Auto; please hold. Ring-Ring! Ring-Ring! Hello, thank you for calling Vegas Luxury Auto; please hold. Mr. Dubai! Yes Jackie! You have a call on line 1 and another on hold; line 2. Thanks Jackie! Hello this is Dubai, how may I help you? Hey Duck, this is Will, what's up playa? Hey bro; what's going on? I'm looking for AC is he still there? Yeah but he's in the conference room with that Detective Ricky chic. Ok, tell him that Dylan and Barbie are heading out for

Puerto Rico tomorrow. Ok Will; I'll let him know. Thanks Duck; be easy brother.

Across the hall from his office; Duck could see Coop and Amanda in a heated discussion through the glass window. Here Ricky; you need to take this money; I owe you this for being a good friend. I don't want it AC; I'm only telling you this now because we had a deal. Yeah we did Amanda and this is a token of my appreciation; you have to take it. I insist! Ok, how much is in the bag Cooper? Its $10,000 like before. This is too much money; I'm not feeling right about this. Hey it's yours; now what's going on with the Chief; is there anything new? Well, that's why I came here AC. Spit it out Ricky; is it bad. I'm afraid so Coop; we had a meeting a week or so ago. This case is about to go before the grand jury soon. Hold up Ricky; how the fuck is that possible? Apparently you didn't pay taxes on any of these businesses you own for one. For two; there's motive for murder in all three Delgato cases. What kind of motive Amanda? Chief Espinoza is calling it a hostile take-over and charging you and your crew with the RICO Act. What the fuck!

I hate to say this AC but you guys need a good lawyer. Chief and the D.A plan to charge you all with several murders, money laundering and murder for hire. The tax evasion case is separate from the RICO case. You will take the full hit in the tax case and all of you will be charged with the RICO act; that in itself carries a life sentence. This is some bullshit, that son of a bitch don't have any evidence on me! We have enough AC and the D.A seems to think so too; we're working on the final steps now. So how can we get out of this situation Ricky? Get a good lawyer Coop and hope for the best; I'll help you anyway I can but this case was in play before I signed on. Damn, this is some BS! I'm sorry to be the bearer of bad news, but you guys should really be careful from here on out. Thanks Ricky; I appreciate you telling me this; I'm in debt to you. Amanda stood up from the table, shook Coops hand then walked out of the room. AC got up then closed the door behind her, then paces back and forth for a few seconds, looks at his cell and dials Jerms number.

Yo this is J; what up! Cool J; what's poppin cuz? Who this; Coop? Yes sir! My man; how you? Bruh I need that lawyer we spoke about! Alright; when you need him playa? Like yesterday nigga; these fuckers done got a case on me and the crew. Damn; say word! Word J! Ok I'm meeting him for lunch anyway; I'll have him call you. Thanks J; what's his name? Oh; it's Dennis Baldwin. Cool, I'll be waiting for that call. Alright; later AC; hit me up after you speak with him. No doubt J; will do.

Knock-Knock! Yeah it's open! Hey bro; Will called for you. Oh yeah; what did he want? He said that Dylan and Barbie are leaving for the club in Puerto Rico tomorrow. Ok cool! Is everything ok Coop? Not really Duck; that Espinoza is about to present our case to the Grand Jury. Damn AC; that aint good brother. I know; tell me about it. Do you think the Grand Jury will indict? It looks that way Duck; but I have a bad ass lawyer from L.A that can make things happen. Why take that chance AC; let's put that Kamikaze in play. Damn; you're right Duck; get Loon on the phone! Hold on; I'll call his ass right now bro.

Ring-Ring! Hello; Adult Video store! Loon! Yeah; whose this? It's Duck knuckle head. Oh what up fool? AC's here with me and he wants you to make that Kamikaze call! Say no more; when and where? Hold on; I'll let AC tell you. Loon; it's time! I'm ready Coop; is that Espinoza still the mark? Yep, make it happen as soon as possible; they're close to getting us indicted. Say what; indicted! Hell nah; I aint going to the pokey for nobody. Make it happen then bruh! Don't worry Boss; it's a done dada!

October; 1998.

Ripe garbage pierced the air as Walt lay on the side walk just across from the Clark County Court House. Defendants, Witnesses, Citizens, Lawyers and Officers passed him by while walking to and from the large Pistachio Green building. News Vans, Police cars, Taxi cabs and Limos jammed curbside as they parked alongside the walkway in front of the 65, concrete steps, that led up to the House of Justice, which stood protected behind 12 huge concrete columns. His card board box, silver shopping cart and soiled clothes, fit comfortably amongst the trash cans and commercial dumpster that sat behind the city library which faced the court house entrance. Walt, now snug and camouflaged under his home made box condo, waited patiently for the opportune moment.

Hey Chief; do you have any news for me today, any good cases? Nothing right now Katie, but you will be the first person I call when I do. Awww, come on Chief Espinoza; you're not walking down these 65 steps for nothing. It's the middle of the day; I know you're working on something big. So come on; give a girl a clue. Mrs. Strong; please get that microphone and camera away from me. I told you that I had nothing and I don't. But Chief! Katie, don't push it now! Pow! Pow! Katie jumps at the sound of the live rounds then screams at the top of her voice. Oh my God, get down! Get down! Pow! Pow! Everybody down; Chief are you ok? Chief! Several officers ran up the steps to check on Chief Espinoza as the others continued to fire in the direction from which the shots came. As they got closer to the pile of card board boxes, Walt's warm breathless body lay still under his smelly clothes with a rifle tucked up under his corpse.

Chief! Chief; are you ok? Someone, go inside and get the paramedics! Hurry! I'm ok Katie; I just have a flesh wound; did you officer get the shooter? Yes Chief! Bring that motherfucker to me; now! He's dead Chief. Then get his I.D; who the hell was it? There wasn't an I.D Chief; he was a homeless guy. God dammit; fingerprint his ass then; I want answers. Yes Chief!

Hey are you getting all of this on camera? Yes Ma'am! Ok let's roll in 2 minutes! Katie don't you put this on the news! Chief I have to! Dammit Katie! Officer; get me out of here! Hurry! The officer helped Espinoza to his feet while making sure to hold pressure on the flesh wound in his right forearm. Ok; live in 5, 4, 3, 2, 1! "Hi this is Katie Strong with breaking news!" "Good afternoon Las Vegas; as you can see I'm live in front of the Clark County Court House." "Right here in this very spot where I'm standing; someone just attempted to take the life of our Police Chief; Espinoza." "Luckily the shooter only grazed the Chief's arm and he will be ok." "The Shooter however did not make it." "After the shots went off, several officers who were in the area, secured the shooter then fired several shots at him, bringing the culprit to his demise."

"We thank God that Chief Espinoza is going to be ok and that the officer caught the shooter." "Once again if you're just tuning in; Chief Espinoza has been shot but it is not serious." "He only has a flesh wound; the paramedics that are on staff here at the Court House are tending to him at the moment." "This is Katie Strong; live from the steps here at Clark County Court House." "I'll be right back after these messages." Ok camera man; let's walk down to the Van; we can do the next segment there. Yes Ma'am.

Hey Mick; turn that radio up please! Yes Mr. Cooper! "Hello we're back here at the Clark County Court House where someone attempted to take the life of Chief Espinoza." What the fuck does she mean attempted; I thought you said this guy was a sharp shooter Loon! That's what he told me AC! God dammit Loon!

"In other news; today is October 15th and the doors of the all new beautiful Bellagio Casino will open in just 3 hours." "I had a chance to take a tour of the place last night and it is just awesome; you guys have to see it." "This is Katie Strong and I will see you guys later today at 5 o'clock!" "Have a Good day Las Vegas!"

Mick; just stop here in front of the club and let us out. Yes Sir! Thanks Mick; go over to herbs and have them wash the limo too! Ok Mr. Cooper, no problem. Manny, Loon, let's go inside and talk this thing out; we need to put plan B in motion. We're right behind you AC!

Will greeted his boys at the door as they entered Club Dolls. What's up Fellas; I just watched the news; how in the hell did that fool miss! Wasn't he a damn sharp shooter? That's spilt milk now Big Will; let's go to the office so we can plan our next move. Coop; you guys go ahead; I'm gonna get a picture of beer. Did you all want something to eat? Yeah man; have the cook make some wings. Alright Manny; I'll be there in a minute. AC entered the office then took a seat behind the desk as Manny and Loon sat in the two chairs in front of it. Ok Capo; this damn Espinoza is really going to be coming after us hard now. Loon; you should have checked that guy out before you sent him on that damn mission. My bad Coop; dude said he was prior Army. Don't apologize; let's just fix this situation.

Coop opened the desk drawer and took a blunt from Will's stash, lit it then proceeded to inhale. Daammnn; this is some good smoke; you wanna hit Manny? Hell yeah bro! Ok hold up! AC; took one more long toke before he passed it to his Capo. Here- Thanks Boss! So here's the deal; we need to gather all the corrupt information we have on Espinoza and his crew; that includes the mother fucking politicians too. They wanna go to war with AC; then I'm going to give their ass a war! I already have the tape I bought off that Detective Ricky; Nina has the Judge and The Chief dead to rights with prostitution.

Is that going to be enough AC? I sure hope so Loon; if not I got 10 Million in bribe money set aside. Some damn body will take it. Here's the wings and beer fellas! Thanks Will! Yeah no problem, so what we come up with? I was just telling them that we have two options Will, give our lawyer all the corrupt information we have on the Chief and his crew or pay some body 10 Million to let us walk.

Damn bruh; you acting like you know we're going to lose. Loon if what Detective Ricky told me is true; we done lost brother. Well if that's the damn case AC; why in the hell are we still here in Vegas. Gas up that 20 Million Dollar Phoenix Jet and let's leave the damn country fool. I'm with Loon AC; let's just kick rocks player. What; and leave everything that we built behind! Will, you and Loon need to chill for a minute. Trust me soldiers; there's a way out of this mess. Do they have any witnesses Coop? From what I understand, they have a pretty solid one Manny.

That's who we need right there AC; that damn witness. Yep; you're right about that Loon. How about Ricky; do she know who the witness is Coop? No she don't Will. Knock-Knock! Knock-Knock! Who the hell is it? It's Fat Boy Will! Come in; it's open! Hey man here's my drop for the week.

What's up guys? What up Fat Boy! Aint much folk, about to trick off with some of these girls then I'm out of here. But here's a thick envelope; business is good on my side; yall be easy. You too man! AC, Manny, Loon and Will responded.

Ok this is how we're going to play this thing guys. Let's hold all the corrupt information until we see who the witness is. If it's somebody that we need to worry about then we make our move by offering up the 10 Mill or the corrupt officials. If it's some buster, that doesn't know shit, we'll have Hector dump on his ass that same day. Why can't we just dump on all they asses Coop. Because Loon; if they know something then we need to discredit their ass with the corruption info. And if that's the case, whoever it is will be law enforcement.

Now if that fool is a snitch; we handle that fucker by the street code. Give that fool a dirt nap, send a signal to the streets, you dig? That's how we handle that brother, do you understand now Loon? Yeah I got it! Cool! Now what if none of this works AC? It will work Loon, the odds are in our favor no matter which way the case goes. I sure hope you're right AC! Trust me Will; we got this, besides, this is just in case; we still don't know if we're even getting charged with anything. That sounds like a solid plan Coop but as your Capo I'm going to have Hector and the squad posted; just in case we need to make a break for it. Where are you going to post them at Manny? In the court house brother; Hector has people everywhere Boss. See; that's why I made your crazy ass Capo; give me some of that beer Will! Loon; go get some of those strippers and let's have a damn party; I need to see some ass and titties!

Dammit LT; it's been 13 days since I've been shot at and no one even has the first damn clue about the shooter. I'm sorry Chief! Well; did you all run his prints? Yes Chief but there was no criminal record. Run them again, this time try the Government data base. Yes Chief; I'm on it now.

Knock-Knock! Come in Captain; what is it? I was thinking Chief; that's probably some of the Sin City Seven's handy work. Why would you say that Captain; AC doesn't know that we're building a case on him. Are you sure about that Chief Espinoza? How would he? I don't know Chief but these criminals are pretty savvy these days. Well it's worth looking into! Do me a favor and expedite those prints we have from the shooter. LT's running them through the

Government data base. Call in a favor to the FBI; tell them we have a possible cop killer here. Yes Chief! If it is AC's work; this guy is more than likely prior military. Tell our friends at the FBI to check the Armed Services Data base first. No problem Chief; be back in a few. Thanks Captain; let me know as soon as you get a reply. I will Sir!

Espinoza gets up from his desk holding his wounded arm. Outside of his office he could see the LT and Captain chatting at the Lieutenants desk through his office window. Chief takes a seat on the corner of his gray steel desk and gazes at the bulletin board of photos. How are you feeling there Espinoza? A soft female voice startled him as it sounded from behind. Oh; hey Mrs. Rollins; I'm doing pretty good, it's just a flesh wound. Glad to hear that Chief! Yeah it could have been much worse. You're a lucky man Chief; did you get the name of the shooter yet? No Ma'am; Captain and LT are working on that now.

Do you have any idea who would want to see you dead Chief? Ha-ha! Probably 90% of the criminals in Sin City Ma'am! Wow; and I thought they hated me; the Prosecutor! Oh I'm certain they do Mrs. Rollins. Well it comes with the territory; huh Espinoza? Yes; I'm afraid so

Ma'am! Do you have any idea who it might be? Not really; the Captain was saying that it could be these guys. Who; the Sin City Seven up there? Yep! Hmmm, what does your gut tell you Chief? It feels the same as he does Mrs. Rollins. Then you should follow your gut Espinoza; do what you need to do! Get me all the evidence you have on this damn crew and I will make sure the judge signs a warrant for their arrest. No one shoots at an officer in Las Vegas and gets away with it! Yes Ma'am, and what about all the evidence we need for a RICO case?

I'll take care of that Chief; get me what you have; these criminals are going down! Are you sure we have enough Mrs. Rollins? I'll make it enough, now I expect those documents on my desk as soon as possible. Call your Detectives and tell them to bring you what they have! Ok; I will take care of it Ma'am. Excuse me Chief! Yes; what is it Captain. Your shooter name was Walter and he was a Vietnam Vet. God dammit; it was Cooper; I fucking knew it! Chief get me those documents; NOW! Yes Ma'am! Excuse me Captain! Oh sorry Ma'am! Attorney Rollins, storms out of the office angry and irate.

Chief we have a problem. Yes; we have a big problem Captain. No; you don't understand Chief. What don't I understand Captain? If AC ordered this hit; that means he knows something; which jeopardizes our case and your under-cover agent. I just spoke to my UC and their fine Captain. Well, we have a leak somewhere Chief; that's for damn sure. Then you better find it and plug it Captain because I am not about to lose this damn case. Do you understand me? Yes Chief! Good, now get out of my office; I need to think.

Espinoza leans back over his desk, pulls out the top center drawer and retrieves a hand full of darts. So, you want to shoot at me, huh Andy Cooper. Chief stood up then took five paces away from his desk then faced the bulletin board. Took a dart in his right hand then threw it at Coop's picture. Thump! This is my city, you thug. Thump! He threw another. Las Vegas aint big enough for both of us AC; you're going down punta. Thump! Three yellow darts now sat in the center of AC's photo as Espinoza continued to take out his frustrations. Thump! Yep, you and your squad are going down Cooper; mark my words. Thump!

Hello! Yeah I'm in the hallway Nina; which place is yours? Uhhh; the one that says Nina Sanchez! Oh ok! Winston; you're such a clown, hurry I've been waiting long enough. I'm coming sugar plum. Really; sugar plum? You have to find another name Winston; you're not gonna be calling me sugar plum. What's wrong with sugar plum Nina? I can see I have my work cut out! What do you mean by that? Meaning; I'm gone have to train your square behind. Nina's Town house door slowly opens then in walks Winston. Damn girl; this is a nice place you have here! Thanks Winston; come in and make yourself comfortable. The dark Vegas night illuminated by a rainbow of neon lights danced in Nina's panoramic window that overlooked Sin City from 46 stories up.

She gracefully walks towards her guest as the moon rays, mixed with flashing red and blue neon lights shimmers off her smooth Latin skin. Nina's Red satin robe swayed open as she walked; exposing her fit naked body to Winston. Umm; is all this for me woman? I can remember when we first met; you told me that I was too short. Shhhhh! Nina places her right pointer finger over her sexy thin lips to quiet him as she pushes the power button on her remote to turn on the sound system. A faint Cinnamon aroma fills the air as the music joins the romantic atmosphere she was now creating. You know; I've been thinking about this night all week Winston. Oh really? Ummm-hmmm. Haven't you been thinking about me too? Oh yeah but I had no idea you were this fine. Thanks Winston; was that a compliment? Baby it's the truth. Well sit down, take those clothes off.

Nina pushed him back towards the couch then straddled him once he fell down while unbuttoning his shirt. You're not scared; are you Winston? Ha-ha! Me scared! Yes? Of course not woman! Oh turn that up Nina, I love that song. Sure. "Hit me" "All the chronic in the world couldn't even mess with you." "You are the ultimate high, you know what I'm saying baby" "Now check this out." Damn Nina; you're looking sexy as hell tonight baby. Isn't this H-Town? Thank you baby and no; it's Jodeci. Oh shit; that's right; I knew that. Umm-hmmm.

"Take my money, My house and my car's" "For one hit of you, You can have it all, baby." Nina pulls off Winston's shirt then throws it on the floor behind her couch while he slips off his slacks. Ohhh! What's wrong Nina? Damn, big

313

things do come in little packages huh? This is all beef cake right her baby; now stand up and bring that pretty shaved pussy here, let me taste it. Nina rose to her feet, now standing up in her couch while her pussy sat right over Winston's forehead. He leans back, opens his mouth and sticks his tongue on the tip of her clitoris.

"I can't leave you alone" "You got me feenin" "(Got me going crazy)" I can't leave you alone" "You got me feenin" "Girl, I'm feenin' for you." Oh poppi; go slow poppi. Like this baby? Yeah that's it poppi. Winston stroked up and down her sugar walls; inside then out then back to the top. Uhhhhh. Yes poppi. Nina reaches down and grips the back of his head with both hands as he continues to sooth her soul and licks her funky emotions. Winston palms her firm left butt cheek with his right hand while massaging his dick with the other; all while sucking on her, now juicy, wet pussy.

"Spend my last dime" "(All of my Money)" "For a drop of your wine" "(And you know, oh)" Ummm. Your tongue feels so good poppi. Winston grabs Nina gently by her waist then guides her wet womb down on his 9 inch surprise. Tsssssssss, Ohhhh shittttttt, Winston. Ummm-hmmm. Ride this horse girl; come on you can do it. Nina bit her bottom lip as the veins popped out of her forehead. What's wrong baby? Am I too short for you now? Umm-umm! No words could exit her mouth, only moans and groans as he bounced her up and down his shaft. Ummmm, Ummmm, Ummmm. Nina groaned in unison every time she bounced up then back down. Whose dick is this Nina? Huh? I said; whose dick is this Nina? It's yours poppi! Wrong answer! Winston grips her waist a little tighter then shoved all nine inches inside her until her ass smacked his balls. Ugggghhhhh! Ohhhh poppi! I said whose dick is this? It's my dick poppi! Yes; say it again baby! Thisssss, isssss, myyyy, Dick poppi! Yeah baby; this is yours, all yours, now get up and turn around; let me hit it from the back.

Ok poppi! She jumps up then walks behind the couch as he follows. Nina bends over the couch while Winston lifts her satin robe and drapes it to the side then slides his black love in her throbbing vagina. Oh God! Hold on poppi; let me catch my breath first. Ugggh! I said hold on poppi! Shut up and take your dick woman, come on stop whining. Ugggh! Uggh! Uggh! Ugggh! Oh yeah; this is nice baby;

look at this juicy twat. Uggh! Uggh! Yeah; just how I like it girl! Winston stroked and stroked as she threw it back, in and out, in and out then back and forth they went. Ugggh! Ugggh! Ugggh! I'm Cuming poppi! I'm Cumin! Her juices flowed heavily on his Johnson while he continued to stroke as her body trembled and jerked from pure pleasure.

Ahhhh, that was good Nina; you're a little freak aren't you. Ha-ha. I am when I need to be poppi. That's just how I like it baby, a woman in the streets and a freak in the sheets. What do have to drink in here? I have some cold beers in the fridge. Great; can I have one? Sure; I'll be right back. Ok, take your time baby. Winston walks back around to the front of the couch to retrieve his slacks, reaches in the front pocket and pulls out a small purple baggie. This is really a nice place though Nina; I love that panoramic window overlooking Vegas. Thanks poppi!

Winston slides up to the coffee table then empties the white powder from the baggie on top. Here's your beer poppi; what are you doing? Oh; I'm about to do a line; did you want some? Nah; I don't snort poppi. Come on; don't tell me you never tried it! Nope; only weed. Well, you should try a line; I do it every day, it makes my day go by so smooth. He reaches in his wallet for a credit card then chops the cocaine repeatedly then separates the pile into two lines. Ok baby; this is mine and that's yours. Nah I don't think so! Just try it once Nina; if you don't like it; I'll never ask again. Alright just once; you go first! Sure just watch me.

Winston holds his finger over his right nostril, leans over the table then snorts up one line. Ahhhh! Yeah, just like that Nina; now come on, you try. She takes off her satin robe, kneels down beside him then leans over the table. Take your time baby, put one finger over your nostril then snort with the other. You're gonna love this high, I guarantee it! Ok, I can't believe I'm fucking doing this. Nina places a finger over her left nostril, leans over the line of cook then snorts away. Yeah, that's it baby, how do you feel? Thump! Oh shit; Nina get up! Nina; baby get up!

Hello, thank you for calling Angel's Escort's, which girl did you want to see this evening? Hey; is that ILona working? Yes see she is; when and where did you want to see her Sir? Umm, around 10 tonight; I'm over off Tropicana and Boulder Highway. Okay; I will be happy to book her for you; how much time did you want to spend? I was thinking an hour. Great; that will be $500 and she will be there at 10 pm sharp Sir. Ok thanks! Is this Phil? Yes is it; whose this? Hey Phil; this is Georgia; you just forgot about me when ILona started working; huh? Ha-ha! Well; I actually thought that you moved back to Atlanta; the last time we spoke you were thinking real heavy about moving back home. Oh I was drunk out of my mind that night Phil, but its ok I don't mind. Enjoy your date! Thanks Georgia! You're welcome!

Ring-Ring! Hello; ILona speaking! Hi Lona; this Georgia! Hi Georgia, how are you? I'm fine honey; you have a date at 10 pm tonight with Phil; one of the regulars. Oh ok; I remember Phil. Well, be ready around 9:30p pm; the driver will be downstairs at The Towers waiting at that time. Ok thanks Georgia! You're welcome and be sure to come straight to the office after your date so you can drop off your 50% split. 50; why 50? Because that's what the split is tonight honey. I think you're making a mistake Georgia; Nina always charges 40%. Well, I aint Nina; am I honey? No you're not! Glad you can see the difference; I will see you later Lona. Yeah ok! Click!

No that bitch did not just hang up on me! These damn girls are so spoiled. Ring-Ring! Hello; thanks for calling Angel's Escorts. Hey; is Nina there? No she's not, may I help you? Oh this is her sister Denna; do you know where she is. I called her mobile but I'm not getting an answer. Yeah; she went on a date with that Winston guy. Ok thanks Georgia; she must be getting her groove on; I'll call her tomorrow. You're welcome Denna.

Ring-Ring! Hello; thanks for calling Angel's Escorts; how may I help you? Hey Georgia; how are you doing? I'm fine and who is this? This is Will over at Dolls. Oh; Hi Will; how are you doing Big Sexy? I'm fine baby; I need you to put Rebel on your roster tonight; she wants to try Escorting. Ok no problem and who is this Rebel? She's one of the girls who moved down from Thailand last year. Umm; Thailand huh! Yep. Well, these perves are gonna love her honey; I'm putting her down now. Thanks Georgia. No problem, anything for you Big Sexy.

Ring-Ring! Thanks for calling Angel's Escorts; which girl did you want to see tonight? Hey this is Fat Boy; is this Nina? No it is not. Then who is it? It's Georgia; Mr. pop belly! Ha-ha! What's up Red Head? Nothing much just working; what are you calling here for? I need two of your girls over here at my detail shop. And what for? Why do you think Georgia! Listen pop belly; I don't won't no BS out of you. I am not sending our girls to no detail shop, car wash or whatever you call it over there Mr.! Come on Red head; its convicts 3oth birthday and I wanted to surprise him with some pussy. That boy been out of the pen 4 months already and I don't think he had no sweet essence yet! Ok, ok, I'll send this new girl Rebel from Thailand and Vicky from Germany. Thanks baby; I swear I will take good care of them. I know you will pop belly; it's gonna be $1800.00. Damn Georgia; why so damn much? Because I aint supposed to be doing this; that's why Fat Boy!

Hell; I don't see why not; I'm paying for pussy and they're whores. So that shit sounds right to me Red head. Yeah but you aint in no house or hotel; are you pop belly? Damn girl; alright just make sure they're here by 9:30 tonight. Ok; gotcha covered pop belly; later!

Hello; thanks for calling Dolls; how may I help you? Yes may I speak with Will please. Sure; please hold. Will line two! Yeah this is Will. Hey Big Sexy; I have your girl scheduled for a 9:30 call tonight make sure she's ready around 9. Where should the driver pick her up from? Oh she's over at the Towers with ILona and Vicky. Great that's perfect because she will be doing a double booking with Vicky tonight. Cool, good looking out Georgia; I really appreciate it. No problem honey, talk to you later.

Ring-Ring! Hello! May I speak with Vicky please? This is Vicky. Hi Vicky; Gerogia here! I'm calling to let you know that you and Rebel have a double call at 9:30 tonight. The driver will be there around 9 to pick you guys up; please be ready when he gets there. Ok thanks Georgia! You're welcome honey and make sure the driver brings both of you guys by the office to pay your 50% after the call. Wait; I thought it was 40%. No, tonight it's 50% hun; it's only 40% when Nina's working and I'm not Nina. Wow; ok I'm sorry I didn't know there was a difference. Well it is; let me know if that's a problem; I will be happy to send another girl in your place. No; it's no problem. Good; I didn't think so! Click!

The night was still young but it was evident that it would be a normal Thursday evening over at Angel's. Georgia lit her Virginia Slim cigarette; inhaled then brushed her red Shirley temple curls away from her freckled face as she gazed through the most recent Las Vegas Show Time Magazine. Ring-Ring! Oh my God this phone is ringing off the hook; I might need some more girls. Ring-Ring! Hello; thank you for calling Angel's Escorts; which girl would you like to see tonight. Hey is this Georgia? Yes it is and who may I ask is calling. No you may not! Excuse me! Listen Georgia; I don't know how you do things where you are from but we have rules that we go by. The next time one of my ladies call me; complaining about you raising your cut. It won't be my voice in your ear; it will be my foot. Hold up; who the hell- Did I tell you to speak bitch; just remember what the fuck I said. This is my business, not yours; I'm the Boss! Oh my God; I'm so sorry AC! Click! AC! AC, are you there?

November; 1998.

Ring-Ring! Ring-Ring! Hello; this is Chief Espinoza! Good Afternoon Chief; the judge signed the warrant! Yes; how long do we have to serve it Mrs. Rollins? You have thirty days Espinoza; so gather your people and start putting an arrest plan together. What are we charging them with Ma'am; if you don't mind me asking? We're charging AC with tax evasion and violation of the RICO Act; on the charges of Murder, Murder-for-Hire and Money laundering. What about the other 6 Ma'am? They're being charged for violating the RICO Act as well Chief. That's great dammit; we finally got them Mrs. Rollins! Don't start celebrating just yet Chief. I still have to try all of them in court. My advice to you is to keep this tight lipped and close to the vest as possible. You also may want to bring your Under Cover in for a debriefing so that they will be abreast of the situation.

I will call my UC as soon as we hang up Ma'am; can you come down to my office in the next hour to join the briefing? Yes of course; I can be there Chief. Thanks; I'll let the Captain and LT know, so that they can join us also. Alright sounds like a plan to me Chief; let's get the ball rolling. Great, see you in a few Ma'am.

Ring-Ring! Ring-Ring! Hello! Hey this is Espinoza! Hey Chief; what's going on? I called to tell you that we got the warrant and I will need you in my office in the next hour for your debriefing; it's time to bring these bastards in. Roger that Chief; see you one hour!

Hey LT! Yes Chief! Get in here! Alright give me a sec! Espinoza; now filled with excitement from the good news; stood in the door way of his office; over-looking the chaos that was going on in his precinct. Officers and criminals strolled through the hallways as the phones rang constantly while Detectives work their suspects for evidence as they sit in holding. Yeah Chief; what's up? We got the warrant; I just got off the phone with the D.A. You're kidding me right! Nope! Holy Shit; let's go get those Sin City Seven bastards. Hold tight LT; we have to do a briefing; the D.A will be here in an hour. Go tell the Captain he needs to join us and I will see you guys then. Ok Chief; no problem; we will be there sir! Yes! LT calm down; keep this thing quiet; remember who we're dealing with now; we don't need anything or anyone fucking this up. Oh sorry Chief; see you in a few. Yeah, see you in an hour LT.

A since of pride came over the Chief as he continued to stand in his doorway. He was just a few more steps away from getting his man. All the long man hours, hunches and sacrificing was about to pay off. Chief Espinoza was about to be the man that shut down the Criminal Enterprise of the infamous Sin City Seven. The thought of him placing AC in handcuffs; made his dick hard. He stood there day dreaming about the look that would be on AC, Manny, Loon, Will, Nina and Denna's faces the moment he brought them in. His heart races as he reach for the pack of cigarettes he kept in his top shirt pocket. I got here as fast as I could Chief! Damn man; you startled me! Oh I'm sorry; I drove over here right after we hung up. You didn't blow your cover did you? No; I was alone when you called. Ok cool; come in my office and have a seat, the D.A, LT and Captain should be here in a few minutes.

The Under Cover Agent followed Espinoza in the office then took a seat in front of his desk. So this is finally it, I'm happy it's coming to an end Chief; I miss my family. I know you do and I appreciate the sacrifice you made by going under cover and putting your life at risk. It's no problem; I was just doing my job. He sat patiently in the chair in front of the Chief's desk; legs crossed, foot shaking and sweating profusely. The white collar of his shirt was stained from sweat as he sat up to remove his black suit jacket to get more comfortable. Are you sure you're up for this? Oh I'm very sure Chief! Good; because the D.A will want to know everything you got.

Don't worry Sir; I've been waiting on this moment for a long time. Me too son, me too! Hey Chief; congratulations! Thanks Captain; you and LT, come in and have a seat! Sure! Cap and LT walk in and notices the stranger sitting in front of Chiefs desk. How are you doing sir? I'm fine LT. How are you young man? I'm fine Captain. Well Gentlemen; I see the gang is all here! Hi Mrs. Rollins; we're all waiting on you. I'm here now; so let's get started! The D.A shuts the office door behind her, walks over to the window to close the blinds then heads over to the bulletin board.

Ok officers; I'm sure Chief Espinoza has informed you that the judge signed the warrant for these seven individuals on this board behind me; one Andy 'AC' Cooper, Emanuel 'Manny' Ortega, Dubai 'Duck' Patel, Lionel 'Loon' Massey, Nina and Denna Sanchez and William 'Big Will' Tosi. Collectively known as the Sin City Seven; the Don or Boss of the Crew; AC will be separately charged with Tax Evasion in addition to violating the RICO Act for the charges of Murder, Murder-for-Hire and Money Laundering. The other six members will also be charged with violating the RICO Act; these charges carry a term of life in prison. Make no mistake officers; we tend to throw the book at these guys and put them away for a very long time. Chief do you have something you want to add? Yes Ma'am. Ok the floor is yours Chief.

Everyone; I like you to meet my Under Cover Agent; Mickey Bradshaw; upon my request he came to Las Vegas via the LAPD. Mick has successfully infiltrated AC and the Sin City Seven. He has been AC's personal driver for the past two years. Mick knows all there is to know about them and their operations. He knows locations and major players in the crime syndicate; it is because of this man's two year sacrifice; that this case, even exist. Without him we would be no-where. On behalf of the Clark County

District Attorney's office; let me say thank you for your service Mr. Bradshaw. You're welcome Ma'am but I was just doing my job. And a good job it was too son! Thanks Chief! Hey; we at the precinct thank you too Mick! You're welcome LT, Cap!

Alright Officers; we need to come up with a strategic plan to arrest all of these guys on the same day at the same time. We only have a month before the warrant runs out, so let's make it count! Mick is there a time when we can get all of them together at once? I think so Chief but let me double check; I should have an answer in a day or so. They usually gather up about every two months or so for some kind of celebration. Well you all work on that; I'm heading to court, I have a case to try! Alright Mrs. Rollins; I'll call you as soon as we have our plan in place. Thanks Chief and rest assure Mr. Bradshaw that your name will not appear on any documents in this case; I will have you listed as C.I, our confidential informant. Oh thanks Ma'am! Don't mention it; it's the least I could do Mick; later guys!

What you doing back in here Chocolate? Minding my damn business; you need to mind yours Candy; oh whoring ass! Hold up Choc; I know you're not still tripping over me and Loon! You damn right I am; you know we we're fucking around and you had to just try him out, huh? It wasn't even like that girl; he came on to me! So what; you could have said no bitch! Choc it's not even that serious; he doesn't give a damn about us anyway. All that nigga care about is the woman that's around there with him now. What woman! Denna that's who! When did she get here? Hell; I don't know; she was up front with him when I walked in a few minutes ago. See; that's some bull shit; he said that they weren't together anymore. Choc just forget about him; why are you tripping over Loon's ass anyway? Fuck you Candy; don't tell me about my business.

Don't get mad at me; I was just trying to look out for your dumb ass! Excuse me! You heard me Choc; old dumb bitch! Call me out my name one more time Candy and I will drag your skinny ass all over this damn video store! Bam! Candy slams her locker, stands up and walks over to Chocolate and looks her dead in her brown eyes. Old dumb ass BITCH! Wap! Wap! Thump! Candy falls back into the lockers from the two swift smacks; Choc delivers to the right side of her face. Oh no you didn't, you dumb bitch! Umm! Umm! Candy kicks at the air twice as Choc dodges her both times. Get up Candy; ol skinny ass ho! Umm! Umm! She kicks and misses again.

You don't want none of Choc; bitch! Ugh! Take that ho! Ahh! Candy groans from the kick Choc delivers to her ribs. Yeah stay your skinny ass down on the floor where you belong. You done lost your mind; tying to fight me, skinny ho. Candy remains on the floor curled up in a ball with her knees to her chest. You're lucky I like you Candy or I would cut your stupid ass. Chocolate looks down at her, shakes her head then walks back over to her locker. Candy reaches in her boot; jumps up from the floor then runs up behind her. Ugh! Ugh! Ugh! Three swift jabs later, Chocolate lay on the floor bleeding from her right kidney as Candy stands there, shaking the blood off her butcher knife. Now, whose stupid; dumb bitch! Oh my God, help me, someone help me! Shut up and die slow ho!

Hey what the fuck is going on in here? Denna, Loon, help me, help me, I'm bleeding! Candy what happened? Candy; do you hear me talking to you? What did you do? Candy looks at Loon as if nothing was coming out of his mouth. Everything was silent, his lips were moving but there was no sound. Candy looks around at the mess and Denna, leaning down over Choc trying to stop the bleeding with a white towel. Her vision began to get blurry and the room starts to shake. Candy! Candy! Candy! Loon shakes Candy repeatedly by her arms trying to wake her from her trans. Loon forget about her and call 911; this girl is losing too much blood; she's not going to make it; if we don't hurry! Ok, ok, I'm calling. Candy drops the bloody knife on the floor then runs out of the dressing room. Hold on Chocolate; help is on the way baby; Loon did you call them? Their on the way Denna!

Keep the pressure on Denna; I'm going to find Candy, so I can find out what happened. Ok, go ahead I got her! Loon exits the dressing room to find Candy sitting in the hallway on the floor in front of one of the peep show booths with her head down between her knees. Candy what the fuck just happened in there; you better hope that girl don't die. I'm sorry Loon but we were arguing over you and it just escalated. Over me; are you two stupid! Both you know that Denna is my woman; don't you repeat what you just said to anyone. Do you understand me! I said do you understand me Candy! Yeah, yeah I got it! Is she going to be ok? Yeah, soon as the medics get here; she's probably gone need a blood transfusion; you stabbed her in the kidney. Tears fell continuously from her eyes as she sat on the floor reliving the scene in her head. I'm sorry, I didn't mean to stab her; it just happened, she was kicking me and I had to defend myself. I understand that Candy but how come you stabbed her from behind if you was defending yourself?

I swear I was Loon; she was walking away and that's when I took the knife from my boot and stabbed her. I didn't mean too; I hope she's going to be ok. Hello! Hello is anyone here? Yeah back here Sir! Hi; we're responding to a stabbing call! Yes the victim is in the dressing room. Ok thanks; this way guys! The three paramedics rushed to Chocolate's side. Thanks for holding the pressure on her wound Ma'am; you can step aside now; we have it from here. Ok guys; you're welcome. Denna leaves the medics to attend to Choc's injuries then exits into the hallway to join Candy and Loon. What happened in there girl? They were just arguing Denna and it got out of hand. I wasn't talking to you Loon! What happened Candy?

It's like he said Denna; she was getting the best of me and I felt I had to defend myself; so I stabbed her. Damn;

do you always keep a butcher knife with you at work! Yep! Why; you don't even need it Candy! You girls dance behind a fucking glass for God's sake. Who do you have to protect yourself from in a fish tank all by yourself? People are crazy around this part of town Denna; you never know when someone might try you. I guess; well, I'm headed out to the Ranch Loon; please keep your crazy bitches in line. This is the last thing we need! Alright baby; call me when you get out there! Yeah of course, and get rid of that knife before the cops come. Oh shit; I'll see you later baby; let me go handle that! Loon jumps up from the floor and runs into the dressing room to retrieve the weapon.

Candy, get yourself together and fast honey; the cops will have some questions for your ass. Yes Ma'am! Denna looks down at her bloody hands, shakes her head and heads to the ladies room to clean up before she leaves for the Ranch. Ding! Ding! The bell over the entrance rings as customers walk in the store to meet their adult needs and fantasies. Candy, take this knife to my car and put it in the trunk, put it in a plastic bag first. Come on hurry; I have to help these customers. Ok, thank you Loon. Don't thank me yet girl; the cops haven't got here yet. Thank me if they leave without you. Alright Sir; we're taking her to UMC, so we can keep an eye on her during the blood transfusion. Ok fellas; thanks for getting here so fast. No problem man; just doing our duty!

Wow; what happened here; is she ok? Yes Sir; just a small incident; how can I help you today? I was looking for the latest Jasmine St. Clair flic, do you have any? Sure; Jasmine's flix are on isle 7. Thank you man! No problem sir; glad to help! Ring-Ring! Hello; thanks for calling Vegas Adult Video! Hey man; do you have any of those Heather Hunter Vagina's? Yes we do sir; they came in last week. Great; I'm on the way! Ok see you when you get here!

Hello Sir! Hi officers! I'm Detective Briggs and this is my partner Casey. We're responding to an assault call! Oh yes, we had an incident earlier with two of the girls but everything is taking care of now. Oh really; well let us decide if it's taking care of. Where's the Victim? She left about 30 minutes ago with the paramedics, they took her to UMC. Ok that's fine; we're glad she's ok; can we talk to the suspect? Excuse me Detective? You know the suspect; the one that stabbed the victim! Oh we don't know who did it; she got attacked from behind. Wait; hold on cowboy; you just said that two of the ladies had an altercation. Well that's what I thought until I asked the victim what happened. What exactly did she say? She said that she didn't see who stabbed her; they attacked from behind then took all her money. So now we have a robbery also? Yes detective!

You stick around Sir; we're going to question the victim; we'll be back to speak with you later. No problem detectives; I will be right here. Come on Briggs; let's head over to UMC. Right behind you partner.

Hey Mo! Yeah baby; what is it? Make sure you cook some extra steaks; Hector and Diego will be joining us too. Damn AC; how many niggas you got coming over. Just eight! Are you sure; it sounds like more to me. Nope; it's Manny, Duck, Loon, Will, Denna, Nina, Diego and Hector. That's eight and we make ten! Alright; I'll get started, what time are they coming? I told them to be here at 7. Damn Coop; it's 5:30 now! Then you better get down stairs and get to cooking. Yeah I'm going.

I'll be down in a minute; I need to shave. Oh are you coming to help me? I wasn't but I can if you need me too.

Nah, I'm good. Monica exits the master bedroom and heads downstairs to the kitchen. The sun rays beamed through the large windows and lit up the white leather furniture, marble tiled floors, Julius Caesar Statue and Stainless Steel Kitchen appliances.

Coop made his way downstairs then stood in front of the statue. Hey Mo; come here for a minute! What you want boy; I'm trying to cook. Just come here; I need to show you something before everyone gets here. Alright; I'm coming. AC pulls Caesar's arm down to open the elevator door to the vault. What is it now AC? Follow me! Why are we going to the vault Coop? Just shut your trap and come on. See; I'm burning your steak, keep acting up. You better not woman; I'll make you eat it too. Ok grab those two empty brief cases off the table. The vault was filled to capacity, every shelf was stacked to the ceiling and only a little room was left on the floor. Money was everywhere, even in the trash cans. Ok I got them, now what?

Give me one of them! Here you go! Thanks; now open yours and put 5 million dollars in it; I'm doing the same with mine. AC what is all of this money for; what are you up to? Nothing baby; this is bribe money. God damn nigga;

who in the hell are you trying to bribe; the President? Monica shut up and put the money in the brief case. I am but who are you bribing? Nobody yet; it's just in case we need it. Is there something you need to tell me AC? Yep, I got word that the LVMPD might be making a move on me. If that happens I may need to pay off some people; if and when that day comes, you give them these brief cases upon mine or my lawyer instructions. Do you understand? Yeah I got it. Good, and Mo, don't do anything stupid. Just hand over the loot; ok. Ok, I got it.

Hey hold your head up, what's wrong with you girl? Nothing; I just don't want you to leave me, that's all. I'm not going anywhere Monica; this is just a safety precaution. It's a damn big one AC. Aww, come here baby; give me a kiss. Stop it; I don't want a kiss, I'm going back upstairs. Ok, I'm gone hang down here for a bit, send Manny and them down when they get in. Sure no problem.

AC closed the brief cases then reaches under the table and pulls out a box of Cuban cigars. He gazes around the vault at some of the billions of dollars he had accumulated over the years as Boss of Vegas. A smiled dawn his face but inside he still felt empty. It was that reoccurring feeling that he couldn't shake. A whole as big as his fist pierced his heart, he could still see her face, smell her perfume, feel Sabrina's tender touch. But it was no match to the feeling that killed his soul, the very reason his heart was now so cold. Just to see them run to his arms and call his name whenever he came home. How was he to regain that Father Role once more; he just wanted his kids to call his place home. Hey Coop; where you at brother! Hey Capo, in here; I was just getting the Cubans out.

Oh yeah; it's been a long time since we all smoked on one of those. Yes it has Manny. Damn Boss; we need another vault don't we? The money comes faster than the lawyers can wash it Capo and Ducks car lot aint even hiding 20% of it! Well, I'll look into some other methods tomorrow; see what I can come up with. Thanks Capo; how's the family? Everyone is good man; thanks for asking. Yo; what yall fools doing down here! Hey Loon; what's up bruh? Shit; this damn vault! I'll be damn AC; is this all ours? Yes it is Loon and this aint all of it. Damn; I'm about to go find me one of these Mansions too; fuck that apartment bruh! Ha-ha! I'm not laughing Manny; I'm serious as a heart attack. I know you are Loon; that's why I'm laughing. Well, I'm calling Rose tomorrow don't she got a Real Estate connect or something like that? Yep and where is Denna? Oh she will be here in a minute; she went to pick up Nina. Cool; they need to hurry so we can have a meeting before Hector and Diego get here. Brothers; what's going on? Will, Duck, come join the party! Damn right; yall know yall can't start with-out us Coop! You know it; Death before Dishonor Will; we can't have it any other way. We're just waiting on the girls. Oh they were pulling up behind us AC! Great we can get this thing started then. What's up Manny? This paper Duck; look at it, isn't it pretty! Lord yes it is; wow is it all ours? Yes Sir!

I don't know about you Will, or you Duck but I'm buying me a Mansion tomorrow. Loon what in the hell are you going to do with that entire house? Man me and Denna are going to make babies to fill it up! Ha-ha! Ha-ha! Hey what are yall fools laughing at; there's gonna be some little Loon's and Denna's running around. Man you crazy; Denna aint having no babies boy! Yes she is Duck, how you gone tell me about my woman fool. Yeah, I'll believe it when I see it Loon. Ask her when she gets down here then Duck; if you don't believe me. Ask me what?

Oh hey Denna; this boyfriend of yours telling us that yall buying a mansion tomorrow and are going to have five babies to fill it up. Excuse me Duck, what did you say? I said; Loon- Hey girls, never mind that, come grab a Cuban, we've been waiting on yall. Thanks AC; hey fellas, it's good to see just the crew all together again without these outsiders. Yep and look at all this fucking money baby! Calm down Loon; it's only money poppi. You're lucky you're my lady Denna; that's the only reason I let you talk to me like that woman. Hey Will, hand me your lighter and pass this cutter around. AC places his cigar to his mouth, twirls it to let the flavor roll on his tongue and waits for the others to follow suit.

Alright, are you guys ready? Nope; hold on AC; I have to pop this Martel baby! Oh shit; I forgot to pull it out Manny. I got it brother, don't worry. Loon; give everyone a glass will you. Sure; no problem Manny; where they at? Look under the table man. Oh, I see them. Now we can make it official; Will, tap the bottom of the bottle baby, bless it for us. Tap! Pop! Manny tops off everyone's glass as AC passes the lighter. Sweet Cigar smoke filled the air as the seven held their glasses high while Coop begun to speak. Here's to our success and may we continue to be successful running Sin City, let no man come between us and no money tear us apart; it shall now and forever will be; Death before Dishonor! God dammit AC; I'll drink to that! We'll all drink to it Loon! Cheers!

Alright, here's what's on the table soldiers. I got 10 million set aside for bribe money; just in case that indictment comes down. I told Monica what to do if anything happens. All of you guys should be taking extra precautions around your people; I still don't know what kind of evidence they have or if they even have a witness. All Detective Ricky told me was that Espinoza was building a case and he had all of our photos on his bulletin board. Damn, why that fool got to come messing with our thing, can't we pay his butt off Coop? I wish it was that easy Duck but this guy is a hard ass.

Well, he probably knows that we were behind that attempted hit on him by now. I'm sure he does Will, that's why we need to have all our ducks in a row if they come knocking. I still say we get in the Jet and leave the damn country; look at all this money; we don't need no more Coop; we got plenty. We can never have too much money Loon! We got enough man; let's just do it. Calm down Loon; we may not even get charged with anything. Manny; those fools are going to charge us bruh, believe that shit. I say we just wait it out Coop and go by the plan we have in place. That's exactly how we are going to play it Nina, cool and in control, like always. Well that's enough of that BS, let's go upstairs and kick it; my baby got it smelling good up there with them steaks too. I sure hope Mo can cook AC; I can't stand no burnt steak bruh. Shut your ass up Loon; I'm gone make sure yours is charcoal. Come on Coop; don't play with my food man. Ha-ha! Bruh I'm just messing with you. Hey; you can die like that boy; a steak too! Loon; get your ass on the elevator. I'm coming Denna, I'm coming.

Hey Red; what's up girl? Hey Shooter; what you doing over here? Oh; me, Asia and Malibu have a meeting with Will; is he in? Yeah he's in the office. Ok thanks Red! You're welcome. Damn; where them ho's come from; I aint seen them in 3 weeks! Hey Remy; you know they've been working out of town. Shit; they ass need to stay gone; it's too many bitches in here already. Girl you crazy; what you drinking? Let me get a double of Crown baby and a Corona for Derek, he'll be inside in a minute. Ok, got you covered baby. Thanks Red! No problem Remy. Hey, my girl told me that Chocolate got cut up over at the Video store. Damn, not gangsta ass Choc! Yep, that's what I heard baby. Who did it? I don't know Red; they didn't tell me all that. Well, is she ok? From what I heard, she is. Good, I'm glad to hear that; here's your drinks baby. Thanks! What's up Red! Hey D; how you doing hun; Remy has your drink. Cool, appreciate that. Thank you baby! You know I got you white chocolate. Muah! Hey; yall two could have stayed home for that now. My bad Red; I was just giving my man some sugar. Yeah, um-hmm.

Knock-Knock! Come in; it's open. Hey Will! Hey girls come in and have a seat, close that door behind you. How's everyone doing today? Good! That's what's up, well; let me cut to the chase. I called this meeting to tell you all that I'm ending the check cashing gig. Why Will? Too much bull shit Shooter, and wherever there's BS the cops soon follow. So is this going to be our last week then? No Malibu, last week was your last week. It's done, over; it was good while it lasted, we all made some money and now it's time to end on a good note. Damn, so it's back to the stage huh boss? Yep, you and Asia are back on the schedule starting tonight Malibu. Damn, aint that a bitch! Calm down Malibu, it's not that serious girl. The hell it's not Asia; you may like shaking your ass but I don't. What time do we have to be on the floor Will? In one hour Malibu! I need some drinks; come on Asia we got time for a few shots. Take it easy Shooter; I'll see you around. Ok Malibu; take it easy girl. Come on Asia; let's go!

Shooter; Loon is expecting you at the store tomorrow, he said take tonight off. Thanks Will! You're welcome; did you want a drink before you leave? Yeah sure! Ok just tell Red; I'm paying for it. Alright thanks; I appreciate it. No problem. Ring-Ring! Hello! Hey Will; Rose is on line two. Thanks Red! Hey baby what's up? I was just calling to check on my man; how is business over at the skin factory? Ha-ha! Did you just say skin factory? Yeah, that's all I could think of. Was it funny? Nope, stick to hustling Rose, comedy is definitely not your thing. So did you miss me already big man? Yeah, a little. I miss you too. What are your plans for Thanksgiving Rose?

I don't know, I might bake a ham or something; why you ask? You should come with me to Manny's; we meet over there every year. Count me in baby; I would love to. Ring-Ring! Hold on Rose, my other line is ringing. No go ahead and take it baby; I'll call you later. Ok Rose, later. Hello! Will you have a girl up here name Candy; she said Loon sent her. What the hell are you talking about; Loon didn't tell me anything about a girl! Well, you want me to send her to your office or not? Hold her there for a minute; let me call Loon. I will call you back. Ok, got you.

Ring-Ring! Hello; Vegas Adult Video! Loon; who the hell is Candy? Oh shit; my bad Will; I meant to call you but I got busy. Well, who is she? That's the chic that stabbed Chocolate; she needs to lay low for a while. The po-po's want to question her. Damn; thanks for the heads up, can the bitch even dance bruh? Yeah man; she sexy and got some good head too! Bye man, next time give me some kind of a waning. Alright my bad Will! Yeah, yeah, bye. Ring-Ring! What's up Boss? Send her back! Cool! Hey baby; just go to the office; Will is waiting on you. Ok thank you. Um-hmm. Damn who was that pretty little bitch? Some girl name Candy that Loon sent over. Is she gonna be working here too? I have no idea Remy.

Excuse me! Yeah what's up Shooter? Can I have a Long Island; Will said he's paying for it. Sure baby; I can do that. Hey Shooter; how you been girl? I'm hanging in there Remy; how about you. Same here girl; and how is your girl Choc doing; I aint seen her in a minute. Choc is still in the hospital Remy. Really; I didn't know that; what's wrong? She got in to it with one of the girls at the store; the chic stabbed her in the back three times. Damn is she going to be ok? Yeah they gave her a blood transfusion and put her on bed rest for three weeks. I am so sorry to hear that; tell her I asked about her and I will be praying for her speedy recovery. Thanks Remy and I will make sure she gets your message. Alright Shooter; one Long Island Ice Tea! Thanks Red! Yep!

So you're Candy? Yes Sir! Call me Will baby. Yes Will. Can you dance? I think I do ok. I sure hope so; because if you can't; I'm sending you to work for Nina at Angel's Escort or with Denna out at Angelica's Ranch, that's where I send the ladies that can't dance. That way; all you have to do is lay on your back or get on your knees. You understand. Yep, loud and clear! Ok; here are my house rules. You have to be on the floor 15 minutes before your shift start to sign in with the Dj. Your hair, nails, make up and hygiene must be 100% at all times. All stage sets are three songs per girl. No fighting, no stealing and control your damn drugs and alcohol limit. If you break any of my rules; I will fine you or fire your ass. It all depends on how I'm feeling that day. Do you have any questions? No; I got it. Good, go see the house mom, she will give you four new out fits and two new pairs of shoes, one pair of heels and a pair of boots. That's just to get you started; I require all ladies to change at least four times during their shift.

So keep your wardrobe up to par and don't come to work in your damn slippers, pajamas or sweat pants. Always, always and I mean always come to work looking and smelling sexy. The same goes for when you leave. You got that Candy! Yes Will. Alright, get to work then.

"Happy Thanksgiving Las Vegas; this is Dj Glenn and I will be with you for the next two hours but I have to leave after that; got some good ol turkey, stuffing, greens and macaroni and cheese waiting for me at the crib. Baby if you're listening; I will be home soon!" "Right now Sin City,

I'm all yours, it's a nice 65 degrees out, the food is smelling up the kitchen and family and friends are gathered to celebrate another Holiday." "So without further a due, here's an all-time favorite, Happy Holidays to you by The Whispers"

Emanuel Junior! Yes Ma'am! Come here! I'm coming, hold on a minute. You see this Nina; he tells me to hold on a minute. These teenagers today; I tell you, they have molasses in their pants. Ha-ha! Sophie you're crazy girl. I'm serious, I'm not laughing. Yes Ma'am! Here; take these turkey wings to the garage so your father can deep fry them. Wow Sophie; he has gotten big, how old is he now girl? 18 Nina but he thinks he's my father. Damn, he's almost bigger than Manny. Yeah that's because he eats up everything in the house. Ok ladies; are you all ready to sample one of my sweet potato pies? Ummm, they smell good Monica! Thanks Denna, come on a try it. No, no, no, no desert until after dinner ladies. Come on Sophie! Nope, that's the way we do it in the Ortega household Mo; sorry.

Well I guess we have to wait Mo! Sorry Denna! Alright Sophie; your house, your rules baby! Thank you Monica, now can you give me a hand with this Macaroni? Sure no problem. I don't do much cooking girls, so I brought three bottles of wine. That's fine Rose, we can use some of that right now! Great, I have Merlot, Pinot and Chardonnay. Which one? Let's do the Merlot! You got it Nina! Oops hold on girls; Sophie is it ok? Sure Rose, a little wine never hurt nobody. Ha-ha! You heard her girls; where's your glasses. Hold on; I'll get them! Thanks Karen!

Here you go pop! Thanks junior! You're welcome. So big man; you're a senior now huh? Yes Uncle Duck. How are your grades? There ok! What's ok, junior? Huh? Answer your Uncle AC, junior, you're not deaf. I am pop! B's and C's Unc! That's cool but what happened to the A's? I'll tell you what happened; those fast little girls he's been sneaking over, that's the problem. Manny cut it out; you did the same thing when you were his age. Whatever Loon, mind your business and play pool. Will; do you believe this hypocrite getting on his son for doing the same thing he did. Loon; shut up and break already; you're just trying to put off this ass whipping.

See; now I have to run the table on that ass for your big mouth. Whatever; just break fool! So where's your homeboy Anthony; junior? Oh, he went to Miami for

Thanksgiving this year Uncle AC. Ok that's cool, have you two decided where you all are going to college? We're coming to work for you Unc! I don't know about that junior; I think your father has other plans for you. What's that Coop? Your son says that he and his friend Anthony wants to work for us. What kind of work do you think we do son? I know what yall do pop; I'm no slow leak. Ha-ha! AC do you hear this? Yep; that's your son. I don't mind Junior because a man has to make his own decisions and he also has to live with them. It's your mother that you have to worry about; if she's ok with it then I am too. Well Junior; I guess you and Anthony better start applying to colleges. Why you say that Unc; she won't mind. Nephew; I've known your mom forever; trust me junior; you're going to college. Man that's not fair; if I'm 18 I can make my own decisions. Ha-ha! AC, listen to him, all grown up now. I'm serious pop! I know you are son, go inside and get the seasoning for me.

Hey Duck; what's up with that special order man? It's on schedule Coop, will be delivered next month. Cool, that's what's up! So Will; you and Rose are kind of serious now I see. Yeah she's cool Manny, for now anyway. I think the chick got problems myself. Loon you think everybody got problems. She do Will, watch and see! Man you need to handle this ass whipping problem I'm giving you, 8 ball off the rail then corner pocket. Nigga if you make that shot; you can have all the money I got in my pocket right now. Ok bet it up; AC yall heard him right? Yep, we heard him!

What you waiting on Will, take the shot bruh. Just have my money ready Lionel! Will leans over the table, pulls back his cue then releases it on the que ball. The que taps the eight ball off of the far rail and banks it back down the left side of the table and into the left corner pocket. What! Give me my money- Damn Loon, you just got whipped brother, pay the man. I'm paying him AC; good shot man, you got me, here you go. Loon stands up, sticks both his hands in his pockets then empty them on the floor. Jingle-lingle-ling! What the fuck! Ha-ha! Loon you aint shit! There you go Will; 75 cent playa! Man, fuck you! Ha-ha! I said everything in my pockets! Ding-Dong! Ding-Dong! Bam-Bam! Bam-Bam! Who the hell is that, knocking on my garage door? Bam-Bam! Open up!

Ding-Dong! Junior, go answer the front door son! Yes Ma'am! The fellas leave the garage and enter the house with the ladies. Sophie was someone ringing the door-bell; they were just knocking on the garage door like crazy. Yeah junior went to answer it. Ding-Dong! Are yall expecting anybody else Manny? No, everyone is here AC. Fuck! What is it Coop? Mo, Rose, Sophie, Karen, go sit in the living room. Crew you know what it is. Click-Click! Simultaneously Nina, Will, Denna, Manny, Loon, Duck and AC reach for their weapons then head to the door. Junior; get upstairs, now! Ok pop!

Who is it? Emanuel Ortega this is Chief Espinoza; I have a warrant to enter your premises; we can do this the easy way or the hard way. Kiss my ass Chief! Is that you AC; come on and be smart about this thing man; I'm sure you guys are cocked and ready to fire on us but let me assure you that we are too. Well, I guess that means some of us are going to die this Thanksgiving day Chief; are you ready to die? I don't know about you but we are all prepared to go. You don't mean that Cooper; just tell your crew to put the guns down and you all come down to the precinct with us, post bail and you can get back to your Thanksgiving dinner.

You said you had warrants Espinoza? Yes I do Cooper! Read them to me; prove it! Ok one sec! Chief pulls the warrant from under his bullet proof vest. Ok it reads; This warrant is issued for the arrest of Andy 'AC' Cooper, Emanuel 'Manny' Ortega, Dubai 'Duck' Patel, Lionel 'Loon' Massey, Nina and Denna Sanchez and William 'Big Will' Tosi for violating the United States Rico Act. I also have a separate warrant for Andy 'AC' Cooper for Tax Evasion. So what do you say AC; lay down your guns and face your charges like a man. Coop looks at the crew, shakes his head to say yes and they all agree. Capo; get the lawyer on the phone and tell him to be ready to post bail. You guys put your guns in the closet, Mo come here baby! I'm coming baby, I'm coming. Come on AC open up, this is your last warning or we're breaking it down.

Hold your God damn horses Espinoza; we're coming out, unarmed. You got five minutes Cooper! Officer's; keep your weapons pointed at this door! Roger that Chief! What do you need me to do baby? Remember that bribe money we packed? Yes! Get it and keep it close, grab another 10 million for bail. Ok baby. And Mo; I want you to get your ass over to the mansion as soon as we leave. I don't know if they have a warrant to search it or not. Just make sure all of our valuables are locked in the vault with the money, can you handle that? Yeah I got you covered baby. Sophie! I'm right here hun. Keep Junior upstairs until we leave; we'll be back in a few hours, you girls finish dinner. Ok Manny.

Ok soldiers you know the routine; Death before Dishonor! When they get us in interrogation; don't say a damn word. Let's go; this punk ass Chief wants a war with us; let's give it to him. I'm gonna make sure this bastard never wears a police badge again. This is my fucking city! Manny you talk to our lawyer yet? Yep; he's taking the Jet here from L.A, he will be at the station in no less than two hours. Mo; make sure Rose and Karen; keep their damn traps shut. I got you covered baby, don't worry. Alright Chief; we're coming out; lower your guns; come on soldiers.

The energy and excitement over fills the precinct as the officers escorts the infamous Sin City Seven into their holding cells while the Chief meets with detectives Briggs and Casey, as well as LT and the Captain in his office. Ok Briggs; you and Casey take Loon, use interrogation room 1.

Captain; you and LT take room 2 and start with Duck. Roger that Chief; did you want us to get AC too? No Cap; he's all mine; you guys go try to shake the others up and see if we can get them to testify against AC before their lawyer gets here. Roger that Chief! Alright let's get to it; we don't have long people!

Ok officer; sit him down; you can take the cuffs off. Are you sure Detective Briggs? Yeah; we can handle it from here. Ok; I'll be outside the door if you need me. Thanks officer! So Mr. Lionel Massey; it looks like you're going to be going away for a long time Sir. Shit; as long as you will be there with me Briggs; it will be worth it. Damn; you got a fat ass! Bam! Casey slams her hand down on the table. Whoa, you're a feisty one, aint you. You watch your mouth Mr.! It's ok Casey; I can handle it, he's a pussy cat. So I guess she's the bad cop, huh Briggs?

Enough of the bullshit Loon! That is what they call you; right? Yep! What they call you Briggs; juicy? Ha-ha! You don't have any reason to be laughing buddy; we got your whole crew for murder and a ton of other charges. Oh really; is that right Casey? Yeah; she is right Loon. Man I don't have time for this crap, can I go now? The only place you are going is prison Mr.! Look Briggs; I don't know what you two are talking about. Oh yeah! Briggs places a folder on the table in front of Loon that held several crime scene photos. See these pictures; we know that you all are responsible for this bank robbery and the Delgato brother's murder. And these pictures, oh yeah; we know you all are responsible for these bodies too; the ones we found in these poor people's back yard. We ran the DNA on the bodies and guest what Loon? What Briggs?

Every last one of these people worked for the Delgato's! Who the hell is the Delagato's? Don't play stupid with me Lionel! He looks up away from the photos then at Briggs. Damn; I sure hate this happen to these folk but I can't help you. Mr. Massey we know that AC is responsible for all of this; all you have to do is testify to it and we will put a good word in for you with the D.A. Fuck you and your D.A, Casey; I want to speak with my Lawyer; get out of my face!

If you don't do this Loon; you're going away for a long time! Bitch didn't you hear me; I want to speak to my lawyer! Fine; suit yourself! Briggs jumps up from the table then follows Casey out of the room. Officer handcuff him and take him back to holding. Ok Detective.

Did you get anything detectives? No Chief; he lawyered up! Ok; get William next and press him hard and where the hell is Ricky? I don't know Chief; we haven't spoken to her today. Alright Casey, I'll call her; you guys go ahead and work on William. Yes Chief!

Mr. Dubai Patel! That's my name motherfucker. Look at this piece of shit LT; he thinks he's hard core. I see that Cap.! Listen to me Duck; I was going to offer you a deal but you can kiss my ass now. The Captain takes a seat across from Duck at the table then lay out the CSI photos. I don't want you to say a word Mr. Patel, just look at these pictures and know that we know. Yeah he's scared now Cap, look at him sweat. LT walks over to Ducks side then leans in close to his face. Dubai glances over the photos, looks across at the Captain then turn slowly towards the LT. Puh! You dirty bastard, you gone spit on me! I just did LT and I'll do it again, you bitch made nigga. God dammit! LT calm down; go outside and cool off! Yeah, take your chump ass outside, like your Captain said!

You just sealed your fate Mr. Patel; no deal for you son. Man forget your deal, I want my lawyer; you buster ass mark. Officer; take Mr. Dubai back to his cell. Ok Cap!

William Tosi; let's go! Man I aint going nowhere; I'm staying right here in this cell until my lawyer gets here. Detective Briggs, Casey you need to come over here. What is it officer? Your suspect refuses to leave the cell. Dammit; these bastards are starting to piss me off. Sit down Briggs; I'll handle it. Are you sure Casey? Yeah I got it. Casey walks over to the holding cell and stands beside the officer. We need to speak with you Mr. Tosi; about your charges. Lady you can speak to my lawyer, I'm gone lay my big ass right here on this bench and take a nap. Don't you want to know what you are charged with William? Nope but I'm ready to get back to that big Thanksgiving dinner that yall bitch asses interrupted. Now leave me the hell alone and speak to my lawyer when he gets here.

Casey what's going on over there? Tosi refuses to come out of the cell Chief; he lawyered up. Dammit, so we don't have anything this far? No we don't Chief. Shit, go question Emanuel, maybe he will talk. Ok chief!

Captain, are you ready for Denna Sanchez? Hold on officer; give us a minute. Ok sir. LT help me lay these pictures out on the table, I want them to be the first thing she sees when she walks in. Ok Captain; you think it will work? I sure hope so; we need something before we run out of time.

Over a dozen photos lay upon the desk, showing, the bodies of Bobby and Vinny, their cousin Victor, The bones of the bartender, House mom and Madam of the ranch from 1996. There even photos of Dolls, The Ranch, Vegas Luxury Auto and the building off Sahara blvd. where Angel's Escorts is located, The Adult Store and The Towers. You can bring her in now officer. Ok LT!

LT go stand by the wall behind her chair and I will sit here across from her. Don't say anything when she comes in; let's just watch her reaction. Roger that Cap. The door to the investigation room opens and in walks Denna. Immediately she surveys the room and notices the LT standing against the wall and the Captain sitting at the table. After accessing the situation she walks over to the table and gazes over the photos as she sits down. Her facial expression remained calm and unaffected from the pictures. Inside she grinned while looking at them because this was no way near the body count that they had accrued during the past three years. She knew she was dealing with amateurs who only thought they had something.

Yeah Ms. Sanchez; as you can see; we have you all dead to rights. This is your first and last chance to come clean. The person we really want is AC; if you testify to him being the Boss of this Sin City Seven and calling all the shots; we will give you a deal. This means you won't have to spend the rest of your life in prison. You don't have to answer right now; look over these pictures and think about what your future looks like. Me and the LT will step out for a few minutes and give you some time alone. When we come back; we expect an answer from you. This is the only chance you'll get Ms. Sanchez.

The Captain stood up and looked down at Denna to see if she understood. She looks up at him, places her handcuffed hands over the pictures, bit down on her bottom lip then looks back down at the photos. Good, you go ahead and think about it; we'll be back in three minutes; come on LT. They exited the room then waited outside with Chief Espinoza as they watched her through the two way mirror. So; do you think she's going to come clean Captain? I think we got her Chief; look at her; she's definitely thinking about it. I hope so, we need this. Ok we got 30 seconds left; come on LT; let's head back in. Right behind you Cap.

Well Ms. Sanchez; I hope you had enough time to think about your future and what you want! Cap sat back down across from her. LT walks over to her, leans down and starts talking in her ear. So is Andy 'AC' Cooper; head of the infamous Crime Family, known as the Sin City Seven? Denna looked over at him then turn back to face the Captain and reaches for a pen that lay on the table. Ok; that's a good idea Sanchez; here write your statement on this legal pad. You won't regret this. LT go get her something to drink; water or something. Ok Cap! Denna pulled the pad in front of her then starts writing slowly with her right hand while the cuffs gripped her wrist. The Captain anxiously awaited as she wrote her statement as the Chief nervously watches from the other side of the two way mirror. Denna places the pen on the pad then slid it back to the Captain. He slid the pen off the pad and began to read. "I WANT MY LAWYER; YOU PUSSY ASS PUNK!"

Bam! The Captain slams his hand on the desk, stands up and walks towards the exit then turns around to look at her one last time. Muah! Denna blows him a kiss while keeping a serious look on her face. Bam! He exits, slams the door and walks over to Chief Espinoza. Well; what did she say Cap? She lawyered up too Chief. Dammit; we only have two people left that can turn on him, we need someone to talk! I'm going to get some coffee, call me if anything changes. Ok Chief.

Emanuel Ortega, aka Manny; that's what they call you right? Yeah that's me; damn you got a fat ass, what's your name? Don't you worry about my name scum bag! Calm down Briggs; don't give him the pleasure. Oh ok; it's Briggs huh? This is not a game Mr. Ortega; you can kiss your wife and son good bye. You need to start talking or you will be going away for a very longtime. Knock-Knock! Yeah; what is it officer? The judge is about to do the bond hearing; I need all inmates; including yours detectives.

Aint this some BS! I'm sorry Detective Casey but I'm just doing my job. Well ladies, maybe next time huh? Shut up Ortega; get up and let's go! Ummm. Just in time for my wife's turkey dressing.

December; 1998.

"Good Morning Las Vegas; and Happy Holidays!" "I'm Katie Strong; reporting to you live; on this 8th day of December from the Clark County Courthouse." "Media from all around the State is here today for the arraignment of The Las Vegas Crime Syndicate known as the Sin City Seven. The organized crime group is believed to be ran by this man, whose picture is on your television screens to the left of me." "He goes by AC aka Andy Cooper; a military vet and entrepreneur who rose to power through a hostile takeover that he and his soldiers implemented against the now deceased Delgato Crime Family."

"The SC7 was indicted last month for violating the United States Rico act under charges of Murder, Murder-for-Hire and Money Laundering." "The Boss or Don of the crew has also been charged separately with charges of Tax Evasion." "Today; all seven of them are expected to enter a plea of Guilty or Not Guilty in this case." "Stay tuned as we will continue to bring you breaking news as the first day of this trial; get on its way." "I'm Katie Strong; this is your news at 11." "Have a good day Las Vegas."

Good Morning; District Attorney Rollins; how are you today? I'm fine judge; thanks for asking. You're welcome! Good Morning Attorney Baldwin; how are you today Sir.? Fine your honor! Great; are your clients ready to enter a plea? Yes your honor. Ok court is in session; will defendant William Tosi please stand? Good Morning Mr. Tosi; you are charged with violating the United States RICO act under the charges of Murder, Murder-for-Hire and Money Laundering; how do you plea? Not Guilty your honor. The Court recognizes that the Defendant; William Tosi has entered a plea of Not Guilty. You may be seated Mr. Tosi.

Will defendant Nina Sanchez please stand. Good Morning Miss Sanchez. Morning Judge. Miss Sanchez you are charged with violating the United States RICO act under charges of Murder, Murder-for-Hire and Money Laundering; how do you plea? Not Guilty, your honor. The court recognizes that the defendant has entered a plea of Not Guilty. You may be seated Miss Sanchez.

Will defendant Lionel Massey please stand. Good Morning Mr. Massey. What's up your honor! Mr. Massey, you have been charged with violating the United States RICO act under the charges of Murder, Murder-for-Hire and Money Laundering; how do you plea? Guilty; your honor! The court erupts with disbelief as cameras snap and mumbles became louder than usual. AC while sitting down at the defendants table; kicks Loon in his right ankle. Ouch! The court recognizes that the defendant entered a plea of Guilty. Guilty! Hold up your honor I said Not Guilty; you tripping! Are you sure Mr. Massey? Umm-umm. Attorney Baldwin clears his throat and stands. Your honor, my client wishes to change his plea to Not Guilty. Very well Attorney Baldwin; the court recognizes that defendant Lionel Massey has entered a plea of Not Guilty. You may be seated Mr. Massey.

Defendant Dubai Patel; please stand. Good Afternoon Mr. Patel. Afternoon Sir. Mr. Patel you are charged with violating the United States RICO Act under the charges of Murder, Murder-for-Hire and Money Laundering. How do you plea Mr. Patel? Not Guilty your honor. The court recognizes that the defendant Mr. Patel entered a plea of Not Guilty, you may be seated Mr. Patel.

Will defendant Denna Sanchez please stand. How are you today your honor? I'm fine Ms. Sanchez; thanks for asking. Your welcome your honor. Ms. Sanchez you are charged with violating the United States RICO Act under the charges of Murder, Murder-for-Hire and Money Laundering. How do you plea Ma'am? Not Guilty judge. The court recognizes that the defendant, Denna Sanchez, has entered a plea of Not Guilty.

Defendant Emanuel Ortega please stand. Good Afternoon Mr. Ortega; I see you're no longer working at the Towers sir. Afternoon your honor, no I left some time ago. Well it's good to see you again Mr. Ortega, just didn't think you would be in my courtroom. Good to see you too judge. Ortega you are charged with violating the United States RICO Act, how do you plea sir? Not Guilty your honor. Very well; the court recognizes that the defendant has entered a plea of Not Guilty.

Mr. Andy Cooper; please stand sir! Yes your honor. Mr. Cooper; you are here facing two charges today sir. The first one is a Tax Evasion charge; you may enter your plea here today for that charge but it will be transferred to the Feds. You also have been charged with violating the United States RICO Act under the charges of Murder, Murder-for-Hire and Money Laundering, how do you plea on the 1st charge of Tax Evasion? Not Guilty your honor. The court recognizes that the defendant has entered a plea of Not Guilty for the charge of Tax Evasion. How do you plea for the RICO Act charge Mr. Cooper? Not Guilty your honor. The court recognizes that the defendant has entered a plea of Not Guilty for the RICO Act charge.

Mrs. Rollins; does the prosecution have anything they want to say? Yes your honor; we ask that the court appoint us a December trial date. Attorney Baldwin; do you object? No your honor! Very well; trial will begin at 10:00 am; two weeks from today. Bam! The judge slams down his gavel to adjourn court session. Court is adjourned.

Loon what the fuck was you thinking? My bad Coop; I'm higher than a kite; I smoked a blunt before court this morning. Man you a fool, you need to be on your A game from now on. I'm sorry AC; it won't happen again. It better not! So what's the next move Baldwin? You guys should stay off the street and lay low Coop. Take this time to rehash everything from the past three years and make a mental note of anything that can help or hurt this case. Ok man we can do that! Great and I don't care what it is, just make sure I know. The last thing we need is any surprises; so think hard. Hey man, do you really think you can win this thing. Of course Mr. Patel, that's why I'm here; I'm the best that money can buy. I sure hope so buddy because if you can't, it's not gone be good for you bruh. Is that a threat Mr. Massey? No, a fact! AC places his right hand on Loons chest. Loon chill with that, come on yall, let's go to the Mansion and hash this thing out. Alright guys; talk it over and meet me at my downtown office Thursday morning. I should have the case files by then so we can see what the prosecution has. Ok Dennis; we'll be there man. Great; see you then AC.

"Good afternoon Las Vegas, this is Katie Strong." "I'm here on the courthouse steps, just leaving the court room." "All seven defendants have entered a plea of Not Guilty." "The first day of trial is two weeks from today at 10:00 am." "I will be here to relay all the news and to keep you up to date on this Epic Criminal case involving Las Vegas most notorious crime family; the Sin City Seven, whose leader Andy 'AC' Cooper was also charged separately with Tax Evasion; more to come on that as this case evolves." "Have a great afternoon Vegas and Happy Holidays; until next time; I'm Katie Strong."

Morning traffic crawled down Las Vegas Boulevard as AC, Manny and Loon turned onto Charleston Blvd in Coops Rover. Nina, Denna, Duck and Will followed close behind in Will's Tahoe, pulling onto the parking lot, of Attorney; Dennis Baldwin's Vegas office. The crew exits their vehicles and make their way to the one level, red brick building that sat nestled just off the North end of the strip; only a few blocks from the courthouse. AC, Manny, guys come in and have a seat in the conference room; I'm just getting back from the courthouse. I have the prosecution's documents. Take your time Baldwin, we aint in no hurry. Thanks Coop, there's some coffee and Danishes' in the break room if guys want any. Cool, appreciate that.

Well, I don't know about yall but I'm about to take him up on that offer. You guys want something? Yeah Loon, just bring enough for all of us. Damn Manny, get your ass up

369

and help me then fool. Alright I'm coming; you're such a pussy sometime Loon. Look Capo, I only have two hands; I'll get the Danish and you can get the coffee. Yeah, yeah whatever; just keep walking. A large maple wood table sat in the middle of the conference room, photos of past President's, dressed its walls. 8 chairs sat on either side while one sat at each end of the huge table. Stale piped tobacco filled the air, mixed with the aroma of fresh brewed coffee and hot apple cider.

Ok folks; I kind of glanced through these documents and it seems to me that the D.A is trying to hang her hat on several murders that she thinks are tied to you all. I know that much Dennis; what's the name of the witness they have? There's no name here AC, all it says is C.I which means confidential informant. Whoever that bastard is they can't hide forever. You're right about that; this person has to take the stand at the trial. Their entire case is built on them. Alright soldiers, I have lemon, cheese and raspberry Danish, who want what? Just sit them in the middle of the table Loon. We'll help ourselves. Ok Coop, what did I miss? Nothing bruh; we just talking about the witness! Oh yeah; who is it? Don't know yet Loon, they have it confidential. I don't like this AC; it's not too late to get on the Phoenix, and get the hell out dodge bro. Loon we aint running; this is our city. Ok I'm just saying.

Alright Baldwin; show me why we're paying you $35,000.00 a day. I'll be glad too, Mr. Cooper. I made each of you a copy of the case files; so we can go through them together. Once we're done, we can compare what they got against what they don't have. Anything that you guys can think of; that may hurt us during this trial; tell me now, right here, today! You sure you want to know it all Dennis? 100% sure Manny! Ok, but if it leaves this room Mr. Baldwin, you may not. May not what Denna? Leave this room Sir. I assure you Ms. Sanchez that whatever you all tell me, will go to the grave with me. I'll remember that Dennis; now let's get started.

Just one second Manny; let me grab a pen. AC! What's up Will? Turn to page two! What's on page two Will? These fuckers got Pharaoh and Monk's murders down here. You kidding; how could they have tied us to them? I don't know Coop; we need to find out who their damn witness is. Just relax guys, most of this case is circumstantial, that's why they turned into a RICO so they can pile on all the charges they can. Well take it from me Dennis; they aint got no kind of evidence on none of these charges brother. Let's not talk so fast Will; we still don't know what the witness has or who they are yet.

I don't know who in the hell it could be Capo, everyone checked out didn't they? Yep, there wasn't any leaks AC, our people on the payroll cleared everyone. Well, I guess we will know soon enough. Dennis; earn your money; take us through this document, page by page. Let's see what Espinoza thinks he got. Ok everyone, I want you to read page two and tell me if they can prove what it says, and if so, how and who?

The only way they can prove those murders are, if they were there when it happened. And I know for certain there's no evidence on Pharaoh's murder, I have the tape from the club. Not to mention they'll never find the body. So you can check that one off Dennis. Ok AC; are you sure? 100% sure man; what's next? This next charge is for the murders of the Delgato family. The D.A states that you ordered a hit on Vinny, Bobby and their cousin Victor so that you could take control over their business empire. How true is that Coop? The question you should be asking

Attorney Baldwin is; can they prove it. Well; can they? Man, I was nowhere near either of those murders.

That may be true AC but you do own all of their businesses. How are you going to explain that to the prosecution? I'm not; that's why I'm paying your ass; what else is on here? This is serious Mr. Cooper; it gives you motive to see the victims dead, the D.A will drive this point hard to the jury. I inherited the business Dennis; Vinny and Bobby hired me a few months before they died. That's how I came to own the businesses. No one else on the payroll had the balls to take it over; so I stepped up. Can you prove that in court? Hell yeah, they can check payroll if they want. Ok I can use that. Alright then; what other crimes are they charging us with?

It says here; that all of you were involved in Paco's murder. He's the guy that ran the North Las Vegas Swap Meet. Damn; how the fuck did they link that to us? It says here Manny, that the C.I reported this to the Chief. Loon stands up then addresses the room. We need to find out who this informant is; this guy can sink us! So, can they prove this, guys? With this damn informant on their said; aint no damn telling what they can prove Dennis! I agree

AC but that's why we're here now to see what they can prove based on what you guys know. From the looks of this document, our chances are looking slim; even if they ain't proven shit. Be honest with me Dennis; can you get us out of this mess or do we have to handle this thing our way? I can handle it AC; let's just get through this document first and figure out our defense after that. Ok man; continue.

Duck; they have the car lot down here for money laundering. Yeah I see this bullshit. The only way that they can charge you with this, is to go through your accounts and find some discrepancies. Did anyone come by the lot and audit your books? No, not that I know of! Well, in order for them to charge you, they had to find something. Alright; I'll ask my employees if anyone came by asking questions. Ok Duck; as soon as you find out; let me know. We have trial next week. This isn't looking good AC; we still can get on that Jet bruh. Loon chill; let's see what else they got. Ok but Rio sure looks good right about now. Loon; sit your ass down so we can finish. Ok Manny but yall know I'm right.

Go ahead Dennis; continue. Sure, Mr. Cooper. This is the thing that will stitch it all up for the prosecution AC. What's that? This Tax evasion charge! It says here that LVMPD detectives checked the business tax returns and no taxes were paid on any of the business since the Delgato's has been deceased. Did you pay any taxes AC? Man, does it look like I gave a damn about some taxes! There's no need to yell Mr. Cooper; I'm on your side remember. Then you better figure out how to get us out of these charges, if you want it to stay that way; Attorney; Dennis Baldwin!

Keep your head AC; we're just reading through the case to determine our defense; that's all we're doing here. What does this mean Mr. Baldwin? What's that Nina? It says that all seven defendants have been charged with conspiracy to murder Chief Espinoza. The D.A is saying that this case gave all of you motive to murder Chief Espinoza and that you ordered a hit on his life but failed at your attempt. Man fuck the D.A; they can't prove that shit; that bitch is trying to pin everything on us; aint she? It looks that way Ms. Sanchez. Go ahead Dennis! Sure, Mr. Ortega!

Loon and Denna, the D.A has charged you both with a video store murder. For who? I know they're not talking about old timer? Yeah that's the one Loon! Man; we aint kill that dude; this case is a bunch of BS! It's beginning to look that way Mr. Massey but I still have to prove your innocents. How can they just pin murders on us like that Mr. Baldwin? That's why they charged you all with violating the RICO Act Denna; it gives them the power to add on any and all conspiracies. See that's why I hate the police; their just as crooked as the criminals! I'm afraid you are right about that Will, I see it all the time in my practice. Are we done yet Dennis; we have some moves to make before trial. It's one more charge here AC and we're done. Ok let's hear it!

The last charge is for the murders of several of the Delgato former employees. It says here that several skeletons or human remains were found in a Vegas suburb; that match the DNA of those employees. The coroner also stated that each victim had a bullet hole in the back of their skulls. Again motive has connected you all to these murders because you all are now actively running the Delgato's business. AC; Rio sure is going to be nice bruh; when are we leaving? Loon chill; can you win this thing Dennis? It's going to be hard Mr. Cooper but I think we can. One last question before you guys go, though! What's that Dennis? It really would help if any of you had some dirt on law enforcement or any politicians. Do you have any dirty cops or government officials on your payroll? Yeah we got a few. Good; tell me what you got Coop!

I have a detective that has been giving me information about this case while the Chief was building it. That's good. We can use that; did you pay her anything? Yeah about $40,000 or more! Cool; now we're getting somewhere, did she give you any evidence. Well; I bought a towers tape from her that had some crucial evidence on it. Was it crucial to this case AC? Hell yeah; we all can go down if they get this tape. Alright what's her name? It's Detective Amanda Ricky; the Chief brought her in from New York to work this case. Great, is there anything else? Yeah I have something! Ok; what you got Nina?

I witnessed Chief Espinoza and Judge Kennedy having sexual relations with two of my escorts at our annual political party rendezvous. Excuse me Nina; did you just say Chief Espinoza and Judge Kennedy? Yep! Well damn; will the two girls testify if you asked them to? Of course they will; without a doubt. Ha-ha! What's so funny Dennis? This is it guys; we got them by the balls. Don't get so happy Dennis; I don't want to use this information unless we have to. What do you mean AC; this will blow the case wide open. That all depends, Dennis! Depends on what AC? Who the informant is! Explain Mr. Cooper. If the C.I is from the streets; it won't matter who the informant is, they will win, even if you try and out the Judge, Ricky and the Chief. The only way we can use this, is if the C.I is on their team, a Cop, DEA, Detective, FBI or something. Then we can use Detective's Ricky dirt, The Judge and Chief's sexual exploits to discredit this case. That's pretty damn smart Mr. Cooper you should be an Attorney. No Dennis; that's your job but I shouldn't have to tell you that. Come on guys let's get out of here; Dennis we'll call you later. AC heads for the exit as Manny, Loon, Denna, Will, Duck and Nina follow.

Manny call Hector and tell him to start making moves; if this thing goes south; we need to be ready. Calling him now Coop. Hey Will, you guys meet me at the Mansion. Ok AC; see you in a minute.

Hello! Hector; what's up homie? Who is this? Manny amigo! Hey homie; what's up Capo? Yo, we need you to put your soldiers in place at the court house. I can do that amigo, how many you need? Three should work Hector. Alright; they'll be the three armed officers in the hallway just outside the court room. Thanks my man; appreciate that. No problem; just call me on my cell when you want them to dump. Cool, my wife Sophie will call or Monica; AC's lady. That will work amigo; who are the targets? Hec you can pop the bailiff, D.A, Judge or anybody that's gone stop us from walking out of that court room. Say no more homeboy it's done. Thanks Hector; later! It's done AC; we just have to tell Mo or Sophie to make the call. Ok Capo; let's get to the Mansion so we can get our business in order. Manny, Loon and AC get in the Rover then follow Will, Duck, Denna and Nina to Spanish Trails.

Upon arrival Mo greets the crew at the door. Hey Baby what did the lawyer have to say? We read over the charges but the name of the informant wasn't in there. Damn; so what are we gonna do now AC? Sticking to plan baby; just have the money with you when we go to court next week. Yo Coop; where's your bong man; I need to smoke! Look under the bathroom sink Duck. Thanks bruh! Mo; what do you have to drink in here sis? Almost everything Nina; what do you want? Some tequila girl! Come in the kitchen; I have a new bottle of Jose'! Right behind you girl! Did you want some too Denna? Yeah, I'm right behind you guys.

I'm going to hit that bong with Duck; this damn case has got a brother stressed; yall coming. Go ahead Loon; Me and Manny need to go over some things. Alright Coop! What about you Will? I'm down brother; I can use a few tokes. Come on then; let's smoke some chronic bruh. You know we can't play this thing by the book Manny! Trust me Boos; after hearing all those damn charges I knew that was out of the question. Yeah those bastards have us by the nuts Capo. With that being said; how do you want to play this thing?

The first thing we need to do is see who that damn informant is; after that we can make our move. I understand that but what if the informant doesn't take the stand, then we won't know who it is. If they know what's good for them; they better put that fool on the stand. But what if they don't AC? We'll wait until the jury leaves the court room; then Mo will approach the most vulnerable two jurors and offer them 5 Million each to acquit. Boy you a motherfucking genius; what sane person is going to refuse 5 Million dollars, huh! Yeah, I just hope it works Capo; I hate to move to the next step if it doesn't.

It should work Coop as long as Hector's guys are impersonating the officers they can let Monica into the jury chambers. Yeah I think so too but if it don't; there's going to be a lot of dead bodies in that court room, because we're not going to jail brother. You can say that again Boss. That's the last resort though and the Jet is fueled up and on standby just in case it comes to that. AC and Manny give each other a high five then head in the living room to hit the bong.

Let me hit that smoke Loon! Here you go Coop; this is some good green right here partner. AC takes a seat on the arm of his white leather sofa, places the bong up to his lips then inhales. Yeaahhhhh, this straight boy; here Capo! Manny takes the bong, relights the bowl then inhales slowly. Ahhhhhh, this is good shit. Take another hit Manny; I'm about to light these two blunts. Here Duck, take that one! Thanks Loon! Manny, AC, Will, Duck and

Loon sat in the hot box and passed the bong then blunts to the right after every hit. Constantly inhaling and exhaling while the house began to fill with chronic smoke. The more they smoked the higher they got. All their problems faded away as the cannabis sativa relaxed their mines and enhanced their senses.

Nina look at them fools; there over there fucked up! Ha-ha! You aint lying Monica; look at them Denna! I see why; they got two blunts and the bong in the cipher. Ooo wee; AC you look higher than a kite baby. Huh? Coop slowly turns to face the girls in the kitchen as he heard his name. I said yall over there tore up! Oh yeah. The girls all laugh as the guys lay out on the floor and couches after smoking both blunts and the bong. A moment of peace seemed to overcome them all; in this time of turmoil. The weed and alcohol had managed to do what their lawyer couldn't; it made the case disappear, if only for a moment.

"Good Morning Las Vegas; this is Katie Strong reporting live from the Clark County Courthouse." "This is day one of the Sin City Seven Trial." "Las Vegas Mob Boss; Andy 'AC' Cooper and his six soldiers have all been charged with violating the United States RICO Act." "The Defendants all pled Not Guilty to the charges just two weeks ago today." "I will continue to bring you live reports through-out the trial whether it ends today or a week from today."

"If you take a look behind me you can see the Sin City Seven; all dressed in designer suits and the two ladies are wearing the latest Donna Karen." "Spectators all along the streets and steps; are cheering. What sounds like; not guilty as the defendants enter the court house!"

As Defense Attorney; Dennis Baldwin leads the way through the halls of Justice; Chino, Carlos and Poncho give a soft nod to AC and the crew as they enter the court room. Monica and Sophia, following close behind takes a seat in the first row behind the defense while the crew, join their Attorney. Dennis waits until his clients are seated then walks over to District Attorney; Rollins to see if she had any more evidence to enter. Good Morning; Mrs. Rollins are these all the files, do you have anything else I should know about? Mr. Baldwin, if there was anything; I would have sent it to you.

No hard feelings Rollins; just wanted to make sure. There's no hard feelings Baldwin; I just hope that you're not a sore loser. Excuse me D.A; I don't mean to boast but I haven't lost a case yet and I don't plan on it anytime soon. Neither have I sir; so I hope you're ready. And I you; Attorney Rollins! Dennis walks back to his table and counsels AC and the crew. Alright guys, she says that there isn't any more evidence so we know where we stand. If anything comes to either one of you during the trial that we haven't discussed and it can help us. Write it down on one of these legal pads and slide it to me. All seven of them look at Baldwin then shake their heads in acknowledgement. The bailiff enters the court room and addresses the court. "All rise for the Honorable Judge Wilkerson!" The judge enters the court room and takes a sea at the bench. You may be seated!

Bailiff; are we all set and ready to go? Yes your honor! Attorney Baldwin, Rollins are we all set here? Yes; you Honor! Bam! The gavel slams down and echoes through-out the court room. Court is in session; jury prepare to hear opening statements. Prosecution; are you ready to proceed with your statement? Yes Judge! Proceed! The D.A leaves her table and walks over to the jury box to address the 12 jurors.

Today people, the State will prove that the accused; The Defendants now known as the infamous Mob Crew; Sin City Seven; headed by ruthless Crime Boss; Andy 'AC' Cooper. Has together conspired to run the Las Vegas criminal underground through murderous hostile take overs, Murder-for-hire, Money Laundering and Tax Evasion! We will prove that they had motive to do the above and we will show you evidence to prove it all.

Make no mistake people, those seven well dressed, well-mannered individuals that you see over there today! They are cold hearted killers, gangsters in ever since of the word. Those same seven people; took over several businesses in Las Vegas with deadly force and retained that power by doing more of the same. It is your job and your sovereign duty as Las Vegans to punish them to the fullest extent of the law. It is my job to prove to you that they are guilty as charged and I intend to do just that!

Attorney Baldwin; proceed with your statement. Yes, you honor. Dennis approaches the jury. Good Morning, good people of Las Vegas! The D.A gave a compelling statement but what she failed to mention was that. Those seven people over there; all risked their lives, so that you all! Yes;

every one of you up here could have your freedom. Those 5 men and 2 women served proudly as soldiers in our United States Army. The State would have you to believe that these up-standing citizens, war veterans, conspired to murder several of their fellow citizens. When the truth is! These are hardworking people; just like you and I. Those businesses that the D.A claimed my clients took over, was left to them by the prior owners. I will show you evidence where my clients were employees of the prior owners and because of their background. Their fellow employees elected them to run the company and all of its businesses.

Another thing the D.A failed to mention was that the State charged my clients with violating the United States RICO Act. If you don't know what that is, people of this fine jury. I suggest you do your research. But I will tell you a little bit about it. It's the Act that was put in place to catch criminals of organized crime because the courts could never pin one crime on any of them. This law was formed to catch Mob Bosses like Lucky Luciano, The Gambino's etc. Look at my clients; do they look like they're affiliated with Organize Crime. Those seven people over there are American Soldiers who fought for their country and they were all trying to be productive citizens here in Vegas until Chief Espinoza came up with his own vendetta. Today I will prove their innocents and at the end of this trial you will see that my clients are no different than you or I! Thank you; Mr. Baldwin, you may be seated.

The State may proceed with its case against the Sin City Seven. Your honor, the State would like to introduce exhibits A, B and C as evidence. Let me see them Mrs. Rollins! She hands copies of the photos to Attorney Baldwin and the Judge. Ok and who are these photos of Mrs. Rollins? In exhibit A you honor; that's the bodies of Vinny and Bobby Delgato at the scene of their brutal murders during the bank robbery that the defendants set up. Objection you honor; speculation, the prosecution has no proof that my defendants were involved in that robbery!

Mrs. Rollins? You honor, these photos are all a part of showing the defendants motives in taking over the Delagto's businesses. Sustain; Mrs. Rollins I will allow it. But your honor! Mr. Baldwin, please be seated. The prosecution's assistant attorney's walks over to the jurors and hand each one of them copies of the photos.

Ladies and Gentlemen of the jury; in exhibit A you will see Bobby and Vinny Delgato. These two men owned the Dolls Gentlemen's Club, Angel's Escorts, Vegas Adult Video and Angelica's Bunny Ranch. At the present time; all of those businesses are owned by Andy 'AC' Cooper; that guy with the bald head, sitting right over there with the defense.

If you flip to the next two photos, you will see a shallow grave with several human remains. These remains were found off Interstate 15 going out towards Utah in one of the Cities new sub divisions. A nice Las Vegas family hired a pool company to dig up their backyard to install a nice pool for their kids and this is what they found! The Clark County Crime lab and Coroner took DNA samples along with examining the body and matched it to several former employees of the Delgato's! Ladies and Gentlemen of the jury; this was no accident! Each individual had a gunshot wound to the back of the head, some of them had two! The defense tried to paint a Boy Scout background for the seven accused but they're anything but.

Ok, let's turn to the last picture, marked Exhibit C! This ladies and gentlemen of the jury; is Victor Delgato! He was brutally beaten and murdered while serving a brief sentence at Clark County Jail. Victor was the last surviving member of the Delgato Family; he was destined to take over the family business when he got released but those individuals, sitting right over there, made sure that didn't happened! AC aka the Boss or Don of Sin City, along with his Capo; Manny and their soldiers, Loon, Duck, Big Will, Nina and Denna all plotted to take over the Delgato's and did so successfully by murdering off the entire family and their employees. These photos along with that motive and proof of current ownership, points to this and only this!

So people of the jury, when you got back to your chambers and review what you heard so far today, remember one thing! AC and his mob family are the current owners of The Dolls Gentlemen Club, Angel's Escorts, Vegas Adult Video and Angelica's Bunny Ranch. I ask you! What more proof do you need?

Thank you Mrs. Rollins! Attorney Baldwin; the jury is yours! Thanks you honor! Las Vegas citizens of the jury, the prosecution showed you everything but proof! Yeah the Delgato Family is dead and I mourn for them. But did my defendants murder them? Did the prosecution find any of my client's prints at either scene? Did the State find any

DNA, clothing or any kind of physical evidence indicating either of my client's guilt? Don't answer that! Let me!

No they didn't! Mrs. Rollins; the States D.A, wants you to believe that my client's had motive to murder the Delgato Family because they wanted to take over the business. Well in my book people, that is circumstantial. To answer her last question! Yes my client's currently own and run those businesses but not because of what she wants you to believe! In fact, hold on a minute. Your honor; the defense would like to enter exhibits 1-7 into evidence. Ok let me see what you have Mr. Baldwin! Here you go you honor. And here are some copies for you Mrs. Rollins. What is this Mr. Baldwin? There pay stubs for my client's your honor. If you look closely at the dates; you can see that the checks were issued several weeks before the Delgato's were deceased. Ok I will allow it. Bailiff; can you hand these to the jury? Sure Mr. Baldwin! Thank you sir! Ladies and Gentlemen what you have in your hands knocks the prosecution's theory of motive out of the window. My clients were merely employees of the Delgato's before their untimely demise.

The hard truth here is; ladies and gents, that the employees came together and elected Mr. Andy Cooper as the new CEO of the businesses. There never was any hostile take-over, no murders; just some hard working folks trying to protect their lively hoods. So when you go back to your chambers and discuss what you've heard here today, remember this! These seven individuals all worked for the Delgato's prior to them being murdered in a bank robbery and their cousin being murdered in jail. I hate to say this, but bad things happen to people every day. Sometimes you're just in the wrong place at the wrong time or maybe, just maybe, you were in harm's way.

All the court asks is; if there is any reasonable doubt, you the jury must acquit. Will there be anything else Mr. Baldwin? No you honor! Do either of you have any witnesses for today? No your honor! Thank you Mrs. Rollins! Do you Mr. Baldwin? No your honor! Thank you, this court is in recess until 10 am tomorrow, at which time we will hear more from the prosecution then the defense. You both may call any witnesses that you may have at that time. Bam! Judge Wilkerson slams down his gavel. All rise!

"Hello Las Vegas, this is Katie Strong." "Day one of the Sin City 7 trial is over and will reconvene tomorrow at 10 am." "Both sides told a very interesting story and right now it looks as if the jury could swing either way." "We all are waiting to hear from the star witness whose identity has been concealed." "Whoever that person is; I'm almost positive that we will hear from them tomorrow." "After that display from the defense; the prosecution is going to need all of the proof they can get!" "Until, tomorrow morning Las Vegas; have a good evening and be safe out there."

Attorney Baldwin, AC, Manny, Mo, Denna, Duck, Sophie, Will, Nina and Loon exit the court house then walk down the steps. Man AC, I can use a drink right now! Me too Capo! Yo; I got a gallon of Crown in my truck. Damn Will; you always ride around with a gallon of liquor bruh? Loon, don't even start, yall want some or not? Hell yeah, do you have any cups? Nina, don't push it sis! My bad Will; I was just asking. Ring-Ring! Some ones phones going off! Ring-Ring! Oh, it's mine Denna. Then answer it Manny! Hello! My friend; how was everything? Who is this? It's Sam amigo!

Hey Sam, we just left court; it was ok. How are things in Puerto Rico? There good my friend. A lot of sexy girls and plenty of money, like you say! That's what's up. Who is that Capo? It's Sam, AC! Oh tell him I said what's up and don't be trying to fuck all the pussy either. Hey Sam! Yeah, yeah I'm here my friend. AC says to keep your dick in your pants. Ha-ha! It's hard to do amigo, so many women. Well, me and the guys will probably come over for a vacation after this damn trial. Yes, please come and see the business; I guarantee you will love it! I bet we will Sam. Oh, how are Dylan and Barbie doing? Ahh, those two are on the beach every day, they love it here. Ok, tell them we said hello and I will call you later brother. Alright Manny, later my friend!

Alright guys listen up, go home and get some rest; tomorrow is a big day. The prosecution should be putting their star witness on the stand. This will determine which way this case goes. You got it Dennis; we're all crashing after we kill this Crown that Will has. Ok AC; see you guys tomorrow and be ready for anything. You will be surprised at who the State can get to turn against you. Don't worry about us Mr. Baldwin; we got this shit under control, just do your part. Thanks Duck, and I'm sure, I don't want to know what you mean by that. Yeah, you're probably right; see you tomorrow Mr. Lawyer. Yep, later!

Hey guys; let's head over to the RIO Carnival buffet; I'm hungry; my treat! Say what; you don't have to say that twice Coop; I'm in! Loon; that aint no surprise! So are the rest of you down? Yeah AC, let's do it. Cool; Manny drive my Rover, me, Mo, Loon and Sophie will ride with you. The rest you can jump in Will's Tahoe!

Will's; White Tahoe pulled away from the Court House curb and headed towards the light as Manny followed in the Rover. The earlier hours of the present day faded away like sandcastles during high tide. Prison was the furthest thing from their minds as they drove 8 miles down to Tropicana Boulevard then entered the valet of the Red and Blue towering Casino.

As the Sin City Seven, arrive at the Clark County Courthouse accompanied by their lawyer. On lookers rave and shout, guilty and not guilty as they walk up the courthouse steps. Sophie and Monica alike both held on tight to their significant others as they entered the building. Reporters jam the hallways as News cameras flash and film roll. Dennis, AC, Mo, Manny, Sophie, Will, Duck, Nina, Loon then Denna walk through the metal detectors to find; Chino, Poncho and Carlos posted in the hallway same as yesterday dressed in LVMPD uniforms. Manny acknowledges them with a slight nod of the head as the defendants enter the courtroom. Ok Mo; today is the day, have that briefcase ready and wait for my signal. Alright baby, just give me the word. You remember what I said to do with it right? Yeah AC, I remember. Good and don't make any moves until I give you the ok. I got you baby, don't worry. Just remember our next move all depends on their witness. Yep I got that. That's my girl, now go have a seat beside Sophie and stay alert. AC joins Manny and the others at the defense table while the prosecution; gaze through their files, preparing for today's session.

Alright guys, remember to write anything down that we can use against this witness when they take the stand. I want to stop the State in their tracks if we can, before the jury can even hear one word from the witness. You all got that? The crew; looks at Dennis simultaneously and nod their heads. All rise- You may be seated! Good Morning; Mrs. Rollins; Mr. Baldwin! Morning judge! Good Morning, ladies and gentlemen of the jury! Morning your honor!

Bam! Judge Wilkerson lowers his gavel. Court is now in session! Ok today the prosecution is calling a witness; is that correct Mrs. Rollins? Yes you honor! Do you have any witnesses Mr. Baldwin? No you honor! Very well! Ladies and gentlemen of the jury; you are instructed to take what you've heard yesterday from both the prosecution and defense then include what you will hear here today from both sides along with the witnesses testimony and make your final decision of guilty or not guilty. You should also understand that if there is any sign of reasonable doubt; that you can-not and shall not find the defendants guilty. A guilty verdict will only be accepted if there is no reasonable doubt.

Mrs. Rollins; you may call your witness to the stand. Thanks; your honor. The prosecution would like to call Detective Mickey Bradshaw to the stand! AC and Manny; eye brows raised; slowly look at one another when they hear his name. Bradshaw enters the courtroom looking straight ahead then walks directly to the witness stand.

The bailiff swears him in then Mick takes his seat beside the judge.

Manny I thought you knew this motherfucking pig! AC he has been driving for the Towers for two years; I swore he was clean! Loon, Duck, Will, Denna and Nina all look down at the floor then shook their heads in disbelief as Mick stare at them with a look of satisfaction on his face. What's wrong Cooper; do you guys know him? AC looks at Baldwin and speaks under his breath. Hell yeah Dennis, this fool know a lot of shit. What's a lot? If that fool speaks Dennis; we're done for! Ok I got it, relax.

Your honor! Yes Mr. Baldwin! May I have a 15 minute recess to speak with my clients? Why should I grant you a recess Baldwin; you had ample time to speak with your clients prior to trial. In light of the identity of the States witness you honor; we have some new evidence to enter! Excuse me; Mr. Baldwin! I said- I heard you Mr. Baldwin! Mrs. Rollins; do you object to a recess? Yes you honor! But judge, I have critical evidence that will discredit the witness testimony! Both of you approach the bench, right now.

Now what is this evidence that you have Mr. Baldwin? Your honor I have physical evidence of foul play by the prosecution involving officers of the court and State officials. Are you kidding me Dennis! No Sir! Do you know anything about this Mrs. Rollins? No you honor. Alright meet me in my chambers; we're going to a ten minute recess. Both attorneys leave the bench, return to their tables and waits for the judge to order the court to recess.

Ladies and Gentlemen of the court; this court is in recess; we shall reconvene in ten minutes. Judge Wilkerson slams down his gavel, stands up then walks to his chambers as Baldwin and Rollins follow. Have a seat, both of you. Now what is this malarkey about foul play?

Judge; one of my clients witnessed your colleague; Judge Kennedy and Chief Espinoza in acts of prostitution with two ladies that works for Angel's Escort. My client Nina Sanchez runs that business and she was there and witnessed them go in the room. Are there any more witnesses besides your client? Yes judge; the two escorts that participated in sexual relations with Chief Espinoza and Judge Kennedy; agreed to testify if we needed them;

their only a phone call away your honor. Mrs. Rollins; did you know of any of this? No your honor.

So in what way do you think this effects your case; Mr. Baldwin? Chief Espinoza is responsible for building this case your honor. It is my belief that he and Judge Kennedy are working together to take over the same businesses the State is claiming my clients took over. Don't be ridiculous Dennis! I'm serious judge and we also have evidence that one of Chief Espinoza's detectives sold my client crucial evidence. What's this evidence you speak of? A video tape that would vindicate my clients of a murder you honor. The chief was holding it so he could stick the murder on Mr. Cooper. When in fact the footage shows that he was defending his girlfriend at the time who was being held at gun point.

Attorney Rollins; this is your call; it's a big mess! Judge; I would like to file for a dismissal on lack of evidence. Hold your horses Dennis. Well; what do you have to say Mrs. Rollins? I still think we can win this thing you honor. If you want to continue Mrs. Rollins we can, but understand the ramifications here. I understand judge. Very well then let's get back to trial. Hold on you honor; if we are going forward with the trial, I need time to get my two escort witnesses here and I will need a TV and VCR to show the tape, then after we win this case, I want Judge Kennedy, Chief Espinoza and Detective Ricky to be charged. The ball is not in your court anymore Mrs. Rollins, this is my game now, it's 4th quarter with 10 seconds to go and my team is up by 3 points with our best player at the free throw line to take two foul shots. Now if you think you can beat those odds, let's play ball. If not; I suggest you concede.

Time is running out Mrs. Rollins, what's your move? Can I have a few minutes judge; to make some phone calls? Sure, you have two minute. Thanks your honor. The D.A leaves the judge chambers and walks in the hallway to make a call. Hello; this is Espinoza. Hey Chief, this is District Attorney Rollins. Hi Mrs. Rollins; how is the trial coming? I have a question for you chief, and please, be honest. Ok what is it? Is there any truth to you and Judge Kennedy having sex with two escorts while at an event together? ------ Chief! Chief are you there? Espinoza; I need you to answer this; if you tell me the truth, this can all go away right now and it won't get out but if it is true and you don't tell me; there's a shit storm coming our way. Yes- God dammit Chief, why didn't you tell me this months ago? I didn't think it was important! Oh really; not important! Do you happen to remember the young lady that was hosting the party? Barely; Mrs. Rollins! Are you in your office right now Chief? Yes Ma'am. Look at your bulletin board! Ok, I'm looking. Now, does Nina Sanchez look familiar?

Oh my God; her face did ring a bell but I could never put my finger on it. Well, it's too late for that now Chief! Click!

Rollins walks back in the judge chambers and takes a seat. So what will it be District Attorney? I'll offer man slaughter and 5 years in a state prison with 3 years of probation to follow. Hell no Mrs. Rollins; I'm holding the ball here; remember! I want a dismissal or we're taking this thing to trial! Well, you two have 45 seconds to figure this thing out; I'm headed back to the bench; be out there by the time court is in session and let's get this thing under way. Yes judge, we'll be there.

Judge Wilkerson leaves the two in his chambers then walks back to the bench to place court back in session. All rise- You may be seated. This court is now in session. Mrs.

Rollins; the State may address the court at this time? The D.A stands to her feet as AC, Dennis and the others patiently watch her prepare to speak.

At this time; due to new evidence in this trial; the State wishes to dismiss all charges against the defendants. Mr. Baldwin do you accept this dismissal? Yes you honor! Very well; Case Dismissed! Ladies and Gentlemen of the jury we thank you for your service and you are free to go. Mr. Baldwin, your clients are free to go. This court is adjourned. Dennis walks over to shake Rollins hand while AC and the others hug and congratulate each other. Monica and Sophia run to the table to join them. Hey baby; take one of those brief cases to the D.A. Tell her AC says Merry Christmas. Ha-ha! You're so bad! I know. He bends down and kisses Mo on the lips. Now go do it before she leaves. Guys; didn't I tell you I would win it for you! Yeah Dennis; you did alright. Thanks Nina!

Excuse me; Mrs. Rollins? Yes Ma'am; what is it? AC says Merry Christmas! What is this? It's for you; don't open it until tomorrow night on Christmas Eve. We'll be seeing you around. But wait a minute! Have a good day Mrs. Rollins! Monica runs out to the hallway to catch up with the others as they exit the court house. Chino, Carlos and Poncho leave the hallway to escort them outside.

"Good Afternoon Las Vegas, this is Katie Strong reporting live from the steps of the Clark County Court House." "It's a crazy scene down here as you can see behind me." "An unexpected turn came today as the D.A dropped all charges against the defendants known as the Sin City Seven; hold on; here's the ring leader Andy 'AC' Cooper; let's see if I can get a word!" "Excuse me Sir; excuse me; can you tell me why the State dropped the charges against you?" AC stops in his tracks then moves closer to Ms. Strong, so close that she could feel his breath on her nose.

I don't have anything to say to you bitch, now move that damn camera out of my face. "But Sir; don't you want the people to know you are innocent!" Monica walks up behind her. Move your ass out of the way ho; before this be the last day that you ever hold a damn microphone. Nervously Katie steps back, regroups, pulls the mic up to her mouth then faces the camera.

"Well there you have it people, all seven defendants have been dismissed from all charges." "The Organized Crime

Family known as the Sin City Seven headed by Andy 'AC' Cooper seems to be untouchable." "You are witnessing along with me, what could be the end of our justice system as we know it." "I am too, watching in disbelief while AC, his Capo Manny and their other 5 partners in crime, all drive away from the Clark County Court House in their 1998 Bentleys with Red Christmas Bows attached to the grills." "Once again; this has been Katie Strong with your local news, until next time; be safe and Merry Christmas Las Vegas."

THE END

Thank you for reading MADE III. We do hope you enjoyed it. Please check out these other Titles by

ANTWAN 'ANT' BANK$.

And please don't forget to right a review; we would love to know what you think.

Adoration can be defined as fervent and devoted love or simply put; to worship. During our time on Earth we will all experience this powerful thing called Love. This novel will take you on a journey seen through the eyes of four couples and their relationships. For Love we endure amazing things and some of us will go to the limit to keep it.

Love can fill your heart with joy or leave it filled with hate. Adoration explores love at several levels; some of them good; some bad. In Book One of this Series; hearts will break, tears will fall, blood will shed and bells will chime; all in the name of love.

F.I.T.H. has a dramatic plot that sheds light on today's bullying epidemic. Take a look inside the mind of a bullied victim and how fear influenced his actions. *Inspired by True events*

Every School, City and County Library should have F.I.T.H (Fear Influences Thine Heart) on their shelves. It is a must read for any Parent, Teacher or Kid. F.I.T.H. is a Social Drama about a High School Freshman and a Bully. The situation becomes very intense when the bully does not let up. Although the victim tries his best to have tolerance and handle him accordingly, no matter what he tries, nothing seems to work. After several run ins and close calls, the victim is forced to become the Bully's favorite mark, influenced by an ever presence of fear, his life as he knew it; changed.

These collection of spirits; were some of my favorites to mix for the thousands of customers that I served as a bartender back in my 20's. During 1995 - 1996, I worked as a bartender in several Las Vegas Clubs and had a damn good time doing it! I've included a few recipe's; I picked up from fellow bartenders, some from customers and most I've learned from bartending school.

Mixology is an art and if mastered one can make a really good living serving spirits and conversing with the people you serve at your bar. If you're a bartender looking for some new drinks or you're just someone interested in mixing up some new drinks in your kitchen. This book of spirits is for you. Welcome to the Party Life and remember to drink responsibly.

The Cover Girl series is about, an Atlanta; Eye Candy photographer; name Malakhi Jones. Pronounced (*Mal uh Ky)*. This short story and many others to come; will take you inside a day in the life of a hot photographer and his daily encounters with several of the industries sexiest Magazine Models and Video Vixens.

While these events are Fiction; anyone in the industry knows; what goes on at the shoot; stays at the shoot! Malakhi is at the top of his game and is connected with every Men's Magazine Publisher, Casting Directors, Hip Hop Artist and Talent Managers in the industry. Getting a session with him is like winning the lottery; when it comes to being an eye candy Model, in the ATL. Any Model knows; that once the session starts and that camera flashes; all rules will be broken to obtain that success; if not! Then keep dreaming.

This title only available in ebook and sells for 99 cents.

In book 2 of The Cover Girl Series; Malakhi ventures on an on location shoot, with the Sexy Chocolate, Video Vixen; Lola Love. Her enticing aura almost proves to be too much for the A List Photographer but in true Malakhi fashion; he prevails. The two meet up, downtown on Peachtree street Atlanta; at one of the Cities five star hotels.

Together, they will create magic for the camera and hot lustful memories in their Jacuzzi Suite. They say a picture is worth a thousand words but only the photographer and the model knows; what exactly goes on, between those poses.

Above title only available in ebook and sells for 99 cents.

Millions travel to the City of Angel's every year in search of that one shot at stardom. But most fail and find themselves caught in the underbelly with the homeless, the drug attics, prostitutes, thieves and murders. Candy and Joe unfortunately are no different than most and end up living in a different hotel every other night; doing whatever needs to be done just to survive.

Above title only available in ebook and sells for $1.99.

PRINTHOUSE BOOKS

Read it, Enjoy it, Tell a Friend!

www.PRINTHOUSEBOOKS.com

Atlanta, Ga.

These Titles also available from PRINTHOUSE BOOKS.

www.PrintHouseBooks.com   Visit site for free previews.

Remember to leave a review!

MADE III

www.ingramcontent.com/pod-product-compliance
Lightning Source LLC
Chambersburg PA
CBHW031958060726
47497CB00015B/278